DEER FALLS
VOLUME 1

AUTUMN'S FALL
CHRIS'S CROSSING
IAN SENSE

SOUL FIRE
PRESS

SAMANTHA LADY

Deer Falls

Editor: Jeremy Soldevilla, Kevin R. Dungey
Cover design: MJC Imageworks

ISBN 978-1-945146-45-9
ebook ISBN 978-1-945146-46-6

Published by
Soul Fire Press

an imprint of

CHRISTOPHER MATTHEWS PUBLISHING

http://christophermatthewspub.com

Boston

Printed in the United States of America

For my hero, Charmaine,
All ways and Always,
Mom

For Laurrie,
Who never doubted

For Anna,
My smart and kind baby sis

For Michael,
Who has made peace
with her own run

Acknowledgments

Great appreciation and a warm thank you to Kevin R. Dungey, my angel in editor's clothes.

Much gratitude to Jeremy Soldevilla, my final editor, at CMP/Soul Fire Press. Thank you for being the beacon for lost, first-time authors

Prologue

"Vera Drexell, you have a visitor." I hear my name called over the intercom system of this place I live now. It surely isn't my home.

I'd tell you how old I am, but I quit counting about thirty years ago, and have never had the desire to add it all up. I was born in 1919, you can do the math if you're interested.

I moved to these parts at the tender age of thirteen. Roy stood in my front yard one day, defying my Pop, and said he was here to marry his daughter. Pop went for his shotgun, and I went for Roy. I ran and wrapped my whole body around him, nearly knocking him over. We ran until we found these hills, then never ran again.

It was the falls that made us stop here. That, and the first deer we ever got together. Roy shot and pieced it out, and I cooked it up. Us playing the man and wife roles. We didn't stop for forty years. Then he just died in his sleep one night. I still miss that boy.

Roy and I bought the hills around here, worked hard, raised babies, and watched a whole lot of other people come 'round to settle in and keep us company. I've out lived all those early timers now. Well, except for one of my boy's friends, Reggie. He must be nearing eighty by now. I've outlived my own three children. The last one passed on ten years back. Any grandkids I have moved away years ago. I wouldn't recognize them if they stood on my front step wearing name tags.

I've watched many families bloom and wither over the years, and have learned to enjoy each blossom for its God-given uniqueness. There are sad stories of course, but the happy ones shed light on why the sad ones were necessary. I think a little good comes from every bad. The bad just helps the good burn a little brighter. It's as it should be.

Book I:

Autumn's Fall

One

I'm at the height of hating this pitiful excuse for my life right now. I grab a loaf of bread from the store's shelf. Of course, it's the cheapest brand that the Food Mart offers. "It's on sale this week," Mother said as I left the house earlier.

I wouldn't even be here this morning if Mother and I hadn't have had another fight last night. We both stormed to our rooms so we didn't have to see each other. So, there was no trip to the store last night.

Now comes the worst part: checking out. I hate this, paying with the food stamp card! I walk hesitantly, watching for any other customers who may be making their way to the checkout so I can let them go first and save myself some humiliation. Every clerk here knows we pay cash for everything except for when we buy food. It would be so much better if Mother would use a debit card all the time, but she's too cheap! She has told me countless times, "I won't give the bank the last few dollars we have in the month, for the privilege of letting them hold our money." I'm always afraid my timing in line will be off, and that someone from school will walk up as I'm paying. It's pure torture, I tell you.

Ah, man! Beehive hair lady is running the checkout! She's the worst! She wears that big phony smile of hers as if she's on camera while snapping her gum and filing her fire-engine red nails between ring ups.

I plop the bread down and toss in a pack of sour apple gum—my lame attempt to normalize my purchase.

"Good morning, Autumn. How are you today, dear?" The register beeps. "One-o-nine, honey."

I do a quick check. Nobody is walking up to join the line, thank God. I pull out the food stamp debit card and swipe it fast. I watch

Beehive lady's face, and there it is: 'The Look.' She goes through her normal routine of the widened eyes, the pinched lips, the flared nostrils, and now . . . the sniff. She acts as if I've stolen the bread money from her purse or as if I'm a dirty bum on the street who grabs at her as she walks by. I watch her two-finger the loaf of bread to bag it. I grab it from her two fingers. My only chance of saving any steam in my self-esteem is to refuse the freebie bag. I want to tell her that poverty is just a rash and not contagious. Instead, I snatch up the gum from the counter.

"So, I seen on the work schedule that yer momma's name was scratched through. She's sick, I guess?"

"Yeah, I guess so," I say as I walk to the trash can by the exit door. I unwrap a piece of gum and toss it in my mouth.

Beehive lady tells the approaching cashier, loud enough for me to hear, "Rita did that girl a disservice by keeping her. She should have given that baby up for adoption or somethin'. Why, she can barely put food in that girl's mouth. Everybody would have forgot by now, how she showed up here with a babe-in-arms and no ring on her finger. Plain and simple stupidity on her part if you ask me."

The sour gum makes my mouth water, and her sour words make my eyes fill. I turn, looking straight into Beehive lady's face. She's leaning against the counter with her arms crossed. A glance at the other cashier shows me that she is ashamed that I've heard the remarks, which Beehive lady obviously meant for me to hear. My eyes threaten to spill their tears, but I stare steely-eyed at Beehive lady. If I say anything, tears will flow. Instead, in my head, I say a lame prayer or curse. 'May your sour words give you lock-jaw, you old hag. Amen.' I turn to leave, and as the door closes behind me, I hear her say, "Weird kid."

My prayer was powerless. Go figure. Next time I'll bring a doll and a pin.

The entire four blocks home I do my usual coulda-woulda-shoulda thing. Why don't I ever stick up for myself? At least I'm not smoking pot under the school bleachers or beating up the littlest kids at school like her precious Rod does! I replay Beehive lady's words in my head. 'Adoption or something' and 'No ring on her finger.' Was her 'or something' abortion? Did she honestly believe it would have been better if I had never been born? As for Mother's marital status, well I've asked about that hundreds of times. Mother won't discuss it. I don't even know my dad's name.

My hands are still shaking a little from anger as I cross my yard and run up the stairs to my house. I sling the bread on the table a little too hard, so Mother does that squinty-eye thing she does when she's trying to read my mind. I'm good at duck and dive, so craftily, I shift her focus.

"The girls asked me to go to the mall after school. I need four or five dollars." My heart ticks off the seconds waiting to see if she believes my lie. I need to gather whatever money I can, while I can, for later use.

"I don't have it this week, Autumn. I'm sorry."

"Please?" Sometimes begging works, especially if Mother is tired. I figure she's not on top of her game since she called in sick at the Food Mart. Something she never, ever does.

"No, Autumn. I said I can't."

"Why not? You never can Mother! Which means, as usual, I'll skip lunch today so I can get a coke or something at the mall. Either that or my friends will have to pay my way! It's embarrassing! I never pay their way. And I don't even consider eye make-up from the 99-cent bin!" I slap my thigh in utter frustration. "I hate this! My friends are sick of it too. They didn't ask me to go anywhere with them for half of the summer!" I slap angry tears from my eyes, plop down on a kitchen chair, bury my face in my arms and cry. The humiliation of poverty invades my life on all fronts for real. "God, I hate my life."

"Honey."

I hear Mother's chair scoot back, then I feel her hand on my shoulder. "Autumn, I hate this too. Don't you know I'd give you the world if I could?"

Her touch infuriates me even more. I shake her hand off my shoulder and stand up. I stare at her without a flinch and say coldly, "No. I don't know that, Mother. You won't even give me my dad."

By the look on her face I know I've hit a home run, but it's nothing to cheer about. I raise my voice, "Instead, I have to hear people talk behind my back! Maybe I should ask one of them who my dad is because it seems to me that the whole town knows more about my life than I do! At least then I could be in on the joke," I burst into big, heavy tears before I can finish, "and know why they're laughing at me."

"Autumn, who is laughing at you? What happened?" She tries to hug me. I step back and shove her arms away. I can't stand her right now. Her long, stringy hair and that old threadbare robe she's had my entire life, make me sick.

"Don't! 'Cuz, right now I really hate you!" Through clenched teeth, I add, "You are such an embarrassment!"

Mother's mouth gapes open in shock. I continue.

"You, with your '70s skirts and hippie hair! No wonder my dad never comes around! God, you've never even been on a date. Doesn't that tell you anything, Mother? Your weirdness is like a wall that keeps everybody away, and I'm stuck in your prison!"

I can tell I've ticked her off by the way her back stiffens, but then her face drops from hurt feelings. My words are true, and she knows it. I'm hoping that maybe this time, she'll break down and tell me about my dad. I wait, but as usual, being true to herself, she avoids the dad issue.

"Go to your room, Autumn. Get ready for school." She points at the table. "There's your lunch money. Oh, and by the way; consider yourself grounded. Maybe next time you want to discuss a problem, you'll do it civilly."

"Perfect, Mother," I say, staring into her eyes, "That solves all of our problems now, doesn't it?" I turn and go to my room, slamming my door behind me. I can still hear her voice through the door.

"For being only fifteen, Autumn, you know how to solve all of life's problems, don't you?"

"Whatever!" I crank up my hand-me-down stereo to full blast. A song is playing that I love to dance to, but I'm in no mood for that. I honestly cannot wait until I'm eighteen. I know that teens worldwide say that, but I can honestly say that my life will be better. No more airing dirty laundry, as I call it, at the local Food Mart. I'll get earrings when I want to. No more welfare handouts, and goodbye to the humiliation every time a person lays eyes on me!

If Dad knew how I was living, he'd take me away. I know he would. What dad wouldn't? He probably doesn't even know I exist. That would explain all the secrecy, and why he's never come to see me. It's not fair! He's my dad, not hers! What right does she have, to keep us apart? I'm old enough to make my own decisions about him now.

I stand in front of my closet looking for something to wear. Today is the first day of school, but I'll be wearing last year's clothes. The reality is more than I can handle. Tears gush in a flood down my cheeks again. I sit on the end of my bed. I hate the pants I'm wearing, they fit funny, so I kick them off. I grab yesterday's jeans off the floor and tug them up over my hips. Size 9s and they're getting too tight. "Great." I grab a shirt, put it on, and leave the tail out. Everybody will recognize these as my old clothes. I dig around a box of throwaways at the back of my closet. I pull out a baggy teal sweater that I barely remember. I sniff it, drown it in perfume, shake it out, and slide it over my head. It looks almost fashionable with my shirt tail and cuffs hanging out.

The bathroom mirror makes a mockery of my best attempts to get human. My eyes are red and puffy. I hold a cold rag over them for a few minutes while I calm myself down. It helps. I tell myself that the day will get better. I feel a headache coming on and take aspirin. I snatch my mascara from the drawer and dribble a few drops of water in the dried-up tube while swirling the brush around. I manage to get some color on my eyes. They are that dark blue color they turn when I get so angry that I cry. They're almost pretty, which doesn't fit with the rest of me. I brush on blush, paint on some of Mother's lipstick, an Avon sampler–free, of course–and push the tube in my pocket. I pick out my large silver hoop earrings and check the chipped spot to make sure my hair covers it. It does. Back in my room, I grab my school supplies. I won't be taking last year's book bag. I grab my purse, think twice, then leave last year's most recognizable accessory slung across my unmade bed.

I tell Mommy Dearest goodbye by slamming the front door. That's all she'll get from me today. I walk, feeling the satisfaction of my goodbye when it hits me; I didn't even have my tea and toast! All that Beehive hair lady drama for nothing! Naturally.

I start across the footbridge that crosses the river that runs from the Falls—Deer Falls. Deer Falls is the name of my high school, the Food Mart, the mall and, oh yeah, our town. You'd think someone could come up with at least one original name around here.

The river divides Old Town from what everybody calls Uptown. I live in Old Town. The river is this geological line that divides Old Town from Uptown. It's a line that tells the world; 'stay away! Autumn is bad news,' but it is my welcome place here in Deer Falls. It lies between Mother's self-made prison walls and the world's walls. A place where the walls don't quite touch. A place between push and pull. It's my secret place.

The Falls are crazy-loud this morning. The water is in full force, gushing down from the cliff and busting up on the rocks below, mimicking my turbulent life. The Falls and I have an understanding. Today it's like we are familiar faces exchanging glances during a disaster. There is pity and sorrow for the other, but we are each intent on our own survival.

I see a flash of color from the corner of my eye. It's the girls, the group I hang around with. Jen is waving her arms and yelling something. I can't make out her words over the noise of the Falls, but it's obvious that she's calling me.

Jen is the chattiest of the three of them. She is the reason I'm even accepted by them at all. Her shallowness is the polar-opposite of my overly analytical nature. I only endure so I won't be one of those girls that sulk in the school halls alone. You know, the type that nobody notices? It's also Jen who pays my way at the mall when I can't, which makes me think she really must like me as a friend. I wonder sometimes what her dad is like. He spoils her rotten with clothes, electronics, money, and I imagine with hugs. I jog over to them with a big smile on my face, which is expected of me if I'm going to be one of them.

Jen doesn't take time to say hi, she just starts jabbering away. "So, me and Mom went to the Gap last night to get this handbag," she displays it to all, "for my outfit today, and guess what!" She finally takes a breath, and an honest smile crosses my face.

"What?" I ask, chuckling while trying for enthusiasm.

"They are having a sale on all accessories!" she squeals. "We have to go after school!" Her words are a demand, but her eyes question me.

"Um . . . I can't. I'm grounded."

"What! Why?"

"I had a blow-out with Mother this morning. I called her the B-word."

"You did not!" Jen says shocked.

"No, but I wanted to."

We all laugh at that, and I make ground with the group.

Jen asks, "Well, then we'll hook up this weekend. Will you be off grounding by then?"

"I don't know, maybe."

The girls are excited about the new school year. They giggle and chatter like they always do, but today they're all about teachers they hate, boys they like, and of course, their new outfits they love. I get by on a smile and a nod of my head. They're so caught up in their excitement, that they don't really notice that I'm not participating.

I'm actually very good at letting others think I'm part of the game, even when my mind is a million miles away, contemplating the questions of life, like, how did such a silly species land on top of the food chain? Surely it was the long arms that aided in escape from predators. Giggles break out, and I join in. Yep, I'm a natural at hiding my thoughts and feelings. It's Deer Falls' greatest lesson to me.

So far, I haven't heard anyone mention Ian Taylor. Ian is cute, nice, and wasn't dating anyone when school let out last year. Of course, his name would never pass through my lips. That's a set-up for rumor disaster! Plus, a lot can happen over the summer, and he could be seeing someone now. It's not like I got to hang out much this summer so that I'd know. No, I won't get my hopes up. Does Ian even know my name? I wonder.

Thoughts of Ian naturally progress to my appearance. Do I look okay? Suddenly I choke inside. Oh God! What if I have a dirty spot on my jeans? I didn't check! I picture myself sitting down on a glob of peanut butter. Now I feel like everyone's eyes are on my pants. I inch my sweater down over my rear, unnoticed. If someone sees something, I'll act all shocked and mad. I rehearse a good response in my head. Everyone giggles again, I don't know what about, but I join in. First stop, bathroom.

I'm hoping I'll be lucky enough to have a class with Ian this year. First period came and went. Nope. Second period was just as boring as first. So, now, here I sit in third period, the tardy bell has rung, and I've given up all hope.

Then, he walks in! Since he's late, most of the desks are full. He looks around and plops down in the desk next to me. He leans over, smiles, and says, "Hi."

My face instantly goes crimson, a plague of my fair skin, but I manage a smile and a "Hi" back.

He turns and starts sparring with the kid on the other side of him. How could I think he sat down there because of me? God, I'm such a dork!

I do manage small talk with him during class, and we roll our eyes at the teacher's over-played enthusiasm for world history. I glance at the clock that reads fifteen minutes 'til lunch. My stomach growls. I didn't have breakfast and–dang it!–I didn't grab my lunch money! This day has got to be the worst day ever invented! Dear Diary, today, Sept. 5th, never happened. Amen.

There's a knock on the door, so the teacher stops talking. Everyone has suddenly found new interest in her as she goes to open the door.

Through the crack of the door, I see the paisley skirt. No! My heart stops, then kicks in with heart attack force. Mother! I'd know that ugly brown and green paisley skirt anywhere.

Immediately, I slump down in my chair and try to hide. I pencil in a carved message on my desk from who knows how many years ago. T-H-. I can hear their voices, but can't make out what they're saying. I-S-. Any second now the teacher will call out my name. B-I-. I'm only a few breaths from Ian seeing who I really am and losing any hope of ever getting another friendly "Hi" from him. T-E-S. I hear snickers around the room. Someone lets off with a wolf whistle, someone else says, "cougar," and growls. The class cracks up.

"Autumn Riley?" The teacher calls. I look up, and there stands Mother. She's wearing the long hippie skirt and has a bandana tied over her long, straight, blonde hair. She looks as if she just hitched a ride out of Woodstock! I underline THIS BITES. I grab my stuff and stare at the floor as I walk to the front of the class. I refuse to look at anyone, especially Ian, as I make my escape from Hell.

Why did she have to come to my class? Anyone else would have just sent the office aide! No, not my mother! I spot our car in the parking lot. I can't miss it. It's a maroon Saab that sticks out and looks like a bloody rat. I climb in and slump down. I put my feet up on the dash, which I know drives Mother nuts. I don't want to look at her face or hear her voice, so I buckle my seatbelt to fend off her usual 'buckle-up, Babe'.

So much for this school year going better than last year. Nobody will ever forget the sight of hippie woman blasting in from the past. My stomach is sick, and I just might throw-up. My mouth is doing that tingly-watery thing. Don't think about it. In my side window, I see my reflection that's a sickening copy of Mother's blonde hair, blue eyes, and too-thin lips. A tear slides loose. I swallow. I look beyond my reflection to the sign in the distance. The bloody rat comes to life as I read, 'Deer Falls High School Welcome Back!' The car moves forward and the words 'Go Bucks!' leave my view.

The ride home is silent. The air is electric with my anger. It bounces around the car like needle-sharp arrows. I send hundreds, no, thousands of them, all aimed at her. I wonder what is so important that she has pulled me out of school, but I'm enjoying torturing her with my silent arrows too much to ask. Revenge has won over curiosity. I know I'm being hateful to her, but it feels really good.

I jump out of the car before it's completely stopped. I purposely close the front door, knowing that she is only steps behind me. I make it through the living room and almost into the kitchen when I hear the door open.

I get out PB and J and start spreading them on bread. I can feel her eyes drilling my back the whole time. I take a bite and turn to go to my room, leaving the mess on the counter. Mother is leaning against the archway of the kitchen; her arms crossed. Is she mad? I make eye contact. No, not mad, but something . . . something I've never seen before.

"What?" I ask.

"Autumn, I'm sick."

Two

*I*t is obvious that by *sick*, Mother doesn't mean throw-up sick. She starts to reach for my hand, then stops herself.

"Come here, Autumn, we need to talk."

I follow her to the couch, taking in the view of her ugly canvas shoes below her hideous paisley skirt. Being at such close physical range to each other feels like forcing the wrong ends of two magnets together. I scoot away to a more comfortable distance as I settle in.

"What?" I ask.

Mother sighs. "Honey, I have to have surgery. A hysterectomy. I spoke with Dr. Jacobs this morning, and we can't wait."

I'm so disgusted and angry with her, yet now I'm expected to have sympathy for her? I'm not even close to being civil with her! I can't help but lash out at her, the doctor, anyone at all.

"Wait a minute here, I don't get it. You've been just fine. Now, all of a sudden, you need surgery? Did you even bother to get a second opinion or are you just gonna believe some quack that makes his living on the welfare dollar?"

Somewhere inside of me, I think that if I can argue her out of this little drama of hers, then we can get back to our normal, 'happy' home. Mother closes her eyes. She has that exasperated look she gets when I'm trying her patience.

"I've been sick for a long time, Autumn. I haven't said anything sooner, well, because I didn't think it was this serious. Doctor Jacobs said he won't even know the full extent of damage until the surgery. I know, and my body knows, that this is necessary. I'll be in the hospital three or four days, maybe less."

My heart does a leap. Three or four days of total freedom! I fight off a smile.

"After that," Mother continues, "I'll be bed-ridden for a couple of weeks. It could actually be a month or more before I can return to work full-time."

She looks up from her hands to my face. I sense something bad is coming. My joy of temporary freedom flees, and I brace myself. How serious is this? They do these surgeries all the time, don't they?

"I have to go to a care center for a few weeks, and you have to go to a foster home, Autumn."

"What?" Pure fighting instinct kicks in. "No! No way, Mother! I'm not going anywhere. You go wherever you want, but I'm staying right here."

I start to stand, but her hands grip my knees before I can move. I try to pull away, but her grip tightens to the point of pain. Her eyes are level with mine, her face only inches from mine. Her stare alone would freeze me in place. She is serious and in control.

"Autumn! Listen to me. First, you can't stay here alone, it's illegal. Secondly, if I'm not working, then we don't have rent, food, utilities. Nothing!"

Her head drops as she mumbles, "I can't take care of you." Her voice cracks, but she continues. "You have to go. I'm so sorry, honey." I watch tears fill her eyes.

In that instant, my whole world of security, my place in the universe is gone. The room goes surreal and whitish. I have a sensation of floating without ties to anything real. There's no one to reach out to, no one to chase after me. I am totally and utterly disconnected. I find Mother's face and stare in disbelief. My surroundings are reduced to slow motion, while my thoughts are in hyper-speed. I've never considered losing my home before. I mean, sure, when I'm eighteen, when I choose to storm out and leave her behind, but not like this. Home is a given, a place that is always there no matter how bad I act. Memories of the morning flash through my head. I see Beehive hair lady standing with crossed arms and a smirk on her face. Her voice floats through my mind, 'adoption or something' and 'can't even put food in that girl's mouth.' Next, I see my tears of humiliation and frustration about my old clothes. Then the angry, electric arrows whiz by that were aimed at Mother only minutes ago. As the images and emotions swirl in chaos around and through me I wonder; how did I not see this coming?

Everything begins to catch up with time again. Mother's voice becomes audible, but I miss most of what she is saying. I look at my hands, they still clutch the PB & J sandwich. This surprises me, it seems almost funny. My throat closes, so I toss the sandwich on the coffee table. The table wobbles in protest. I would laugh at its weakness if I weren't so weak myself. I slump down into our battered couch in defeat. I am suddenly exhausted. The only thing I have a grip on is the reality of my unknown dad and my miserable life.

So, what will a foster home really be like? I've heard that the state buys those kids school clothes. Mother won't be around to embarrass me anymore. Do I want to go? Would it be better? Can I detach myself from her this easily? Do I actually hate this woman enough to cast her aside? Is this really hate that I feel or just anger and disappointment? I think of times that I've disappointed her, and on purpose at that. Can I rebuild 'me' from this? Alone?

I watch Mother wipe tears from her eyes. She sniffs. Her world is destroyed too. My heart hurts for her sadness and for my destined loneliness. All of this, while my life-long anger at her refusal to tell me about Dad still burns deep inside. It's part of me, that anger, and I've created who I am around it.

Guilt creeps in from my selfish thoughts of being free from her. I look at her through my guilt, my anger and our shared sorrow. My heart answers me; No, I can't detach my life from hers that easily. The comparison of my home to a foster home brings more clarity. Both are humiliating, but at least at my home, I'm familiar with our beat-up relationship. I have to fight for my home, this home. It is the only tolerable part left in my world. If this is gone, then I will melt into nothing. I'll just be dead air floating out there. A ghost girl haunting the streets of Deer Falls.

Anger builds at the injustice of it all. The more I think about how easy it is for the law and agencies to push families into oblivion, the angrier I get. It no longer matters to me what is fair or right or just. This is about survival. And the world doesn't know how hard I can fight! I'll start with Mother. I'll fight in the way that I know best; by appealing to Mother's guilt and sympathy.

I sit up on the edge of the couch. Mother's eyes watch me. "Mother, hear me out. You don't understand. There is only one foster home in town that takes teens. Janey Freeze's house. Janey always acts so superior to the kids that go there, as if it's her own good nature taking them in and not her parents doing it for the money. She tells those kids' tragedies at school as if it's a pitiful drama, and she's the queen with the goods. It's disgusting! Everybody at school will be talking about how you couldn't take care of me and that my Dad won't have anything to do with me! Trust me, it won't be in a sympathetic way. I'll be a joke, and seen as toxic!"

Tears sting my eyes as I picture Janey announcing in the halls every one of my most hurting and personal issues. I picture her pointing out the proof by the fact that I had no school clothes this year. I imagine her voice. 'I took her shopping, and she picked out three new outfits. Doesn't she just look so great now?'

"Please, please don't make me go there. Please!"

"Autumn! Don't do this to me right now. I mean it. I can't take anymore!" I watch her face crumble into tears. "Do you think I want to do this? When our rent is overdue, we'll get evicted. It will take me months to save enough for rent, deposits, everything needed for a new place! We have no choice here!" Her voice breaks on her last words as she buries her face in her hands and sobs hard. I watch this and think of all the times I've tried to break her. I'm relieved that I never succeeded.

I've never seen her cry like this in my entire life. She is broken. Mother has just become human to me. She is fighting life and the world, just like me. Her surrender to defeat scares me to my core. In my worst rages against her, she has always been safe enough to fight against, because I knew deep-down, that she'd be the rock that could handle my anger. But now, she is as vulnerable as me. I don't know what to say or do. The only thing I can think of is to continue, to get her angry enough to fight.

"Mom."

Her head pops up. I see a lost dream in her face, her dream of a loving daughter. My heart drops again, landing in more guilt from calling her Mother lately, instead of Mom. "If you send me to Janey's, I'll run away." Her face drops. "I'll come back here. If they find me and take me back, then I'll run again! I'll find Dad, and I'll go live with him!" I hold my breath, waiting for her response.

Quietly she answers, "You just don't get it do you, Autumn? He's not an option."

Suddenly, the world turns huge, cold, and empty. I am unprotected, exposed to it, with nowhere safe to run.

"Why!" I scream. I fight back my Dad tears. "Why isn't he an option? Is he dead?"

"Autumn!" She raises her hand as if to fend off my questions. "Not this! Not now! Please!"

I didn't really expect an answer. At least I've got her ticked off, and she's not crying as hard. I scoot in close to her. Our knees touch and I reach for her hands. I break through the awkward space between us. This is a new connection for us. She looks at me, surprised. I stare into her eyes ready to plead with everything inside of me. I'm caught off guard for a second. Her eyes have done that thing where they turn dark blue like mine do when I go from anger to tears. I didn't know hers did that too.

"Mom, I know I've been a brat. I've been so mean to you, and right now I'm not even sure why anymore." I can feel my face heat up red in shame. "It seems all we do anymore is fight." I take a deep breath. I have her full attention. "Mom, I didn't realize how close to the edge we were, but now I get it. And I am so sorry, Mom." I burst out a sob but talk through it. "Instead of fighting each other, let's fight together, for us. Don't send me away." I gather myself and continue. "I know that I've been acting like a little kid, but I'm telling you, I can do this!"

"Do what Autumn? Honey–"

"I'll take care of you! No care-center. No foster home. No dad. Just us—you and me."

My eyes search her face frantically. She has a weird expression that I can't discern. It's not only shock but confusion too. Is it disbelief mixed with a glimmer of hope? I tuck my hair behind my ears, ready for battle.

"I'll clean, cook, and nurse you back to health. It can't be too hard, or they wouldn't let you leave the hospital. I'll call the school for my assignments, and I promise to keep my grades up." I search her face for approval. "Please, Mom! I can do this! I'm begging you. Trust me. I know I don't deserve your trust, but I'm asking for it with everything in me. I can do this! We can do this!" I feel the confidence in myself build as I talk. Not only is this possible, but I really want to do this. I have a drive, a burning determination to fight the entire world and win. Every ounce of anger I've had inside of me over the years has just found a new target.

"Mom, how many times have we been late on rent before?" The landlord always works with us. We've been renting from him nearly all my life. And utilities? We'll just have to make do for a while."

We're both quiet. Mother is weighing what I've said. I can feel the possibility buzz between us.

"Autumn. Your plan would demand a lot of hard work and self-sacrifice on your part. Most adults would find it difficult to see it through. Few would make it through to the end. It's a long commitment, honey. Once I'm out of the hospital, I must stay wherever I go. I won't have the health or the resources to make alternative arrangements. It could be 4-6 weeks before I'm close to going back to work. Autumn," she tucks my hair behind my ear and studies my eyes, "I know you don't want to lose your home. I don't either, but I'm not sure you're up to all of this. Besides, you should be living your life with your friends at school and chasing boys." She gives a small smile.

"Mom, I can do this. I want to. Trust me. I swear to you I'll see this through to the end. I may have irritated moments, but I won't quit. I will fight to the end. Fight with me, Mom. If we don't fight, we will lose everything, including us. By the time the state allows me to come back to you, it could be months. I've seen it before with other kids at Janey's house. Most of them leave because they hate it so bad, and they end up in Juvenile Hall. Once that call is made to Children's Services, I can't come back until they see that you have a house and a job for six months. Mom, it could be a year before all of that is back in place."

"I know, Autumn," she says sadly.

I know how much Mom detests government interference, so I use it. "After that, the state will check on us for God knows how long! Do you want that?" I sit quietly. "Mom, I don't want to lose my only family just to be tossed into a stranger's home, who only wants the state's money. Oh, and just so you know," I grin, "the boys I chase run too fast."

After a long silence, Mom says, "We would have to make sure that not one person knows there isn't an able-bodied adult here."

"Yes!" I throw my arms around Mom's neck. It's a shock to both of us, but relief gushes through me, and instantly I feel the doom and gloom lift from my body. Mom holds me tight. This is the first hug I've given her since I was a little kid. I feel her shoulders shake, and I know she is crying. I am ashamed of myself for holding my love hostage for so long. Mom pulls back and smiles shyly, like she has over-stepped her bounds, infringed on my personal space, or stolen a piece of me. Shame makes me look away from her eyes in that moment. I pat her hand, then squeeze it. Without words, I've told her, no harm/no foul.

"Autumn, we need to make a strict budget and put everything on payment plans. We'll need to list every person or agency possible that we'll come in close contact with, then work out a plan, every detail, so nobody suspects a thing. If one thing goes bad, the entire plan could crumble. This has got to be fail-proof, and no slip-ups on our parts."

For the first time in a very long time, we agree, and together we move from this raw situation into a fighting stance. I feel as if I've become an adult over the last hour. I don't care about new clothes, boys or revenge. I'm focused on Mom's illness, our survival and fighting a system and a world that is bigger than both of us.

I'm lying on my bed face up, just the way I landed. Mom is in the kitchen making dinner while I'm taking a nap, or I would be if my brain would stop long enough to obey my exhausted body.

I've realized a lot today. I've got a different perspective on life this evening than I did when I woke up this morning. Everything in my world is different, new, bigger, harder, softer. The things that mattered this morning are insignificant, and things that I never gave a thought to are now prominent. I don't know yet if I like it or not, but it's clear to me that there was good and bad before, and good and bad now. It just seems they are more intense now.

I find there's a lot to be said for the survival instinct. It's what gave us the energy to work out our plan, after bottoming out emotionally. We sat in the kitchen making lists, Mom with her coffee, and me with my tea. Together we created a story, a secret life. We are breaking the rules. I smile to myself. We're regular outlaws. Well, it doesn't stop Mom from lecturing me on the wrongs of telling lies though.

We tell some agencies and people that Mom's cousin will be caring for her and keeping an eye on me. Others, like my school and friends, we say that I have mono–yes, that kissing disease. It was the best we could come up with that would give me at least a month off. I'd be contagious, yet not be in the hospital.

I roll over onto my stomach and grab up Pandy, my stuffed panda bear. I kiss him on the nose and replay that whole 'mono scene.' " I complained, "Great, now I've got mono, and I've never been kissed."

Mom did that squinty-eye thing of hers and asked, "Really?" My mouth gaped open, I almost answered, but then she laughed. So, Mom has a sense of humor. Who knew?

I know everyone at school will be wondering who I kissed. I don't care so long as it doesn't get to the point where I find myself defending my virginity or explaining that "No, I don't have AIDS!" The kids at school love gossip. I hug Pandy to my chest. Dear Diary, will I ever be kissed? Other than by Danny White in first grade?

Mom is scheduled for surgery tomorrow. She has to be at the hospital by 6:00 a.m., which only leaves us the afternoon to prepare and put our plan in place. We go to the library and read up on endometriosis, which is what Mom has. We find out what a hysterectomy entails and what the recovery will be like. We can do it, but Mom will have a lot of pain for a while and will need a lot of help the first week, but gradually she'll be able to do more. She should be back to work in five weeks. She says four. We'll see.

The school will mail my assignments, and I'll slide them under the door after hours. Mom told them that she would be the one dropping them off, but her work schedule conflicted with school hours, so she would do it after hours.

The food budget is skimpy. After paying full rent and working out payment plans for everything else, we're left with $60 for food and anything else for two months. Mom refused to pay partial rent. She said that the landlord is not a business, and not getting the full rent or not warning him about no rent next month would be a hardship on him, and that isn't the right way to treat a person.

Mom wrote a note to the Community Food Bank explaining she was sick. She's leaving her I.D. to verify her signature on the note, so with my student I.D. from last year to show we're both Rileys, I should be able to get help from them.

I lay quietly, going over our plan, trying to see if we've missed anything. We've covered Mom's job at the Food Mart, the hospital, Doctor Jacob's office, my school, my friend Jen, the landlord, the electric company, the phone company, the caseworker at the welfare office, and the food bank. I can't think of anyone else.

I realize that the amazing part of all our planning isn't the story or solutions we've come up with, but that in just a matter of hours, Mom and I have come to know each other as comrades instead of enemies. I think she respects me. I think I like her. This is huge for us, Mom and me.

My eyes open to Pandy staring at me. I toss him aside and look at the window. It's dark outside. My stomach lets out a growl, and I roll off the bed and stagger to the kitchen.

Mom has made spaghetti. A lot of spaghetti! She's filled the huge pot; the biggest one we own! I lift the lid, and my stomach reminds me again that I've only had one bite of sandwich all day. I laugh at the absurd amount of food,

"Yeah, that should fill me. What are you gonna eat?"

Mom grins. "Well, I figured that if you're going to play cook for the next few weeks, I'd freeze some for later. Help my odds of survival, you know."

"Really. So that's how it is? Where's the trust? The love?"

Mom grins and points at the pot of spaghetti.

"Hmm," I say as I set out plates.

Mom pulls garlic bread from the oven and tosses it on a plate.

I tease, "Ya know, it's a good thing your care won't require sponge baths because I'm thinking right about now, you would be in a world of hurt."

"Well, no more than you having to live in the same house with me."

"Touché."

Mom heaps our plates full, and we both eat like starved hounds, throwing all etiquette and manners out the window.

Mom pushes her plate away and smiles with a contented look on her face. She's happy. She could possibly not wake up from surgery tomorrow morning, but she's happy. It is evidence of her strength and courage. I am struck by it.

With a smirk on her face, Mom says, "You know, Autumn, I got to snoop in your locker today when I went to get your books and assignments."

"Yeah? Too bad it was only the first day of school, you didn't get to see my playgirl pin-ups."

Mom laughs. "What is it with that secretary? Talk about the third degree! She acted like she was my mother. Oh, before I forget, if you need help with your homework you can call and talk to your teachers when they aren't in class."

"Well, that's not gonna happen. I wouldn't know how to sound. Stuffy nose? Raspy voice? Dead?" No sooner than it leaves my mouth, I realize what I've said.

We both turn quiet.

"Well," Mom says, cutting through the atmosphere that my blunder has caused, "I better get some things packed."

I watch her grab a red plastic bag with hard plastic handles on it from the bag drawer. "The Riley suitcase," she says smiling. I see that the advertisement on the bag has worn off.

"Very *Vogue*," I agree and smile.

While she packs, I clean up the kitchen. I pull out the Riley Tupperware, which are empty margarine tubs, and scoop portions of spaghetti in them for freezing.

I think back on the day. I feel like I've dug myself out from under a mountain, but now I still have to climb it. I think of how different my life is going to be. No school means that I don't have to worry at all about school clothes. By the time I go back, the newness of the clothes topic will be over. It's a silly, tiny relief, but relief just the same. Also, I won't be seeing Ian Taylor. He probably won't survive the bombardment of female hormones. Maybe he'll forget that he ever sat next to me in World History. Maybe by the time I return, my seat will be full, then I can avoid questions, explanations and his girlfriend's perfume clinging to him.

Knock it off, Autumn! You chose to lay these bricks in Mom's prison wall. You chose to cut yourself off for a while. No self-pity allowed! You will do this, and with no regrets.

My thoughts go to Mom being on the phone with the doctor's office. The doctor's business card was laying on the coffee table, its edges curled and creased. Evidence of Mom's nervousness and fear. Then it hit me. She called in sick to work because she was waiting for the results from the doctor. Waiting to see her fate, while I told her I hated her! Once again, my eyes open to realities in life that I never considered before. Life is not all about me. I am ashamed again of my selfishness and my blindness. I replay Mom's response to my cutting words this morning. She was patient with me, even through her anger and fear.

I put my old life, the old Autumn, behind me right then, and I begin to climb my mountain.

Three

My alarm clock beeps, so I blindly hit at it until it shuts up. It's 4:00 a.m. I roll onto my back, sinking into the soft warmth of my bed. Then I remember. Mom. Sick. Hospital. I have to go.

I climb out of bed and stumble to the bathroom. It's humid. Steam fogs the mirror from Mom's shower. I hear her rummaging around in her room. I turn on the shower and step into the hot spray. Today is the first day of our secret life. I feel a conspirator's tingle run through my body. I recap the final details of today's plan.

We'll walk to the hospital this morning since I can't drive the car back. That will save us five bucks on cab fare. In our world, there are no close friends holding out offers to drive us. On my way home, I'll stop at the Food Mart; my first trip for groceries. I'll make a trip each day while Mom is in the hospital. I can carry it home a little at a time, yet have it done before she is back. I don't want to leave her here alone. I have $30.00 in the food stamp debit card to last three weeks, and $30.00 cash until Mom gets another paycheck in probably six weeks. Out of the cash, I need to get candles, T. P., batteries for the flashlight, and bandages for Mom. The rest can go to food. The water pounds on my back, and I relax and wake up at the same time. I should go to the food bank first, then I can use our money to create meals around what they give us. I'm pleased with myself. I can budget! I can do this! I step out of the shower and think of our fight yesterday over the money to go to the mall. I push away the guilt feeling.

Mom and I leave the house with an hour to spare. It is still dark out and cold. Fog curls through the street, dampening my hair. We walk slowly, a stroll really. We don't talk. I can hear the Falls in the distance.

My secret world is calling out to me. My world that lives between the walls of Mom's world and the walls of the outside world.

I feel uneasy. Guarded. I don't want to share this place with her, this private part of me. I feel close to panic the closer we get to them. I resent her invasion of the most private and safe place I know. I remind myself that physically this is a public place and she is just another passer-by and that I will still have my non-physical secret. The thought calms my panic.

Mom stops midway across the footbridge. We can't see the Falls, and I'm selfishly relieved. They've hidden themselves in the dark and softened their voice in the fog. They are protecting my secret. My panic turns to comfort as I realize the Falls' mutual affection for me. My Falls.

While we inhale the sound of the muffled roar but exhale plumes of white vapor to join the fog, I can sense that Mom is mentally preparing for surgery. I stay quiet. What is there to say anyway? I know that this could all go bad and that right now could be the last memorable moment I ever have with my mom.

I close my eyes. I feel the darkness heavy on my body, and the fog wraps around me like a blanket, yet feels cold and lonely on my body. The Fall's violent rhythm keeps time with my heart's beat. I own each of these sensations.

"Autumn," Mom says softly, breaking my trance. She is looking out over the rail as if she can see the Falls. "You are the best thing that has ever happened in my life. Do you know that I love you more than words can express?"

She turns her face to me. I don't respond, but I see the sincerity in her eyes. "You don't have to do this, Autumn. You can back out. It's not too late yet. I will love you regardless of your choice."

My throat goes tight, trying to swallow down the reality of why she is describing her love to me. I hide the moment's sensation, and her words, deep inside of me.

"I want to do this, Mom." She looks at me more intensely, nods her head gently like she is answering a question in her mind.

"Mom?"

"Hm?"

"I love you too."

She reaches out and takes me in her arms. There is no hesitation in her hug this time. She feels welcomed by me. She steps back, takes a deep breath, and releases a long white plume. She squares her shoulders, raises her chin and asks, "Ready?"

A stern-looking man enters the waiting room. His beady eyes dart around, then land on me. He's wearing a surgeon's cloth hat and coat. He has a matching face mask that dangles around his neck.

"Autumn Riley?" He moves toward me.

"Yes." I don't like this man. I hold my breath from nervousness I guess, or else my body is rebelling against him. I can barely hear him through the swishing and pounding in my ears. "I'm Doctor Jacobs." He extends his hand. I ignore it. This is the hand that gambled with my Mom's life. "Your mom is out of surgery. It went well." I breathe again. I feel dizzy as he rambles on through a well-rehearsed spiel.

"She's heavily sedated now, but she'll be ready for a visit tomorrow. We're holding her in Post-Op for a few more hours to keep a close eye on her. The surgery was more extensive that I had anticipated."

I look at his tiny eyes and think, *A larger gamble than you were prepared for.* "Will she be okay? I mean, is she out of danger?"

"She'll be fine." He smiles like he knew this all along. "She'll be sore for a while, but I don't foresee any problems."

"You didn't foresee how extensive the surgery would be," I remind him.

His polished smile flickers. "Listen, Autumn, she'll be spoiling grandchildren for years to come."

I take offense to his stereotyping of us. "She doesn't have any grandchildren." I thank him, though I don't know why, other than it is a good way to exit before he tries to touch me again.

The further away I walk from the hospital, the more I feel like a traitor. This isn't how I pictured it. I expected to be there when she woke up, to allow us to seal her moment of success together. I wanted my face to be the first thing she saw when she realized she was back amongst the living. I can't shake the feeling that I am betraying Mom by leaving her in a place where she doesn't belong. I've missed our golden moment of proof that we're a team in our new relationship.

Dear God, please don't let her wake up and think that I don't care. Amen. Oh, and let her know that I'll be there to the end.

The gray, weathered boards of the footbridge creak under my weight. I stop at the place where Mom and I stood together only hours earlier. It feels like that was days ago. I stare at the Falls, who reveal themselves in all their splendor now. The faint mist of spray touches my face. Mom's words slide out from the shadows of my mind. *'You are the best thing that has ever happened in my life. I love you more than words can express.'* I almost believe them. I want to, but I don't own them yet. How can I be the best thing to happen to her?

The crashing sound of the Falls calls to me. They provoke me, or maybe give me permission, and I break down in sobs, sobs of relief, but also of shame for how I've treated Mom the past few years. I listen to the Falls' music, a symphony made up of their roar, my relief and my fears.

The sun peeks from behind a cloud, lighting up the scene in a band of golden glow, but ends short of reaching me. It is majestic. I reach out my hand so that it's bathed in gold. I pull it back to me, and it's my normal color again. I push my hand out again and stare at the goldness. The new mixed with the familiar. My eyes go to the Falls that are also gold. It is like the world has shifted, but I'm the only one who sees it. Even the familiar has a different hue now. The Falls' symphony fades along with the golden glow.

As I stand watching, new water courses down the ancient Falls, I feel both strong and weak, old and new. I square my shoulders and straighten my back in honor of Mom, and I take my next step in this new world of mine.

My stomach screams at the smell of melted margarine on my toast. I think twice but add PB & J anyway. It takes me only seconds to demolish the warm, drippy mess. I plunk two more slices in the toaster. I snoop out the cupboards and fridge, taking inventory. Our meager stock would be sad if it wasn't the normal, which I guess is sad in itself.

I wander through the house feeling alone and in charge of nothing. I know the plan: food bank then the store, but I just don't have the umph to face the public right now. I need to do something, though, besides pacing the floors and thinking of Mom being alone at probably the scariest time of her life. Is this the scariest time of her life? Was she scared when she found out she was pregnant? Or when my Dad left her to raise me alone? Did he leave? Or did she leave?

I'm standing in her bedroom. I can smell her perfume and years of burned incense. Her bed is made, her dresser neat, the curtains . . . I take them in my fingers and rub the lace trim. I look, really look. They're handmade from dark blue sheets. The ruffled valance and ties are sewn neatly; evidence of Mom making our house a home. I've never thought of them like this before. I think of the years that she has worked at the Food Mart. So many extra shifts and putting up with Beehive hair lady, just to come home to a brat who condemned her efforts. I push my shame away. It's not productive. I know what is.

I pull down the curtains, the matching cover that hides a hideous nightstand, and strip her bed. I will clean! I'll deep clean the entire house!

I don't have money to go to the laundry mat, so I'll do the wash in the bathtub like I've seen Mom do sometimes. I go to my room and strip it out too. I study my pink curtains with the big bow accents that were made with love, I'm sure, but with limited taste, I think. I hear Mom's voice, and her words sink a little deeper inside of me. Do you know that I love you more that worlds can express?' "I'm beginning to see that, Mom."

I spend the rest of the day cleaning non-stop. I wash bedding, every curtain in the house, windows, cupboards, floors, and scrub the kitchen and bathroom. I vacuum the carpets and beat the couch cushions to a pulp. Dusk is dawning as I hang the nearly dry curtains back in place. When I finally finish, I collapse on the couch more tired than I've ever been in my life. The windows are wide open, and the September air should be chilly, but it feels good on my sweaty skin. The smell of bleach and pine cleaner offer a fresh newness, complemented by the breeze sweeping through the house.

I have pride in myself. A great sense of satisfaction. Tomorrow I'll wash our clothes. My heart is light, and the fresh scents carry me into sleep in the quiet stillness of our home.

I wake to distant shouts and laughter of some grade schoolers starting their day. The house is freezing. My muscles scream from the cold air, old couch and yesterday's workout. The house has an eerie feel about it. It's so quiet that the loneliness sinks into my soul. I miss my mom. I close the living room window and make my way to the kitchen. I close the window over the sink and turn on a burner to warm my hands. I look around the spotless kitchen and see the cold coffee pot. I make a partial pot of coffee that I know I won't drink, but I need it to at least smell like Mom is here. The trick works. My nose doesn't know that Mom didn't brew it, and the normalcy is comforting. I turn off the burner, then walk through the house closing windows and taking in my accomplishments from yesterday. I feel good. The blankets are almost dry and will be out of my way in time for today's laundry.

I'm not sure when they will move Mom to a regular room, or when they'll give her a dose of morphine that will knock her out again. So, I hurry to the shower not wanting to miss my window of opportunity to cheer her success.

On my way out the door, my eye catches a glint from the keys to the Saab. I pause. I pick them up, thumbing the notched edges. I mentally tick off my errands for the day; hospital, food bank, Food Mart, laundry. My heart pounds as I walk out the door.

I turn over the ignition and the Bloody Rat roars to life. It doesn't pass judgment on me for not being Rita Riley. I start to back down the driveway, but I let the clutch out too fast, and it lurches to its death. I push the clutch in again and roll into the street before I can turn the key again. My heart is pounding out of my chest. I look around to see if a car is going to hit me or if the neighbors are watching. All is quiet. I try the key again, and the Rat breathes. This time I rev the engine high and let the clutch out only halfway, and I move down the street.

Every stop sign is a new battle between me, the illegal driver, and the creeping vermin. When I finally reach the hospital, I pick a parking space at the empty, far end of the lot. I figure, if the Bloody Rat lurches, it can't bite another car. My hands are trembling when I turn off the engine. I sit back in the seat and bark out a laugh. I hadn't moved the seat forward! I drove the entire way pulling myself up to the steering wheel while I worked the pedals! I slide the seat forward and sigh with relief, knowing the drive after this will be much easier.

I get out and slam the door. I glance back to check my parking skills. The car straddles the center line perfectly, taking up two spaces. "I hate you." I can hear the 'tick, tick, tick' of its heart beating at me as its temper cools with the engine.

Four

The hospital looms over me. I look at the rows of windows. They feel like eyes that study me with the weight of God's vision. Like they watch and wait to judge. I wonder which pair are Mom's, and there is a strange comfort in that. Then, I wonder if she saw me pull up in the Bloody Rat. I walk through the automatic doors, and I'm instantly hit in the face with a blast of surreality that smells of medicines and antiseptic. Why are hospitals so white? So hard looking? So foreign? Shouldn't people feel comfort coming to a place of healing? Instead, it feels factual, like hard truths that are non-negotiable.

The information desk gives me Mom's room number, and I hurry to the elevator. As soft Muzak accompanies my ride, I think, *Next trip I'll bring roses from the back yard if any are still in good shape. I also need to pick her up some of those romantic mysteries from the library she likes to read.* I shiver at the thought of them, either that, or the place is too chilly.

I step out into a white-tiled hall that suggests an insane asylum. Some nurse's practical shoes squeak on the too-shiny floor. I half expect to hear the tortured wails of the desperate and long-forgotten come from any one of the dozens of closed doors I pass. I see Mom's room number. I draw a deep breath, put a smile on my face, and step in.

Mom is groggy but awake. My smile grows honest, and I hug her tight. Her hair is a sweat-dried mess. Her eyes look nearly as dark as the bruise on her hand from the I.V. She is so pale that she's almost translucent. She looks like one of those aliens I've seen on T.V.

We share relief over her success and discuss her pain level, of which there hasn't been much yet because she's been knocked-out on morphine almost the whole time.

I go to the too-white bathroom and wet down a wash cloth. I ball it up in my hand to keep it warm on the way back to her bed. I wipe the sheen from her face and brush the front part of her hair. I can't get the back, she's not able to lean forward enough for me to reach it. I hand her a complimentary-sized bottle of mouthwash and give her a tray to spit in.

I sit in the visitor's chair. I don't know what to talk about. Life outside this place seems trivial and a whole universe away. All I can think of is that yesterday Mom didn't fit in this place, but today she does. What did that beady-eyed man do to her? I want to roll her, bed and all, out of here and take her home where he can't touch her.

Mom is not really staring at me, it's more like she's drinking me in with her eyes. I move from the chair to her bed and gently sit. I ask with my eyes, in that non-verbal language that moms and daughters share if I am hurting her. Her eyes answer, *I thought you'd never get here!* I feel my eyes get hot with tears. I make a conscious effort not to think of leaving her here or how close I came to losing her forever.

"So, was it a piece of cake?" I tease her, mocking her famous quip when things are tough. She chuckles, and I watch her face wince a little as her hand tightens on her lower stomach. "I'm so glad you came, Autumn." She whispers like it's a conspiracy. "You're exactly what I need. Better than being drugged into oblivion."

Suddenly, the door bursts open, startling us both. A nurse comes squeaking in, way too cheerily and loud.

"Well, look at you! Entertaining guests already! Sorry to crash the party, but it's time to have a peek at that incision and for more sleepy juice."

I instantly hate this woman. I kiss Mom and whisper, "I'll be back this evening. We'll plan your escape."

Mom smiles, and slowly blinks her eyes, which in our language means "yes."

I'm fuming inside as I leave her room. Mom is obviously in pain, and that nurse is treating her like a mentally ill child. How dare she?

I climb into the Saab and slam the door. I crank the engine and yell at the Bloody Rat. "Don't you try anything with me, 'cuz I'm not in the mood! I put it in reverse and back up. "I've heard that people who drive Saabs, sob. Well, in my world you'll be the first thing to get scrapped! You just remember that, Rat."

Rat car heeds my threat. I drive with engine revved high, clutch half out and roll slowly home with only a few lurches.

My spirits are low. I just can't face anybody right now. I decide to run errands later. I just want to be alone, no pretenses of 'life is normal,' no fighting with the Bloody Rat. I need time to think. I'm feeling the weak part of me in this new world of mine.

I keep picturing Mom's transparent skin, then my golden hand at the Falls. I know that she is going through a life shift like I am. I move from weakness to fear. I bounce around in them until I have doubts about my ability to save our home. I have the bathroom floor heaped with laundry and the tub filled with hot, soapy water. I toss in some shirts and blouses first, things that are quick work.

I feel better. My spirits lift a little when they are clean. I fill the sink with bleach water and toss in whites to soak while washing jeans in the tub.

Mom's face just won't leave my head. I wonder if she'll ever go back to her normal self again. Hearing the word surgery, then seeing the after effects are two different things. It's shocking. I'm not so sure anymore that I can handle all of this on my own. So much could go wrong! This isn't like nursing someone back from the flu. What was I thinking when I told her I could do this? What was she thinking when she let me? Four to six weeks of this? Really? Why did I say I'd do this!

I scream out, "This isn't fair!" I sling my half-washed jeans across the bathroom. I feel so helpless. I sit on the floor, my back against the wall and watch the mirror cry sudsy tears of splatter. I pull my knees up, hugging them, and I cry.

A thousand tears fall for a thousand reasons. I let my mind run free, and I count off those reasons. I cry because I'm hungry all the time, sick of doing laundry in the tub, and a little scared to spend the next three of four nights alone. I am lonely, and none of my friends have called to see how I'm doing. Mom ran Dad off, I'm sure, but I'm still trying to love them both. If I recreate Mom and me, then I am a traitor to Dad and my life-long hope of ever knowing him. If I continue my fight to learn who he is, then I am a traitor to Mom and holding back my devotion to her. If Mom dies under my care, can I live with myself knowing that in some way I betrayed her, us? Can our relationship even work with the Dad question standing between us? Every turn I make is a betrayal to Mom, Dad, or myself. Every choice feels bad, deceitful, and turns me into a person that I don't want to be. So, I cry. Until I let everything out, and there are no tears left.

I reach over and pull toilet paper from the roll. I pull beyond the point of 'house rules' length. I keep pulling and pulling, rebellious in my obvious waste. The paper tears off on its own. I shove the huge pillow-size wad to my face and blow my nose. I throw it in the toilet and start pulling again. It feels good to break the rules, even though it will cost money later that I don't have. When I've emptied the roll, I feel a satisfying guiltiness. I smile. I feel like myself again. The old Autumn. The brat. It feels good to be normal.

I look down and see that I'm sitting on a pile of clothes that still need washing. I sigh. I see a familiar brown and green paisley print. I jump up, grab the hated skirt, and go to the kitchen then out the back door.

I'm standing in the middle of the yard when I watch my hands light a match. The frayed hem catches fast, and, within seconds, I watch flames swallow the soft, worn-thin fabric. My heart beats fast in guilt, fear and pleasure. I toss the skirt to the ground and let it die in a heap.

Then, the strangest thing happens; I feel in charge. A new strength, a clean strength fills my entire body. I just rid my life of something I hate! I laugh out loud, pleased with myself. I've made a choice for me, for Autumn, and I didn't waver! I can do this! All of it! I will nurse Mom back to health, I will save my home, and I will find my Dad. I will be true to myself, and if it is betraying anyone else, well . . . I will hope their love is strong enough to forgive me.

As I walk back into the house to finish the laundry, I decide that it is probably best to tell Mom about her skirt while she's still bedridden.

I hurry through the remaining laundry, and before long, I have clothes dripping from hangers in every doorway of the house. Clothes drip in closets and from the shower curtain rod too. I wipe down the bathroom, erasing evidence of the storm that erupted earlier. I put on a new roll of toilet paper without batting an eye.

I scarf down two bowls of rice using up the last of the milk. I realize that skipping meals isn't saving food because I just eat twice as much later. I make a mental note that we have plenty of cinnamon, which will help us get through a long stretch of boring meals. I really need to go shopping. I can't put it off any longer.

I make a call to the Deer Falls Community Outreach, and they give me the number for the food bank. I call and find out they are located at a church not far from my house and will be open until 5:00 today. If I don't make it today, they won't be open again until next week. Guess I'm going today.

I run out to the yard and find some decent roses. It's already 2:00, so I take a speed shower then grab the keys on my way out the door.

I go to the library first because I'm a little nervous about the whole note thing for the food bank. The library is quiet and will ease me back into the public eye while I get my nerve up.

I find some of those weird books that Mom likes, and find out there are videos to help with Algebra. I'll go later and use them instead of calling my teacher.

Later, I find myself standing behind a woman with three young children as she is handed bags of food. I'm embarrassed, and I worry they won't help a teenager with a note from her mom. It doesn't take long to realize that everybody who comes here needs help, and the workers are kind. They give me a box and two bags full of food. There's powdered milk, beans, rice, chicken bouillon, a block of cheese, a block of butter and a huge can of peanut butter that I see her put in the box. I want to cry from relief. The lady asks if I need laundry soap, shampoo, or toilet paper. I accept them humbly. I'm embarrassed to ask, and almost don't, but forge ahead.

"You don't by chance have any candles, do you?"

"Yes! I think we do," she says, eager to help. She rushes off and comes back handing me a box of birthday candles. She is so pleased to help make someone's birthday nice, that I don't have the heart to not accept them. I thank her, like they are just exactly what I wanted, and make a mental note to get more specific in the future.

The Bloody Rat and I fight all the way to the Food Mart. I shut off the engine and sit staring at the sign: Deer Falls Food Mart. I scan the sale items posted in large print covering the windows, trying to figure out how to best spend the $60 we have. I figure lots of bread. We'll be living on grilled cheese sandwiches, peanut butter sandwiches, rice and beans. I go inside.

I push my cart into the checkout lane. Beehive hair lady is finishing up with the customer in front of me. I begin putting my carefully chosen items on the counter. Beehive hair lady is her usual patronizing self, full of fake smiles and completing our ritual with, 'The Look.' Some things never change. I watch her bag up the groceries and plop them carelessly into the cart. She ends with a look of pity on her face. "Well, Autumn, you be sure and tell your momma that she's in all our prayers, honey."

"Thank you, I will. Oh! And you be sure to tell Rod that I hope he's feeling better too. It's too bad he's had to miss the first two days of the school year."

I wheel my cart out, cherishing the look on her face as she's thinking that Rod is skipping school already this year and what she's planning to do about that. I unload the groceries and put the cart back. I slide into the Bloody Rat enjoying how good it feels to stick up for myself. Hey! I just grew a spine! "Piece of cake!" I yell and crank up the Rat.

When I get to the hospital, I park in my usual end of the lot. I grab up the three faded, pink roses and the library books and head into the asylum.

Mom is sitting up a little higher in her bed this afternoon. The color has returned to her face enough that she looks solid again. It's more of a relief to me than I expect. Mom must see the relief in my face because she gives a little laugh at my expression.

Hi, Mom." I stretch over the bed and hug her. She feels thinner to me. I set the books down. "Here. Romantic mysteries, or mysterious love, something like that." I roll my eyes.

She grins at me. "Thanks. They lowered my doses now so I can stay awake long enough to enjoy them. What's that?" She points at the flowers, grinning.

"A little piece of home," I say, putting them into her drinking cup and filling it with water. She takes them and breathes in their fragrance. "Mmm, thank you, Autumn. This is better medicine than anything these people have to offer." She smiles, "See? I knew you'd be good at this."

"Yeah? Well, wait 'til you have your fifteenth grilled cheese sandwich in a row, then tell me how good I'm doing!" I laugh.

"Just having fifteen of them is a miracle!" She grins. "Any problems with the food bank?" She looks a little worried.

"No. They were very nice."

Mom smiles. "Good."

"So, is there still spaghetti left?"

"Yes!" I laugh.

We keep our conversation light. We're just confirming within ourselves and to each other that we are still okay and that we both still want and need our relationship to heal.

My drive home only has two or three lunges in it. I can even let the clutch out all the way sometimes if I have a long enough stretch of road to get my speed up. Maybe I can do this. I smile, then smile bigger. "You are doing this, girl!"

I grab two of the bags of groceries from the back seat and jog up the stairs. It's dark out, and I haven't left any lights on. The streetlight alone lights the stairs. I open the front door and hit the light switch. I yelp! Clothes hanging in the kitchen archway look like robbers.

I drop the bags and rip down the now dry clothes. I'll be locking up from now on. I begin talking loud and laughing like I'm not really, alone. If there is an intruder, they'll hear me and escape before I get to them. I cautiously walk through the house turning on every light switch I pass. I hit the hallway, bathroom, my room, then Mom's room. I breathe a sigh of relief. I check the closets. All good. I go back through the living room and turn on the porch light. The throw rug from Mom's room drapes over the back-porch railing. It can just stay there.

I dread going back out to the car for the rest of the groceries, but I do it. I toss each bag just inside the living room door with each trip. When I get them all in, I lock the door behind me and feel better. I take the bags to the kitchen and am happy with all we've got. I can make this last until the food stamp card renews. I'm especially proud of the small can of coffee I managed for Mom. It's a welcome home treat that I know she doesn't expect. She'll have to have powdered milk in it instead of regular, but I know she'll like it anyway.

I crank up my stereo to drown out any noises. I don't want to hear intruders trying to come in, but then I turn the music down so I can hear them. I yank down all the laundry and take it to Mom's room to fold. I sit on her bed, pretending I'm not alone and that she's going to walk into the room any minute. It helps a little.

I put our clothes away and make sure Mom's drawers are neat and tidy. I hang her hangables, making sure there are no wrinkles. My eyes travel up to the high shelf that tops her closet. She has boxes stacked up there. I know what's in them. They are her old keepsakes, weird stuff that she likes, but won't set out and enjoy for fear of them getting broken or ruined. I pull the boxes down. Maybe it's time for her to start enjoying the little things in life. I open one that I don't remember seeing before. It's full of old pictures, black and whites of her parents, I assume. There are pictures of her as a child and full packages of my school pictures. She's never had anyone to send copies to, and apparently, she can't throw the extras away. So, they sit in this over-stuffed box. I see snapshots of me that either I don't remember or have never seen.

There's a notebook, no, three notebooks. I open one and realize that these are Mom's diaries! I quickly put them back how I found them and restack all the boxes just right. I don't want her knowing that I've seen her private hiding place.

I want to read them out of pure nosiness, but that is an invasion of her privacy. I won't dishonor her trust like that. I'd feel guilty for the rest of my life hiding a secret like that. Besides, what if there was stuff in there about her sex life? *Oh God! Don't even go there!* But then, Mom doesn't even date, so what am I thinking? Then again, the notebook looked old. Then it hits me. Dad! My dad could be in those notebooks! My heart is pounding now. Should I do this forbidden thing? Will she ever tell me about him on her own? The need to know who my dad is, and the possible first clue ever in my life to finding out about him, is too much. I remember the promise I made to myself, that I would find him.

I pull the diaries back out and take them to my own room where I don't feel Mom's eyes on me. I open the first one and begin to read about myself.

> *Oct. 10, 1999 (Almost 3 yrs.)*
>
> *Autumn keeps asking where her daddy is. She has a friend next door whose daddy lives with her. Autumn doesn't understand that she doesn't have a daddy, only a mommy. She'll see strangers in the store, point, then ask if he is her daddy.*

Jan 8th, 2000 (3yrs. next week)

Today Autumn informed me that Elisha's mommy said that everybody has a mommy and a daddy. It's just that sometimes people don't get to see their daddy. For her birthday, she wants to see her daddy. I told her that her daddy can't come to see her, and my smart little girl wanted to know why. I told her that he didn't know where she lives. She asked me why I don't tell him. I said because if he came to see her, it would make him cry when he left. She told me that he didn't have to go, that he could live here. He could sleep in her bed with her and Pandy. I explained that he already had a house and his own bed so he can't live here. She thought about that for a minute, and diary, I walked away before my smart little star could argue the point anymore. We ate cookies and played Chutes and Ladders.

I sit, dazed. I can't read anymore. Not right now. I'm so angry and hurt! I don't get it! How can she do this to me? She tells me she loves me, but she always avoids any questions I have about Dad! What is the big secret? Does he even know I exist?

I feel the old feelings creeping back in. I remember clearly why I've hated her for so long. I grab Pandy and hug him to me. I look into his face, rub his ears and nose. I turn out my light and cry myself to sleep. I wake later by a sound. I realize it's me, whimpering in my sleep. Pandy is faithfully keeping watch over me.

Five

Daylight streaming through my windows brings me fully awake. This is the third morning since Mom went to the hospital. I know she'll probably be there one more day, given the way she looked last night. She is doing better, but I doubt she is well enough to come home yet.

I call the hospital to be sure. The nurse on her floor, the obnoxious one that I can't stand, tells me the earliest that they will release her is tomorrow morning, but only if all goes well—when they can control her pain with Perca-somethings, when her appetite improves, and when she is able to walk a little, then she can come home.

I put on water for rice and pull out bread for toast. Pandy, is tucked under my arm, but I sit him on my lap like a child when I sit at the table. I pull the journal I read last night across the table closer to me. I'm ready to see what it says, and I steel myself against my fears. I feel like I'm on the cusp of a secret that is bigger than me. A secret that Mom has always protected me from. She doesn't know that this secret is what has kept us distant all these years. I need the truth more than her protection.

I think of my hurt turned to anger. I remember that anger turning toward her, but I'm foggy on when it grew into a full-blown hatred. The heat of my hatred, when exhausted, transformed into disgust. They say that love's opposite is hate. They are wrong. I've watched love's decline, and its opposite is indifference. You can't hate a person if you truly don't care. Mom and I, we came so close to no return.

We're both trying so hard to get along now, to heal us. Can we honestly heal, while this secret lives between us? Wouldn't we just live lives of smiles and jokes, with no real depth? Is that good enough? Isn't that just another path to indifference? What if this secret exposes that Mom is the reason that my dad left? Will I be able to forgive her? Will I lose Mom over an already lost dad? Do I even have the right to force these answers?

I consider this new world of mine. I realize that my tough choices can have tough consequences. My next move will affect the rest of my life, I'm just not sure how. My heart beats hard. I open the journal, stepping through the gateway of fear and into the acceptance of consequences for my actions.

Aug. 19th, 2002 (6 yrs. old)

Autumn plowed into my lap today, her face buried in my chest sobbing. Her entire body heaved with gasps of breath. She wailed in absolute agony, "Why doesn't my Daddy love me?" I swear, I heard my heart snap in two. I felt a piece of it lodge in my throat. Diary, I lied to my daughter today. I told her that he did love her, but if he came to see her, then welfare would make him pay money, and he didn't have it. Dear God. Help me here.

I don't remember this particular time that Mom has written about, but I do remember the agony, the utter emptying of myself with tears over my dad too many times to count. My heart breaks now for this child that was me. I want to hug her and tell her it will be okay. I want to give her, her Dad or at least the answers to the questions that she doesn't know how to ask.

July 23rd, 2004 (8 yrs. old)

I've dated a few guys over the past couple of years. I've just told Gary, the latest and the last, that this just isn't working. He didn't understand, and I didn't explain. How could I? How can I tell him that he will not make a good dad for Autumn? How can I explain that seeing him snap his fingers at her, to command her to wait on him like a servant, is unacceptable to me? He wouldn't grasp my reason for disgust, nor would he understand that this is not something I want to see grow in our home. Autumn and I both deserve better.

This woman, my mom, was trying to fix her little girl's broken heart. She was unsuccessful. I feel tears begin to build, and close the journal.

I look around the kitchen. My rice water is at a hard boil, and the bread is in the toaster, ready to be sunk. I look at the clock. It's 9:00. It's getting late, and I need to get ready to visit Mom. I turn off the stove, leaving the pan and the toaster where they sit. I tuck the journals under my mattress. I don't know who I'm hiding them from. Maybe I'm just re-burying words from the past that I never should have known.

I leave the house, but make sure to turn on lights and lock the door. I stare at the Bloody Rat in the driveway. I let it sleep and walk down my street.

The Falls' familiar call is a comfort, so I stop on the bridge to watch them. My secret place reveals itself in that majestic way it has. I take in the tall trees, the thirsty ferns and the relentless flow of water. Its calm serenity and evolving violence rumble deep inside of me as if acknowledging that it knows of my new choices and discoveries. Those which can give me peace or destroy what I do have left.

I think of what I read this morning and look from the perspective of a single mother. Suddenly I realize, I have shaped my Mom's life, not the other way around! This is a shock to me. All my life I have blamed her for everything that is missing in my life—a dad, clothes, a nice house and car. Though, in reality, she was missing these things first, because she chose me over an easier life.

I stare at the Falls in astonishment. I leave my secret place a bit wiser, my soul a little older, and my heart a little softer. I glance back at the Falls and whisper, "You truly are inspirational to me."

When I arrive at the hospital, I find Mom sitting up in bed. She has showered, is eating Jell-O and she has some color to her face.

"Look at you! God, you look fantastic!" I throw my arms around her and can feel her strength. "When are you leaving this nut house?"

She tells me what I already know, but I let her share her good news. She is so happy about it.

"I had help getting in and out of the shower, but managed okay other than that. And . . . I walked to the bathroom and back, with no hand-holding." She smiles a child's proud smile. I laugh.

We visit for about an hour. It's good to see her awake and off the morphine. Her Percocets are kicking in, so I put the T.V. on the weather channel for the soothing music and hand her the partially-read love story.

"I'll have a car here for you at 8:00 tomorrow, okay?"

She smiles and nods. I open the drawer of her nightstand and shove all the gauze, tape, and salve into my purse.

Mom's eyes widen, she gasps. "Autumn! What are you doing?"

"It's fine." I pat her arm and smile. "This is part of our budget plan. The revised plan. Oh, and when Nurse Ratched from *One Flew Over The Cuckoo's Nest* brings in more, take a walk to your closet and stash the goods in your vogue suitcase." I waggle my eyebrows at her.

She shakes her head but smiles. "I've created a monster."

"Oh, and–"

"What now, Autumn?" she interrupts.

I whisper, "Ask for extra supplies to take home with you until you can get to the store."

I hug her tight and whisper, "I love you, Mom."

She tilts her head at me and says, "Autumn . . ." but there are no words to define it all, and I know this.

I leave, waving and blowing her a kiss as I walk out the door in a sassy manner. Mom is smiling.

I walk home with a lift to my step. This is finally my last night alone! I run through last minute things to tidy up before she comes home. I want the house spotless. Also, I'll leave the stereo on so the house doesn't feel so empty and lonely when she steps through the door. I'm excited to show her that I haven't just been a lazy bum but that I've been working hard to bring her home where she is safe and loved.

My thoughts turn to my dad. It would be easier if he were here to help me. I wonder, *what is he like? What does he look like? Why did he leave? Does he even know about me? Why won't Mom talk about him? Was he an alcoholic? A druggie? Gay? What?* Those are the same old questions with no answers that I've had my entire life.

By the time I reach home, I'm determined to find those answers or as many as I can. I'll read every page of Mom's journals if I have to. It's time to solve this mystery!

* * *

Sept. 21st, 2004 (8 yrs. old)

Today Autumn came home from Elisha's house and informed me that my name is now Mom. Apparently, Mommy is for little kids. I don't think I like Elisha very much.

Jan. 15th, 2005 (9th B-day)

Elisha couldn't come to Autumn's birthday party. Elisha's parents are getting divorced, so Elisha and her mom moved out today. Autumn kept checking the front window, in case Elisha came back home.

Later, when I finished setting the table for dinner, I went to call her in. I found her standing on Elisha's porch talking to Elisha's dad. She asked him if he still loved Elisha since she didn't live there now. I couldn't hear his answer. Then she asked if he would go visit Elisha. I called her home then.

I scan the pages of the journal looking for my name, or my age near the date of entries. It doesn't escape me that Mom is logging my growth and questions about my dad. These are topics not entered in my baby book.

Sept. 5th, 2005 (9 yrs. old)

Autumn came home from school today, took one look at me, and burst into tears. She didn't come to me for comfort. Instead, she ran past me to her room and grabbed Pandy. I followed her and asked what happened. She said that the teacher asked everybody to tell the names of all their family members. Of course, she didn't know her father's name and said so. At recess, the kids made fun of her for being too stupid to know her own dad's name. One of the boys called her retarded. I'll call the school tomorrow. What was that teacher thinking?

November 10th, 2005 (9 yrs. old)

I saw Jack Stogavich on the news today. She favors him somewhat.

My heart stops. This! This is it! I read it again to make sure. It has to be him! "Jack Stogavich." I say his name out loud, my dad's name, for the first time in my life. "Autumn Stogavich. Dad! Oh God."

My hands are trembling so bad that the journal is bouncing up and down. I set it down. I stand up. I read the words again.

"Oh God."

I pace the floor. What to do next? I run to the phone and dial the hospital's number, but I hang up before they answer. I stand in front of the picture window and look out, for what I don't know. I yell out loud, "Jack Stogavich! Jack, I favor you!" My voice drops. "Jack, I'm coming to find you."

I grab the keys and jump into the Saab.

"Umm . . . Google! I need the internet! Library!"

I crank up the engine and go. I'm not even aware that I'm driving unless I kill the rat, which happens too often because I'm not paying attention to my driving. My brain is swirling with possibilities and creating its own home movies.

I picture the happy reunion when I finally see Dad in person. There will be tears, he'll tell me that he is so sorry. I will forgive him. He will tell me how beautiful I've become, and that I have my grandmother's smile. He'll cry for wasting so many years. I'll go to his house, a huge yellow house with a big white wraparound porch and balcony. I'll go there for Christmas, Thanksgiving and on the weekends.

Of course, there'll be joint custody. I'll have clothes, a new stereo, CDs galore! I'll have a huge bedroom that I get to decorate however I want!

I think of my bedroom now with the pink, handmade curtains. What will happen with Mom and me? Will I eventually go live at Dad's?

The home movies are running rampant in my head, so I'm surprised when I'm suddenly looking into the librarian's face.

"Oh, um . . . a computer, please. With internet."

"There is a charge of fifteen cents for fifteen minutes. If you go over the block of time, you pay for the next block whether you use it all or not."

"Fine. That's fine."

I find two Jack Stogavichs.

I click on the first one, and my heart drops. He's an inmate. Arrested in 1998. I do the math; I'd have been one to two years old. It fits the 'babe-in-arms' tale. I search the prison website and type in his name. A picture of a stranger in a jumpsuit stares back at me. He looks like a normal guy except for the clothes. He has dark blonde hair, blue eyes, and fair skin like me. This can't be him though, Mom's journal said he was on the news in 2005. Unless . . . he had new charges, or new evidence on his case come up. I read his profile. D.O.B. 7-12-1978, sentenced on 12-15-1998 to life in prison, not parole eligible. His charges are kidnapping, robbery, and murder.

I look at the face of this man. Maybe he doesn't look so normal. This is what a murderer looks like? Is this my dad? He could have been on the news if they were questioning his guilt. He looks guilty I decide, and go back to the list with the second Jack's name. I click on Jack Stogavich.

The screen reads; Jack Stogavich, D.O.B. 6-5-1975, US Senator, Miami, Florida.

I search the internet for articles about this Senator Stogavich. I find a recent reference to the Miami Herald and click on the link.

There's a photo of what looks to be a community speech. I read the captioned names below the picture to find Jack.

He is a big man who towers over the others on the platform. His large hand swallows the hand that he is shaking, as he poses for the camera. His size alone, I think, would give pause to a gang of street thugs. He's huge. I zoom into his face and stare at his eyes. His is a face of strength, determination and power. *Is this my dad?* This photo is black and white, but I can tell he has light-colored hair and light eyes. I look at his nose. I pull my compact from my purse and look at my own face. I touch my nose, then touch the screen where his nose is. I close the website and pay the librarian forty-five cents.

I drive home, pleased with my accomplishments, yet nervous and antsy. Either one of the Jacks could be my dad. I consider both scenarios played out. I think: *Prison visits? No. Senator in Florida? If it is him, then why has he never contacted me?*

When I get home, I immediately dial 411.

"I'm sorry, ma'am, that is an unlisted number."

Of course, it would be. How stupid of me! "Um . . . Can you get me the number of Senator Stogavich's office then, please?"

"Certainly. That number is . . ."

I write down the number, then dial. An operator answers then transfers to Jack's office. As the extension rings, my hand begins to tremble again. I almost hang up when his assistant answers, but instead, I manage to schedule a ten-minute call with him later in the day. I posed as a reporter for *The Miami Herald*. I don't know how I thought of it, the words just came out of my mouth, and they worked.

I pace the floor. *Oh Lord, is he my dad? What if he isn't? How embarrassing will that be! What if he is? Oh Jeez!* I pace to the kitchen and see the now cold pot of water and bread perched in the toaster. I slowly push down the lever and watch the bread disappear. I stare at the bread as it heats up. I watch it shrink in size. I can smell it cook. It pops up, and I yelp. I smear butter over it, take a bite that my throat won't let pass. I spit it in the trash and toss the toast in after.

I grab up the journals. I re-read the entry that may change my life, just to make sure, again, that I have his name right. I do. I scan all three journals for more information about him. His name is mentioned only the one time, in keeping with the great secret that is my dad. I grab up Pandy, crush him to my chest, and sit on the couch staring at the phone.

There is a soft click then, "Jack Stogavich here." The voice is deep, old-sounding. It is gruff with a politically correct, cheerful, yet condescending flair to it. "Hello?"

"Did the call drop?" I hear him call out, probably to his assistant.

"Hello," I manage.

"Oh! There you are. Autumn, is that correct?"

"Yes. Autumn Riley." He doesn't respond to my name. "I'm calling Jack, because, well, ha, I think you're my father." I cringe inside and out. Where's my quick thinking now? There's dead silence as he processes what I've said.

"Who is this? I thought this was an interview!"

"I am Rita Riley's daughter. I am fifteen, and I believe that you are my dad."

"Now you listen here, I don't know what kind of prank you're trying to pull—"

"This isn't a prank—"

"I don't know who put you up to this, but somebody will pay. I don't know any Rita Riley, and if you ever call here again, I'll have you arrested for slander and harassment! Do I make myself clear?"

The phone goes dead. My hand is shaking so badly that I can barely hang up the receiver. I run to the bathroom and get sick.

I find myself walking, I don't know where to. I just know that I can't sit staring at the walls. Suddenly, I realize the mist of the Falls is sprinkling my face. I watch the water cascade over the cliff's edge from up high. I focus on a spot. There, on an imaginary single drop of water. I let my eyes follow it all the way down. Falling, falling, until the drop shatters over the rocks below, into a million pieces, and is swept away by the turbulence. A single drop that is insignificant, broken without care, then cast aside by the grand scheme of the river. I heard once that part of these waters goes to the city sewer system. How appropriate.

Something catches my eye. I look closer. There's movement down below me. On the river's shore stands Ian Taylor. He raises his arm and waves. I lift my hand, palm forward. *How silly,* I think, *that I can lose a lost dad, and a little later feel my heart rise because Ian waved at me.* "God, I'm pitiful!"

I turn and walk back home.

I pick up the journals and take them back to their hiding places in Mom's room. I open the box and thumb through the faces of the past.

Mom, young and laughing at every turn. Me at one of my birthday parties. Our lives' stories lay at my fingertips. Stories with a missing part. The journals revealed a secret all right, one I'd be better off not knowing, more than likely. No, that isn't true, I had to find out about my dad, or it would have destroyed me.

Dear diary, this is what I know about my dad: 1. His name is Jack Stogavich. 2. He is either a murderer or a liar who doesn't want me. Amen.

I tidy up Mom's room and place scented candles around the room. I bring in a water pitcher and glass for her nightstand. I look at the knick-knack boxes in her closet but decide that to display them now might draw suspicion to her journals. I don't want her to know that I've betrayed her trust.

I pull out a stick of incense, which I hate, and set it up in its holder on the dresser. It is a peace offering of sorts to Mom. I'm ready for her to come home.

Six

oday is the day! Mom is coming home. I'm more excited than I thought I'd be. Nervous too. I wipe down the bathroom, again, now that the shower steam has cleared. I check for missed crumbs on the kitchen counter and pull out the can of coffee for display next to the pot. I make my bed and kick my dirty clothes into my closet. I rearrange the candles in Mom's room, again.

The first thing I will do is make her a cup of coffee. I go back to the kitchen and pull out the Riley Tupperware. I fill two tubs; one with sugar, the other with powdered milk. I dust the counter with my hand to get the spilled granules. I set the tubs on the table, then arrange her favorite cup and a spoon at her usual place. I know she'll be surprised. She'd never guess that coffee would even cross my mind, much less that I'd buy it on our meager budget. I wonder what she is going to do when I pull up in the Bloody Rat. Will she be mad? Or refuse? I remind myself that I am responsible for my actions, there is no turning back now. I look at the clock: 7:40. Time to go!

Nurse Ratched insists on wheeling Mom out of the hospital. I argue, but it's hospital rules. She tells me to have our cousin bring the car to the front doors. I look around, I'm at a loss. Mom seems intrigued. She's got that little controlled smile of hers and those raised eyebrows that say, "Well?"

"Well, I'll just go . . . now," I say pointing at the door. The nurse gives me a funny look like I'm a nut job or something.

I pull the Rat up to the pick-up spot and turn off the engine. Mom spots me first. The look on her face is, well, I'm not really, sure. It kinda shifts from surprise, to fear, to humor. All three roll across her face. I take a deep breath and open the passenger door like it's the most normal, everyday thing to do.

I help Mom out of the wheelchair and start her toward the car. Nurse Ratched starts to object, but I interrupt her.

"Oh, my aunt stayed at the house, getting a surprise party ready." I smile in Mom's face and say, "Surprise! Ha-ha."

I get her in the seat and grab the seat belt.

Old woman Ratched won't let go. "I thought it was a cousin?"

I quickly make my way around the front of the car to the driver's side. "Oh, actually it is. We just call her Aunt Dorothy, don't know why, we just always have. Aunt Dorothy and Uncle Bob."

I close my door and can hear her say something about hospital rules, liabilities and not being held responsible. I start the engine while she's still talking, pretending I can't hear her.

She knocks on Mom's window, "Are you even old enough to drive?"

"Well, now, if I wasn't, Aunt Dorothy would be here, wouldn't she?"

I rev the engine high, let the clutch out slowly halfway, and we make our getaway.

Mom laughs out loud, grabs her stomach, but still laughs. "Who taught you to drive?"

"Well, you did Mom. I've watched you do it all my life."

She laughs again. "Well try not to burn out my clutch, okay?"

I grin. "What? This? Aw, this is nothing, you should have seen me two days ago."

"Hmm," she says still smiling. "Autumn, as your mom, I think it's important to tell you that you should stay away from a life of crime. You are the worst liar!"

"That bad huh?"

"Yes! I've always known when you were lying! You stammer and hop from foot to foot. It's crazy."

"Now wait just a minute here!" I raise a finger in the air to make my point. "I remember once you came running out of the bathroom, in a big ol' fuss, looking for your lipstick. You dumped your purse out on the couch, getting madder by the minute, but of course, I had it in my hot little hand. I didn't know what to do, so I threw it into the pot of chicken soup you had on the stove."

"What? Why?"

"Because you had me trapped in the kitchen, and you were headed there to third degree me!"

"No way. I would have found it when I stirred the soup."

"Nope. You'd been called into work, which is how the whole fiasco started anyway, and you shoved the soup, pot and all, in the fridge! For three days, I sweated that soup! Every time I'd hear the refrigerator door open, I'd go into this panic, and I heard that door every single time! I hate your chicken soup by the way."

Mom laughs. "Well, it served you right. I wonder how I never found that tube?"

"Oh! That's the beauty of this story! You saw a pinkish hue in the noodles and decided it was bacteria! You told me to dump it out, and then we scrubbed the entire fridge out."

We both laugh and barely noticed that we are home. I shut the engine off.

"You know, Autumn, that doesn't really count. You didn't have to lie, so there was no fancy foot work. But, thanks for telling on yourself," she says with a grin.

"Fine," I say, feigning anger.

Mom looks at me, "So, from here on out, let's keep it real. Come what may, we'll work it out together. Okay?"

I look down at my hands in my lap and pick at a nail while I consider her words. I look at her face, "Then tell me about my dad, Mom."

Mom's breath catches in her chest, her smile drops. I'm not ready yet, Autumn." She opens her door and winces in pain trying to escape my questions.

"All right, Mom," I put my hand on her arm to stop her. "Wait, I'll help you." I get out and go to her side of the car, and together we climb the stairs and enter our home.

The moment Mom steps into the house, the mood lightens. She looks at the living room, then at me in pleasant surprise.

"Honey! It's so clean! It smells so fresh! She makes her way to the kitchen. "It's spotless!" She looks at me, "I have to admit, I did not expect this." She laughs, "You've never been big on cleaning. Thank you, Autumn."

She is embarrassing me with her praises. "I told you I could do this, Mom."

She squeezes my face between her hands, "Yes, you did, didn't you?"

"I did all the cupboards and drawers." Then I laugh. "And the fridge. And look here!" I rush over to the coffee pot and grab the can of coffee, displaying it in true *Price is Right* form.

Mom gasps, "Coffee! Oh, Autumn, I think I love you more right now than even the day you were born!"

I laugh and pull her chair out, helping her to sit. "I want you to get the full effect." I use the hand-held opener and crank until the lid is half opened. I stick it under her nose. "Sniff it," I say with a grin.

She takes a deep whiff and fake faints. "There is nothing like the aroma of a freshly opened can of coffee. There really isn't. I know Moms would say that baby hair is best, but they're all lying. That right there," she points to the can, "is what keeps women running hearth, home and the world."

I'm smiling as I make a pot for her. "Just so you know, this is your reward for the clutch-burning sacrifice this morning. Coffee instead of cab fare."

"And a wise choice that was, Autumn!" She gives me a look that says, 'not really, but what's done is done.' I know in an instant that my driving days are over.

Mom drinks her coffee while we talk about the past three days. She didn't like Nurse Ratched either.

"She is obnoxious, rough, and I don't think the other nurses care for her much either."

I tell Mom about doing laundry in the tub and about my would-be intruder. I thank her for our fancy curtains and told her I never noticed how well she could sew. We discuss how the budgeting went, and I set the remaining twelve dollars on the table. I'm handing her the rule of the house. She smiles and tells me I may as well hang on to it since I'll be the one shopping. Her trust and belief in me puts me on top of the world. We tell each other everything that happened over the last few days. Well, I don't mention that paisley skirt; I don't exactly know how to put into words why I even burned it. And, I definitely don't mention the journals.

I see that Mom is hurting. With all our talking, I had forgotten about her pain. I see her face startle, she grows pale, then flushes red. "Come on, Mom, let's get you to your room."

"I can barely wait to see it, Autumn. You really have done a great job here. So, how much crud did you find in the cupboards and fridge?"

I laugh, "Now there's a memory I don't want to relive!"

Mom sneaks a peak at the bathroom as we're passing by. She stops and points. "I must use it now! Hurry, while it still sparkles!"

She holds the counter as she makes her way to the toilet.

"Help?" I ask.

Her face flushes as she nods. "I can get the clothes, it's the sitting and getting up part . . ." she gives an embarrassed, weak smile.

I help her down, then leave to give her privacy. I'm embarrassed for her and hope this gets easier between us.

I go to her room to pull back her covers and fluff her pillows. I light the candles, and the room gives a warm welcome. *Perfect*, I think. "Ready?" I call out.

"Okay."

I open my bedroom door so she can complete the tour on her way to her room. As we make our way toward her room, she stops at my door.

"Hey! That room is carpeted!" She's taking a jab at my previously wreck of a room.

"Yeah, I installed it two days ago," I snip. She laughs.

We get her changed into a nightgown and settled in her bed. I unpack her bandages and put them with the stockpile in her nightstand.

Pointing to a stack of library books, I say, "Let's see, we have romance," I waggle my eyebrows, "mystery, adventure with a half-naked hunk on the cover, and a how-to book called, *Exercise for the Infirm.*

"I'll take the romance and toss in the hunk for good measure." She grins and rubs her hands together in anticipation.

"You are absolutely pitiful. You know this, right? Hey, are you hungry?"

"No, but another cup of coffee to share with my hunk would be heaven."

"You're a bottomless pit, woman." I leave the room and call over my shoulder, "With no shame to your game!" I bring her coffee and set it on the nightstand. "Mom, I really missed you."

"I know, honey. I love you too." She grins.

"Well, I have laundry to do. If you need me, I'll be elbow deep in the bathtub. She opens her book, and in the glow of her fresh room, she looks better, more content, than I ever remember seeing her before. I've done well.

I kneel beside the tub watching the water gush into the suds. I play with a softened clump of detergent, rubbing it in my fingers, trying to squish the granules. I think of how I've managed to take the fear out of coming home for her.

I think she is impressed with how I've stepped up by cleaning, planning and following through with a budget that will carry us through, and how I learned to drive, which saved us money. She sees now that I am capable of doing this, that I'm not the brat she knew. I think she knows that she can depend on me, and she can feel safe and comfortable while she heals.

I swish my hand in the water, making more suds, then turn the faucet off. I hear a noise from her room. It takes me a second to realize that she's choking. I rush to her room. She's holding her stomach and vomiting over the side of her bed. I race to her, but she's done by the time I reach her. "Mom!"

"Oh. Autumn. I'm so sorry."

There are tears in her eyes, I'm not sure if they're from the vomiting, the pain in her stomach caused by the force, or because she has spewed coffee over the blanket, sheets and throw rug.

"Mom, it's okay. Are you in pain?"

"It's easing up now. Autumn, all your hard work! I'm so sorry." She's crying over the mess.

"Hey, I've gotten really good at this cleaning thing. Piece of cake." I smile and help her out of the bed. "Come on, let's get you into some clean clothes." We go to the bathroom where she cleans up, and I find a baggy T-shirt for her to wear.

"Here, go in my room for a while. I'll get your room good as new. I'll put clean sheets on your bed, and you can use my blanket tonight."

"No, what will you use for a blanket?"

"I'll be fine. I'll figure something out."

The reality of our situation hits me. It's time to get serious. I help her into my bed and pull the covers up over her. She is shivering. "Are you cold?"

"A little. The meds maybe. I think they made me sick."

"Sure it wasn't my wonderful coffee?"

"Not a chance."

"Well, you're on a one cup limit for a couple of days."

"But I told you! It's the meds!"

"I feel like I'm arguing with a child here! One cup!" I laugh. "Try to sleep."

"Yes, Mommy Ratched."

I strip her bed and grab the throw rug. I wash the sheets first; they're quick work. The rug is next, then the dreaded blanket. My mind flashes back to a few days ago, the first time I washed this same blanket. It was heavy, hard work, and I already feel the same muscles start to object. I'm going to be sore tomorrow.

When I finish, I peek in at Mom. She seems to be asleep. I take the washing to the kitchen and drape the blanket over the table, then turn on the oven to help it dry faster.

I rinse out the old drip pan from under the sink to use for a sick pan. I take it to my room and quietly sit it on the floor near Mom's head. She opens her eyes.

"Hi. I have fresh sheets on your bed, do you want to move?"

She tries to raise up, but grunts while doing it. She rolls on her side and slides to the edge of the bed, and I help her up. Sweat has broken out over her upper lip. I tell her it's med time.

"No, Autumn. Just Tylenols. Let's see if that works."

I argue the point that she really needs the meds, at least for a few days, so she can move those muscles. We compromise on Tylenols now, supper, then meds on a full stomach.

She snatches her pan up, in frustration, as we get her to her feet. Like a child, she mumbles, "A lot of good supper is going to do if I just puke it all up."

I ignore her irritated remark. I've won the battle. I remember the nurse saying that part of the conditions of her release were movement, pain control, and appetite. She did well, motivated by getting out of the hospital, so I know she's capable now. I won't allow her to slack up. I smile to myself and think; *It's me or Nurse Ratched, Mom, and she's not getting you back.*

"I'll start supper now. What do you think? Rice okay?"

She shakes her head, "Just some toast. And coffee." She stares me down.

I grin. "Rice and toast, then coffee."

We make our way to the hall, and I point my chin toward the bathroom. It's more of our non-verbal language. She nods her head. I help her down onto the toilet and leave to get the blanket off my bed and spread it on hers.

I call from her room, "Mom?" Do you think you can eat rice?"

"I don't know. I just agreed to it for the coffee. You should know that I'll feel bad spooning it under the bed."

I poke my head in the bathroom and laugh. "Fine, your wish is my command."

"Really? Then I wish to be relieved of this throne."

Her sense of humor is back. I laugh and help her up.

The next day, I see that she is still in severe pain. Her lip breaks out in sweat when she moves, but she refuses the heavy meds. She eats Tylenols like they're candy.

As I get her ready for a shower and remove her bandages, I'm shocked by the cut that underlines her stomach. *This is where they cut my mom open and pulled her insides out!*

I wring out a soapy cloth and hand it to her. I think she is rubbing too hard and say so. She laughs.

"Autumn, the incision doesn't hurt that much, it's actually the torn muscles inside that hurt, and my lower back where they cut fibroids from my spine."

My face must have gone white because Mom says, "Okay, okay. Here, sit down. Sorry. TMI, huh?"

I nod my head while sitting on the toilet. I start to feel a little better by the time she has finished washing the incision area.

"Better now?" she asks.

"Yeah."

"Wimp."

"What?"

She grins. She puts a sanitary pad over the incision, and we tape a plastic bag to her, covering the whole area. This way the water pressure from the shower won't hurt, and the plastic keeps the area dry. I toss a folded towel in the tub as a no-skid pad and turn on the shower. I get clean, loose-fitting clothes for her when she's finished. We replace the bandages, and she eats more Tylenol.

Each passing day, Mom is moving her arms and legs more freely. Her stomach muscles are healing and, by her fourth day home, she is walking slowly, but not hunched over. Progress.

By the end of her first week home, she isn't subconsciously guarding her stomach with her hand anymore, unless she moves wrong or too fast. After a week and a half, her incision area still needs care, but we ran out of gauze and tape two days ago. So, we're using sanitary pads, secured in place with T-shirts tied around her hips. It doesn't work the greatest, and I'm washing T-shirts two or three times a day.

* * *

It's been three weeks since Mom came home. I'm sitting on the couch watching T.V. while Mom takes her laps through the house. She sits on a kitchen chair we put in the living room for her. She still hurts a little when she tries to get up from the old, sunken couch.

"How many laps today?"

"Thirty." I could have done more, but I'm feeling lazy."

I smile. "Thirty is good."

"I'm going to go soak in the tub."

"Need help?" I ask.

"No, I'm pretty good at inching my way in and out. I can handle it."

Mom is getting better, and we're getting along pretty well. I think it may be time to raise my dad questions again.

I still don't know which Jack Stogavich is my dad. I'm scared to find out, but I've made a pact with the new me. I will find my dad. I'm not stupid, and I know whichever it is, he won't be playing daddy.

I think back to my call to the senator. I'm embarrassed by the thoughts I had of shared custody and being spoiled. A dream life is not to be my fate. Yet, in the back of my mind, there is still this glimmer of hope. What if he just never knew about me?

I hear the bathroom door open. I give Mom time to dress and settle in her room. She is sitting on her bed, her lamp is on, and she has a book in her lap. I sit down next to her, my back against the headboard. She pats my leg.

"Mom. Can we talk?"

"Okay," she says hesitantly.

I sit quiet for a minute, then ask, "What was my dad like?"

Mom lets out a sigh.

"I mean, what happened? Were you married to him? Was he abusive? An alcoholic? A druggie? What?"

"Honey, I really don't know what to say. Autumn, we were both young. Our lives were going different directions. I don't want to talk about it, really."

"I know his name."

Mom's head snaps in my direction. "What do you mean, Autumn?"

"Jack Stogavich," I say, and wait.

"How—who? Has he contacted you?" She looks panicked.

"Does he know I exist?" I ask hopefully. She doesn't answer.

"I found your diaries when I was cleaning."

"You read my journals?"

"I found his name. I googled it. But there are two of them, Mom! I don't know which one is my dad! Please! I need to know!"

"Autumn, listen to me, very carefully. You don't know what you're dealing with here. You're a pup, and he is a pitbull. He can, and will, rip you apart! You stay away from him!"

I stand, with tears in my eyes. "Just tell me, Mom! Is he in prison or is he a senator?"

She says nothing. We stare at each other. Fear, anger, betrayal and hurt fill the room. I start to leave, then turn to her. "Just so you know, I burned your paisley skirt!" I slam her bedroom door, then the front door as I storm out of the house.

I run, then walk. I'm doing that coulda-woulda-shoulda thing I always do when I'm angered to tears. Later, when I calm down, I'm glad I left before I said any of the hurtful things I came up with. I don't really want to hurt her; I just need answers.

I roam the streets for an hour or more before making my way back home. When I walk up the steps, I see that Mom's bedroom light is off. I go in the house and sit on the couch. I turn the T.V. on low and pull out my algebra.

I try, but I can't concentrate. I keep thinking about all I've lost since my life spiraled into this pit three weeks ago.

I'm not seeing my friends at all. There's no school for me now, so I never leave the house. I'm not getting this algebra on my own. I'm tired all the time, exhausted emotionally and physically. The laundry is endless. Clothes, sheets, blankets and her disgusting bandages, and don't forget her underwear! All I do is cook, clean, do laundry and wait on her hand and foot! I haven't turned in a single assignment this school year! This isn't a challenge anymore, it's just drudgery. Then, of course, there's the dad thing on top of it all.

I'm startled by Mom's voice. "I'm glad you're keeping up with your school work. I wondered."

I look up into Mom's face. For a second, dread fills my heart. What does she want now? Her hair is a mess, her face is puffy from sleep, and she has stuff in the corner of her eye. I'm disgusted. I close my eyes and lean back into the couch. I feel the old familiar hate for her flooding in. I haven't changed at all. Nothing has.

"Well, I just got up to use the bathroom. Goodnight, Autumn."

I keep my eyes closed, and just sit there. I hear the toilet flush, the water run in the sink, and finally her bedroom door close.

I'm angry and sad, but I also feel a wave of something come over me. A yearning maybe? Or, is this what loss feels like? No, loss would feel empty, and I feel full. Overflowing, with something I don't have a name for. Exasperation only starts to describe it. I'm going to explode from the inside. I walk to the door and step out into the night.

The sky is a black-blue, broken up with lighter silver-gray clouds that are backlit by a full moon. The clouds are so close I feel I could pluck them from the sky. The yard and street are both lit in eerie suspense like an old black and white horror movie. Everything, even the cold air, is still. The only sounds are my footsteps on the damp pavement and my pounding heart.

I can make out the distant roar of my Falls. Their call pulls me closer. I stare at the moon as I walk. The clouds try to hide it, but the moon wins. I drink in the calm, yet shiver from its eeriness.

I hold on to the bridge railing as I face the Falls. The Falls are also set in classic black and white. The only color is a faint ring of rainbow in the mist that clings to the phosphorescent-edged Falls. I become part of the scene and am all in black and white. All natural color is gone from me, but it feels normal. I sense a methodical, eternal belonging confirmed by the relentless crashing of the water. I feel the sound crashing in my chest, and it beats down the explosion locked inside of me.

I tilt my head up. The moon draws closer, or maybe, I am pulled to it. As the clouds gently pass, I have the sensation that it is me that moves, while they stand still. I hold the fragile feeling. My body hums from the pulse of the water, the pull of the moon, and my floating. I spread my arms in what must be flight, a cool welcome from the night, and a release of my soul. I feel more alive in black and white than I ever have in color.

"Hi, Autumn."

I startle, and a hand grabs my arm. The majestic moment is gone, as if I have awakened from an incredible, compelling dream. The echo of the Falls recedes to their place. I sense a grief at the loss of the moment. Of what might have been.

I'm guided down, from where I had been standing on the next-to-top rail. I see Ian's face. His brows are furrowed in confusion—maybe concern? I'm confused too. What is happening here?

Ian reaches a finger up and wipes a tear's trail from my cheek that I didn't know was there. I say nothing and leave him standing on the bridge, as I make my way back home.

In my room, I kick off my shoes, crawl into bed, and curl myself around Pandy. I can't put a title to my feelings. I whisper in Pandy's ear, "I'm a stranger to myself."

Seven

I wake in the morning chilled from damp clothes. The Falls have left their mark on me. What exactly happened last night? I replay the scene in my mind. Would I have done a carefree fall off the bridge if Ian hadn't stopped me? Ian stumbled into my secret place, broke its barriers and saved me from myself.

I shiver, unsure if from the cold or from what could have been. I grab fresh clothes and head for the shower. I pull my thoughts to the present day, a new day, and a fresh attempt at Mom's and my relationship.

I make my way to the kitchen smelling coffee and pancakes before I get there. I'm surprised to see Mom at the sink doing dishes, and I'm very happy to see a stack of pancakes on the table. My stomach growls.

Mom turns and smiles. "Therapy. I can't sit another minute in that bed!"

"Do you feel okay?" I head for the pancakes.

"Great. I haven't taken those pills in over two weeks, Autumn, and I'm feeling so much better today than I did just last night. Crazy huh? I'm officially on the mend I think."

"Well, don't overdo it."

"I'm not."

I smear government butter on my pancakes and sprinkle sugar over them since there is no syrup. I hop up on the counter beside the sink while Mom does dishes. I take a bite. "Mmm . . . How do you do that!" I ask around a mouthful.

"Do what?"

I point my fork at my plate. "Same mix, but yours taste so much better!"

Mom laughs, "Because I'm a mom, it's what we do. We make the unbearable bearable." Her face loses its joy. I know she's thought of our fight last night. I ignore the blunder.

I point at her lingerie bag lying on the floor and raise my eyebrows.

Mom laughs, "I guess I could do my unmentionables in the bathroom, but at least it's one job you can cross off your list. Yeah."

"Hallelujah!"

"Autumn, I know this has been really hard on you. I'm sorry for that. I really didn't think it would take me this long to be able to move around normally again."

"It's okay, Mom. I just get tired and overwhelmed. I'm not throwing in the towel. Well, unless it's in the bathtub." I grin.

"You know, I couldn't have had a better, more compassionate nurse. Thank you."

I nod and drop my head in embarrassment; yet, I'm glad she said it.

Mom adds, "Besides, nurses don't cook, clean and wash underwear."

I give a short snort of a laugh and jump down. I slide my plate under the water, then hug her. "I'd do it again, Mom. Just not right away."

"Honey, I still need help with laundry and the big stuff like vacuuming and heavy lifting. I can't go back to work yet, but we're getting closer."

"I know, Mom. Hey, since you're feeling better today, I think I'll go to the library and exchange your books. I need to get out of the house for a while, ya know?"

"Sounds like a plan. I'm ready for a new hunk." She grins.

"Don't fix lunch. My treat. I'm thinking toasted PB and J, or maybe grilled cheese sandwiches."

Suddenly the phone rings. It's loud and obnoxious, a foreign sound in our house these days. I answer it. It is the school. They want to know if my homework was turned in because they haven't seen it. My eyes shoot to Mom's face. She is leaning against the archway to the kitchen, waiting to see who is calling.

"Well, I was too sick to bring it, and our car wasn't running. But it will be there by Friday. Okay. I'm getting better, slowly. Thank you. Bye." I hang up the phone and look at Mom.

"Autumn! You haven't turned in any homework yet?"

"Mom, I've been so busy, and I'm just not getting the math."

"You should have called the teacher, then. They said they would help."

"Mom, how will the teacher help with algebra over the phone? I've been too busy to go to the library and use the teaching tapes."

"And, you lied to them, Autumn! We agreed—"

"No Mom, I didn't lie. I said the car wasn't running, and it hasn't been since you came home," I say sheepishly.

She shakes her head. She's disappointed in me.

"And, I am feeling better, I guess. So that's not a lie either."

Mom hugs me and says, "Okay, I'm just worried the school will get suspicious and cause problems for us. I can help you with the math. I'll brush up on algebra, and we'll work on it together."

I grin at her. "No offense, Mom, but I get really ticked off when I'm doing algebra. I think the tapes are safer, for both of us."

"Yeah, probably." She chuckles.

"I'll take my math to the library and work on it today. I better cancel our lunch date and take a sandwich with me." I moan, "I'll probably be there 'til I graduate."

"Autumn, I'm very proud of you. You've done what a lot of adults couldn't do the past few weeks. The stress, the work, putting up with me." She smiles. "Focus on your schoolwork now."

"I have everything else ready to turn in, it's just the math, Mom. It's all good."

"Well, when we're all done with this mess, you can take an entire week off. Just laze around, and I'll wait on you for a change."

"As tempting as it is to have you wash my undies—no thanks! I'm outta here ASAP! I need civilization!"

I grab the library books and my math book and stuff them into my backpack, arranging them so their corners don't stick through a gap where the seam has come apart. Mom hands me a wrapped PB and J sandwich, and I set it on top of the books, and head out the door.

It must have rained last night after I got home because there are puddles in the street. I jay-walk across the road but pause half-way across to let a car go by. It comes to a stop, blocking my way. It's a big, black, fancy thing with tinted windows. The rear window hums as it slides down.

"Autumn? Autumn Riley?"

The face is familiar, then it hits me; this is a fatter version of Jack Stogavich! The senator! I look back at the house to see if Mom is watching. She isn't. I want to run, but my feet are frozen in place.

The front door opens, and the driver gets out. I step back. He opens the rear door, and Jack gets out of the car. My heart is pounding, my mind is racing. *Dad?* Obviously. Pitbull! Fear. *What does he want?*

He is disturbing. His very presence interrupts the air; this huge man whose door was opened for him, and who now stands on the wet street in a three-piece suit. He doesn't fit in this neighborhood; he doesn't belong on my street. He looks as out of place and wrong standing here as he would be wearing the title Daddy.

"What do you want?" I ask summoning up every ounce of bravery I own.

"I want to talk to you, Autumn."

"I don't want to talk to you," I say and start to walk away.

"Do you know who you're dealing with here, young lady?"

I stop and turn back to him. "Yeah, I do. A pitbull, and I don't plan on getting bit."

He laughs. "I came to give you something to help with college, or . . ." he looks around in disgust at the houses on my street, settling his eyes on mine, " . . . whatever. Also, to tell you there will never," he lowers his double chin and stares unblinking into my eyes, "never be contact between us again. I'm a very powerful man with a lot of friends.

You and your mother will forget you ever heard my name. Do I make myself clear?"

"Don't worry, Jack, I don't think we like you much either."

"Ahh," he smiles. "A win-win. Nice." He takes a piece of paper from an inside pocket and hands it to me. He gets back in the car, the driver closes his door, then gets in himself. The car rolls away. I stand, trembling, and staring.

His presence resonates in the air even after the car has turned the corner and is out of sight. A chill runs down my back, the hair on my arms stands up, and I shiver. In his wake, I feel a calculated callousness. I have no doubt that he can and will make good on his threat. I look at the paper in my hand. It is a check for fifty thousand dollars!

The check trembles in my hand, my mouth starts tingling and watering. Oh God! I'm gonna puke! I run to the house and burst through the door, heading straight to the bathroom, where I barely make the toilet in time.

"Autumn!" Mom yells. She's in the bathroom immediately, her hand on my back.

I am vomiting hard. It won't stop. "Oh, honey."

I shove the check toward her. "I hate him." I get reprieve from my sickness and sit on the edge of the tub, crying.

"Him who?"

I point at the check, and she looks at it for the first time.

"My dad."

"Oh God! What did he do to you, Autumn?" She darts to the bathroom door, checking to see if he's in the house. "Where is he?"

I flush the toilet, splash water on my face, and bury my face in a towel.

"Every time I talk to that man I puke!"

"Every time?" Mom asks.

I yell, "I called him, Mom! I had to, you wouldn't tell me anything about him! I have a right to know who my dad is!

No, you don't!" Mom screams back. "How dare you go behind my back like this! Especially after I told you not to contact him!"

"I do have the right! He's my father! And for your information, I called him before you warned me!" I lower my voice, "He is my father . . . even if he doesn't want me." I crumble onto the floor in tears. I just fold up into myself, in a helpless heap.

I feel Mom's arms wrap around me, tight. I cry into her shoulder like the child I am right now. She leads me to my room and sets me on my bed. I kick off my shoes and hide from the world under my covers. Where it is safe. Where Pandy lives. I feel the weight of Mom's body on the bed. She lies on top of the covers but spoons my body with hers. She lets me cry. She doesn't try to shush me. She just lies there, tight against me, arm around me, protecting me from a ghost.

When Pandy has caught my last tear and there is no more in me, I lie quietly, my breath gasping in unexpected hiccups that break the silence.

I feel Mom move. She leaves the room. My back misses her warmth. I pick at the fuzzy balls on Pandy's ears. Mom returns to my room with a hand full of candles and sits cross-legged on the floor in front of me. She lights a match. I see its shine on my nose. She touches the match to a wick, and it sucks up the flame. I can smell sulfur and wax. I watch the flame with Mom's face as the backdrop.

She lifts a candle and hands it to me. I look in her eyes. They are pools but say nothing. They're just quiet. I take the candle and hold it to hers, they mesh and become a joined flame. I pull mine away, letting the wax drip where it will, watching its tears build, then fall. She takes my burning candle and hands me another unlit one. I hold it to the flame. I slightly raise my head from the pillow and look at the candles burning, arranged on the floor. They'll fall over I think, but they don't. I stand my candle with the others and pick up another unlit candle. Mom picks one up too. Together we light them from the same flame. I watch her face inches from mine, her eyes are changing, but I'm not sure how. We stand our candles with the rest of the burning candles. I lay my head on the edge of the bed and watch them burn. When I open my eyes again, the candles are gone. Mom sits there, cross-legged in front of my face. She holds a cup of tea out to me.

"I found a lonely bag. Drink, baby."

I close my eyes. Dear diary, what I know about my dad: 1. His name is Jack Stogavich 2. He lives in Florida 3. He is a senator 4. He is scary 5. He wishes I had never been born. Amen.

The next time I wake, it's night. The house is dark. Mom is curled up behind me again. Somehow, she knows my eyes have opened.

"Are you hungry?"

I shake my head no. I roll over and lay my head on her shoulder. Her hand brushes the hair back from my face. After a while, I say, "It's for college, or whatever. The check."

"Well, we're not cashing it," she says firmly.

I tilt my head up and look at her. "Why not?"

"Because, Autumn . . ." she sits up in bed, and I do the same. "It is a payoff. It is a cashier's check and untraceable. It buys our silence for his career. He got off cheap, and he knows it. More importantly, Jack Stogavich doesn't hand out money freely, even if he owes it. He will one day return to remind us that he gave that money to us, and it will not be worth the fifty-thousand then."

We both sit quietly.

"We met in college," Mom says.

I sit up straighter, slowly, not even breathing, afraid of breaking Mom's voice.

"I had seen him around. He was a football jock. Popular. He was very handsome back then. I had gone to a frat party, and he was there. He wasn't with a girl, so I decided to talk to him. He was funny, charming, smart, and he held my eyes in his when we talked. We were an item for a year. When I found out I was pregnant, he told me to get an abortion. He told me he never loved me, that he was just killing time. Later, I learned that he was quite the playboy while we dated."

I watch shame and embarrassment from years gone by run across Mom's face. She had been naive. I also see that she had been in love with him.

"When I called my mom, she told me to either take care of it or to lie in the bed I had made. I never returned home. My choice made me unwelcome there."

"Your mom abandoned you?" I couldn't comprehend this. Moms don't do that. "And Jack—what a creep! He can't just walk away from you, me, his responsibilities like that! Like we never existed! Well, he's about to find out that Autumn Riley is alive and well!"

"Autumn! No. Pup-pitbull, remember? He's a senator, honey. He's untouchable."

Cold reality hits me again. I was nothing in my father's eyes, but a paid-off problem, swept under his royal rug. My eyes fill with tears. I am powerless.

Mom grabs me and folds me into her arms, where we both cry.

"Autumn, I'm so sorry. God, I'm so sorry."

We cry for ourselves and each other. The pain is all mixed together. It is honest and real and cloaks us. I feel the weight of Mom's heartache. She was thrown away by those she loved and by society. I, too, was guilty of throwing her away. I carry the shame of that, yet together we carry the shame of illegitimacy. Her by choice, and me by birth.

I think of my own recent choices and how they have affected our lives. Have those choices been worth it? Have I caused us senseless pain in getting my dad answers? I search my heart. An emptiness is gone. The place where the 'Great Dad Questions' always lived, is replaced with hurt and anger. But this is okay. Because I don't have to be angry at Mom anymore. Just maybe, through all this pain, we have saved us.

Eight

Mom goes to the kitchen to heat up frozen spaghetti. I stay in bed. About the time the aroma makes it to my room, Mom comes in with two plates. We sit up against the headboard and eat quietly. I finish every noodle.

"I'm a mistake. I don't belong. I shouldn't have been born, Mom."

She looks at me, takes my empty plate and stacks it on hers, putting them on the floor.

"No, Autumn. You're my daughter."

"A daughter who is a constant reminder of a painful time in your life. A daughter who made you an outcast. When you look in my face, do you see him?"

"Honey, I chose to have you." She turns fully toward me. "I chose you. I have never regretted that choice. I don't think about the pain or the scrutiny of others who cast judgement on me. I chose back then, and still choose today to be left alone, Autumn, rather than defend my reasons to people who could never grasp them." She grabs my hands and squeezes. "When I look in your face, I'm not seeing him. I'm seeing a beautiful, smart, sometimes funny, young lady that I can't imagine my life without."

"Do you ever wish you hadn't gotten pregnant? You had to drop out of college, you lost your family, your whole future went down the drain. I mean, look at us, Mom! We get food stamps and a state medical card! Because of me," my voice cracks, "you live a life of poverty and loneliness."

"Autumn! Stop it! You are not the mistake here! Don't you see? You are my healing and independence that rose from that. You are my sanity, the reason my life is good. He is the mistake. He is the one that is to blame for running from his responsibilities. He is the plague on my life and society. Not you. And my parents? Honey, I could have continued living a sheltered, spoiled life under their wing, but it would have been the life they dictated for me. I chose my own life. Mine and yours. I have never been ashamed or sad for that decision." I see a power move across her face. "You are my victory, Autumn! The power and victory for women to choose throughout society."

I am stunned by her conviction and this adamant strength that I never knew she possessed. She is not some slighted, lonely woman that I always thought she was. No, my Mom is an icon of force for her beliefs and values! For the first time in my life, I am truly proud to be her daughter.

"How did you get so strong, Mom?"

She sighs and looks up at the ceiling. She scoots back against the headboard. "Freedom, Autumn. Freedom to make my own decisions and living by my convictions. The freedom to be true to myself makes me grow stronger in who I am." She looks at me, "You know, you have that strength too."

"How do you figure?"

"Well, look. You chose to nurse me back to health, even though you were scared. You chose that rather than to live in a gossip's house and become the latest tragedy. Apparently, you don't like gossips, so you took the harder road, rather than fighting, or entangling on her terms. That was strength. When you decided to find your father, you knew it might hurt, you knew I'd be upset, but you had to have your answers. That was courage. And, when you drove the Bloody Rat, yes, I know you call it that, that was bravery."

I hug my mom. "Thank you, Mom, for everything."

"Piece of cake, honey," she whispers.

I chuckle. "You know what?" I ask.

"What?"

"I think tomorrow I'll go to the library. I'm knocking out this algebra once and for all."

Mom smiles, "I have no doubt."

I spend all day at the library. Thank God, they don't charge by the fifteen-minute block for math tapes! But, I nailed it!

When I get home, Mom is hanging up the phone.

"Who was that?"

"Nobody. So, how'd the math go?"

"I rocked it." I grin, "I got it all down, Mom! I even did next week's assignment. Hope I did the right problems. Algebra is no longer an enigma for this woman of victory!"

"Sounds like we should celebrate."

"What do you have in mind?" I plop down on the couch beside her.

"Well, I still can't work the clutch in the car, so how about we call a cab and go out for dinner?"

I look at her, "How?"

"Our talk last night made me rethink some things. One being, why am I sitting in fear of a man who is obviously scared of us? So, I took a cab uptown today and cashed the check."

"You did?" I bounce up and down squealing, "We're rich!" I hug her tight.

Mom laughs at me, "Autumn, we're not rich. This money won't go as far as you think, but we'll be able to get you some school clothes, upgrade our furniture, maybe buy a washer and dryer, and have some to invest in our future."

"Clothes for you too, Mom!"

"A few things maybe."

"Can we go to the mall first? Please? I want to wear my new duds to dinner! I'm so excited!"

She laughs again, "Okay, one outfit! It's been a long day for me already. I've run around more than three days' worth of laps here."

We call a cab and head to the mall. I end up with three amazing outfits, make-up, and a gift for Mom. Mom got a couple of outfits too. We change in the mall restrooms. Mom's outfit is just some conservative sweater and slacks with a jacket, but she looks classy. It's so far removed from her normal hippie wear, that she looks like she's jumped through a time warp! I'm so pleased with her style, I'm nearly in tears as I look at her.

"Stop it. It's just a pair of pants and a sweater!"

"No, Mom, it's so much more than that," I say, remembering the day she picked me up from class.

We call another cab and go to dinner. We decide on the café since we have our shopping bags with us. Our dinner is quiet, cozy, and the food is wonderfully greasy. We have a dessert that is a splurge and a sure sin against our consciences. It's a huge chocolate brownie covered in ice-cream, chocolate syrup, whipped cream and a cherry. Oh, and sprinkled with nuts, of course.

"This thing is so fattening I'm going to have to go back to elastic waistbands," Mom says.

I pull her dessert to my side of the table and fake a serious look. "This is for your own good Mom, and for the good of the world; leave the '70s elastic waistbands buried."

She whips it back to her side, "Autumn, don't ever step between me and my chocolate again. If you do, you'll be grounded 'til you're eighteen!"

I smile, "Well, I have a confession to make."

Mom raises her eyebrows. "You burned out my clutch last night while I slept?"

"No." I laugh. "Listen, this is serious." I take a deep breath. "Mom, a month ago I was so angry with you." I drop my head; I can't look her in the eyes. "I think I even hated you, because I blamed you for running my dad off, then hiding him from me."

"Autumn—"

"No, Mom," I stop her with a raised hand. "I need to say this. I wouldn't cut you any slack. I had been hurt by him for so many years, but I still held on to hope. So, I had to blame you to help myself believe in that hope. Well, I remember the first day of school before you told me you were sick; I felt my whole world was a mess. I didn't have new school clothes, the best jeans I had were dirty, but I wore them anyway. I blamed you for that."

I watched Mom's eyes tear up, she pushes her dessert away. "That morning, in my anger and hurt, I told myself that I couldn't wait until I was eighteen so I could leave and never come back. I thought you kept my dad from me just to keep me for yourself, and I also thought that I could do better supporting myself than you did. That was only a month ago, but it feels like years. I realize now that you've only wanted the best for me. I don't know how you've gone through what you have, and continued to love me when I was so mean to you."

Tears roll down both of our faces, which we wipe away quickly. "So, . . ." I pull out two small, dark blue, velvet boxes and set them on the table. Mom's face questions what this is.

"While you were getting your new outfits, I got something that will always remind us both of how important we are to each other, and what we have come through together."

I lift both lids and display gold pinkie-rings. Each ring is a half heart, that when held together reads: Victory Forever. I pull Mom's Forever ring out and slide it on her pinkie finger. She picks up my Victory ring and slides it on mine.

" 'Til death do us part." I giggle, embarrassed.

"And beyond. Thank you, Autumn."

We look at the new, permanent addition to our bodies.

"Mom?" What would have happened if you hadn't become sick, or if we had gone our separate ways, me to Janey Freeze's house and you to a care center?"

"I think, Autumn, that we would have found each other, made our relationship strong and come through it. It would have just been later down the road. I think that we were meant to travel this life together. We complement one another. We cause each other to question ourselves and to grow."

We pay our bill and wait outside for a cab. The air is cold; winter is setting in quickly this year.

"We need coats, Mom."

She sighs. "We need a lot of things, Autumn. Oh hey! Let's grab a paper and go through the ads for furniture and stuff."

"Okay, but I'll need a soda to get me through it. Let's stop by Food Mart on the way home."

"Real creamer for coffee!" Mom adds.

That night, regardless of our huge meal and sinful dessert, we munch on snacks while in our pajamas. Me leaning against Mom's headboard shoulder to shoulder with the ads spread across our raised knees.

"Autumn, I've been thinking. What would you think of us opening a small business?"

"Really? Well, yes! What kind of business? A clothing store! Then I'd always have the latest fashions!"

Mom laughs, "Well, I think to start a business with that kind of inventory would take more money than we have. I was thinking more along the lines of a little ice-cream shop, or a soda and coffee shop for shoppers in the mall. Maybe have desserts available or cold sandwiches. Something not too expensive to open up and a place where kids could hang out at the mall."

"I love it! When?"

"I saw a small unit available when we were at the mall, and if you want to work there, help me run it, then I think we could make it successful. It has a partition up, maybe we could put video games in there, and booths and tables in the front area."

"I think it's an awesome idea, Mom! You could get out of Food Mart! That'll kill Beehive hair lady."

"Autumn—"

"I know. Just kidding."

"No, you weren't. Be nice."

I wake up early and start coffee for Mom. I make a cup and wave it under her sleeping nose. Her eyes open, and with a moan, she rolls onto her back.

"Get up! We need a big fat bacon omelet, and the mall opens in . . . one hour! Get Uuuup!" I pull back her covers, and she tries to grab them back. I win, and we're at the mall shortly after it opens.

We spend hours at the mall shopping, and at a hair salon, where we both get haircuts, highlights and lowlights. I'm amazed at some of the clothes Mom has bought herself. She got professional stuff, but also some very cute things that pull years from her face. With her new clothes and the new haircut, she looks sassy. We go by three units that are empty and throw around business ideas. It's the most fun I ever remember having with her.

When Mom gets tired and needs to rest, we head for home with a mountain of bags.

I dump them all out on my bed and squeal like a two-year-old. Mom is standing in the doorway, laughing at me. I do a high dive right in the middle of the pile, and the bed lets out a loud crack. All laughter stops instantly. I slowly turn my head to Mom, not even breathing. Her eyes are wide, her hand covers her gaping mouth. She gives me her hand, and as we carefully pull me free from the pending disaster, the bed collapses and I'm nearly buried in the falling headboard.

We're laughing so hard by the time I'm free of the bed, that Mom can barely get her question out. "So, was there a bed in those ads?"

I answer, "I don't know, but I think I'm sleeping with you tonight." Tears of laughter are rolling down our cheeks. We're both bent over in pain, but we can't stop laughing. We're contagious to each other.

Mom sits on the floor where I join her.

"A ring doesn't buy you passage into my bed! Put your mattress on the floor." We collapse in peals of laughter again.

I can barely squeak out, "Mom, you're a tough sell!"

"Tylenol!" Mom laughs. "I need Tylenol! Oh God, you're killing me right now, Autumn. Stop it!"

I crawl away on hands and knees to get away. I don't dare look back at her because she has gone into another deep fit of laughter, and I am barely catching my own breath.

I get to her room, grab the Tylenol and water, and compose myself. I slide down the wall beside her, and hand her the medicine and say, "Wow. That was exhausting."

I turn my head toward her, and she's started again! "shht-shht!" I hold my finger up. "I can't. No more!"

I turn my face away and ignore the bouncing of her shoulder next to mine. I won't look at her. I scoot away so I won't feel her bouncing, and that takes her over the edge. She lets loose with more laughter, sending me back into hysteria.

Later, once we've gotten control of ourselves, we get the busted bed frame out to the backyard. Mom helps me make up my mattress on the floor, and we have a pizza delivered.

While we're sitting watching T.V. and waiting for supper to arrive, I think about our laughing fit. The hysterical laughter was a release that we both needed. After years of hurt, anger, stress and struggles, it was the perfect medicine. I can't see where breaking the bed was funny enough to cause the laughter it did, but I think it triggered another phase in our healing together. I have climbed my mountain. The mountain that had me buried just a few weeks earlier.

The pizza arrives, and we opt to eat it in front of the T.V. Mom says it is our 'farewell to arms,' since we were furniture shopping tomorrow.

"Really? *A Farewell to Arms*?" I toss her a look. "Never read that book."

"Hmm," she grunts in disapproval. "It's a classic. So, you have to. It's a literary law."

Suddenly, I point at the T.V. My father's face is plastered on the screen. "Oh. My. God!"

"Shh!" Mom turns up the volume.

'The Florida senator was arrested today on charges of racketeering, tax evasion and several counts of murder in connections to the Cuban drug cartel. The senator's assets and accounts, in excess of $120 million, have been frozen. Authorities say they are asking that bail be denied, for fear of him leaving the country to avoid prosecution.'

I look at Mom. She has a small, satisfied smile on her face. She takes a bite from her pizza and tosses the crust in the box. She dusts the crumbs from her hands and says, "Huh."

By the look on her face, I know she is happy with herself. "Mom?"

"What, Autumn?" She looks me in the eye, straight on as if to say, bring it on.

"Honesty, no matter what. Remember?"

She just looks at me.

"Did you—what did you do, Mom?"

She picks up a piece of pepperoni and holds it in her fingers, thinking. "I made a phone call," she answers and pops the morsel in her mouth.

"To whom?"

"An old friend, Autumn." She wipes her fingers on a napkin. "A friend who told me if I ever needed help to call. I needed help."

I sit back into the couch, "Wow."

"It is over. We never have to worry about doing favors for Jack Stogavich."

"Was he set up?"

Mom smiles, "No, Autumn. He is just plain and simply caught. The pitbull is collared and caged."

"Will he get the death penalty?" I feel sick, knowing my search of him brought this on.

"No, honey, they were Cuban nationals, drug lords. Castro can't extradite him, or he'd have to admit there is a cartel that Castro himself is very likely involved in."

The enormity of it all hits me. Us, an illegitimate fifteen-year-old and a single mom on food stamps, sitting on a broken-down couch in Deer Falls, stopped a corrupt senator and touched the life of a dictator of another country! It is overwhelming.

"I . . . life . . . I'm not ready to be a grown up yet."

Mom hugs me. "I know, but you are on your way. It's up to you who you want to be and the type of person you'll become. I think you have an honorable start on it." She smiles. "Shoot, you've rocked algebra! Nothing can stop you now!" She kisses the top of my head.

I spin my victory ring around on my finger and think of how I have become victorious with Mom's help.

The phone rings and we both jump. Mom answers it, and I think to myself, what is this? A confirmation call?

Mom hands the phone to me. "Hello?"

"Hi, Autumn! I've missed you so much!"

I look at Mom. "Hi, Jen. What's up?"

"So, the girls are in so much trouble! Julie ripped a pack of cigs from her dad, and they got caught smoking!"

"What?" I can't believe my straight-laced friends would do anything like that. I picture them in their cheerleader outfits, pom-poms flashing and a cigarette hanging from their lips. I stifle a laugh.

"They were smoking in the park, and one of Terri's mom's friends saw them! She ratted them out. They said they were ready to puke anyway and threw them away before they left the park, but . . . they're both still grounded, maybe for life. Who knows?"

"So, who are you hanging with now?"

"Well, that's why I called, I haven't really been hanging out at all. I don't know, this year is just different. I don't like to go places with Julie and Terri anymore; they're always trying to do something to get in trouble, ya know? Autumn, when are you coming back to school?"

"Well, I was hoping on Monday, if Mom says it's okay."

"Really?"

"Hey Jen, tomorrow is Saturday. Do you want to go to the mall together?"

"Can you? Are you well enough? Well of course you are, or you wouldn't have asked me. That would be so great!"

I laugh, "Yeah, Jen it would." I look at Mom, asking permission with my eyes. She nods yes. "Hey?"

"Yeah?"

"My treat this time."

"Okay! 10:00? At the footbridge?

"Great. See ya then. Bye."

I jump up, hug Mom and run to my room yelling, "What am I going to wear?"

The next morning, I settle on my Lucky Jeans, and a cute top, with matching socks and my DCs. My hair is spritzed out, and I have a lacy ribbon holding it out of my face.

Mom hands me forty dollars. "No piercings or tattoos," she says.

"Ah, Mom," I whine and run out the door, giggling.

Jen is already at the bridge when I get there, so I run across, giving the Falls just a glance on my way by. I feel great! I'm adorable, and I know it. I've never felt so confident meeting a friend before. I catch up to Jen, and we hug.

"Look at you! OMG! How cute are you?" Jen squeals, "Turn around! Ha! Lucky jeans?"

I laugh, "Come on. I have so much to tell you!"

I tell Jen that my dad died and left my mom and me some money. I stopped her consoling with, "It's okay. I never knew him, Jen." I made up a story about a fatal car wreck, and she believed it. I don't know why I lied, I just didn't want to go into the whole story or become the center of gossip. I self-consciously work my victory ring around my finger as we walk. I tell myself, "Honesty. Come what may."

I stop walking and look at Jen. "I lied. That story isn't true. The money came from my father, but I don't want to talk about it." I hold my breath, waiting for her to yell at me for lying, and storming off in anger.

Jen smiles and says, "Okay." As simple as that! I want to laugh and cry all at once!

"Let's go have fun," I say.

"You're on!"

We bounce from store to store, giggling like the teen girls we are, trying on outfits and looking at make-up. I show some of the outfits I bought with Mom, and Jen gives me some great ideas on accessories. We go to the music store and listen to CDs and critique the outfits of the rock stars. We play games at the arcade, then settle for a rest at the food court and eat burgers and fries.

"Jen, thanks for always being my friend. I know it wasn't always easy for you. Me being the odd duck and all," I say embarrassed.

"Well, you just always seemed so sad and serious. You were never mean to anyone, and so I thought you could use a friend. Besides, the girls were so jealous of you! It drove them crazy, and I kind of liked that." She giggles.

"Jealous? Why?"

"Autumn, you're gorgeous!" She laughs. "Everybody thinks so. You've just always been so quiet and shy that nobody asked you out! You didn't know?"

"No." I drop my head, embarrassed. Then I look to make sure she's not lying. She isn't, and I'm shocked. "Well. Ha! Well then, that changes a whole lot, doesn't it?"

"Absolutely," she says, as she tosses her trash, making a two-pointer shot.

We part ways at the footbridge where she continues down the street, and I start across the 'great divide.'

I stop at my usual place and watch the Falls. The sky is bright, this afternoon. I take in the view of the tall trees on the cliff's ridge and the few that survive by clinging to the cliff's wall. The ferns are huge and look like they reach their arms out to the water. Everything is so alive in its own vibrant color. The air is fresh and cool. The mist's fingers reach out and brush my face. I close my eyes and absorb the power of the water's roar. I let it fill my soul with sparkling, clean clarity. I can sense it coursing through me, clearing every doubt from every crevice that has ever caused me embarrassment, shame and isolation. I say goodbye to poverty, hatred of my mom, jealousy of my friends, and to the desperation of knowing my dad. The flow carries away my fears, pains and limitations. I'm held firm in the Falls' healing music. I open my eyes, and the beauty of this place tells me I belong. It lets me know that I love, and am worthy to be loved. For the first time ever, I love me.

I realize that the Falls have always been here, reflecting whatever I have gone through. The thought hits me; the Falls don't change, I do. I change and perceive my emotions in them. I realize that all of life is like that. A mirror of myself. When I am okay with myself, then the world is okay with me. Jen's words and my relationship with Mom come to mind. It was me who changed and made my life better.

I make a pact with myself that from here on out the world will treat me as the kind, smart, resourceful and happy person that I am. A person who belongs. I look at my victory ring.

"I am victorious!" I yell out to the Falls.

Nine

I walk into the house ready to show Mom the ideas that Jen had for accessories. When she hears me come in, she walks toward me from the kitchen.

She hooks her finger at me, "Come here. I want to show you something."

I grin, intrigued. "What?"

She leads me out the back door, and in the middle of the yard, she has a fire going!

I laugh. "Oh wow, Mom."

There's a blanket spread on the ground beside the fire with two bags sitting on it. One is a small, brown paper bag, the other is a large black garbage bag.

"What is this?" I ask.

"Don't worry, I found a spot where someone already had a fire," she says, grinning.

"Hey! Is that my bed you're burning?"

"Just the frame."

She grabs my arm and drags me down on the blanket, where we sit between the two bags. She reaches around me and grabs the small bag. She pulls out the makings for s'mores, and I laugh. We roast our marshmallows and scoop them on our crackers and chocolate. I lay back squishing my mini-sandwich together, take a bite and giggle.

"This is too much fun!"

We eat, laugh, add parts of my bed to the fire, and talk. I tell her about the cute, yet reasonably-priced jewelry, head scarves and hair clips I got to match my new outfits. We laugh at the ridiculous plastic banana that Jen wanted me to get. "What? It's a banana clip," I mimic.

"So, you had fun I take it?" Mom asks.

"Yeah, I guess."

"What?"

"Well, I don't know, I mean I'm glad she is my friend and all. It's really her that invited me to hang out with the girls. She was always the one who paid my way when I couldn't. It's just that she's so . . . giggly, I guess. It's as if she doesn't think about anything but the immediate moment. I don't know how to explain it. She's very young, I guess." I smile because she's my same age.

"Superficial maybe?" Mom asks.

"Yeah, I guess that's it."

"Well, honey, sometimes people exaggerate happiness and focus on the shallow things to hide pain. They overcompensate. Also, it could be that you're a little too serious sometimes. I mean, you'll never be giddy, it's not in your nature, but you can joke around and have fun."

"I know, and we did that today."

We sit and watch the fire. A smoke trail rises into the sky.

"You know, Autumn, maybe Jen has secrets like you do. Maybe you can help her with that."

"How?"

"I don't know, but you've proven yourself a resourceful gal. You'll figure it out. Sounds like a better way to say thank you to a friend than paying her way at the movies. She has that area covered. A true friend gives in ways that the receiver can't get on their own or may not even realize they need."

"Like your old friend that you called?"

"Hm . . . sometimes. Subtlety is better though, where the person doesn't realize you're helping them. That is called grace and finesse."

"I like that."

"Me too."

"Thanks, Mom."

"You're welcome, Autumn."

"Oh, did you know that Jen has an uncle that's a fireman?"

Mom looks at me, not knowing where this is going.

"Well, yes, I think he volunteers there but owns a construction business too."

I nudge her and smile. "He's kinda good-looking for an old guy, don't you think?"

"He also has a good-looking wife, Autumn. What are you getting at here?"

I grin. "Not anymore he doesn't. They're divorced."

"No! I don't need any complications in my life, Autumn."

"That's exactly what you do need! Jen said he's been coming over to their house almost every night just because he's alone. He eats dinner, watches T.V., and Jen's parents keep telling him he needs to meet someone."

"No, Autumn. They're saying that because he's a pain, and I don't want him hanging out here!"

"Too late. You have a date with him tomorrow night at the Sizzler!" I laugh.

"That's not funny. You call Jen right now and tell her no."

"Mom, he asked her about you. He knows you from the Food Mart. Jen heard him talking to her parents. She told him that you were one of her friends' moms and that you were single. He doesn't drink, he plays baseball, and likes to go to the river." I sing-song, "He has a boooat. Please, Mom? What can it hurt? One date. He has a job and volunteers. He might even have his own month in one of those fireman calendars! Ha-ha. He could be famous!"

"Why didn't he ask me himself then?"

"He's shy, and you haven't been at work for him to flirt with either, you know. This could be fun for both of you! Go. It would give Jen's parents a night off."

"Oh, I hate this! I can't believe you did this to me! One date, Autumn. One. That's it, and I mean it! If he gets all hurt because I tell him no more, it's your fault!"

I raise my palms in the air. "I accept responsibility for the man's broken heart."

"Hmm."

"He's a nice guy, Mom."

"They're all nice 'til you get to know them," she snaps.

"Ouch, we'll work on that attitude." I re-direct toward the big bag. "So, what's that? You're not planning on roasting a pig or someone are you?"

"Funny." She pulls the bag over, and I try to peek inside, but she won't let me. She reaches in, feels around and whips out one of her old skirts. She flings it on the fire, and I burst into laughter.

We take turns burning our old clothes piece by piece, creating our passage into our new lives. Mom tosses the last item on, and I jump up and run into the house. I return to the yard, holding Mom's old white blouse by the shoulders and walking it to the fire.

"No, Autumn! That is still a perfectly good blouse!"

I dodge her and run to the fire tossing it on as I pass.

"I can't believe you just did that! It was fine." She walks fast to the house, I run to catch up.

"What? Mom, what are you doing?"

She heads through the kitchen, and I run past her and block my bedroom door. I'm laughing.

"No! What?" I try to close the door, and she jets past me. She's rummaging everywhere. She pulls the blankets off my bed, digs around in my closet, then looks between my mattress and the wall. She digs her hand down and whips out Pandy.

I'm stunned, then instantly angry. "No! Absolutely not!" I lunge for her, but she sidesteps me, swinging Pandy behind her. She races out the door, me on her heels screaming. "This is not funny anymore! I'm not playing!" I catch up to her at the fire. I try to grab Pandy, but she's too quick.

"I'm not playing either, Autumn."

I can't believe this. She could ruin everything we've built up in one move. I feel like my life is on the cusp again.

Tears burn my eyes. "Mom, if you do this I will not forgive you." It's silly really, I don't know why I'm so angry over a stuffed bear. It's just that he's been with me my entire life. He is the brother or sister I never had."

"Autumn, Pandy goes." Her eyes are dead serious. She is willing to gamble everything over a toy!

"I've had him my whole life!" I yell. "This is like throwing away a part of me!"

Mom's voice is a low growl almost, a tone I've never heard before. It is cold and loathing. "I've watched you curl up countless times with Pandy, sobbing. Your heart broken over that man, Jack!"

This is a woman I don't recognize.

"You cried for him, begged me to bring him to you. He didn't deserve even one of your tears! For years I've watched your heart break over and over again for that self-serving man, while you clung to a toy for comfort!" Tears stream down her face. Her eyes plead with me to understand something she can't explain. Something she dare not put into words. She envied Pandy the comfort I sought from him, instead of going to her.

I scream, "I wouldn't have cried to Pandy if you would have just told me about my dad!" I feel my anger flair. "Instead, you kept him a secret all of my life!" It was out. Finally. My truth.

"How was I supposed to tell a little girl, my daughter, that she wasn't the center of the universe, that her daddy didn't love her or want her? Especially when she was the center of my universe? How? Tell me, Autumn! Because that has plagued me for years. Give me the answer if you have it."

I feel the pain in full force. My own pain of the past and Mom's pain of watching her daughter's devastation, whom she couldn't rescue. I crumble into a heap on the ground, sobbing. I feel Mom's arms tight around me. I wear her tears. My heart's last piece of hardness shatters. I feel the weight of Pandy on my lap, where Mom has put him. I dry my face with his paws. I rub his fuzz-balled ears and look at his hard, plastic nose, where the velvet wore off long ago.

"I used to pretend that my dad gave him to me. I kept Pandy close, to show my dad that I still had his gift when he came to visit me. Turns out, when he finally came for a visit, all I could do was throw up." I look at Mom. Her eyes show hurt, and honest love. I know then that she is right. Pandy represents a lost wish, a pretend comforter. Pandy has got to go if I am to completely move on in my life, and leave my Daddy, Jack, in the past.

"I'd use his paws to wipe my tears away, and pretend they were my dad's hands."

"I'm so sorry, baby girl." We stare at Pandy.

"Autumn, all the times that you wouldn't let me close to you, he gave you the comfort I couldn't. He was my helper. I have a love for him too, you know."

I lay Pandy gently on the coals. We watch his fur melt, then the cloth peels back and burns away. His stuffing smokes and catches flame. "These are the last tears that I will ever shed over Jack Stogavich."

We sit and watch until the coals are nearly gone. "Mom, wait here a minute."

I feel her watching me as I walk to the house. I come back out with the old drain pan that seconds as a sick pan. I scoop up the ashes where Pandy has laid. "Let's do a proper burial. A burial of the past."

"What do you have in mind?" Mom asks.

"Come on."

Mom takes hold of one end of the pan, I hold the other. Together we walk to the Falls. We don't go to the footbridge. This time we walk up the mountainside trail that runs alongside the face of the Falls. When we get to the top, we go to the river's shore at the head of the Falls.

I ask, "You planned on making me face Pandy all along, didn't you?"

"I wasn't sure how to approach it, or how to even put it into words, but the opportunity presented itself. I took the leap. Are you ready, Autumn?"

I nod my head. Together we spill the ashes into the river. At first, they just dust the top of the water next to the shore, but then I watch as the current carries Pandy over the edge.

"Bye, Pandy."

I feel a loosening of a heaviness that had always been there, but that I wasn't aware of. Something that I always thought was a part of my body. A lightness expands my chest where the heaviness used to sit. It's like taking the biggest, deepest breath of air I've ever taken in my life. I look at Mom, my mouth agape.

"Freedom, Autumn."

* * *

It is Monday morning and my first real day of school. I get up early to prepare. I've tried on four outfits, and settle on the one I picked out last night. I'm so excited I can't stand it! I try three different hair styles and do my make-up twice. I look at myself in the full-length mirror, admiring my size 8 Lucky jeans. Yes! Size 8! The dark purple tank top and oversized lavender pullover hit my hips just right. I slide the shoulder of the pullover down a touch. Perfect. I'm wearing lavender socks that have purple hearts on them with my purple Chuck Taylors. My wild geometric earrings match my bangle perfectly. I've topped it all off with wildly-spritzed hair and a purple lace tie to pull my hair from my face.

I look in the mirror, and I look like the other girls at school. I look normal, finally. I can't help but smile at the mirror. It's time to go. For the first time ever, there's no self-talk on how to survive my day at school. I'm just excited to see everyone, and yes, to show off my great fashion sense. I kiss Mom goodbye and pounce out the door.

When I get to the bottom stair, I see Ian Taylor standing on the sidewalk. My heart stops for a second, then beats double time.

"Hi, Autumn," he says, as he reaches for my hand, then pulls it back self-consciously.

"Hi, Ian." I smile and take his hand in mine. I feel a tingling go through my hand, up my arm, and all through my body. I'm catching every electric arrow he is sending my way. It's the best feeling in the world!

As we walk hand in hand across the footbridge, I can feel the walls of the great divide tumble behind me. My secret place is gone. I look back as I hear the Falls' cheer.

Dear diary, today, Oct. 10th happened. For real.

Book II:

Chris's Crossing

One

I wake with a gasp.

Craig is dead.

My sleeping mind has reminded me again. Is there no escape?

My heart beats fast. The constant tremble that vibrates my body has become a normal, automatic function. I turn my head and see Mom sleeping in the seat next to me. I remove the blanket that she apparently draped over me and carefully climb over her to the aisle. I make my way to the head, at the back of the bus. The smell of the exhaust is heavy back here and makes me nauseous. It has a sickening, soapy odor that isn't like anything I've smelled before. I've endured this stench for three days and two nights solid. I leave the head and make my way back to my seat.

The driver, in a monotone voice, announces, "Deer Falls."

The bus slows, then tilts and rocks one wheel at time, as it pulls into the depot. I touch Mom on the shoulder. "Mom. We're here."

She jumps up, folds the blanket and grabs the bag of untouched snacks from the floor. I pull her suitcase down from the overhead rack. We descend the steps into fresh air. In spite of not wanting to be here, I'm relieved to see a faded sign welcoming me to Deer Falls.

The driver opens the luggage compartment of the bus, and I point out my box. Everything I'll need for the next two and a half months is in that box.

When Craig was murdered, Mom was afraid that I'd be next. So, five hours after his funeral, we were on this bus. She could be right, you know. It's hard to say because I don't know who shot my brother. My twin brother. Maybe, they meant to kill me instead, though I can't think of a single person who would want either of us dead.

Over the summer, Mom will find us a new neighborhood. Meanwhile, I'll be staying here with my grandpa, whom I've never met.

Mom said he used to be military and then a cop, but he's retired from both now. I'm a little scared to meet him, and more scared to live with him.

Craig's voice teases me from inside my head because that's where he lives now. *"Check out that old man. You could be from his loins."*

The old man is tall and thin, but far from frail. He has a ruggedness about him that could easily be meanness. *"If so, then you were first,"* I remind Craig.

Mom's short legs scuttle up to the old man, trapping him in a hug.

I hear Craig's laugh.

The old man's eyes lock on mine as we size each other up. He pats Mom, then steps back, his eyes never leaving mine. We both know immediately that we don't like each other. I'm sure he's thinking 'Young punk,' just as I'm thinking, 'Old fart.'

Craig makes a foul noise and laughs.

"Grow up!" I snap at him. A blunder of course, because he can't.

It is obvious that Mom loves her dad and that he tolerates her. Since I'm only an extension of her, I know my place immediately.

The bus pulls out, leaving a farewell of soapy exhaust in my face. To the side of the depot is a bare patch of dirt with three cars and an old beater, green truck. Grandpa points to the truck's bed, and I toss my box in. It lands hard, so for the hundredth time, I'm glad my CD player is on my person and not in that box. I open the passenger-side door, and Mom slides in. I climb in beside her on the cracked and ripped vinyl bench seat.

"Nice ride," Craig puts in sarcastically.

"Daddy! I can't believe this thing still runs. Chris, your grandpa had this truck when I was a girl."

Mom laughs that tense, making-nice laugh she has for strangers in awkward situations. I glance over her head at Grandpa. His face twitches like someone just scratched fingernails down a chalkboard. This is apparently why I've never met him before; they just don't click.

Mom must be really scared if she's leaving me with a person she's not close to. I wonder if she knows something I don't. Did the cops tell her they have a suspect? For the hundredth time, I search her face for a hidden truth. Nothing. She continues to chatter away while Grandpa and I stay quiet.

Maybe this will be easier after she leaves for home tomorrow. She'll go back to the city she knows, to her familiar life at work, and busy herself by finding us a new place to live. I'll listen to CDs and get used to Craig not being in this world anymore. Grandpa, he'll just keep double-clutching this ugly, old beater. However, for tonight, we are three separate worlds forced together. A family minus Craig.

The truck bounces into the pitted driveway. Grandpa kills the engine, and the truck stops by rocking on its heels. He is out of the truck before it settles. I get out and climb over the tailgate, grab my box and jump down. In front of me stands a narrow, two-story house in need of paint and washed windows.

"Chris, I grew up in this house. Daddy? Is my old room available? Chris, I think you should sleep in my old room."

"He sleeps wherever he wants, except for my room," Grandpa growls.

"Oh, good! You'll sleep in my room then."

"I'll check it out and see, Mom," I say, casting a look at Grandpa.

His eyes might have almost smiled at my defiance of Mom, but I can't be sure. Maybe I'm worth a second look to him. Do I care? Probably not. *Just ten weeks*, I remind myself.

When I walk in the house, I expect to see cobwebs and to be knocked over with old man smell. Instead, the house is neat, and while I detect a hint of old, stale books, it's barely noticeable. I figure Grandpa must leave the windows and doors open a lot. I'm glad.

The furniture is heavy wood and old-fashioned. Grandma's flair of decor is obvious. She's been dead since before I was born, so this furniture and the duck wall paper in the kitchen are at least 17 years old.

"Creepy," Craig says. *"Do you think there are ghosts?"* he asks.

I let out a tired sigh. I'm tired of Craig's voice, of strangers too close in that sardine can of a bus and of this sadness and trembling inside me.

"Grandpa, can I go find a place for my stuff?" I raise my box a little, for display. He waves a hand toward the stairs, while Mom follows him to the kitchen, chatting nervously and nonstop.

I hear a bird tweeter, then Craig's voice. *"Look Chris! She's doin' the pudgy parakeet!"* Craig laughs. It's what we call it when she's excited and twittering around. Or, we used to—we still do I guess.

I carry my box upstairs and see the stairwell is lined with black and white photos of ancestors long gone. Death defines my life. Craig's dead, open eyes flash across my mind. His empty stare accusing me of living. I breathe deep and continue up the stairs.

The door at the head of the stairs is open. I see a bed and a nightstand with a book that holds a pair of glasses, and beside those, a beer bottle. I turn right and glance down the hallway which has four doors on the left and one on the right.

The door on the right turns out to be a long, narrow closet. I pull a dangling shoestring to light the room. It holds boxes of what I guess are Grandma's things. The bathroom door is open and is the first room on the left. I open the next door and find an old, dusty sewing machine sitting on a table. Beside it lays a dusty and faded bundle of folded cloth.

"Like I said, creepy," Craig whispers. I ignore him.

I back out of the room, touching only the door knob and close the door. The third door is obviously Mom's old room. I go toward the last door on this side of the hall. I hear a drum roll and Craig's voice, *"Wayne! Please show us what's behind door number five! A newwww car!"* I hear canned applause.

To the right side of the hall, across from the last door, is a small reading nook. The shelf is full of old books. There's an overstuffed chair and a rocker, both of which share a floor lamp and a view out a window, which overlooks the front yard. I can picture Grandma and Grandpa sitting here together reading, as Grandma rocks in her chair.

I open the last door, and relief floods in. The room is small but neat. The comforter on the bed looks new. The navy-blue curtains have sun-faded lines that run the length of the folds. On the window sill sits a small, glass ashtray with a note: 'Open window when in use.' Here's an obvious difference of opinions between Mom and Grandpa. I don't want to upset the household more than it already is, so I hide the ashtray under the mattress since I don't smoke anyway. I try out the bed. It's not great, but it'll work in a pinch.

I retrieve my box from the head of the stairs and begin to make the room mine. I put my clothes in drawers and hang some shirts in the closet. I stack up CDs on the nightstand. The last thing to put away is the gun. The gun that murdered Craig.

I hold it in my hands. The ever-present tremble in my body moves through my hands to a full-on shake. I see smudges of fingerprints on its black side. I wipe them off with my thumb, wondering whose they were. Mine, Craig's, or the murderer's? Its oily smell brings the haunting images back to my eyes. Craig lying on his bed, eyes open, looking at me. Blood is everywhere. The gun is lying on the floor. I pick it up and stuff it down my pants, though now I wish I hadn't. The next picture is Mom screaming, crying and closing Craig's bedroom door.

I push the gun deep under the mattress, my face burrows into the new smell of the comforter. I shouldn't have picked it up, I know. At the time, I was running on instinct, it was the natural thing to do. I wasn't thinking about evidence or anything like that. I just knew that this piece of metal was the last thing my brother saw before he died. I wasn't there to help him, we had no goodbyes. I only have the last thing Craig saw, and maybe touched. I had to pick it up . . . I just . . . had to.

I go down the hall to the bathroom. The tub-shower combo is clean but old. The medicine cabinet has a mirror for a door and hangs over the sink. I avoid looking in the mirror as I open it. Craig's face is always in mirrors now, which is kind of weird because even though we're twins and others can't tell us apart, we don't really look the same. Now, when I look in a mirror, it's Craig's face staring back at me, not my own.

The medicine cabinet has shaving stuff, aspirin, Bengay—I chuckle at that. I close the door, avoiding Craig's face, and go downstairs.

I stop midway on the stairs when I hear Mom's voice.

"I came home from work, and the house was quiet. I knew the boys were probably at the bowling alley. That's where the kids hang out. I started dinner when I saw Chris walk in the front door. I asked where Craig was, and he shrugged his shoulders. He said Craig didn't go to the lanes with him. Chris went upstairs, then I heard him call me. His voice sounded strange, so I knew instantly that something was wrong. When I got upstairs, Chris was standing in Craig's room. I had to move around him to see what he was looking at."

Mom sobs, and I hear Grandpa's voice mumble something that I can't make out.

"Craig, my baby, is laid out on his bed. At first, my mind doesn't register what my eyes are seeing. There's blood everywhere! Part of his neck is just . . . gone! Like some animal tore his neck out! That was my first thought." Mom cries harder, yet tries to compose herself enough to talk.

I see the scene flash before my eyes again. Craig's body is lying at an odd angle, unlike his usual kicked-back manner. His feet skim the floor, and his head isn't on his pillow. His eyes are looking at me, almost like he is lifting his head to see me. His neck is a mess, blood is splattered on the wall above and beside him. I hear the very soft tic, tic, tic of blood as it drips into a puddle on the carpet. I remember feeling like my own heart was bleeding out in time with Craig's dripping blood. Unlike Craig's, though, my blood finds its way back home. I feel like I'm going to be sick, but Mom's voice gives nausea a pause.

"The officers said he died instantly but that he still partially bled out because of how his body was positioned." Both Mom and Grandpa are quiet for a bit. Then Mom adds, "Daddy, six days ago Chris found his twin brother brutally murdered. They were inseparable. I think Chris is in shock. He's quiet, which I would expect, but he hasn't cried. It's as if to him, Craig isn't dead."

I hear Grandpa's low mumble again, then Mom's reply. "No, no. There wasn't a gun, no evidence at all. They don't know who did it. They spoke with Chris, but he said neither of them had any enemies, and I believe him. Those boys were good kids. They were always happy, cutting up and teasing all the time. Everybody loved them. They lit up a room when they walked in. Their friends, jeez, like thirty kids in all, said Chris was at the lanes with them all afternoon, but that Craig didn't come. They said that was a little odd since the boys were always together."

"Daddy," Mom's voice cracks and she clears her throat, "Help my boy get through this. Please. I put in a transfer at work, but I need time to find us a new neighborhood." She breaks down in sobs again. "His life is never going to be the same. I'm so scared that whoever killed Craig, will come back for Chris. I have to get him away from everyone he's ever known."

I'm sure Grandpa is feeling awkward with Mom, and I'm sure he doesn't want to take on a kid he's never met. I'll make it easy on him. I won't cause trouble, and in two and a half months, I'll leave him to his normal life again.

I back up the stairs quietly, then turn and climb the rest of them to the top. I don't know what to do. I go to the bathroom and avoid the mirror while I splash water on my face. It feels good. I go to my room and lie on my bed. I think about never seeing my friends or school again, or never going to the lanes. The world feels overwhelmingly big and empty. I put on a CD that was Craig's favorite and sing along with it in my head.

The next thing I know, Mom is waking me for dinner. I didn't realize I had fallen asleep.

* * *

It's morning. I wake up feeling alone. Mom is going back home today. I go downstairs, and she is very clingy. She keeps hugging and touching me, but I'm okay with it. She's made me a bacon and cheese omelet, my favorite, for breakfast.

I know she misses Craig and hurts, but I can't help her with that. Craig talks in my head and looks at me from the mirror. I listen to his music, and nobody knows this, but I also wear his clothes. I can't make him leave me, to go be with Mom. I don't want him in my head, but I don't want him to leave either.

We drive Mom to the bus depot. We hug and say goodbye. She looks worried from the bus window. And lonely. I smile as big as I can and wave. I hope it helps.

When the bus pulls away, Grandpa and I both let out a huge sigh. We look at each other. We're in the truck and gone before the bus exhaust clears.

On the ride home, I ask Craig, *"What now?"*

"Chill, Chris, I've got this."

Two

I 've spent all morning in my room just tossing up and catching my ball. My mind won't stop hitting replay on the scene in Craig's bedroom, even going as far as the smallest detail. I keep seeing his face and body, and I wonder what life will be like without him here. It seems unnatural or foreign, impossible even. It's like this is somebody else's life, some stranger's story seen on T.V. I'm shocked every few seconds as I realize this is real.

I tell myself to go shoot some hoops, but that would require going to a court. People would be there, and I don't want to be around anyone. I've had enough of people the past few days on the bus. People tick me off. I can't comprehend how the world just keeps going on, business as usual, while for me it has stopped dead. I feel forced to move, breathe, even to sleep. I don't understand why people aren't stopped in their tracks. It doesn't register how they can't sense that my brother is dead when it floods from my pores. I want to scream it out loud. CRAIG IS DEAD, YOU IDIOTS!

I see the long, black bag on the gurney being rolled past me to the ambulance. The rises in the bag are Craig's feet, chest and head. I wonder, *is he still bleeding?* I'm standing on our lawn staring as the ambulance doors close, the flashing lights go still, and it quietly rolls away. Craig is helpless. My other face, my other body, my other self is going away. No sirens, no alarms. Nobody notices that half of me is dead.

I get up from my bed and walk out to the hall. I stand looking out the window of the reading area. I sit in the rocker and close my eyes. The motion is comforting, but the soft squeak of the chair doesn't allow my mind to leave the space.

I open my eyes and reach for a book on the shelf. *Dracula*, by Bram Stoker. I open it. It smells old. The copyright date reads 1897. I've seen this movie with Craig. I didn't know it was written so long ago. Now, Bram is dead and so is Craig. I stare at the shelved books; each one I reach for is dated from the late 1800s to the early 1900s.

I lift up a huge white Bible, that is yellowed with age. Inside, our family tree is handwritten in neat penmanship. The writing looks feminine; undoubtedly Grandma's. I see the names of dead people whose photos probably hang in the stairwell. I see Mom's name, then mine and Craig's. Every name has a space for D.O.B. and D.O.D. I get a pen from my room and write June 1, 2017. on Craig's D.O.D. space. I stare at my writing; it looks wrong on this page with the neat penmanship. My writing doesn't belong on this page any more than Craig's and my name belong with a list of dead strangers.

I close the Bible and ask myself, *Why am I here in this strange town, with a stranger I've rarely heard stories about? Why did Mom bring me here when I need my family?* The answer shocks me. Craig was her son, my twin. To look at my face is to see Craig's face. Mom simply can't handle it. Tears blur my eyes as I realize she needs to grieve without my face, Craig's face, always in front of her. My heart drops, it feels heavy. How long will she need to be away from me? Will my face always drag this tragedy to the front of her thoughts? Have I lost Mom along with Craig? I take a deep breath and let it out. I look at the surrounding area. There's a small crack in the ceiling. Is this my home for good now?

I get up and go downstairs. Grandpa is in the kitchen.

"Hungry?" he asks.

"Uh, yeah, I guess so."

He pushes a plate across the counter toward me. It holds a sandwich that's stacked like half a foot tall, with chips heaped next to it. My eyes go big.

"I s'pose your mom made nice little polite sandwiches." It is an accusation, not a question. I don't answer.

"Men need food, plain and simple."

I pick up the plate and thank him. I take it to the table, wondering how I'll ever get my mouth around this monster. Grandpa grabs his and takes it to the living room, where he sits in front of the T.V. I watch him cradle the plate on his lap, push down the top of the sandwich so it's a manageable size, then devour a quarter of it in a single bite. Impressive. I move to the living room. This feels all wrong like I'm breaking rules by sitting on the couch with food on my lap. I smash down my sandwich, and amazingly get my mouth around it.

"Onions!" Craig sounds the alarm. I pull rings of onion out and lay them on the plate.

"Thanks," I tell Craig.

I sneak a glance at Grandpa, but he doesn't say anything about wasting food. He finishes his lunch in record time and sets his plate on the coffee table, then puts his feet up next to the empty plate. While he watches the news, my mind flies back to home and to our glass coffee table.

At home, a drink is only allowed in the living room on a coaster, and then only when non-family is visiting. I nestle into the couch, relaxed, but cautious. I put my feet on the table and eat fast like a man should. It feels barbaric. It feels right.

"Shhhooot. Now, this is what I'm talkin' 'bout!" Craig says.

I chuckle out loud. My eyes dart to Grandpa. He gives me a look like I'm nuts, but goes back to his news. I quietly finish the sandwich, but I can't force down the last few chips, even though I dare not waste more food.

I pick up Grandpa's plate with mine and take them to the kitchen to rinse off. Grandpa comes into the kitchen and hands me his glass. I rinse it, and he belches.

"You get full?" he asks.

I give a stupid grin. "Yeah."

"You don't like onions." Again, it's an accusation.

I wipe the sink dry, avoiding his eyes.

"Not really."

"Anything else you don't like?"

"Old man smell drowned in Bengay?" Craig offers up.

"Sissy voice in my ear?" I snap back at Craig.

"No, I'm good. Sorry, I didn't mean to waste food."

"Well, that's why I'm asking, so we don't waste in the future. So, if there's anything else, let me know now, 'cuz I like to cook."

"You do?" The picture in my head of this mean-looking old man puttering in the kitchen is just all wrong.

"It's what happens when you're retired. You're reduced to old man and woman's work. Can't be helped."

"I don't like seafood."

"What kind?"

"All of it."

"Hmm. What about river food?"

I look at him, not sure if this old guy is serious. "I-Uh . . . "

"I fish. I do okay at it. You may have to suffer through some trout at some point." He's staring me down now.

"Or, I could make a sandwich."

He snorts. It's the first laugh I've heard since I got here. "You'll eat my trout."

I'm outside with my ball in the dirt driveway. I'm going through some moves that are second nature to me. I hear a noise and see Grandpa in a shed that sits in the back yard. I walk over. He's rummaging around, climbing over dusty, rusted junk.

"Neanderthal cave," Craig states.

"Grandpa, what are you doing?"

He pulls at something leaning against the back wall and wedged-in by junk.

"Grab that end." He points.

I climb over a mountain of crap and see a basketball hoop.

"Wow! Cool!" I help him dig it loose. It's dirty and covered in spider webs. I brush them off with my hand. We get it outside, and he goes to a faucet and turns on the hose. I spray it down and see that the net is like new. Grandpa goes to a bench just inside the shed door and grabs a jar of bolts and a drill. I grab a step ladder, and we hang the hoop on the side of the shed.

I toss the ball and hear the familiar 'whoosh' of the net and grin. Grandpa snags the ball, and unlike the old man that he is, he leaps and makes two points. I laugh, and the game is on.

We're nice to each other at first, sharing and taking turns. Then it gets pushy and rough as we play. Before long we're both mad and shoving each other to get at the ball. At one point, he trips me! I can't believe he's done that! It becomes an all-out war then. I'm not sure who won, we lost track of points, but he was first to plop down in the grass. I lie out next to him. We're both breathing hard and are all sweaty. I spot blood on his elbow where I knocked him into the shed's wall and point at it.

"Maybe you should hang up your jersey and leave this to the young guns," I say, grinning.

He grunts. "You think of that scratch as damage?"

I laugh. It feels good. It's an honest, clean laugh, my first in a long time. I watch clouds roll by and feel the cool grass on my back. I feel good, then my heart drops as I realize that Craig's not with me. I see blood-spray on Craig's cheek. I throw the picture out of my mind.

"Grandpa?"

He looks at me.

"Thanks."

He grunts out a "Yep," then gets up, and I follow him into the house.

During my shower, I stretch out sore muscles that I've neglected for a week now. It was a good workout with Grandpa. My body was craving the exercise.

I head downstairs and realize that I am welcome in this place. I think I even like it here. It's different for sure. It's . . . manly. I like the roughness of it. I've lived with a female all my life in a house full of untouchables and polite manners, which mark a woman's world with a woman's rules. This place is more comfortable, more natural. I can breathe here.

When I hit the bottom stair, I see Grandpa sitting at the dining room table. He has a lamp on the table that reminds me of the aliens in *War of the Worlds*. Its long neck is stretched and bent around to position the bubble head just inches from the work Grandpa is doing. I walk to the fridge and pull out a beer. Grandpa stares me down.

"For you."

"Nice pass, kid, but you don't want to see my block."

I grin and put the beer back, then grab a soda. I sit in the chair closest to him and pop the top of my can.

"What are you doing?" He is working on some tiny glass vials.

"I like to pan for gold. I make necklaces out of what I find, and sell them."

I pick up a glass vial filled with water and gold flakes. There's a fine gold chain attached to a gold cap that seals the top of the vial. It looks professional.

"These are pretty cool. I've never seen anything like them before. Where do you sell them?"

"I have a friend that sets them up at the senior center and sells them for me." He looks a little embarrassed, then like he's challenging me.

"Oh. Go to the senior center often do ya?"

"Shut up."

I chuckle.

"I get twenty bucks apiece for them. Vera, that's my friend, she gets half the money."

"Half!"

He looks at me. "I don't need the money, but she does. Plus, it gives me an excuse to play in the river."

"Hm, you surprise me."

"Why? Think I'm too old to make something nice?"

"No." I grin. "I thought you were too mean."

He grunts. "Maybe I am."

"Can I go gold hunting with you next time?"

"It's called panning, and it's boring work," he glances at me, "for some."

"Oh." I assume that's a no.

He looks back down at his work. "I guess you can tag along as long as you don't whine."

"When?"

"Tomorrow work for you?"

"Yep."

"Good. We'll take a pole with us. When you get bored, you can earn your keep by getting us a trout."

Craig laughs and sings, "Let the good times roll," complete with music accompaniment. I hear him laugh even harder as he fades into the distance—wherever that is.

It's late. My clock's glow reads 2:11 a.m. I can't sleep. My head is spinning with everything that's happened the past week: Craig's murder, his funeral, a three-day bus ride, Mom gone, and meeting Grandpa. Weirder yet, Grandpa ends up being an okay guy. I wish Craig could have met him. I bet we would have spent summers here instead of in the city. Maybe that's why I can't sleep because there's no city noise, no hum of life being lived. But then, I did sleep last night. Well, I was sleep-deprived from the bus trip, too. Actually, I hadn't slept since Craig died. I think I remember hearing that having no sleep for a week or month would kill you. Oh wait, it just makes you crazy, that's right.

The streetlight's beam shines in through the curtain. I miss my mom, my room, my city, but I miss 'Chris-n-Craig' the most. I see the blood on the wall and Craig's open eyes. Jeez, it was like he was looking right through me!

I rub my eyes trying to erase the image of his face. *Craig, who did this to you? Why?* He'll just be another statistic of unsolved murders in the city. Nothing but a case number, because I picked up the gun, the evidence! *Why didn't I just take the gold chain you always wore?* The image of his half-missing neck pops into view. *Oh.*

I sigh, close my eyes and keep them closed. I'm so tired of seeing that scene over and over again. I'm tired of hearing his life drip into the carpet. I'm tired of hearing his voice when I least expect it. I wonder if I'll ever see my own face in the mirror again. If not, will Craig age with me, or stay seventeen?

A single tear slides down my nose. I've given up only one tear when I saw Mom sobbing. I take a deep breath trying to exhale my guilt. His smell is still in these pajamas.

The black gun stands in mid-air pointed at Craig. Craig's smile drops. Fingers appear on the gun. Craig's mouth is moving, saying something.

I wake up gasping for breath. A dream. The clock reads 4:35 a.m. I go to the bathroom. Was he trying to show me who killed him? Is this really Craig in my head? Is this my imagination? I just don't know. I think I may be losing it. I rinse my hands, managing to avoid the mirror. I crawl back in bed, where sleep finds me again.

Three

Craig isn't here today.

Grandpa takes me to see the falls, Deer Falls. They are awesome. Loud. We walk up a trail that leads to the river above the falls, then hike another half-mile or so until we come to a bend in the river. Grandpa says it's a good spot for panning and wastes no time in finding his first flakes of the day. He was right about how boring panning is no matter how cool it is to find money lying in a river. He points me up river and tells me there is a big boulder, "good for hanging a worm." I grab the pole and cup of worms and head upstream.

I walk quite a way and wonder if I missed the boulder. I figure if I don't see it around the next bend coming up, then I'll just hang out a while and throw the worms in the river to fatten the fish for next time. As I make my way around the bend, I see it. The boulder is huge! I laugh because there is no way anyone could miss it.

It sits in the river, so I hop on several smaller boulders to get to it and climb up. I look over the edge of it and see a deep pool where the river has carried out the bed in front of it. The pool's depth gives the water a dark color, too dark to see the bottom. I wonder how the boulder hasn't rolled into the pool.

I sit down and bait my hook. I've never fished before. I'm just a city boy. I can find any street, get you to any rave, and dance like nobody's fool once we're there. I can earn cash on the b-ball court and catch any girl's eye, but this yee-haw country stuff is all new.

I toss the line. It doesn't drop. The worm swings around the end of the pole in what must be a terrifying ride. I unwrap the line, and the worm takes another terror-filled ride straight down, plunging into the water. I reel him in and put on a new worm. The first one I figure has paid his dues, if not died of fright. Eventually, I get the hang of casting and reeling in, and I see why so many guys like this sport. You don't have to do much to play it.

The sun is getting too warm, but I stay on the boulder, hoping and not hoping, to catch supper. Pizza would work just fine for me. I lay back on the rock and notice how quiet it is out here. The trees look majestic against the sky, and the river has a smell of its own. This place is fresh and alive. I fall asleep in the warmth of the day.

Sweat trickling down my face wakes me from an unexpected nap. The pole has no fish and is missing the worm. Looks like pizza tonight. I strip off my shirt and jump into the pool. I touch bottom and guess the pool is about a dozen feet deep. The water's cold is a shock, but a good one. I swim out a way, where the current isn't too strong. The water feels good, refreshing, and I feel free from . . . myself. I make my way back to shore, grab up the pole and my shirt, taking a long look across the river. It's wide. I wonder if anyone has ever swum across it. I doubt it; it's really far. I begin my trek back down river.

When I catch sight of Grandpa, he's sitting by the river's edge, playing with his pan.

"Did you get rich?" I ask.

He squints up at me. "Did you get supper?"

I grin. "No, I was goin' for pizza, but no luck."

"Hmm," he grunts. He holds up a small glass bottle. It has maybe fifty gold flakes swimming in it. "Today has been a good day."

I realize that Craig hasn't been around. There have been no flashbacks, no comments, and no dreams. I grin again. "Yeah, Grandpa, it has."

Grandpa grabs up his things, I hang on to the pole, and we begin the walk home. It's quiet out here. I can almost hear the trees breathe in the breeze. The river is an entity that dominates everything around it.

"Craig would have liked it here," I say.

Grandpa grunts. "It's not like the city. No bright lights or action, but it does have its own way about it. It won't be ignored. It kind of sneaks up on you and grabs you before you even know what's happened. It grabbed me about forty years ago and never let go. So, why do you think Craig would have liked it better here?"

"Well, maybe not better, but better for vacations, you know?"

We walk in silence for a while. Then Grandpa says, "I've been wondering what he was like."

I look in his eyes, trying to measure the weight of the response I should give. I see that he is serious. He's not wanting to judge, he just wants to know what his grandson, whom he never met, was like. My heart is suddenly glad that he, that anyone, has asked.

"Well, we looked a lot alike." I snort out a laugh. "Most people got us confused, but we never saw it. Actually, we had the same build, color eyes, hair, all of that you know, but to us our faces were different. I mean the same general shape, but . . . different expressions. I'm not sure how to describe it."

I go quiet for a minute. I remember Craig and me with our friends.

"He carried me. He was the funny one, the smart one. He was loyal to me. We fed off each other like we were a show, I guess. We'd feed cues to each other, and the other would just run with it. It was only natural for us, growing up as twins and being the center of attention of little old ladies in the supermarkets." I smile as I remember the laughter of our friends.

"We always had fun. Wherever we went, we were a team." Quietly I add, "We were just 'Chris-n-Craig.' "

Grandpa has a serious look on his face, but he's not condemning me or disbelieving me.

"So, now I'm not sure how to act, how to be 'Just Chris.' I'm not sure who I am without him giving me cues. I don't know how to do life with half of me gone."

Grandpa stops walking, so I stop. We look at each other. "Son, it'll come to you. It will."

I nod my head, but I don't believe him.

"For now, just breathe, until you don't have to remind yourself to take in air anymore."

I study his eyes and feel the truth of his words. My brows furrow in deep contemplation. "Now that makes all kinds of sense to me."

On our way home, Grandpa asks if I want to go to the café for dinner. I don't. I'm not wanting normal strangers around me doing normal things.

Later, I hear grandpa on the phone. He calls out to me, "Chris, what kind of pizza were you tryin' to catch out there today?" He gives a crooked grin like Craig does. Did.

"One of those humongous Hawaiian flat bellies that your wimp of a pole couldn't handle." I tease back.

Grandpa speaks into the phone. "Hawaiian, I guess. A big one. Yeah, that'll do. Yeah, I guess so, cola." He looks over at me with a question in his eyes. I nod. "Okay, thanks." Grandpa hangs up the outdated, wall-mounted princess phone, and says, "They said it'd be here in thirty minutes." He tosses a twenty on the table. "I'm hitting the shower."

"What, you're not paying with all that gold you found today?"

"Naw, I save that for the whiskey and women."

"Really. Are there many available 70-year-old women in these parts?" I ask as he climbs the stairs.

"Gotta beat 'em off with a stick, kid."

I laugh. The second real laugh I've had in a long time. "At least that pole's good for something," I mumble.

"It's good for keeping young'uns in line too," he adds as he goes out of sight.

"Good ears, G-pa!"

He appears back on the stairs far enough to lean down and see my face. "Gee Paw?"

I grin. "It fits you; you aren't quite grand yet."

He grunts, and goes back upstairs.

My own shower didn't help my tiredness like I thought it would. I'm still feeling the effect of being sleep-deprived for most of the past week. I go downstairs, and see G-pa already munching on pizza. I look at the box and recognize the pizza franchise.

"G-pa, I hate to tell you this, but that pizza should have been free."

"Nonsense."

"Seriously!" I laugh. "That's this company's ad campaign. 'Thirty minutes or it's free.' Unless people out here in the backwoods don't hold people to their word," I say to get a rise out of him.

"Well that little punk," G-pa scowls.

"Here, I'll call and complain."

"No, leave it."

I look at G-pa, confused. "Why? If you were ripped off . . . "

G-pa holds up a hand to stop me. "It's probably the only money that kid sees from his job. I know of the family. Leave it be, Chris."

"Regardless, you can't let him go around ripping you off!"

"It won't happen again; I promise you that. But what good is it for him to lose his job over fifteen bucks? Naw, that family needs him to work, for the money and to keep him out of trouble."

I squint, sizing him up. "You tryin' to work your way to grand status?"

I plop down on the couch and grab a piece of pizza. I grab the liter of soda and chug it down until I can't take the burn anymore. I prop my feet up on the table like G-pa, and we go through our barbaric ritual of ingesting sustenance.

When I'm stuffed full, I go upstairs. Man, I'm beat. I lie on my bed. It's still light out when I crash.

The water is dark, heavy and cold. Not only can't I get to the surface, I can't even find it. My lungs are hitting max, and panic pumps my heart hard. Something touches then grabs my foot, but I jerk loose. I don't know what it was, but I sense it is horrific. I swim in the opposite direction. Panic! Lungs! Those thoughts make up my world. My arms are tired, and I'm not gaining enough distance, I know it is right behind me. I see a faint light. Surface! I stroke as hard as I can, and my feet finally give me some push. I glance under me and see that it's Craig reaching out for me! I grab, but our fingers don't lock, he's falling into the dark deep. My lungs need air! I burst through the surface and gasp for air.

My eyes open, I find myself sitting up in bed, breathing hard. I rub my face to erase the dream. My clock reads 1:01 a.m. I look down at my feet that are trapped and tangled in the sheet. I kick myself free and escape to the bathroom. Craig's face stares at me from the mirror. I flip him the bird and go back to bed.

I lay awake for a long time, afraid to go back to sleep, yet afraid to stay awake where Craig can haunt me. I have no true escape. I go downstairs and eat cold pizza and watch infomercials.

I wake in the morning to G-pa cooking breakfast. The T.V. is off, and my comforter is over me. I feel silly. I get up, and G-pa hands me a cup of coffee.

I grin. "Um, I don't drink coffee."

"Why not?" He looks at me like that's the craziest nonsense he's ever heard.

I shrug my shoulders and take the cup. It is sweet and milky. It's actually a pretty good way to wake up. Better than other methods lately.

"You know, Mom would have a fit if she knew you were giving me coffee."

"Better than giving you beer." He squints at me, "And I'd tell her."

I smile. I get his double meaning. "I know you would."

"Besides, she doesn't scare me. Now her mother, she could scare the bejesus right out of me. Wouldn't even have to raise her voice to do it either." He shakes his head like it's all a shame. "She's been gone twenty years come October, and there's some things I still won't do."

I chuckle. G-pa really is funny. "Like what?"

He glances my way, and I only make out part of his mumble.

"You still can't what?"

"I can't leave the toilet seat up."

I laugh, picturing all the times Mom would yell about the same thing, and how Craig and I would point fingers at each other.

G-pa ignores my laughter and hands me a plate of eggs, potatoes, sausage and toast, heaped so high I'll never see the bottom of it. I give it my best try.

"I'm going uptown for a few things today. You want to come along?"

Panic hits my chest. "No. If it's okay, think I'll just go down to the river for a while. I kind of like it there."

"Suit yourself. Watch that current, it'll sweep you over the falls."

"Okay."

"Want to take the pole with ya?" he asks.

"No, you might need it uptown today." I grin.

"You're gonna try my trout some time, you know."

" I can't wait," I mumble.

G-pa laughs a full-on laugh.

After he heads out, I grab my CD player. I've been listening to Craig's CDs. I'm not sure why. I guess I hope that if I keep playing them, maybe my aching heart won't be so hollow. Like pushing on an aching tooth; when you quit pushing, the pain seems less intense. I don't know if this works, but I have to try something, anything.

As I walk along the river, I turn off the music and listen to the quiet. Man, this river is wide. It looks calm and almost flat like you could walk across it. I remember last night's dream, and I'm not sure I can go in again. I bend over to touch a finger to the water. Cold! Too cold! Nope.

I walk on, making my way to the boulder. I wonder why nobody else comes up here. Maybe this place is too dangerous. Or, maybe there's a really cool swimming hole below the falls that everyone goes to. I'm glad no one comes up here. I like it here.

I sit on the boulder and watch the river flow by. Fish jump every once in a while. The sun is getting hot, and the water sparkles as it dances under its light. It is calling me. It's time to go in.

I flash to my dream. I'll be leaving my sneakers on. I pull off my shirt and take the leap. The current is there, but not too strong near the shore. I paddle around and flip on my back and let the current carry me a little, while I watch the sky and tree tops. I begin to swim toward the center of the river. The current shows me who's boss pretty quick. I make my way back to the shore. The sun feels good as it warms my cool body. I walk up river back to the boulder and sit in the sun. I stare at the opposite shore, and wonder, could I make it across?

Four

"Chris, wake up. We're going uptown."

G-pa's face is poked around my door.

I groan. "Whatever happened to just breathing?"

"You're breathing. Come on, get up. We're going to the café for breakfast, then to get you some summer clothes. I'm sick of looking at that same pair of shorts all the time."

"I have other clothes I can wear."

"Five minutes." His tone is a military command. His face pops out of view, and my stomach tightens.

I do not want to see people. I pick up my shorts, and the odor of river wafts up. I toss them in the corner and grab clean jeans and a shirt, tossing them on my bed. I jump in the shower, and the soap wakes me up faster than I can say 'Zestfully clean.'

Downstairs a cup of coffee is on the table, already made. G-pa is fiddling the truck keys in his hand while standing at the open door. I slam down the coffee, and before I know what's happened, G-pa is double–clutching us to town.

I find the café busy, hectic and too loud. It's full of smiling faces that I try to avoid so I don't have to fail at acting normal.

The mall is overwhelming, even though it isn't busy at this early hour. Cheerful people living life like Craig isn't dead about sends me over the edge. We go into a store that is geared toward teens. A bubbly, peppy clerk approaches. I freeze like I've entered gangland.

G-pa tells me, "Grab whatever suits you," while he stops the clerk in her tracks with his meanest expression.

I pick up a pair of cargo shorts and a tee, pushing them toward G-pa. "These will work," I say.

"Get more," he demands.

"Really, this is good."

"You need a whole wardrobe," he answers.

Finally, I get it. Craig and I dressed alike. He is handing me a new identity. Whatever identity I want. My heart pounds and my hands begin to shake. G-pa sees this and kindly looks away. I feel my eyes sting, and G-pa goes to a rack and pulls down some shirts, then hands them to me. I grab two pairs of jeans and various styles of shorts on my way to the changing room.

Craig meets me in the tiny rom. He is staring at me from the mirror. I look away.

"You're a punk, Chris!" he yells.

I don't respond. I feel ashamed because I do want to be rid of Craig, but only because I'm not sure if any of this is real. This craziness, his face, his voice, even his death all seem conjured up in my head. What if I'm really just a lunatic and none of this is real? I look back at Craig in the mirror. I reach a hand up to my face and watch it touch Craig's face. He grins, I do not. A chill runs down my spine.

"So, what—you'd just toss me away like that? You tell that old man to mind his own business! Tell him, Chris! Tell him! Be a man for a change and stick up for yourself. Who is he to tell you who you are?"

I put on the new clothes and look in the mirror. Craig shakes his head in that way he has when he sees something ridiculous. He snorts a laugh at me. I stand nose to nose in the mirror. *"We're done here, Craig."*

I step back and pick up the remaining clothes. I can't help but glance at the mirror. His hair is shaggy, his nose a touch wider. Wait. It's me! It's my face! I touch my cheeks, my nose and my lips. I look down my body at the shirt and jeans I'm wearing. This isn't Craig! Relief hits me hard enough to make me sway. I smile. It's my smile, not Craig's crooked smile. I take inventory of myself. I'm more filled out than the last time I looked at myself. I think of the huge meals G-pa swears by and chuckle. My chest feels like it's expanding inside. It's excitement, actual joy! My smile grows to a size I had forgotten the feel of. I stand up tall and look at what the world sees. I pull the tags off the clothes I have on, and walk out of the changing room, leaving Craig's clothes behind on the floor.

"You're a PUNK!" Craig screams from wherever he is now.

I don't look back at the mirror. Self-doubt wells up inside, fighting for my joy's space. This isn't over, but then Craig never did let a fight go until his opponent surrendered.

I step out of the tiny room, and G-pa's gruff face makes me smile. His eyes brighten. "I need a haircut now."

"I was getting a little concerned about that, thought I might have to wrestle you in your sleep."

He takes me to his barber, which is a big concern to me. A younger guy starts to cut my hair though and seems to know what he's doing. The place settles into its routine and turns calm.

"Seems to me that I remember you asking me what we should do when you stepped out of our life and into hick country. I told you then that I had this whole mess handled. Why the disloyalty all of a sudden, Chris?"

I glance at the mirror and see my own face. I grin. The barber sees me and says, "Is it looking okay?"

"Perfect," I answer, staring down my own reflection in defiance.

G-pa gives a nod of approval when I'm finished and pays, leaving a generous tip to the young barber.

"Money well spent," he chides me.

We head for the truck, and G-pa points at my shoes. "Those look a mess with the rest of you looking so sharp now."

"Yeah, yesterday I jumped in the river with them on."

He gives me a puzzled expression and then shakes his head.

"What? We city folk are squeamish about things in the river, G-pa." He barks out a laugh as he opens the door to the shoe store.

On the way home, we stop for gas. The smell of it is an old familiar. It sets me more at ease. I feel like I belong here sitting in this ugly, beater truck, with this skinny old man, who looks at times like he'd just as soon bite my face off as to look at it. Even so, I know that under his rough exterior is a 'Grand' pa, who cares about me.

"G-pa, that was a lot of money to spend on clothes. Are you sure you can afford it?" I'm ashamed to spend his retirement money and scared to pry into his personal finances.

I get a nasty look for my inquiry. I've crossed the line.

"I'm sorry, I just—"

"I'll let you know if we're out of money."

"Okay."

G-pa sighs. "I have two pensions, and I have investments. I'm not rich, but I won't run out either."

"Okay."

We bounce into the driveway, and he's out of the truck before it's done rocking. I've either made him mad or embarrassed by my prying. I grab the bags of clothes and climb out feeling like . . . like a punk. I go inside and see G-pa is setting up his jewelry work.

I don't say anything and go straight upstairs. I open drawers and see my old clothes and some of Craig's. I wait for Craig's voice as I pull his clothes out and toss them in the box I had packed to come here. Craig is ignoring me; he must be mad at me too. I pull tags off the new clothes and put them in drawers. I change into simple shorts and a tee.

"I'm going to the river, G-pa."

He doesn't say anything. Not even a grunt. He just keeps working.

"Do you want me to take the pole?"

He looks up from his work. "No, that's all right. We'll leave the trout for another time."

"G-pa . . . "

"We're fine, Chris." He waves his hand toward the door like he is shooing me away. "Go swim."

"Okay." I don't feel that we're fine. Maybe he needs some time alone. I close the door gently behind me.

I stop and watch the Falls. They are so tall and powerful. I walk to the foot of them and know that if I stood under them, they would crush me. The spray hits my body and cools me. The sound is deafening. I think about what it would be like to be swept over the cliff and thrown down this monster. I can see why they are the town's namesake. They are violent, strong, imposing and demanding of respect. They are beautiful. I climb the trail to the top of the cliff and watch the deceptively calm water slip over the edge to its destination.

I continue up river, along the shoreline, beyond G-pa's panning spot. I pass by the boulder and continue to walk until I'm hot and need a rest, so I sit beneath a tree, looking out over the river.

I look down at my shorts, I touch my freshly-cut hair, and I remember seeing my own face twice in the mirror. Is Craig gone from it for good now, or will his face unexpectedly pop up again? If he is gone from the mirror, does that mean he'll be gone from my head and dreams too? In some weird, cosmic law thing, does he have to go because I told him I was done? Will I finally stop seeing him dead? Is he even a ghost? Is this all just my imagination? Have I gone crazy? Will I ever be free?

Man, I have got to escape this torture. That single thought brings with it a barrage of guilt and shame because it means leaving Craig behind. It makes me a traitor to my brother. I think of the good times with him and let myself sink into the old familiar me, the 'Chris-n-Craig' me. It is heavy and warm. My brain rejects it with a jolt, telling me that Craig is dead. Like the flip of a switch, I'm half a person again. I feel cold, unshielded and empty. I know that I have to be 'Just Chris,' but I'm not sure how to do that or if it's even possible.

My eyes skim across the river's surface, and suddenly I need to swim across it. I need to conquer it. I know that if I do this, something inside of me, untouched by Craig, will be born. The wound left by losing my other half will somehow heal over. Maybe I will be scarred, but I will be functional again. I will be a separate person, a whole person, and not 'Chris-n-Craig' minus Craig. I jump up, run to the water and dive in.

The shock of the cold water blows all thoughts from my head except for the here and now. I surface and holler out. I get my bearings, target the opposite bank and swim. I am determined to make it. The only sounds I hear are the splashes as I stroke and the thumping of my heart pounding in my ears. My skin is numbing to the cold, and I feel a burn start deep in my muscles. I keep pumping out the strokes. It feels like this is taking forever! I see that the bank isn't getting any closer. I find my target and realize I'm being carried downstream!

I turn around and head back to the shore. As I get out of the stronger current toward the river's center, I make pretty good time. I climb out tired and disappointed but glad I caught my trajectory-to-tragedy before it was too late. The image of the falls flashes in my head. I need to be stronger, faster and smarter than the current. I need muscle and a plan.

Don't forget scuba gear and a prayer," Craig snips.

My heart startles and then drops in disappointment. Yet, I'm also glad to hear his voice. I feel my 'Chris-n-Craig' identity take over again but force myself to push it aside.

My arms are trembling from exhaustion, but to shut Craig up, I drop down and do pushups. My arms burn and shake with effort.

On my way home, once I get to pavement, I jog.

I'll build up my God-given tanks, thank you. But Craig's not around to hear.

When I get home, I run upstairs, grab my ball and go out to drill and shoot hoops. I'll work my body into the ground if I have to in order to cross that river! Nothing else matters. This is my only task in life now. I have to cross it, or some part of me will die, maybe the only part of me that's left.

Tonight, G-pa and I cooked steaks, baked potatoes and even a pie. Craig called me 'Mr. Stewart' as in Martha Stewart, but other than that, he kept quiet.

After dinner, my stomach is stuffed, my body is tired, but I still sit in front of the T.V. with G-pa. He's put a tape in his VCR. I grin.

"You know they make better machines for this now."

"This works fine."

The movie starts, and it's in black and white. I look at G-pa.

"They make these in color now too."

"Not the good ones they don't."

We watch *Phantom of the Opera'*. It was actually a good movie. Good enough to stay up for. I'd never seen a real black and white movie before. The lighting and shadows along with the filters they used made the whole thing work. I was drawn into the drama and suspense more than with color movies. It was pretty cool. G-pa says he has a lot of the old movies like that. His favorites are the horror movies. He says nothing compares to *Dracula, The Mummy, Frankenstein, Psycho,* or *The Birds*. He says the stories draw you in, and before you know it, you're living it.

G-pa rewinds the tape, and I go upstairs. I decide to sleep in my boxers. Maybe Craig won't visit tonight if I don't wear his pjs. I turn out the light, climb into bed and stare at the streetlight shining into my room.

Walking down our school halls, it's crowded, and people are bumping into me rudely. Craig is beside me. He has a scared look on his face that sends alarm through my entire body. The crowd grows thicker. We're getting packed in. We push and shove our way through bodies and begin to run—the only way you can run in dreams—slow and not getting anywhere fast. The hall stretches out in front of us for what could be a mile, it goes forever. The crowd is now chasing us and is right on our heels. I'm running as fast as I can, but moving so slow. Craig falls, so I reach down to grab him. He has somehow hurt his neck. He gets back up, and we run again. Suddenly, his neck explodes, spraying blood everywhere. I jolt awake.

Just a dream.

I lie back down and let my heart slow as I stare, again, at the streetlight shining in my room.

Five

I wake to G-pa's voice downstairs. I get up and listen at the head of the stairs. I can tell he's on the phone. I start down as he appears at the bottom stair.

"Here." He holds out the phone to me. "Your mom."

"Hi, Mom, I just woke up."

G-pa goes up to his room, and for a few minutes, I can have my old life back.

Mom asks how I'm doing, if I'm okay here, and then tells me she has a couple of houses to look at next week. She thinks they may be too close to my old neighborhood though. She wants me in a school where I don't know anybody.

I tell her that I'm fine, about the clothes G-pa got me and that I've been swimming a lot. She asks how I'm really doing with all of this. I tell her I'm angry at whoever killed Craig and that they destroyed my life too. I ask if the cops have found his killer. Her voice breaks as she tells me they don't have a single lead.

I feel bad for asking. She isn't handling this any better than I am. We give each other our love, end the call and Mom is gone again. Two thousand miles' worth of gone. She is driving down my city's streets, seeing familiar places and faces, while I am in a different world. I sigh and hang up the phone.

G-pa comes down and points at an empty cup sitting in front of the coffee pot. I make a cup and sit at the table. G-pa beats eggs for French toast.

"G-pa."

He looks over at me. I can tell he's afraid I'm going to talk about my phone call.

"You were a cop. Do you think they'll ever find Craig's killer?"

"Hard to say. I spoke with the lead detective on the case."

"You did?" I'm shocked that he got involved.

"He said they don't have a lick of evidence. There was no forced entry, nothing stolen, no drugs were found, and everyone they've interviewed said that you and your brother were well-liked and good kids. He really doesn't have anything to go on."

"So that's it? They aren't going to do anything?"

G-pa pulls his pan off the burner and sits down. "Chris, what would you do if you were them? Where would you look for answers?"

"I don't know; I'm not a cop."

"No, you're not, but you were the closest person to him, and if anyone could guess who did this, it's you." He looks straight into my eyes, searching to see if I have any ideas at all. I don't, and I feel helpless again.

G-pa puts a hand on my shoulder and says, "Son, they aren't closing the case. They are waiting."

"Waiting! For what?"

"They're waiting for another crime, where the bullets match the one in your brother's case. Maybe someone will know or see something then."

I know this will never happen because I have the gun.

G-pa must see my disappointment written on my face, because he says, "Chris, there are almost always links between cases. Someone who kills will do other crimes. We just have to be patient."

I think of the killer's next victim. Who will it be? One of my friends, my mom, or me?

"G-pa, what if they never find him?"

"Then I am confident that he will be caught for something else and end up in prison anyway."

I sit back in my chair and rub my face in frustration. It doesn't feel like justice to me, but it's better than nothing. There is some comfort in G-pa's words.

"Get some clothes on. Breakfast will be ready in a minute."

I wash my face and brush my teeth while avoiding the mirror. It's become a habit, so I make myself look. It's me. I hear a loud crash and jump. Then, I realize that G-pa has just thrown the pan into the sink. He's angry and frustrated too. It's a weird comfort to me.

I'm poking at my breakfast, wondering if I can even swallow the bite in my mouth. G-pa is watching my every move without actually laying an eye on me. I break the silence. "Why did you become a cop?"

He squints at me, trying to see if his practiced, pat answer will work. It won't. "I wasn't a 'cop.' I was a police officer."

"Oh, sorry."

"I was a kid heading for trouble. I stole a car."

My head pops up in full attention. "You? You stole a car?"

"I was your age, and it was the neighbor's car. The guy was a police officer, of all things."

I chuckle.

"He told my pop he didn't want to turn me in, and after Pop gave me a lickin', I remember to this day, he gave me two choices: I could either go confess to the 'Po-lice'," he says it slowly so I get it right next time, "or, sign up for the military. I chose the service, and turned eighteen with my rear planted in Korea."

"You were in the Korean war? Wasn't that back in the '50s?"

He nods. "I got persuaded to be a M.P. It wasn't a bad job. Mostly, I just got drunk American GI's back to base, so I stayed for twenty years. I was in my late thirties and not ready for the retirement rocker, so I joined the police force. I guess it was in my blood by then."

"How old are you, G-pa?"

"Old enough to lose track and for it not to matter."

I bark out a laugh.

He squints at me, which is an 'almost' grin for him. "Somewhere in the mid to far end of my eighties," he answers.

"Well, you don't show your age on the court, that's for sure."

"I can hold my own. I don't have a foot in the grave yet."

I eat my breakfast and am surprised it goes down so easy now.

"I have to go to the Food Mart today. You can ride along."

It's not a question. I swallow hard. "When?"

"Now."

The old beater truck bounces and squeaks into the parking lot and rocks to a stop just before crashing through the store's plate glass window. Big red letters scream in my eyes. Today's specials are only six inches from kissing G-pa's bumper. He is out of the truck and at the door before my brain even registers that we didn't actually hit the window. I get out and squeeze between the truck and window, making my way into Food Mart.

G-pa already has a cart and is squeaking the wheels toward an aisle. The man has energy like he's outrunning the grave! I shake my head and jog to catch up to him.

He tosses items in the cart as he goes. No comparison shopping here. He snatches a can of cooked apples and gives it a disgusted look.

"Using these in Vera's pie would be a dirty trick."

"You're baking a pie? For Vera?"

He doesn't answer but pushes the canned apples back on the shelf. He makes fast work of hitting every aisle, and before I know it, we're in the check-out lane.

"It would have taken Mom an hour to fill a cart like this. I'm impressed."

"I know what I like," he grunts

The cashier is a tall, slender woman with stiff, blonde hair piled high. She has claw-like nails and is snapping her gum vigorously as we set out items on the counter.

"Mornin', Reggie," she says, drawing out G-pa's name. "And how we doin' today?"

She starts ringing up the items before G-pa answers with a nod.

"So, who is this handsome fella you got with ya today?"

My face heats up. *Did she just—? —Is she—? What the—?*

"Oooh, a blonde!" Craig says and laughs so hard he chokes.

"My grandson. He's married."

"Darn it! Guess my niece will have to keep lookin', huh?"

"Dibs on the niece!" Craig blurts out.

Claw-woman cackles out a laugh that proves she's a demon-witch. I look at G-pa; his face twitches, and I bark out a laugh that I cover up with a cough.

"Grab those," G-pa snarls at me as he points to the cart full of bags. He pays and still beats me to the door!

"Take the cart back in."

"Why do I have to?"

He gives me a look, and I obey. The cashier is leaning against the counter with arms crossed, just waiting for me to come back through the door. She gives a wave of her claws, and I shove the cart into place. As I go out the door, I feel the hair on the back of my neck stand up. I rub my neck in protection against her gaze. I slam the truck door and half yell, "GO!"

G-pa doesn't disappoint me.

"That woman is the mother of our pizza boy."

I shake my head trying to clear the images stuck there. These are the townspeople he keeps subjecting me to? "Is this the only grocery in town?" I ask, ticked off at him.

"There's one other. It's worse."

"Good God," I sigh.

I'm not happy about G-pa dictating the events of my day. I had plans of my own to have another go at the river. Reluctantly, I help him peel and slice apples for pie. While I learn how to make pie dough and noodles from scratch, I also learn a little about Grandma.

G-pa learned how to cook by watching her. He still uses her cookbook with butter-stained pages and writing in the margins. G-pa squints at her scrawled writing.

"A pinch of salt. A pinch," he says as if he's teasing her.

"When my Lily died, it took me a long time to act normal. Well, nothing's been normal since, but to get as normal as it goes, I guess."

I go quiet. I know what he means.

"So, what did you do when your heart sank because your mind just told you for the hundredth time that she was dead?"

G-pa looks at me, then back down at his rolled dough.

"You mean after I recovered from losing my mind, or during?"

Suddenly, I know, that he knows exactly where I am at and what I've been going through.

"During."

G-pa nods. "At first, I'd see her; just a glimpse here and there. Then I'd see her full-on, standing right here at this counter. Sometimes I'd see her from the corner of my eye, sitting in the truck while I was driving. She'd disappear when I'd remember that she was gone. Knocks the wind right out of ya, that does. Every time, every single time, ya just have to force the breath back in. I guess it was just my brain's way of getting me used to the idea that she was gone, a little at a time. I'm pretty sure that if I'd have felt the brunt of all that shock at once, or had the pain hit in one blow, I'd have gone insane and never found my way out the other side of it. Maybe, my heart would have just stopped beating from lack of breath. I've heard of that; perfectly healthy people dying from grief. I think they overdose on shock and pain."

G-pa goes quiet, but his hands stay busy cutting out lasagna noodles. He just shared the most personal and vulnerable moments of his life with me, a kid. I'm probably the only person he has ever told this to. I watch this old, tough, hard-cast man roll out another ball of dough, and I know I have to share some of my own secret with him to keep us balanced.

"I hear Craig sometimes."

I watch his face and hold my breath, wondering if he will think I'm crazy, and if so, what he plans to do about that. He only nods, like he knows this happens to people. I'm so grateful for that small nod of his head, that tears well up in my eyes.

G-pa is watching, without looking at me again. He busies himself rolling up long strips of noodles into wax paper and putting them in the fridge. He gives my tears time to stop.

"What do you two talk about?"

"We don't really have conversations; he just smarts off like we used to. I usually ignore him or tell him to shut up."

I glance at G-pa, to see if this is dangerous territory. G-pa has a soft smile on his face.

"Well, I think that sounds perfectly normal given the circumstance."

I let out a sigh of relief. I finally have someone who can tell me I'm not crazy. I venture further.

"I see him, too. He just pops in front of my eyes when I least expect it. Only . . . well, it's always him dead. I see the blood and his eyes and stuff. It hasn't happened for a few days now."

G-pa squints his eyes at me. "Why do you think it stopped?"

"I don't know. He was in the mirror too. I mean, I never saw me anymore, so I stopped looking. Then in the store, when I tried on the new clothes, it was my face. Craig was gone, and he hasn't shown back up in the mirror since. I still hear him sometimes, but not as often. I don't know if he will come again. It's only been a couple of days."

"It might be the end of it or it might not. I guess this is just your own process to deal with this tragedy. He was your twin, Chris. The mirror seems a logical way to say goodbye."

"I've been scared to tell anyone. I didn't know if he was haunting me or if I was going crazy."

"Chris." He pulls me to him and hugs me, then pats my back. Tears burn my eyes again from someone, anyone, understanding me. His coarse voice whispers, "We all go crazy, and we're all haunted sometimes. It's part of life." He releases me but avoids my eyes. He busies himself with the food again.

"Do you know that some of us hang on to the haunting, for fear of letting our loved one go?"

I shake my head, no. "I think it would be guilt that would make me keep Craig around. I'd feel like I was cutting him off."

"That sewing room upstairs, it smelled like my Lily for a long time. I used to go in there just for her scent. She didn't use perfume, she smelled like actual flowers." He sighs. "Real flowers. She said perfume had a fake chemical smell, musty or sour. She thought it was obnoxious or pungent. So she used flower oil extracts." A smile spreads across his face. "She said, 'A lady should smell sweet and tender so that when she leaves a room, she leaves an impression, not an odor.' That sewing room held her sweetness for months, maybe even a year. Maybe Lily kept her scent alive that long for me, so I wasn't alone. Like how Craig stayed in the mirror for you, helping in the only way he could."

I move to the table and sit down. G-pa brings two cups of coffee. I fix mine up so I can drink it.

"I'd like you to meet someone."

I look at G-pa, and my heart starts racing. "I don't need to see a shrink."

G-pa chuckles. "No, I mean Vera. I want you to go to the senior center with me."

"Oh," I say, relieved.

"I need to drop off some jewelry and take her that pie."

"G-pa? Are you sweet on Vera?" I grin.

He plays mad and stands up. In his gruff manner, he begins to clean up the mess in the kitchen.

"Go make yourself presentable. Oh, and try to use grown-up words. People judge you by how you dress and how well you speak. So, don't embarrass me."

I give him a laugh and a salute, and then run upstairs to make myself 'presentable.'

Six

I've been swimming this river nearly every day for a month now, and I still can't reach the center without being carried downstream. Its's so frustrating! I work out every day; even my arms and legs are showing my effort, but it's not working fast enough. I only have five more weeks until I go back to the city and to Mom.

I can't ignore this desperation that burns in my chest. I know that if I make it across this monster, then everything 'Craig' will stop. I live in this state of anxiety wondering when his voice will scatter my thoughts if I can sleep the night through without nightmares, and I hate his 'pop-up dead scenes.' I'm sick of this, both literally and figuratively. The 'Craig' moments are less often now than at first, but I'm a nervous wreck waiting for his next surprise visit. And so, I will continue to fight this river.

Today I am trying something new. Instead of swimming directly across or at an angle, I'm swimming upstream against the current. It takes me a while to find the exact spot where I match the river's strength, but I'm doing it. My arms burn, but I haven't drifted from my place. I'm pumping it out hard.

My mind drifts to last night's dream. I block it out at first, then think maybe if I let it play out while my body aches, it will stop the ache in my heart. Maybe I can burn the dreams out of my life.

I see the dream clearly. Last night was so real. I saw the veins of the leaves, the porous holes in rocks, and dust in the beams of light shining through the clouds. Craig stands on a mountain top. At first, he is a dark silhouette against a pale blue sky, but he becomes clearer. I can see his skin tone, then the shine in his eyes. I recognize the shirt he's wearing; I have a teal one just like it. He is saying something, but I can't hear him. I try to read his lips, but I can't make it out. I'm yelling without sound. 'What? I can't hear you!' Then like dreams do, I realize that I'm on a different mountain, and he's actually far away. That's why I can't hear him.

I know there is a deep valley between us. I don't see it; I just sense it. These are huge mountains we stand on. I yell across what is now a dark gap that divides us. 'What Craig? What?' Craig is flailing his arms and screaming loud, but I hear nothing. He is agitated and pointing. Is this a warning? I suddenly fear the murderer is behind me. I turn to look, but there is no one. I'm confused and turn to look back at Craig. I slip. I'm falling; falling for a long time. I know I am about to die. I wake before I hit the darkness's floor.

The ache in my body brings me back to the present. I'm breathing in gasps—oh, I'm crying. I swim toward the shore close enough to touch ground. I'm sobbing like I haven't since I was a child. I sit in water waist high, lay my forehead on my arms and watch my tears make small rings as the river carries them away. Ashes to ashes . . . falls made of tears.

Every day now, I jog to the river, swim, do three sets of pushups and a hundred sit-ups, then I run home, where I shoot hoops and practice shots I've never tried before. I'm building up my core, arms, legs and lungs. I'm pleased with how long my workouts last now. I go full-on for four hours, as hard as I can. Some days I run twice and do extra core work.

I barely start my ball workout, when I feel eyes on me. I turn and see a kid standing in the driveway. I recognize him. He lives like three houses down.

"Hey. How's it goin'?" I ask.

The kid nods. "Name's Ian. Want to join me on the asphalt?"

My heart beats hard. My head yells, *Too many people! Too many questions! Don't start up with anyone around here. Five weeks and I'm outta here!*

Ian, though, looks like he has secrets of his own. Plus, why is he standing in a stranger's yard, without his friends? The panic subsides some, to a caution level. It feels like . . . this could be safe.

"Chris," I tell him, and fist bump him. "I'm kinda lying low here. I don't want to get in a game."

"Naw, just us. At the park. Nobody goes there. They go to the school for hoops."

I shrug my shoulder, "All right, I guess. It's better than trying to dribble on this stuff." I kick at the grass.

Ian laughs. "Well, yeah."

"Let me go tell my G-pa." I jog into the house, grab two power bars and two sodas. "G-pa, the kid down the street asked me to go shoot hoops at the park. I guess I'll go."

G-pa looks up from his jewelry work. "Which kid?"

"Um . . . Ian. He lives three houses down."

"He's not a bad kid. Kind of a loner though."

"Perfect. I'm not looking for a crowd." I smile.

G-pa gives me a grunt. "You're about four hours from burgers frying for dinner. If you show up after that, you're on your own."

"I'll be here. Thanks, G-pa."

I jet out the door and hand Ian a power bar and soda. He has the ball and is dribbling on the street. "So old man Tanner is your grandpa?'

I study Ian's face to see what public opinion is of G-pa. "What? You know him?" I come off a little defensive.

"Not really, seen him around in that old truck."

We both chuckle.

"Yep," I say with a sigh and a grin.

It turns out that Ian is pretty good on the court. I'm better, though. I show off using some of my fancy moves, nice fake-outs and make some shots that surprise even me.

Ian is on the team at Deer Falls High. He said they ranked fifth in their division of twelve teams. Not great. The team has mandatory practice, and once in a while, they play a game at the school during off-season, but Ian is probably the most serious about it. I think of my old team last year. We played all the time, nearly every day. We made regionals.

I tell Ian I'm here for the summer, that I stay busy, but if he wants to grab me to practice some time, I'm cool with that.

A few days later, I come home from my swim, and G-pa says that Ian had stopped by. Panic hits me.

"Did you tell him where I was?" Crossing the river is my own private deal. I don't want anyone to invade that part of my life.

"Nope. You go there every day. If you want him to find you, you'll tell him about it."

I smile. How does G-pa just know the right things to do and say all the time?

"Thanks."

He grunts out a "Hmm."

Tonight, G-pa has made a mound of popcorn.

"Movie night." He barks in his tone of accusation.

"Yeah? What are we watching?"

"Well, since I've seen them, you pick one out and put it in the machine. Just make sure it doesn't have any color in it."

I laugh. "Do you own any color movies?'

"Nope."

"Okay. I think I saw *Frankenstein* in there. That would be good with popcorn."

The movie was good. The shots of the full moon, the fog, and the Jacob's ladder snapping electricity must have been high tech stuff when the movie was filmed. The characters' makeup was dramatic and fantastic. I really got into it. The dark corners of the lab had mysteries and secrets that the imagination couldn't conceive, yet you knew were lurking in those shadows. I cheered for the doctor's success as the horror of his project appalled me. It was ALIVE!

When the movie ended, I was excited over the thing. "That was great stuff, G-pa!"

"Yep. They don't make 'em like that anymore, that's for sure."

"You know, I've seen remakes of *Frankenstein*, done in color, with modern actors. I could take it or leave it, but this black and white demands your attention."

"You aren't gonna have nightmares, are you?" G-pa teases.

Suddenly my forgotten world of Craig and the dreams slam back on me.

G-pa's face tells me that he has seen my shift.

"Naw," I say, trying to smile. "I'm heading up to bed. 'Night."

He studies my face but doesn't say anything. I can't get away fast enough. I go upstairs, glancing at the black and white photos of all the dead people hanging on the wall as I go.

G-pa calls out. He has an apologetic tone, "Maybe next time we'll watch Marilyn Monroe. You just might fall in love."

"Sounds good," I say, as I round the corner of the staircase and start down the hall.

Craig is smiling. He has that look on his face that says he is proud of himself like he just did something over-the-top. He is in his bedroom. There's a blue-striped shirt turned inside out, crumpled on the floor. His comforter is pulled up over the pillows, in his signature half-job of bed making.

I see the gun. It's floating in the air as if it's lying on its side. Fingers appear, wrapped around it. I try to see who is holding the gun. I know what is about to happen, I can feel my heart pound. Craig's lips move, but there is no sound.

I ask him, "Who, Craig! Who's holding the gun?" I know that if he tells me before he is shot, then I'll know who murdered him. My voice doesn't fill the room. Our words don't make a sound. I strain hard, staring, trying to look up the hand, up the arm, to see a face, but the hand fills in slowly. I see the knuckles appear, the wrist, a wrist band. It is my hand! I see my fingers tighten. My pinkie finger is on the trigger.

I hear the shot ring out in a huge explosion. Craig's eyes are wide in shock. Blood sprays, and I hear it splatter the wall beside him. Craig sits on the end of the bed. I hear the squeak of bed springs under his weight. Blood pumps on the wall in a long streak. Craig's eyes go from shock to surprise, then to anger. They ask me, 'How could you be so stupid?' The gun falls to the floor with a solid clunk. Craig slowly slumps back onto the bed, his eyes looking at me but not comprehending, not seeing anything, ever again. I hear the tic, tic, tic of his blood pooling in the carpet.

I wake to my own screams.

My door bursts open and G-pa is scanning the room with raised gun. Light from the hall shows him we are alone, and he lowers his gun. He turns on the light and hurries to my side.

I grab him and hold tight. I hold on for dear life. I'm crying and yelling, "I did it! I killed Craig! It was me! Oh God! I killed my own brother!"

Guilt and pain hurl through my body. It feels like a knife in my gut, my chest and head. I can't sit still; I rock and churn, I'm shaking violently. G-pa is strong and pins me down, he wraps himself around me. I hear sounds coming from deep inside myself that sound like an animal. This guttural moan-wail won't stop. I manage, "Craig! I'm so sorry!"

"Chris!" G-pa yells in my ear. "Chris! You didn't do this! He lowers his voice. "It was a dream, son. You're okay." He shakes me, and I see his face is nose-to-nose with mine.

"It was a dream. It's okay."

I look at him, hoping he is right. He releases me. I realize then that he's not right. I remember now. I picked up the gun after it went off and left the house. I walked in a daze, and when I returned home, I went to Craig's room like I always did if he wasn't with me. That's when I called Mom.

"You found him, Chris. Craig was dead when you came home. Remember?"

I stare at G-pa, wanting to believe him, wishing I could. I remember the shooting now, not in dream form, not by Craig's voice in my head, but in real-life memory.

I shake my head, tears fall fast, but all sound is locked inside of me now. I move off the bed. G-pa sits up and watches me. I reach under the mattress and pull out the gun.

G-pa's eyes grow big, then his face drops in disappointment, maybe sadness, or maybe in the pain of betrayal.

I lay the weapon on the bed. "I remember now. It just went off."

I am still on my knees beside the bed. I bury my face in the new-smelling comforter and cry. My body trembles. I feel G-pa's hand on my back, quaking from his own sobs.

G-pa and I sit on the couch. I curl up like a small child hiding in my comforter. I tell him my story, in detail. How Craig didn't go to the lanes with me that day. How I had gone without him because I wanted to see if a girl that I liked was there. She wasn't, so I came back home. I told how I had surprised Craig by barging into his room, where he stood holding a gun. I got excited over the gun and grabbed it to check it out. It was so cool. Then it just went off. In a split-second, Craig was dead, and my life was changed forever.

"I remember picking up the gun from the floor and thinking, 'This is the last thing Craig touched.' I remember his touch still warmed its metal. I held it to my chest, absorbing that touch, the warmth of his life still present. I put it in my special box in my room. Then I walked, like a zombie or something I guess. I must have ended up back at the lanes. When I came home and found Craig, I was shocked. Somehow, I had forgotten that he was dead!

"Until tonight, I thought I found him, saw the gun, and picked it up, then called Mom. That's not what happened, though. I don't understand how I could just forget that I killed my brother! How? How does that happen?" I wipe tears from my face, while G-pa watches me.

"Shock, Chris; you were in shock." G-pa lets out a long breath. "So where did the gun come from? Why did he have it?"

"I don't know, he never answered me. I killed him before he could."

G-pa reaches over and puts his hands on my shoulders. "Chris, this was an accident. That's all; a horrible accident."

I look at him, "Mom! Oh God! How can I tell her that I'm the one who shot Craig? I can't face her! She'll hate me! I can't ever go back to her." A new wave of sobs burst from me.

"No, she won't." G-pa shakes my shoulders. His eyes desperately search mine; his whole being bores into my core. "She won't hate you because you're not telling her."

"I have to!"

"No. We're not telling your mom or the police."

"What? Oh God! I'll go to prison!"

I notice the trembling, that low vibration is back that plagued me the first few days after Craig's death. I watch my hands shake. Strange, I hadn't noticed when it stopped before.

"We're not telling anyone, son. Going to the police is the lawful thing to do, but not necessarily the best or right thing to do, in this circumstance."

"But they'll keep looking for the killer! No. Mom, she needs to know what happened!"

"No, they won't keep looking. They don't have a case until this gun shows up. Listen to me, Chris, this was an accident. By telling, it will only make things worse for everybody. Your mom would have to live with the pain of knowing what happened. She'll also watch her only son go through an investigation that could take months, watch you be locked up and possibly tried and found guilty. She is better off not knowing by whom or why Craig was killed than to lose both sons."

"What if the police find out?"

"They won't. If they suspected you, they would have charged you, or at least not let you leave the city. Remember, you have a strong alibi. All the kids at the bowling lanes say you were there all afternoon. There was no evidence at the house. Believe me, when they talked with you, Chris, they were seeing if you were a suspect. They ruled you out."

We both go quiet for a bit, just thinking over all this mess.

"Chris, the police have nothing on this case without the gun. I'll get rid of it. You can never, ever, tell anyone what happened. Can you live with that?"

I consider all that G-pa has said, especially about Mom losing both sons. To live with this secret is something I can't carry. Tears fill my eyes.

"I can't do this, G-pa. I love that you want to protect me, I honestly do, but I have to tell them."

G-pa sits back on the couch and rubs his face.

"I already hear Craig's voice, there's the mirror thing, and the nightmares. I just can't, G-pa. I might go nuts. I mean honest-to-God-crazy."

I stare at him, pleading, hoping he understands. I'm praying he knows that I understand what he is sacrificing for me. I can't put him in this position.

He sighs. "Listen to me. You feel responsible for Craig's death—"

"I am responsible!"

"Not entirely. Craig had a loaded gun, Chris!" G-pa punches the couch. "Stupid damned kids!" He closes his eyes and rubs the back of his neck, as he blows out a frustrated long breath.

"Look, this was not a malicious or criminal act. Don't you dare confuse your remorse with guilt! The police will piece together a story as best they can from the evidence, and I'm telling you that it can, and probably will, all go very wrong for you. It's a huge gamble to tell them. The good that will come from it is setting right here in front of you now; someone who believes you and knows you are sorry. I forgive you! This is as clean as it gets, Chris. The pain and sorrow you feel in your heart right now won't go away because you throw yourself to public scrutiny, looking for forgiveness. You have me for that. I believe you, and I forgive you, and I hurt with you!"

He sits quietly for a minute, then softly adds, "Gambling with prison, or breaking your mom's heart again will not take away this tragedy. It will not bring Craig back."

I sit motionless, taking in all that G-pa has said. I hadn't fully realized all of my reasons for wanting to turn myself in. Now that he has mentioned my need to have people believe me, forgive me, and to have it all go away, and to just have Craig back, I know he has nailed it. If he is spot on with my feelings, then maybe he is right when he says the 'best' and 'right' things to do are to just stay silent about shooting Craig.

"You don't see Craig in the mirror anymore, do you?"

"No. Not since the day I got the clothes."

"When was the last time you heard his voice?"

I consider this, "It was when we were at the Food Mart."

"That's been what, five weeks ago?"

I realize what's happening here.

"Okay, so the voice is probably gone for good too. Tell me about the dreams. All of them."

I tell him about the drowning dream, the mob chasing us in school, the mountain where I fell, and then about tonight's dream with the gun.

"Chris, don't you see? These dreams were just a progression of events so your memory would come back. You blocked out the shooting, but your subconscious knew. These dreams show your fears and anger at who did this. You didn't know who killed your brother, so it was a mob. Everybody was out to get you both. Remember? Even your mom feared you were a target. The drowning was just you trying to save him, but you couldn't. The mountain was you feeling the separation from him, your acceptance of that. The last dream only means that you are finally strong enough to know the truth now. I think you are grieving and healing. I don't think you are going nuts. If anything, you are coming out the other side of grief's insanity."

I study this old man's rough and weathered face. I study his eyes. Saying nothing, I stand up and go upstairs. I blow my nose and splash water on my face. I look in the mirror. I see me. I've heard every word G-pa has said. I know he is right about all of it. If I turn myself in, the police will create a story around the evidence. However, right now, I can't even hold my own gaze in this mirror. Deep inside of me, there is a hard stone sitting in my chest, and it blocks my breathing. These things will never change if I don't tell the police.

I go downstairs and sit beside G-pa on the couch. He hasn't moved.

"G-pa?"

"Yes, Chris."

"I have to."

Tears fill his eyes, and his shoulders drop. He nods his head and looks at the floor. "Then let me talk to them. It's morning there by now; that detective I spoke to before will be in."

I nod my head yes, and feel more fear rise from my stomach than I've ever felt before. This is true terror. This is not a movie that I can later laugh at myself about.

G-pa picks up the phone and dials a number he had written down and tucked in his wallet. My heart races. It's not too late! Tell him to hang up! I fight myself to let him continue. G-pa and I stare at each other, each of us waiting for the other to say *stop* or to reveal that this is all a dream that we wake up from. I can hear the ringing from the other end of the princess phone.

"Homicide, please." G-pa continues to lock eyes with me, waiting for any sign to disconnect the call and this spiral I've entered.

"Detective Morris, please." I see G-pa's fingers tremble around the phone.

I turn and walk up the stairs, leaving him to the task that I'm not man enough to do myself. I soak in a long, hot, skin-burning bath. When I've cried and washed my cowardice away, I get out and return downstairs. G-pa is sitting at the dining table with his hands folded on top of it. He looks up when I cross the distance between us.

"They don't believe you, Chris."

"What?"

"They think that because of all the witnesses at the bowling alley, and no history of trouble in your past, that you are just having a hard time with this. Detective Morris told me to get you into counseling."

"Counseling?! But—"

G-pa holds up his hand to stop me. "Chris, please. Let this thing be. You turned yourself in; let it go now."

"But what about the gun? I have it!"

"He wouldn't let me tell him. I started to, but he cut me off. He knew what I was going to say, Chris. Those calls are recorded, and he stopped me. He said that calling in was a brave and courageous thing to do, that in his opinion, most adult men wouldn't be so brave. He said that you were a good kid and that society needs you to be the man he is confident you will become."

"Chris, he knows if you did this, it was an accident. He also knows that if he investigates this, then your record, reputation and family will never be the same."

"But—"

"Christopher! Let this rest!" G-pa shouts and slams his hand on the table in anger.

I suddenly realize that I've been given a pardon by the police. I gambled, and I won. I have done all I can. "Okay. As long as I have you to, you know, talk with."

"Anytime, son. I'll be here."

I grab him, hug him tight, and cry like a child from relief. I pull myself together finally, and ask, "What about the gun?"

"You let me handle that. I know places in these mountains around here where it will never be found." He looks at me seriously. "I promise you, it will be dismantled and distributed in pieces over this entire mountain range, in places where a vehicle can't go. You put it out of your mind. It will never be found in a hundred years."

"I want to go with you."

G-pa stares at me, thinking, then nods.

I feel calmer but full of sadness by what I did to Craig. I lie down on the couch, pull the comforter up to my chin and hope this trembling stops soon.

G-pa walks over and peeks over the back of the couch at me. He pats my trembling leg and says, "I'm ready for a hot meal."

I hear him clanking things around in the kitchen, then I smell lasagna being re-heated. In only minutes, I wake up to a heaped plate full of steaming, hot food, served by a strained and weathered face. I see more love and kindness in that face than I've ever seen in it before. My trembling has stopped. I am safe.

Seven

*I*t's an irritating sound that brings me back to the world. I sit up and rub my face. G-pa isn't around. There's that noise again. What is that? I push off my comforter and get up from the couch.

My sleep-befuddled mind finally figures out it's a drill. I look out the kitchen window and see the shed door is open. The noise grinds again. I go investigate.

G-pa is wearing a pair of safety goggles that have flapping rubber ties hanging from the sides. He looks like a bubble-eyed fish with antennae. I raise my eyebrows and suppress a laugh.

"What?" he asks.

I shake my head. He is all business. He has the gun broken down and is drilling out the barrel. My chest explodes as reality and memory flood back to me.

"What are you doing?"

"Security measures. Drilling out the barrel so if a bullet is ever run through it again, which won't happen, then the marking on the bullet won't match up with . . . old bullets."

"Clever." It's all I can choke out of my tight throat.

He nods and lays down the drill. He plugs in a grinder and starts on the side of the barrel. He's taking off the finish, the outer layer of oil and polished metal.

When he stops to reposition the gun, I ask, "Isn't that overkill?"

"When it was fired, the metal heated up, and it can burn your prints into the top layer of oily residue. Forensics in large cities can pull those prints now."

I'm shocked. I'd never heard this before.

"Also, with the finish sanded off to bare metal, the gun will deteriorate sooner. It'll be years before it's gone, but I'm giving it a head start."

G-pa starts grinding out stamped–in serial numbers. The noise is too much, too soon for my short nap on the couch. I pat him on the back in thanks and head back to the house. I count my blessings that he used to be a cop. "A Po-lice officer," I correct myself.

My tense muscles start to relax under the heat of the shower. I remember Craig's laughter, his cutting-up and pranks. My heart drops. I miss him so much. I remember the look in his eyes from my ultimate screw-up. I place my hands on the wall in front of me, and my back catches the water's flow, as my tears fall. "Forgive me, Craig. Please?"

I assume that G-pa and I are going on a hike today. I'm not wrong. G-pa isn't wasting any time dumping any evidence against me. He's fighting hard for me.

We bounce around in G-pa's beater truck for about an hour, leaving Deer Falls behind us. Neither of us talks as we turn down side roads, then onto old dirt roads, that wind their way up one of the mountains.

G-pa slams on the brakes and grinds the gears into reverse. The road dust we have stirred up floats in through our open windows. He backs up to an overgrown road and kicks the old truck into granny gear. We make our way up a steep path that wouldn't be called a road even in its prime. Tree limbs batter the truck as we pass through.

"What is this, an old wagon trail? Jeez!"

G-pa grunts.

When we come to a rusty gate blocking the path, he cuts the engine off and climbs out. He jumps the gate like a ten-year-old on an adventure. I can barely make out the letters of warning on a rusted, lop-sided sign. I'm pretty sure, though, it reads 'No Trespassing.'

I follow him over, where the road has become a one-lane foot path. The birds call out a warning of human intruders.

"How far are we going?"

"Just over the top here to a small pond on the other side."

"How do you know about this place?"

"Old friend of mine; he died about ten years back. His family owns it now. They don't do anything with it."

We get to the top, and G-pa stops. There's enough of a clearing to see the surrounding mountains. G-pa takes in the view that he probably hasn't laid eyes on in a decade. He points out a direction and mumbles, "Over there."

We walk downhill through trees until I see a small stagnant pond, a depression filled with water, really.

G-pa chuckles.

"What?"

"This was the attempt of two greenhorns trying to dig a well. It took an old-timer of these parts, my friend's dad, to ask us why we were digging when there was a natural spring just east of here."

I smile, but I know that me, a city kid wouldn't have known any better either.

G-pa begins digging with his hands, and we lift out a good-sized rock. He pulls two sandwich bags from his pocket and uses them like mittens. He pulls the ground-down barrel from a trash bag. He pushes the nose of it deep into the hole until it's buried in the mud. He rolls the rock back in place and hands me one of the bags. "Don't leave prints, hand or foot, anywhere.

We pack mud around the base of the rock that is half submerged in stagnant water and decaying leaves. When we finish, I can't tell that anyone was ever here.

"In time, the water will help break down the metal." His eyes show a certainty that gives me relief I hadn't expected.

My throat tightens. He is smart and making sure this never comes back to haunt me. I've never felt so protected in my life. I really wish Craig could have known G-pa. Mom has always been vague about her relationship with him. She just said they didn't get along very well, or that he lived too far away. It was never really an issue, we never really thought about him. He was just some distant relative that wasn't part of our lives. My eyes burn. I turn away from his face and look out over the view of mountains in the distance.

G-pa pats my shoulder and picks up the bags he brought, including the trash bag that still holds the gun's grip, slider and clip. We walk in silence back to the truck. What is there for either of us to say?

G-pa rips down the mountainside like a maniac, faster than the old springs on the truck can possibly bear. I give him my best 'REALLY?' look, as I hold on tight to the dashboard and broken arm rest. We get to the main highway, and he drives civilly again. I relax my grip and sit back in the seat.

"Where to now?" I ask.

He points to a mountain that's about twenty miles ahead. We ride in silence for a while. I consider how this all feels more like a real funeral for Craig than when his body was laid to rest. I feel like I have turned a corner, like something inside of me, inside of this pain, has shifted.

"G-pa, do you think Craig will leave me alone now?"

He squints at me but doesn't say anything.

"I mean, except for the recent past, I see him all the time. I see him dead way too much. His eyes look at me, but he doesn't say anything. He just . . . " I search for the words, ". . . looks right through my soul." I shiver, understanding the depth of truth I just spoke.

"That's a lot for a person to carry around by themselves, Chris."

"Sometimes, my chest is so heavy that I can't breathe right."

I look out the side window at the view speeding by. We turn off onto an access road that will soon wind us up this new mountain of his. I sigh.

"Well, you wouldn't be the first to make yourself sick over grief. People tend to remember only the good parts of a loved one when they're gone. It's a distorted memory of who that person really was. You have to learn to live without Craig, so maybe if you remember his human side and don't turn him into a saint in your mind, it will be easier. Craig, as much as you loved him, and still do, wasn't perfect. Nobody is."

I look at G-pa. He's right. That's exactly what I've been doing. For some reason, it's what I thought I was supposed to do, to honor Craig. I think of the little irritating ways he had about him. How he always had to win at everything. How he was sloppy in the house, and it drove Mom crazy, but he'd shrug it off. I think of how he had become distant to me, going his own way and secreting his activities from me. To me, it was a form of betrayal.

"He stole my girl one time."

G-pa looks at me. "Stole her? Really? Or was it that twin's game where you do swappies?"

I catch the smile in his eyes, but I still don't think it's funny.

"Borrowed, I guess, but he talked me into it. She went for him afterwards. He was supposed to give her back. So that means he stole her. It was a trust thing that he betrayed."

"Hmm. Better that he got stuck with that girl than you, I 'spose."

"It ended up being a short romance. Served him right."

"More to the point, we may be getting somewhere now. I've seen people forget another's faults and go so far off track by it that they try to live out the loved one's life. They live their own life but pull double duty, finishing up tasks of the deceased. I've seen people marry the spouse that's left behind, trying to fulfill what they felt was unfinished business. So, what happens when the grief finally subsides? They're in a trap, Chris. Sometimes the trap is so deep, they no longer live their own life. By the time they realize what has happened, they can't get back."

"Go ahead and love Craig, miss him and remember the times you shared, the good and bad, but keep in mind that your life didn't end when his did. And don't you ever feel guilty for living."

I watch G-pa's face as he drives. His is a face of wisdom. The lines, creases and age spots all show a face that has weathered throughout a long life and gives him earned character. His is a face that knows the exact place my soul is stuck. He has been here himself.

"You know, Chris, when it gets too rough, that's the time to pull out those funny memories you have. The ones that make you laugh out loud. Release some of those happy brain chemicals they talk about these days. It doesn't all have to be pain and reverence."

G-pa goes quiet for a minute. He gets serious again. "Maybe you shouldn't focus on what Craig can't do now." He sighs. "Chris," he looks in my eyes and studies me, then looks at the road again. "Craig is in a new place, doing new things. He has moved on, and you can't change that, only how you view his death. It was his time to go, whether you had a hand in it or not, I believe it would have happened anyway."

He looks at me again. I stay silent, stunned by what he is saying.

"He will always live right here," he pats my heart, "and right here," he taps my head. "So, you see? He's really not so very far away."

"Do you really believe that? That he would have died anyway?"

"I believe that God is in control of birth and death. I believe that every life has a purpose, if not many purposes, and we all have freewill to arrive at our purpose in our own time."

"So, Craig reached his purpose in life early?"

"I would have to say so."

"What was it, his purpose?"

"Only God knows that, and probably Craig, too, by now."

Tears burn my eyes again. "I just miss him so much. It's not fair."

The truck comes to a stop, and I finally notice that we've been on another dirt road. G-pa kills the engine. G-pa gives me a nod of his head and speaks to the steering wheel. "Well, son, maybe he'll leave you alone when you're ready to ask him to."

I bark out a laugh through silent tears. "That's a lot to ask of me and a lot for me to ask of Craig."

G-pa smiles and pats my leg. "I know." He opens the door and gets out. I get out and watch him grab a shovel from the truck bed. He has the trash bag with gun parts in his hand. I follow him over the ditch and up a fairly steep hill.

"This is BLM land."

"BLM?"

"Government. They started logging it about ten years ago, but the public screamed about destroying the view from the freeway over there." He points out a tiny black line that looks about three inches long from our position.

"You'd only see this spot for two seconds as you're zipping down that highway!"

G-pa chuckles. "Yep, people were of the thinking, 'give the government a minute, they'll take a decade.'. They didn't want to see any of this changed in the years to come. They can't touch this area for another fifty years now. Unless, of course, Deer Falls becomes a mega metropolis." He chuckles.

I smile.

We walk through brush and small trees until he finds a larger tree. He shovels out dirt about three feet from the trunk. He digs until he finds and uncovers roots. He digs a hole under the roots and shakes the gun parts out of the bag. Again, he puts bags on his hands before touching the metal pieces. He shoves them into the hole under a mass of roots.

"As this tree grows, the roots will grow around these pieces," We look at each other and suddenly, I feel even safer than when we buried the first part of the gun.

On the drive home, G-pa is quiet. I run over the things he said about remembering Craig's bad points, not living his life for him, and living my own. The heavy burden of being the one left alive is becoming lighter. I glance over at G-pa. Is he right about death's timing? Do we die no matter what, if we have met our purpose? Aren't we all, just guessing about life after death? I think his rationale makes as much sense as any other I've heard. I know it makes me feel better, and right now that's sanity insurance for me.

I wake up when my head bounces off the window as G-pa does his infamous driveway dive.

"Hungry?" He asks giving me that generational crooked grin, as I rub my head and scowl at him.

"Amused by that are you?"

"Welp, gotta get my entertainment where I can these days."

We barely start fixing dinner when the phone rings. It's Mom. She tells me that she may have found a house for us, but it won't be ready for a month. I guess my days in Deer Falls are numbered after all.

Mom said people keep laying flowers in the yard for Craig as a memorial.

My heart hurts for her. I wish I had something I could say to make her pain go away. I'm at a loss. The main thing on my mind will only make it worse for her. G-pa is right; she doesn't need to know my secret. She doesn't need to know that one of her sons is the cause of her mourning. Guilt floods in, and I end the call.

"Mom, I love you. I'll be home soon." It's all I can come up with. Before she hangs up, I add, "Hey, Mom, we're going to be okay."

G-pa and I eat dinner on the couch. We're quiet. It's been a long day. I clean up the dishes, and G-pa gets out his jewelry stuff.

"G-pa, you know that room upstairs has good light."

He looks at me, not understanding what I mean.

"Grandma's sewing room."

He looks at his hands. They hold a tiny gold chain and they are frozen in place.

"It's sitting there the way she left it," I say quietly, treading softly. "Maybe you could turn it into a work space."

He swallows hard. "Maybe it is time that I changed that room."

"I mean, only if you want to. It would be a good place to tinker around in, to put your jewelry stuff in."

"Lily's scent left that room long ago. She's not there anymore."

"I'm sorry about that, G-pa. Hey, never mind, I was just bored and thinking out loud."

"I kept it like it was, hoping she'd come back to visit." He smiles a sad smile. "She took on other things to do long ago. Who knows," he looks up at me, "maybe she's got Craig by the hand, or the scruff of the neck, showing him that you're okay, not alone, and are sorry. Maybe Lily is helping him to move on."

"Maybe I won't hear his voice anymore now."

"Maybe, Chris, maybe. Come on, cleaning out the sewing room is a good idea."

G-pa and I pack up the sewing machine and boxes of cloth. We move hundreds of spools of thread and dozens of coffee cans filled with buttons, snaps, zippers and eye hooks. We haul everything to the storage closet and stack it beside Grandma's other boxes filled with clothes and knickknacks.

I wonder who, if anyone, has packed up Craig's things. Has Mom? Did she go in his room with the blood? Did she clean up the . . . stop!

I look at G-pa. He quickly averts his eyes. I think he is afraid I'll mention getting rid of Grandma's things. I suddenly know that would do more harm than good, for this old man who is still madly in love with 'his Lily.'

I smile, dust off my hands, and we move to the door. G-pa pulls the dangling shoestring, storing away his memories for now.

I go to the sewing room. As I wash off the table and move it and the chair closer to the window, I know I was wrong for suggesting this.

I pull back the curtain to look out. The window is fogged over with years of dust and grime. I wash it, and the setting sun's last light puts the room in a soft glow.

The room is too large, too empty. Even I can feel it. Grandma is gone now.

Eight

oday marks eight weeks since Craig died. It doesn't feel like two months. It still feels like he just died. Does this sadness ever go away? I miss him. I still carry guilt, only now, I remember the real scene, and how it all went down. I just want this all to stop so I can get on with my life.

Guilt eats at my core. I hurt everyone I come into contact with, it seems. First Craig, and Mom, and now G-pa. He hasn't been the same since we cleaned out the sewing room last week. He doesn't use the room either.

I drink a cup of coffee and eat a Power Bar. I'm ready to go swim. I'm evaluating my progress and the three weeks I have left to cross the river when there's a knock on the door.

G-pa doesn't get visitors, and we look at each other, casting blame for the intrusion. I open the door. It's Ian.

"Hey, Ian."

"Ready to shoot some hoops?" He spins the ball on his finger and grins.

"Oh, well, actually I'm busy this morning. How about I catch you around noon?"

Ian's face drops in disappointment, but he recovers quickly. "Okay. You want me to stop by and get you then?"

"Sure."

"Okay, guess I'll catch up with you then." He turns awkwardly and leaves.

I close the door, and G-pa is staring at me.

"What?"

He shakes his head as if to say, 'Nothing.'

"I'm busy! I have my swim and run before b-ball. I don't want to mess up my routine or to be distracted while I swim."

G-pa just sips his coffee and looks at me.

"Aw, man. Bye." I head out for the river.

"You're becoming a regular Opie Taylor, Chris!"

It's been a while since I've heard Craig's voice, so when he speaks, it startles me. My heart drops. He's back. Then anger takes over.

"Why'd you have the gun, Craig? What were you into? What about those times you were ducking out of the lanes lately?"

"Before long you'll be sporting a straw hat and sippin' on 'shine."

"Why didn't you just come to the lanes with me? Where were you going? What were you doing?"

"Ian looked all sad that you put him off."

"Who were you mixed up with? You left me, Craig! You failed me first by shutting me out of your life! I didn't fail you. What I did was an accident, but you left me on purpose."

"Shut up, Chris! You were busy chasing that little blonde skirt, so don't talk to me about loyalty. You were too caught up to see beyond your own nose."

"I thought we were a team, Craig! You didn't even tell me what was up, man; you just dissed me!"

I reach the river and dive in. My strokes are long, rushed, and full of rage. Before I know it, I'm being carried downstream.

"You can't swim this thing, Chris. It's suicide. No crossing for you, little brother."

I turn direction and head back to shore. I monitor my strokes, my pace against the current, and I feel my anger burn as my strength catches fire. "Oh, I'll cross, Craig, just you sit back and watch me! You just watch me, Craig!" I scream.

A week ago, we buried the gun, and now I feel safe. A week ago, I wasn't sure I'd cross the river, now I know I will. A week ago, we cleaned out the sewing room, and G-pa hasn't been the same since. So today, while

I'm feeling more safe and sure, G-pa has grown old and quiet. He's no longer mimicking ten-year-olds hopping gates for adventure. Instead, he's withdrawn, and I do all the cooking, or he wouldn't even be eating.

I know it's my fault. I wish I had never mentioned clearing out Grandma's room. I don't know why I did that. I'm disgusted by my cheap shot at going for a quick fix for my misery. I was exhausted with struggling alone in my guilt and sadness. I needed someone else to hurt with me, to take some of my pain. I know why G-pa agreed to do it, too. To show me that one day I will be done with the hurt and that I'll be okay again. He was wrong, I guess. He has shown me that it hurts forever. Just like forever there will be unanswered questions. So, now I guess, I'm holding out for less pain instead of it being gone.

If putting the room back together again would bring back my rusty ol' G-pa, I'd do it. It's too late, though. I can't bring back Grandma's last touch that the room held. The damage is done, and it's killing me inside, just as surely as it's killing G-pa.

I head to the river where the silence is filled with familiar guilt, not this fresh guilt that swallows up my heart.

The water seems colder today. My arms are aching, and my legs are tired already, but I keep swimming. I swim to punish myself and to get this crossing done so I can be normal again. Or like G-pa says, 'As normal as it gets.'

I've been swimming against the current for about twenty minutes. I steer a little further into the current and immediately feel the difference of its strength fighting my body. I'm not beating it and can see I'm drifting, so I steer back out of the current and make my way to shore. I check my watch. I was right—twenty-three minutes. It's a long time to fight the current. I was further out than I've ever been. It took forty-nine strokes to get back to where I could touch toe to the bottom again. I had to have been close to the halfway point and the strongest part of the current. I smile. I'm almost ready to make my crossing from 'Chris-n-Craig' to 'Just Chris.'

I flip over on my stomach and make myself do 125 pushups, even though my arms are wobbling with exhaustion. I jump up and begin my run home.

G-pa's truck is gone when I get there. I'm surprised by that but glad. I shower, change clothes and eat a sandwich. I find a note on the kitchen counter saying: "Senior center, back before dinner." Well, at least he got out and went to see Vera.

Ian bounces up to the door, and I am out before he knocks. We dribble and pass the ball all the way to the park.

"How 'bout you show me that mid-air twist you do when shooting? Man, that's an awesome fake-out!"

I laugh. "Yeah, it is pretty cool, huh? Craig says I look like a confused worm when I do it."

"Who's Craig?"

"Um, my brother. He's not here."

"Oh. Does he play?"

"Not anymore." I move the conversation away from Craig.

"The trick is to double-tap the ball. The first tap is a fake throw in mid-jump, at a 90-degree angle from the net. It sends everyone scrambling the wrong way. It also tells your body how far to twist for the second tap that sends it home."

"Huh?"

I laugh again. "Okay, think of the net at the 12:00 position. Your first tap is done at the 3:00 position. Your hand furthest from the net needs to aim where your other shoulder is; it's like a mid-air marker. You twist and do the second tap when you're facing 12:00. Your shoulders will be at 3:00 and 9:00."

"Whoa, cool."

Ian and I play hard. In about an hour, there are other kids hanging out and watching. Ian introduces me to them, and we hit up a game of 2 on 2. Ian and I win. Ian tried the twist and missed the shot, but he's getting closer. We stop for a break, and I see G-pa's truck parked. He's sitting on the bumper watching us, so I go over to him.

"Have a nice visit with Vera?" I tease.

He ignores the comment.

"I drove by and saw you out here. I went and picked up some cold sodas and some of those candy bars you like."

I smile. "Thanks, G-pa. They're energy bars. Healthy."

He grunts.

"Listen, G-pa, if you're gonna hang with us rad dudes, you should know that people don't care how old you are, they judge you by the cool lingo you use. So, don't embarrass me." I grin.

"Tell me why those girls over there think that punk is so rad."

I laugh. "'Cuz, he says he is, I guess."

"Oh, well, I'm rad then. Think Vera will beat feet to date me?"

"Oh, she'll beat feet all right! You don't want Vera anyway."

"Why not?"

"'Cuz, a rad dude doesn't date a Vera, that's why. No, you need an Edith or a May."

"No Edith! Archie Bunker I am not!"

"So says you!" I laugh.

He squints at me.

"Yes, I know who Archie, Edith, Meathead and even Sally Struthers are. Not all of your tapes are in black and white, G-pa."

"Archie is outdated. I don't know why that tape is still there."

"Outdated? And black and whites aren't?'

"No. Black and whites are timeless." He gets up. Pats the side of the truck like a faithful dog, grabs a bag and hands it to me, and climbs in the truck.

"Dinner in about two hours?"

"Sounds good." I lift the bag in thanks.

G-pa cranks up the truck, waves a hand, and double clutches down the street.

When I get home, G-pa is sleeping through the news. I don't smell dinner, and my stomach protests, making sure G-pa hears.

"Call down there to that pizza joint and see how soon they can deliver."

"What kind do you want?"

"Get one with everything on it."

"A giant half and half sound good?"

He grunts, and I take it as a yes.

The pizza comes quick, and we settle into the couch. G-pa puts in a movie.

"*A Street Car Named Desire*." He whistles and says, "Marilyn is a bea-u-ty!"

I laugh. "Wipe the pizza off your mouth before you embarrass me in front of this bea-u-ty."

In the morning, I wake, ready or not to swim. I go downstairs before G-pa has crawled out of bed. It's 7:30, so I make coffee, slam it down, and head for the river.

My swim goes well. I feel strong this morning and pretty sure I could make it across. Something holds me back, though. Maybe I need to make sure I can make it across on any day and not just on my strongest. Maybe it's too cold this morning. Maybe I'm not quite ready to ask Craig to leave. I get out, do 300 pushups and walk, not run, back home.

When I go in the house, it's quiet. I look at the kitchen counter and see the coffee pot is still on. I check, and it's still near full. I go upstairs, listening for the shower. Nothing. All I hear is the tick, tick, tick, of the cuckoo clock downstairs. I put my ear to G-pa's door. Nothing. I tap lightly. No answer. I think of how grumpy he'll be if I wake him up when he's this tired.

I quietly go to my room and get clean clothes out for my shower. Something doesn't feel right, and I know it.

I go back to G-pa's door, I tap again. Nothing. Craig's bloody body and staring eyes flash.

I can't do this.

"G-pa?" I knock louder. Nothing. I rest my forehead against his door. Tears run down my face.

"G-pa," I say louder. Nothing.

I open the door. He is in his bed. He looks asleep, but my soul knows better. Last night's empty beer bottle sits on his nightstand. His chest doesn't rise and fall with breath. I walk to his bed. He is obviously gone. His eyes are closed. I feel for a pulse and get expected results.

I go downstairs and pick up the phone. Tears fall as I dial. "Mom?"

Nine

The house is quiet. I stop the pendulum on the cuckoo clock. The click of the minutes without G-pa are too loud. I have to stop time's beating heart. This time, I will force the world to pause.

I push a button and hear the whir of the tape fast-forward through nearly the entire movie. I hit play, and watch an excited, but muted Igor flipping switches before the monster comes to life. The doctor's words are clearly seen in a close-up shot, his eyes are wild as he mouths, "IT'S ALIVE!"

A knock on the glass of the front door makes me jump. The coroner is here.

I point to the stairs and go outside to wait. In only what seems a few minutes, but what my numbed butt tells me is longer, the front door opens. I watch another black bag strapped to a gurney, roll across another yard that I call home. This time there are no cops asking questions, no hysterical Mom, and no flashing emergency lights to turn off. The door to the customized station wagon closes.

A man in uniform, covered in a white lab coat, approaches me. In his gloved hands, he has a clipboard. He needs my signature on a form that says he made a pick up. I scribble *Chris Tanner*. I'm surprised when a raindrop falls on the paper form. Oh, not rain.

The man takes the clipboard from me and says something I don't hear. Why hasn't he removed his latex gloves?

I watch the car bottom out on the rutted-out driveway. I stand, emptied. The car is long gone, G-pa is gone, and the cuckoo clock has stopped counting time. I go in the house, sit on the couch and rewind *Frankenstein*. I watch without volume.

The door opens. Ian walks in. He doesn't knock, he doesn't say hi, he just walks in, sits on the couch and stares at the black and white screen with me in silence. I'm not alone.

When the movie has played through, and the screen is just white snow, I continue to stare at it, hypnotized. I feel Ian get up, but don't take my eyes from the screen. I hear his footsteps climb the stairs. I hear the soft click of G-pa's bedroom door as it closes. I hear the ceiling creak when Ian walks down the hall. He pauses, then continues until I hear him directly over the kitchen. I hear his footsteps make their way back down the hall and down the stairs. He has my comforter from my bed and puts it over my shoulders.

He goes to the kitchen, and I hear the refrigerator door peel open. He comes back and sets two beers on the coffee table. He opens one and hands it to me. I take it. He opens the other, and we raise our bottles.

"To G-pa."

We drink. It tastes awful, and I make a face.

"It tastes terrible, I know, but I hear after a while it'll grow on you."

"Kinda like G-pa in that way, I guess."

"Hungry?" he asks.

"I should be."

Ian looks at the cuckoo clock, it says 10:12. I look at him. "It's later than that."

Ian nods his head like he gets it.

He snoops around the fridge and finds something to heat up. I go in the kitchen and see chili in the pan.

"He made that himself. From scratch."

Ian gives me a look of uncertainty.

"It's all good. I can eat it." My eyes blur with tears as I smell the spices fill the air. We sit on the couch and wash down spicy chili with G-pa's beer.

"Is your family coming?"

"Mom is flying down. She'll be here tomorrow."

He nods his head. "I'm staying here tonight."

I look at him. It wasn't a question.

We sit, drinking G-pa's six-pack and talking.

I knew that Ian lived with his dad, but I didn't know his mom is out in California. He said he hasn't seen her since he was ten.

I tell him about Craig; well, the edited version. I explain that his murder is why I'm here. I told him about the blood, Craig's eyes staring through me, and how watching G-pa leave the house today in a black bag was like seeing Craig all over again.

"I don't even know what to say to all of that, Chris. Jesus. I've never lost anyone to death. If you ever want to talk about Craig or your G-pa, I'll listen to your stories. It's all I know to do."

I'm glad he is here.

The next morning, a cab pulls up in the driveway. Mom gets out. The driver pops the trunk for her luggage.

Ian, still half asleep, stands next to me, watching.

"Mom."

Ian grabs the empty beer bottles, puts them in the six-pack, and puts it next to the trash can, which would be automatic cover normally, but I'm so numb that I don't care. The fear I would have once felt by getting caught drinking beer seems trivial now.

The door opens, and Mom's arms are immediately wrapped tight around me. She starts to cry. Ian walks around us and out the door as quietly as he came in yesterday. I feel his calmness slip away as Mom's anxiety consumes. I take a deep breath, adjusting to the changed atmosphere. I don't think she even realized Ian was here.

Mom follows me upstairs as I carry her luggage to her room. She passes by G-pa's room, lightly touching his door, but averting her eyes. She stops at the old sewing room."

"What—where are Momma's things?"

"We, um, cleaned them out."

"But why?" She half whines.

I think of how best to explain, but the truth is too much for me to admit. "So that G-pa could move on, Mom."

She has a puzzled look on her face. "Oh."

"Here, your bedding is fresh. Go ahead and unpack. Are you hungry?"

I need a reprieve from her chaotic energy, even just a minute to shift gears and catch my breath.

"No thanks, I ate on the plane."

"I'll fix you a sandwich anyway."

I go downstairs, and I peek out the door's window. Ian is long gone, and so is my serenity it seems.

I go to the kitchen and stare out through the country-styled curtains at the shed. I can see the b-ball hoop. The first time G-pa reached out to me, he tripped me. I smile. We poured our aggressions out on the grass and walked away bruised and scratched but with cleared minds and hearts.

I'm drinking a cup of coffee when Mom comes into the kitchen. She takes the cup from my hand, pours it down the drain and says, "Oh honey, coffee isn't good for you."

I look at her, then pick the cup up and refill it. I stir in milk and sugar. She stares at me, realizing that I'm not the little boy she brought down here on a bus two months ago. She seems to accept it well enough.

I make G-pa-sized sandwiches for both of us, cutting hers into polite halves. I smash mine down with my hand and sit at the table with her to eat. I think of G-pa's grunt of approval and smile inside of myself.

The day ends up being no more than way too many hours of Mom's uncomfortable twittering. It feels like we are strangers. I see her differently now, and I can't shake the idea that she's seeing Craig when she looks at me.

A call from the coroner's office breaks our stalemate. We learn that G-pa died of an aneurism. They said he died in his sleep quite suddenly and probably didn't feel any pain. They suspected he had been living with it for several years.

Mom and I talk more after the call, but mostly about anything but the obvious: death. I go to bed early.

I lie for hours listening to CDs and watching the streetlight shine its now familiar beam on my curtain. I get up, go to the reading area and in the rocker and pull out the big white family Bible. I run my finger down the list of names 'til I come to Reginald Tanner. I enter August 15, 2017, on his D.O.D. line.

The next day, the third day since I found G-pa, we are surprised when G-pa's attorney calls. We didn't know he had one. He asks us to come to his office, that G-pa had drawn up a will.

Apparently, G-pa had set it up less than a week ago. I knew the only time that he had left the house was the day he visited Vera and stopped by the park with sodas.

The attorney said that G-pa told him he had a bad head and was having terrible headaches, which his doctor had warned him of. He knew his time was short.

I suddenly realize that it wasn't the sewing room making him quiet, it was the headaches! Relief floods over me and opens the door of guilt-free grief. My heart fills with a clean sadness. I start crying, hard. A disruptive cry, so I leave the office. I go to the car and cry every tear I've held in about G-pa. I cry tears that had been hidden even from myself. I have learned what grief is supposed to feel like. It is freer than what I experienced with Craig's death.

Mom gets in the car.

"Daddy left me the house and some repair money. He also left me the truck. He left someone named Vera a lot of money. I guess the attorney was instructed to hand deliver her cash every month. Apparently, she lives in a nursing home, and they'll take it if it's in a bank account. That was sweet of him, wasn't it?"

She hands me a sealed envelope and starts the engine. I stare at the envelope, not wanting to erase his last touch. Mom pulls out of the parking lot as I ease the seal apart. There is a letter. A note really:

Chris, I couldn't be prouder of you, if you were my own son. Keep trying to cross that river. You didn't know that I knew, did you? I'll do my best to occupy Craig and keep him out of your hair. You do your best in caring for your mom for me. She needs you. I'm leaving you some cash for college. You will likely get a b-ball scholarship, but then what would happen if they discovered an 8-decade-old cuss whooped you? So, this is just in case anyone finds out 'your secret.' I have full confidence in you that you will be the best 'Just Chris' possible.

I love you, son,

Gee Paw.

P.S. Turns out you were right, Vera beat foot. I've never seen a woman laugh so hard in all my years.

The money is there for my defense if my secret ever comes out. The b-ball whooping is just his way of razzing me. I pull out a bank deposit slip in my name, for $40,000. I put the slip and the note back in the envelope. I stare out the side window, seeing happy people doing normal things as tears blur them into oblivion. An oblivion they live and play in, though my world has stopped. Again.

Mom tries to break the silence on the drive home. I wonder why she always has to be chattering? Then I think of her life. She's been a single parent for nearly all my life. She lost her mom before I was born and she wasn't close to her dad. I wonder if her habit of busy talk is because she feels so alone all the time. I wonder why she and G-pa weren't closer. I let out a sigh. I'll be more patient with her. G-pa's words slam me in the chest: 'She needs you.'

Tears threaten my eyes again. I've always loved her; I've just never understood her. I reach over and grab her hand. She stops talking mid-sentence. We both are hit with the reality, that each other is all we have in this world, from here on out, it's only us.

"Mom, I love you, and we're going to survive this, all of it, together."

She sniffs back tears, and says, "Okay, Chris."

Once we pull into the driveway, Mom sits and stares at the old house she used to call home.

"I guess it's a good thing Daddy gave us some fix-up money, huh?" Then she bursts into sobs. She lays her head on her arms over the steering wheel, and I let her cry. I don't try to console her; I don't even touch her. I take a lesson from Ian, and I give her silence.

Eventually, we go into the house. I pull out frozen lasagna that G-pa and I made together. I heat it up, and the house smells normal again. I pull garlic bread from the oven, as Mom comes from upstairs.

"I was going through the closet up there; it was so nice to see Momma's things again. All those little figurines she had, I forgot what they looked like. Oh," she chuckles, "and all her costume jewelry I used to play with as a girl. Chris! That smells wonderful! You made this?"

I smile and grab her in a bear hug. "G-pa and I did."

"Really?"

"He was quite the chef, Mom, ruffled apron and all." I laugh.

"I didn't even know that about him," she says softly.

I consider bringing up the subject of Mom and G-pa's estranged relationship when she saves me from asking.

As she searches drawers for a serving spoon, she says, "You know, Daddy didn't like me very much."

"Why?" I ask gently.

"I don't know!" She says this with a choked voice and buries her face in her hands to cry. I take hold of her, wrapping this short, pudgy woman in my arms.

"Mom, he loved you, but he only adored one woman in his life; his Lily."

Mom nods her head and wipes her tears. I carry our plates to the table.

"You know, G-pa absolutely adored her. He talked about her often, and his eyes would light up like a love-sick puppy. Mom, I'm not sure that he ever got over her death. I think that you reminded him of her, of the fact that she was dead. I think on a certain level that was a truth he fought for the remainder of his life. I mean, even last week he still talked about her like she had been here only just the previous week."

"Oh. I guess that makes sense when I consider when he became distant to me. I thought I'd done something wrong or that maybe he just thought I was silly."

I remember how that was my first impression of G-pa, too, but given how G-pa wanted to spare Mom the pain of knowing the truth about Craig's death, I realize that he loved her. It makes sense to me now. Mom wouldn't be able to handle life without me, her only family left to her. He knew what being alone was. His phrase, 'Coming out the other side of insanity,' gives a deeper insight to me. Yes, he loved Mom and wanted to protect her. He had fought my turning myself in for my protection, but also for Mom's.

"That wasn't it, Mom. He loved you, a lot. He told me. He spoke of you in a protective way that only a dad who loves his daughter could."

"He did? Her eyes plead with me to confirm; she wants to believe this so badly. And while he didn't tell me in words, he told me in his actions.

I smile and nod my head. "Yes, Mom, he did . . . Mom?"

She looks at me as she lays a napkin on her lap.

"Why couldn't I stay with you at the motel?"

"Chris! It was for your protection! I was so scared the murderer would kill you too. You were twins! We don't know who or why—" her voice cracks and she clears her throat. "Honey, I explained this to you."

So, it wasn't because to look at me would constantly remind you of Craig?"

"No, Chris! No, honey. I thought of him every minute of every day regardless, of both of you."

She gets quiet and looks down at her plate. She settles her arms on the table in front of her and looks me in the eyes. The look on her face isn't a 'Mom' look, it's an adult to adult look.

"Okay." She sighs. "I was afraid that you would sneak off and go see your friends, or go back to our neighborhood, where the killer could be. I shouldn't have left you alone in a stranger's home, even if he was your grandpa, but I had to stay in the city to keep the police active on Craig's case. For all the good that did."

"Mom, it really was the best thing you could have done. If I hadn't come here, I never would have known G-pa like I did, if at all. We wouldn't have become so close if you were here too. With just us two, we were forced to come out of our shells and get to know one another. He was like the dad I never had." Tears fill my eyes. "He called me 'Son,' and he meant it."

Mom's eyes fill, she reaches and takes my hand. "He was a good dad, wasn't he?"

I stand and go to her. She hugs me and cries in my chest. She's crying for G-pa, her Mom, Craig, my long-gone dad and for the loss of our normal lives. I pull her in closer, let her cry; I take care of her like G-pa told me to.

When she is cried out and has collected herself, we sit in front of monstrous-sized plates of lasagna. She giggles as she looks at it.

"What?"

"Momma and Daddy had a fight. Momma was cooking dinner, and Daddy kept eating everything she opened, cut up or mixed together. It got on Momma's nerves. She told him if he couldn't wait an hour, then to fix a sandwich and leave her alone. So, he did. He made a huge sandwich with everything in the fridge on it!" Mom laughs, giggles until her face is red and tears flood her eyes.

"Momma hadn't paid him any mind; she was giving him her best ignore stance. When she finally saw what he was doing, she took the stuff she had cut up on the counter and threw it at him. Told him to stick that in his . . . sandwich!" She laughs even harder. "Ever since then, he'd make these huge sandwiches to irk her!"

I laugh because I can picture the old cantankerous Reggie doing just that. He'd call it the spice of life. No wonder he called a regular sandwich a 'polite sandwich.'

Our laughter calms, and Mom looks around the kitchen, dining area and living room, everywhere she can see from her chair.

"I love this place, Chris. I have so many wonderful memories here. I hate to sell it."

"Why do you have to sell it?"

"Oh, honey, we won't be here to take care of it. To rent it out while we live so far away just isn't practical."

"Mom, what if we just stayed here?"

She looks surprised for a second.

"Won't you miss the city? Honey, this is a very small community. There's not much for a boy your age to do here."

"Mom, even if we went back to the city, and even if I could reconnect with my friends, I'm not sure I want to. I'd see the places and streets where Craig and I used to go; and as far as our friends, well, I'd always be living in the shadow of Craig's death. I couldn't just be me. I'd always be 'Chris-n-Craig' minus Craig. I'd always be the guy whose twin brother was murdered. I'd see it in everyone's faces forever.

"Mom, G-pa taught me to live my own life. To let Craig, move on, and to move on myself. I don't want to end up in a trap where I'm always thinking what could have been, or telling others that I'm okay.

"I . . . I've made a friend here. He's a good friend. I don't have to entertain him like I always did my old friends. He plays b-ball, and he gives me my space when I need it. Plus, the school here has a team that needs my championship blood." I smile. "Honestly, I'd rather finish school here playing ball and getting ready for college than to spend time in the haunted city."

I watch Mom's face to see if she gets it.

"What about my job, Chris? I can't just walk out. I just got approved for a transfer."

"There are hospitals everywhere, Mom. You'll find work. Couldn't we live on the house repair money G-pa gave you to get us by for a while? I just think a new start would be good for both of us."

"Well, you certainly have grown up over the summer, Chris. Wow."

I smile but wonder if she's changing the subject. The silence between us is long enough that I accept defeat of my idea, when she finally says, "Okay."

"Yeah?" I grin. "Okay then." I take a manly bite of my lasagna, and she shakes her head at my animal behavior.

"The house still needs repairs, though."

"Well, my dear, short lady, you have me for three weeks 'til the school year starts. I'll throw Ian, my friend, in for free!"

She laughs, "This should be interesting!"

* * *

G-pa's funeral is held in a church, whose door I'm pretty sure he had never darkened before. I am surprised by the number of people who attend, but remind myself that he had lived here nearly half a century.

Strangers shake my hand and hug Mom. Many need to tell her who they are before she recognizes them. Many she never knew at all.

I see a nurse wheeling a white-haired woman out the door. I excuse myself, and make my way to the entrance and see them as they reach the car.

I run over to them. "Vera?"

"Yes?" Her fogged, blue eyes are rimmed red. She holds a dainty, embroidered hanky in her frail hand; with her other, she pats her snow-white hair. I wait to see if she recognizes me.

Her eyes light up. "Chris! It is a pleasure to see you again." She pats my hand.

"And you, Vera. Thank you for coming."

"You gave him the best days of his life in over twenty years, Chris. You know that, don't you?"

My eyes burn; I gasp out a choked, "No. I didn't know that."

Vera smiles. "He was like a newborn boy again." She chuckles. "He asked me out on a date! I'm old enough to be his mother, and told him so!" She put her small hand up to her mouth and whispers, "He made my day!"

I laugh. The nurse asks Vera if she is ready, and Vera nods her head. She reaches up and fingers the vial necklace around my neck, then gently pats it.

"You know, he told me you two went up to my property, my son's old place, up on the mountain."

I look at her shocked. That was Vera's land? Her son was G-pa's friend that died! I understand now, why G-pa took care of Vera and visited her so often. Vera gets a twinkle in her eye like she is a co-conspirator.

"He showed me a spot where they started a well."

She laughs. "Well, now, that's a mighty fine spot all right. It has good memories about it."

"Vera, thank you, from both of us."

She waves and the nurse helps her in the car.

I walk slowly to the doorway of the church. I smile. What great drama to liven up Vera's days. G-pa was so smart in so many ways. I just keep finding out new things about him nearly every day.

I peek in the door and see that Mom is surrounded by well-wishers. Most people have left already, and she doesn't look stressed. I go out to the car and leave a note on its rental agreement, telling her I went for a walk and will be home by dinner. I run home, put on my swim shorts and jog to the river.

As I walk the empty shore, where G-pa's favorite panning spot is, his words come back to me. He is right about how this river grabs hold of you before you know what's happened. He's also right about me living my own life. Still, somewhere inside of me, I want to make jewelry and take it to Vera, but that's not my life to live. G-pa will always be a part of me. He left his mark on my life, just as I'm sure he did many other people's. I'll visit him every time I watch a 'timeless' black and white movie, or his outdated Archie Bunker tape. I'll remember his lasting love for his Lily, and measure my own love to that high standard. I will live life to the best of my ability because if not for him, I wouldn't have it at all.

I scan the river. I do a few stretches and a few push-ups while keeping my eyes on the river, I'm daring it. I can feel it in my bones; today I make the crossing.

I dive in at an angle to counter the current's trajectory. My strokes are long, smooth and precise. The river gives way with each stroke, and its chill releases adrenaline through me. Every stroke is a claw tossing the shore behind me and pulling the current to me. My body burns fuel created by weeks of running, swimming, push-ups and sit-ups.

The opposite shore is closer than it's ever been before. My heart races with excitement. The current grows stronger and shoves against my angled body. My arms burn, and my legs start to lose their rhythm. I struggle to regain my focus and get my body back to its machine-like precision before I reach the most powerful part of the current. My legs are aching, and I catch a mouthful of river. The current can flip me and tumble me down river at any moment. My arms feel like they are ripping apart. I check my target spot on the opposite shore. I've drifted! The shore is still a long way off. I fight, stroke, kick, breathe, but still, my target is leaving me behind. I'm being carried way too far. I can't tell how far I have before I reach the falls. Panic rises in my chest.

"Come on, Opie boy! Push through it. You wanna sink like a rock? Maybe drop over the side like the true drip you are?"

"Shut up, Craig!" my brain screams. I set a new marker and focus on it. I'm so angry. I tug handfuls of water behind me. My arms are raw with pain, but I focus on the river that I cup behind me with each stroke. My legs are screaming. I let them yell.

The current begins to loosen its grip on me. It pushes, but no longer shoves me. I've made it through the worst! I see the shore coming closer with each stroke now. Excitement seizes my chest again. I am no further from this shore, then I've been from the other shore hundreds of times. I'm doing this!

My entire body is shaking violently, from exhaustion and cold, from fear and disbelief, and from pure adrenaline. My legs keep dropping, but I fight to keep them raised. They have a will of their own and drop again. I touch sandy gravel with my toe! I slap my trembling, noodle-like arms into the water again and again. I have no strength left in them, they are as useless as my legs now. My feet touch bottom. I walk out from neck-high water, my arms not helping much to get me to shore.

Finally, I am only waist-deep and drop to my knees to crawl onto dry land. I raise my arms in victory. Tears flow out from my physical pain, emotional pain and the pure joy of success. I sit and raise my arms high in honor of myself.

I look at the vastness of water I have just conquered, and I see the current ripple as innocently as a child's dimple. I look to the familiar shore across the river, where Craig stands, staring at me.

My heart catches. I drop my arms in exasperation. He gives me a crooked grin, raises his hand palm-forward toward me, then evaporates, like he was an illusion all along.

The emptiness deep inside of me confirms that Craig is gone.

I sit on this bank as a free man, at last. 'Chris-n-Craig' have died. 'Just Chris' is born.

My soul begins to breathe . . . without my telling it to.

Ian Sense

I used to cry for you at night.
The void you left, just didn't feel right.

Can I go with you? I'll be good!
You shake your head like no mother should.

Why did you leave me here alone?
You don't pick up when I try to phone.

I used to cry for you at night.
But now I lock my tears up tight.

—Ian Oliver Taylor

One

My inner alarm shoots adrenaline through my entire body. Before my mind registers what's going on, I have leapt into action. I've hit the T.V.'s power button and am clearing the back stairs in a single jump as I hear Dad's truck pull into the driveway. It always amazes me how I sense things before they happen. It's pretty cool, really.

I make my way cautiously along the side of the house toward the front. Dad is home early today, which means either he left work early or he didn't go in at all. Either way, I'm sure he's put in his time at Grady's Pub. It would be too big of a gamble to hang around and find out why he's not at work since I couldn't care less anyway. I do need to know, though, if this is a happy drunk or a mean one. I stand silent, listening, with my back flush to the side of the house.

A sure sign that my alarm was on cue is by how long it's taking him to get to the front door. I inch my head around the corner just enough to peek. Dad wobbles, loses his balance, then takes a step to straighten up. This is a bad one.

He pushes at the truck's door but misses it. He takes a quick step forward and closes the door by running into it. I pull my head back out of sight and sigh. At least he'll pass out early tonight. The thought cheers me up some.

I hear him clomp up the porch steps, pausing and shuffling as he climbs. I hear the keys hit the wood floor, then his grunt as he bends to pick them up. I chance another peek. He is on his knees with one hand on the door knob for support. He leans to grab the keys but turns the knob as he does. The door falls open, and he rolls in, cursing. I duck back around the corner as I hear the door slam shut. The eagle has landed.

I give him a few minutes to move away from the picture window. Seconds feel like minutes. After I've waited for what feels like forever, I crouch down and jet out of the yard. I pass the neighbor's house where I know he can't see me, and I breathe a sigh of relief. I let my pounding heart calm down and allow my adrenaline to settle back to wherever adrenaline goes when it's done freaking a body out.

I don't have anything to do, so I just walk. I do this a lot, walking around to avoid Dad, waiting for him to pass out. Actually, now that I think about it, most everything I do is to avoid him. There's b-ball, my job, and just kicking it down at the river. B-ball keeps me busy after school and on weekends during the year. My job keeps me out of the house during the summer and on weekends. The river, well it's my year-round safe place. Dad doesn't know about any of these activities. If he knew, at some point he'd show up drunk and cause a scene. No thanks.

This summer's job is at the deli in the mall. I get to stuff my face, and I'll be able to pay b-ball fees and get school clothes. The bonus is that Dad doesn't go to the mall, so he'll never know I'm working there. It's a win-win. Today is a weekday and my day off, which works for me. I work on the weekends when Dad is mega-drunk. Plus, I like my boss, and working weekends helps her on the shop's busiest days. So, it's all cool.

Summer or winter, there are some things that stay the same, like never knowing how long Dad's bar trip will last, how drunk he'll be when he gets home or what his mood will be when he gets there. I have figured out that hard liquor turns him mean and sends him home earlier than when he drinks beer. Also, he tends to drink the hard stuff around payday. I suppose it's more expensive than beer, so he splurges on payday. Regardless, I spend a lot of time checking the yard for his truck, and too much time creeping around our windows like a Peeping Tom, waiting for him to pass out so I can go to bed.

So, here I am, same ol'- same ol' walking down the street with the warm sun on my face, smelling the fresh cut grass of the neighborhood. I wish I would have remembered to grab my b-ball from under the porch. That's where I keep it for times like this. I glance behind me as I turn off my street, making sure Dad isn't following me. He isn't. He was bad drunk; I figure he'll go straight to bed. For now, I'm in the clear. My nerves settle to calm mode.

I consider my great escape today. I love how the adrenaline shot through my system before I even heard Dad's truck. I know it's weird that I sense things that other people don't, but I make exceptions for myself, well, because it's me. Truth be known, I find it weird that others are caught off guard or surprised by someone sneaking up on them. That never happens to me. It's why I'm good at b-ball too. I just know the moment someone is building up to a crucial instant. I feel when the person is ready to let the ball fly, and I block it. People have asked how I do that. I tell them it's luck and try to blow it off.

I've never told anyone about my narrow escapes from Dad, or how I know things before they happen. I've never heard anyone say they can do this, so I keep my mouth shut about it. After all, it's my weirdness that gives me an edge.

I read in a book once about empaths. I think that's what I might be. I have a heightened sense where I can feel others' strong emotions even if I'm not involved. It goes beyond sympathy and normal empathy. Sometimes the emotions are so intense or overwhelming that I have to remind myself that they aren't my feelings and that I'm only a witness to someone else's. That book said being an empath means a person has a highly developed sense of awareness. I think I developed mine from living with Dad. It's a form of survival for me.

For as long as I can remember I've had to be alert to Dad's shifting moods. They can change in an instant, without warning. Like when he's in a good mood and is talking with me, laughing, teasing me, then, in the next breath, he'll lash out in anger and hit me. I stay on alert around him, watching for the slightest cue like a shift of his mouth, eyes, stance or tone of his voice. My gut usually knows before my eyes do, though. Since I'm always waiting for his blows, I've gotten pretty good at ducking them. I've also learned how to guide his rambling thoughts to keep him in a good mood until I can exit stage left without incident.

I'm not sure when my heightened sense started. I remember all kinds of situations where I have felt anger, panic or fear, then walked up on a situation that could have been very bad if I had not shown up. There have been dozens of cats and dogs, even a squirrel one time, that I happened across in the nick of time and rescued from this guy named Rod. He used to be mean to animals. I don't like to think about it.

There was also the time when I was just a little kid that Mrs. Drexell broke her hip and I found her. She was on my paper route and would always wait on her porch for me. I think she was lonely because she'd talk forever about people I didn't know. I hated delivering to her! One day she wasn't on her porch, so I tossed her paper on the step and got out of there. Then fear hit my heart, and tears fell from my eyes even though I wasn't crying! I went back and found her in her backyard, crying. I'd never seen an old person cry before. She said she knew I would be the only one to come by. After that, I left her street for last on my route, and I'd go inside to deliver her paper because it hurt her to walk. It turned out that I ate a lot of cookies, and got to hear a whole lot about people I'd never met. I keep this stuff to myself because if anyone knew about my sense, then they'd know how weird I am. I'd have to explain what an empath is, how it developed, and everyone would know what my home is really like. That can never happen. The authorities would make me leave home, and I want to be there if Mom comes back to get me.

I'm not a kid anymore. I know Mom probably won't come back. It's been like seven years since she left. I probably wouldn't go with her now if she did come back. I just want to finish school, and next year, when I'm eighteen, I'll get a good job and move out of Dad's house. I used to ask why she left, but Dad would get mad and call her horrible names. I never believed the names were true though. I think maybe he used to hit her too.

We look a lot alike, Mom and me. I have her dark brown eyes and hair, her Hispanic traits. My skin is lighter though because Dad is white. People say I'm lucky to have a natural tan. I guess so. It doesn't matter to me, it's just me and more of my weirdness. See, I have this totally white name, Ian Oliver Taylor, on a Hispanic body. Weird.

I used to wonder what it would be like when I saw Mom again. I'd make up scenes of how it would all play out. Now I understand it's not when, but *if*, I see her again. It would be nice to see her. I could ask her why she didn't take me with her when she left.

I stand on the river's edge, near the Falls' base. The spray is cool on my skin. I scan their height and feel their strength. Their roar is so loud it silences anything or anyone that may be around. I glance around and see that I am alone. Nobody is downstream, on the footbridge, or on the path that climbs the hill to the head of the falls. I step out onto the rocks in the river that are like natural stepping stones. I scope out the area again, all is clear. I hop from stone to stone until I reach the wall of the cliff that runs behind the falls. I climb up the face of the rock wall and hook my toes on the ledge while gripping a crack with my fingers, as I make my way across and behind the falls.

The powerful force of the water rushing past only a few feet behind my back always gives me a rush, like I'm tempting fate. A few more feet to go until I reach the cave. Nobody knows about this cave but me. It's my hideaway when things get crazy at home, and I need to escape.

I reach the cave and hoist myself up. It's dry in here, which is pretty cool when you consider what the front door is made of. I take a quick inventory and am satisfied that no one has found my spot. I have my sleeping bag, candles and lighter, bag of jerky, and a water canteen. My sources of entertainment consist of a book, a deck of cards and my notebook for writing my thoughts or poetry in. I unzip the old shaving kit bag and see my overnight stuff is still there for when I get ready for school from here.

I sit with my back against the wall and watch the water race by my door. It feels good in here. It's cool, dim and quiet; well, except for the roar. I grab my tablet and read a poem I wrote last time I was missing Mom. After I wrote it, I saw how I really felt, and it cleared out some heaviness from inside of me. I realized that I don't really need her anymore, and that's a good thing. I guess I'm growing up. I toss the notepad and stare, hypnotized by the rushing water and its calming roar. This is my favorite place to be. My cave has a comfort and solitude. At home, I am always on full alert. When I am here, I can let even my inner alarm take a rest.

I feel the water's sound rush through my body, clearing away every thought of fear, disgust, anger, betrayal and loneliness. I sit for a long time as it cleanses and energizes me.

I turn my thoughts to next year, my senior year. Finally, my last year of school. When it's over, I'm free. I'm glad and scared at the same time. Glad that soon I'll get out on my own, but scared I can't make it. I guess if all else fails, I have my cave. It gets awfully cold during the winter, though. I do have all next summer to work and save cash for a place before winter hits. Maybe joining the military is my answer. At least I'd have food and a place to sleep for a few years.

I roll up my sleeping bag and stuff everything into plastic bags to keep the damp out. I slide down the cave's mouth until my toes hit the ledge of the rock wall, then I make my way back to shore.

I wander neighborhood streets looking at houses, and for the millionth time, I wonder what those families are like. As I walk by a familiar house, I gaze through the picture window, that's framed with lace curtains, and see the big oval mirror on the wall that sits near the dining table. I don't know who lives there, and I wonder if they have family game night. Does anybody actually have game night like on the commercials? I try to picture the old man and me sitting in the lace-curtained window playing Monopoly. I see the yellow hundred-dollar bills in the old man's hand, and it's just too out there . . . and the image evaporates.

Right now, I just want to go to my room. I end up on my street, debating if I should risk Dad still being up or not when I see the kid who's staying at old man Tanner's place. I figure the kid must be

Tanner's grandson or something, but I've never seen him visit before. Then again, I don't recall ever seeing any out-of-towners visiting Tanner.

Like a magnet, I'm drawn to the driveway. I stand at a distance checking this kid out. I can sense inner turmoil. There's something huge going on in his life that has redefined him. It's something he fears, but it also saddens him. The chaos of uncertainty skirts along his emotions.

The kid feels me watching him and stops tossing hoops. He turns to look at me. His panic slams my chest hard enough that I suck in air. I know he wants to be left alone, so I almost turn to leave, then suddenly I realize he is hiding from everybody, not just me.

"Hey," I say as I walk toward him. "Name's Ian."

"Chris." He fist bumps me.

"Want to go toss hoops on asphalt?" I ask.

He makes a dozen excuses that I rebut, and he finally agrees. He goes in the house to tell his 'G-pa." I was right, Chris is old man Tanner's grandson. Chris comes out and hands me a health bar and a soda. I'm embarrassed by my stomach's lack of control. I haven't eaten today. Chris just laughs at the growl, and it's all good.

We toss hoops for an hour. Turns out, he is cool. He likes to keep to himself, but, man, can he run a ball! Seriously, he's like a pro player or something. He said his school placed third in regionals last year. I know he tore me up on the court, and I'm the best player on Deer Falls' team. I told him he has got to teach me his moves. All of them. He said he's open to practicing with me over the summer before he goes back home. Too bad he's not sticking around, we could really use him on our team.

We get back to Chris's house, and I'm hoping he invites me in to watch T.V. or something, but he doesn't. We part ways, and I feel my insides tighten up as I get close to my house.

I pause in the neighbor's yard and look through shrubbery to check out the scene. Dad's truck is parked crooked. I doubt it's moved since I left. I don't see any movement in the picture window, so I walk into our yard, quietly, as if Dad can hear the grass under my feet. I hold my breath, afraid of him seeing me before I see him, as I creep up the steps to peek in the front window.

The T.V. is on, but I don't see his feet propped on the foot rest of the recliner. I don't know if he's gone to bed and left the T.V. on or if he went to the bathroom. As drunk as he was, surely, he went to bed. I wait, watching for him to come from the direction of the bathroom. No movement at all. His bedroom is off the living room, so his door is only a few feet from the front door. Too much noise could wake him, so I go around the back and come in through the kitchen door. I'm standing in the kitchen, listening for the toilet to flush or for Dad's snore when suddenly, he appears in the kitchen's archway. My heart jumps like a rocket.

"Where you been?" he asks.

"At the park. Playing ball." I swallow, sizing up his mood while getting my heart to not make me die of an attack on the spot.

"You just run the streets at all hours of the day and night like you own 'em, don't you?"

"It's only seven o'clock, Dad. It's still light out."

He looks past me, blinking at the window and see's that I'm right. The room fills with the breath of hard alcohol.

"Doesn't mean you can't stay home once in a while."

I grin, "But Dad! All the fun is out there!" I try to direct his mood more jovial.

"What? Your old man ain't fun?"

By his remark I know I've succeeded in heading off a fight.

"Hey, let's see if there's a movie on," I offer. I'm praying he says no.

"No, I'm too tired. Some of us have to earn a living tomorrow; we can't just do as we please," he says.

"Oh, well, all right. Will the T.V. bother you if I find something on?"

He swats his hand at me, in a dismissal rather than attack, and staggers to his room.

I sit on the couch and turn the T.V.'s volume down, and sit, waiting to hear his snore. It comes before too long, and I let out a breath of relief. I turn off the T.V. and go to the kitchen. The only things in the fridge are mayo and dill pickles. I make a sandwich out of them, then go hit the shower.

I lay back on my bed, staring at the ceiling, considering my day.

I like Chris. I hope I can learn those shots of his. He's got some great fake-out moves too. I grin, picturing myself as the team hero and showing the guys what I can do.

Your sweat, your breath,
Your boozed-up smell,
Now I'm in the depths of Hell.

Your sway, your stomp,
Your crashing gait,
Breaks all I own, I live with hate.

Your slur, your curse,
Your words that cut,
Hides my truth, deep in my gut.

Your scream, your yell,
Your hours of rage,
Imprison me, within your cage.

Your strikes, your blows,
Your hand that's marred,
They teach me, to be on guard.

Your grunts, your groans,
Your women past,
Repel my soul, leave me aghast.

I'm tired, I'm sick,
Of drunk charades,
Do you know the mess you've made?

—Ian Taylor

Two

I started my job at the deli before school was out, so I already have seven hundred dollars saved. I've only spent like eighty bucks, and that was mostly on food and clothes. It's all good though. I'll wear the clothes to school next year. So, I would have spent the cash anyway. I figure I only need a hundred for b-ball fees next year, and everything I earn over that goes for school supplies, clothes, food and mad money. I have eight more weeks to earn all I'll need for next year. I figure I'll earn another sixteen hundred. It'll be tight, but I can make it work.

I got paid today and stocked up on provisions for my 'man cave.' I bought jerky and some pop-top cans of single-serve food. I got candles and another lighter, but also this cool water filtering jug. No more running out of drinking water, I can just fill it up at my front door. I was considering a flashlight too, but I think it would give out too much light, and people would see it glowing from behind the falls. Besides, the candles help to heat it up in there when it's super cold. I got thirty cans of food, enough for thirty overnight stays. Everything I got will stay good for a year; well, except for the chips, and I only spent forty dollars on all of it! I think one more load of food, my old sweat suit and heavy sweater from the thrift store will be all I need to create my comfy home away from home. It feels good to have some security, to be prepared ahead of time. Last year was cold, lonely, and I'd be so hungry all night when I was staying at the cave. It was miserable. Not this year.

I pack my supplies into my backpack, but I also use a durable garbage bag, the kind that has the drawstring for a handle. When I get to the falls, I slip the handle of the bag over my shoulder like a huge purse. If anyone were to see me right now, I'd die.

I make my way along the rock wall behind the falls. It's tricky to sling the bag up into the cave while hanging by fingers and toes. I almost go down, and my heart surges in panic.

"Stupid!" I yell at myself. I should have just made two trips with the backpack. I remind myself of the times I've made this trip in the pitch black of night, and when the wall was covered in ice. I've done this with numb fingers on both hands before. Surely, I can hold on with one hand for the five seconds it takes to sling this bag up into the cave. I close my eyes, take a deep breath, and start swinging the bag in an arc to gain height to get it in the cave. But the arc won't allow me the angle I need to swing it in there. I grab the bag, as close as possible to the cans inside. I throw it, and the falls' water knocks it back, but I had enough power in my throw that the bag lands teetering on the lip of the cave's opening. I push it back as far as I can, then wiggle my pack off one shoulder.

It's too heavy and bulky to swing up like I did the bag, I'll have to hoist myself in while wearing it. Extra weight on my tired arms isn't what I need right now. I close my eyes, breathe, focus and jump. I pull myself in halfway and push the bag out of my way. I work my hips and legs in and let the backpack drop. I lay on my back and let my arms, fingers and toes come back to life. I made it. A grin crosses my face.

I arrange my provisions in neat stacks against the wall. I pull out my sleeping bag and sit on it with my back propped against the opposite wall. I look at my accomplishment with pride and relief. "One bag at a time from now on," I promise myself.

My pop-top cans look kind of small now that I have them here. One can will keep me from starving and is way better than a piece of jerky and a bottle of water like last year, but if I'm going to stay here this year, I won't be doing it hungry! I need about two more trips with my backpack full of canned food. Shoot, if I'm staying in the wild, I can at least have comfort food. Maybe I'll get one of those camping stoves or disposable burners for winter nights. I'd have a hot meal and heat, too.

I fill up the top part of my filtering jug and it works real slow, but it does work. I mix in Kool-Aid and groan. I don't have any utensils to stir it with. No dishes or a cup either. I'll get that stuff from the house; no sense in buying it.

All in all, I'm happy with my hideaway here. I wish it was an apartment, sure, but that's not possible until after next summer when I'm out of school. I'll also need a better paying job than at the deli. I could work weekends through this last year of school. Maybe I'd save enough to move out of town when I graduate. Maybe to a large city like Chris is from. There'd be more jobs to choose from. I could go to a college town and take classes, I could get a degree from a trade school. Mechanic school is my first thought, but instantly I see Dad, greasy and drunk. I toss that idea out.

I check my watch, it's time to meet Chris to practice some of those fancy moves of his. I'm starting to pick up on some of them, but none are perfected yet. I hustle getting my cave put back together, putting things in their bags, and then scale the rock wall out.

Our game went smooth, except for when Chris got mad at my great defense. I just laughed at him, and he shot me the loser sign to remind me who won. On our way home, we stop off for burgers, my treat since I lost.

"I hate to eat and run, but I gotta cut out man. G-pa is fixing dinner."

"You're going to eat again?" I laugh. "Tell him you already ate!"

"Mmm . . . no. He's been slaving away in a frilly apron all afternoon. He'd probably kill me."

I can't tell if Chris is joking or not. Old man Tanner in an apron just doesn't fit.

"It really does have ruffles."

We both burst out laughing.

I do my usual scan of the yard before I let myself be visible from the house. Dad's truck isn't here, but I still feel like something's not right. I feel like maybe he really is home, maybe the truck broke down or something. My stomach feels sick. Well, if he is here without his truck,

I'll spend hours watching for him to come home. He's a mechanic, he'd fix it if it broke, I tell myself.

I cross the yard and start up the stairs as I hear his truck. He's in the driveway before I can jump from the porch. My heart races like a trapped rat's. Why did I ignore my warning? He gets out, and I can tell he's been drinking. The best I can do is act normal, pretend he's not drunk and wait for him to go to bed. He's far from passing out. This is going to be hours of fending off his mood if I can't come up with a way to leave. This is the worst way to catch him.

"Where you been?" he demands.

I open the door as casually as I can. "I was uptown for a while, then to the park. How was your d—"

My words are cut off by his fist landing on the back of my neck. "Liar!"

I stumble forward, feeling every ounce of expertise from his boxing days. I catch my balance before I fall.

"I saw you! At that sandwich place in your little fairy-boy uniform!"

He is standing nose to nose with me. His breath reeks of hard alcohol. This is gonna be bad.

"I got a job, Dad."

He lands one between my eyes, and it's lights out. I must have only been out a minute or two because I wake to find him rifling through my pockets. He pulls out the money I have on me, which I know is over twenty bucks. I grab his hand and try to wrestle it from his fingers. I'm so angry! He punches me hard in the gut. I lose my air, then my lunch. He storms off to my room, and I hear things being tossed around. He's looking for more cash I assume. I get up and head for the door as he yells, "By God, if you're old enough to work, you're old enough to pay your way!"

I run out the door and down the sidewalk. My stomach cramps and I double over. A hand grabs at me, and I swing.

"Hey! Whoa, Ian! Stop!"

It's Chris. He pulls me into his backyard behind his house, and I let him. My nose is a river of red, and I wipe it on my shirt. I slide my back down against the house and hit the ground with a thud. I can't help it—I cry. Chris scoots to the edge of the house and peeks around the corner.

"Nobody is coming. Who did this? We'll hunt them down and handle it." He stares me hard in the eyes.

I'm surprised by his willingness to take on anyone, any number for me. I shake my head. "No, Chris, we won't be handling it, but thanks."

"Ian, seriously, who are they? Where'd they go?"

I don't answer.

"Come on, let's go inside and get you cleaned up. G-pa isn't here; he went to the store."

"No. He could come back any minute. Chris, he can't see me like this. It would just make things worse."

"Why, Ian? How could it be worse? Who did this!" He yells that last part, but I see in his eyes that he has just figured it out. "Your old man? Did he do this?"

I don't answer. You got a rag or something? I'm bleeding here."

"Yeah, wait here." He studies my face. "I mean it. Wait here. Looks like you need some ice too. I'll be right back." He stands up, unsure whether to trust me not to run off.

"Go. This is the safest spot right now." I hear Dad's truck drive by and my body tenses. I'm sure he's going to Grady's to drink up my money. Chris sees this and watches the truck go by, then looks back at me and nods. He's angry. I see it in his face, but I feel it strong in my chest. It's an odd comfort to me. I give him a cheap smile. "Chris." I point to my face, "Still gushing."

"Yeah, okay." He runs into the house. He returns in about two minutes loaded down with a wet rag, a baggie of ice, toilet paper, and two sodas.

"Did you have to bring the whole house out?" I ask. I grab the toilet paper and blow my nose. It hurts, but it's not a broken hurt. I know the difference.

"It's not broken. He hit me between the eyes. Lucky, huh?"

I take the rag and wash up, then set the ice over the bridge of my nose. It hurts, and it's so cold I can't leave it on long enough to numb it. Chris pops open a soda and hands it to me. I put down the ice and drink. I taste blood, spit, then drink again.

"He found out I have a job." I laugh. "My old man just mugged me. Stripped my pockets clean. Got over twenty bucks. Guess I'll have to find a new job now."

"Why would he take your money?"

I study Chris's eyes. It's the honest question of a guy used to a good and fair life. I shrug my shoulder.

"He's got a drinking problem." I force a laugh. "He can't afford it."

"Then maybe he should jump in the ring as a side job," Chris says disgusted.

I look at Chris. He's still angry. "He did when he was younger. Guess he got tired of getting whooped."

"Well," Chris says while letting out a sigh, "maybe we should call the guy that ended his career."

I snort out a laugh, and blood sprays.

Chris's face goes white. I realize the blood upsets him. I feel a punch of fear and grief hit my chest like what I felt that first day I met him. I stare at him, trying to figure him out. He looks away and rubs his eyes. I wipe the sprinkles and apologize.

"So, you've gotten a rare glimpse into the happy Taylor home. You know, Chris, I've never told anyone how it is."

Chris's expression tells me that he isn't judging me, and I know that my secret is safe with him. After all, I've sensed he has secrets of his own and knows how to keep them. I start talking, I'm not sure why. Maybe I just need part of my story documented somewhere in the universe. I'm also not sure why I choose the roach story either. It just popped into my head.

"After Mom left, nobody really cleaned the house. One day, Dad brought home this old refrigerator because ours died. With it came a nest of cockroaches." I snort a laugh of disgust. "I call it the 'year of the roach.' I remember seeing them everywhere. Hundreds, maybe thousands of them. It was bad. They were in the kitchen, in the bathroom, the living room, I even found them in my bed. I complained to Dad, and that's the first time I remember him hitting me. A real hit, ya know. He said if I was gonna nag like a woman, I could clean like one. I honestly tried to kill them all, thousands of them. I remember crying because Dad had hit me, but I was also crying because those roaches scared me. I thought they'd bite me.

"I pulled out this prep table that stood between the stove and the refrigerator. It had hollow legs, so when I moved it, hundreds of roaches came pouring out of the legs. They scattered everywhere! I was smacking and stomping them as fast as I could before they ran and hid in cracks. Man, it was like trying to kill all the ants in a huge ant hill. Impossible. I got mad and threw the table out the back door, and it busted up in the yard. Dad came in and saw the mess and the busted table. I dodged his blow which make him proud. My reward was a can of bug spray. He pulled that fridge and stove out, and I couldn't believe my eyes." I sit quiet for a moment, seeing the scene again.

"What? What did you see?"

I look at Chris. "I swept up three heaping dustpan loads of roaches that day."

"Jeez! That's the most disgusting . . ." Chris stops himself.

I pick at the grass I'm sitting in and say, "I never did get them all. I mean, how could I? So, here I am six years later, still living with roaches, and a drunk dad. I live in a constant disgust . . . and fear." I look at Chris's face to see if he thinks I'm a wimp or disgusting and if I've just lost a friend. He doesn't, and I haven't. I'm relieved. I chug down the last of my soda and smash the can. My stomach growls.

"Good lord, man! How can you be hungry?" Chris laughs.

I smile. "I, uh, lost my lunch when he gut-punched me." I sigh as it hits me, just how bad home is. The way Chris reacted with shock to the situation today, and my story, along with saying these things out loud, has made it all the more real, more in-my-face. I'm less able to ignore it or accept it as normal. I have no excuses for my weird life this time. It just is, and always has been, but it feels different now. It feels more wrong when I see that Chris doesn't really comprehend the things in my daily life. I haven't even told him that the stories he heard today are mild ones.

I see in Chris's face that he is angry again. I feel his anger heat and tighten my own chest. He doesn't understand an adult hitting a kid, or going days between meals, or wearing the same school clothes for three years; it's not in his world, it's nothing he's ever seen. I'd bet he has every year of his school pictures and has family game night. I can never tell him the full impact that Dad has on my life. I've shown him on a personal level, things that he's only heard about at a distance; that life isn't fair. I feel his righteous indignation toward my dad, and at this point, I'll take it. No matter how shallow his knowledge of my life is, I need someone on my side for a change. It feels too good to turn down. I don't have to worry about my story leaking out either, because he's leaving town soon, and he's not open to meeting people around Deer Falls. It works for me and him.

We hear old man Tanner's truck clang and bounce into the driveway. I go rigid and alert, ready to bolt. I watch a cloud of dust float past us.

"Have dinner with us, Ian." Chris grins. "I'll slip you my share when G-pa isn't looking. I'm still full, from the burger."

I'm disappointed that Chris is willing to open my life up to old man Tanner. Chris reads my face and tries to reassure me that my secret is safe. I hear the front door close and know that Tanner is inside. It's my cue to leave.

"Naw, I'm good. Really. I'll go grab a burger or something."

"But your dad took your money!"

"Not my stash he didn't." I grin, shaking my head at his silliness. "I'm smarter than that, Chris."

I leave his yard and walk down the street toward the falls, to my refuge. I'm a little less burdened inside, yet a little apprehensive that Chris might say something to his G-pa. Mostly, though, I'm just relieved to know that in minutes I'll be safe and alone for a while. I'm thinking my pop-top cans of supper are sounding pretty good right about now. Vienna sausages and pork-n-beans make my stomach rumble.

I reach the falls at dusk, and there are people on the footbridge. I hang around the shore, throwing rocks in the water while waiting for them to leave. Every time I glance their way, it seems they are just hanging out, talking and watching me. I move downstream under the bridge out of their view, hoping they'll get bored and move on. It works. I wait until they are on the street, then I cut back upstream to the falls. I do another check; all is clear. I disappear from this world into my crashing world of safety.

I light candles, make Kool-Aid and open cans. I eat with my fingers because I still don't have utensils. When I've finished, I lie back on my sleeping bag and try to read my book. I finally give up, toss it aside, and wonder if I could just live here in my cave. I think about Dad's face, the rage he has toward me, and how today he distanced himself enough from me to actually rob me. Most days he doesn't know or care if I'm around. I could easily live here and just pop in there from time to time, clean the house or leave messes when he's not there just so it looks like I'm still around. Sometimes, I could even sneak in through the back door, in the mornings before he's drunk, so he sees me around. I can shower while he's at work, or use the school showers. That worked last year in a bind. I just told coach that I had to go to work right after school and didn't have time to run home. I smile. This could actually work. I have an alarm on my watch so I wouldn't be late for school.

I roll on my side and reach for the rock that covers a hole I hide my coffee can bank in. I recount my seven hundred dollars. I dig in my pocket and pull out seventy-three cents. I toss it in the can. If I only buy burgers after our games at school when the team goes out, I should have enough to eat on for the school year. I do need to buy more clothes though. Shampoo, soap—that stuff I can take from the house. I'd need more than a hundred bucks every month to eat. I'm gonna have to keep my job at the deli a little longer. I let out a sigh. I hope Dad doesn't show up and make a scene. He wouldn't take my money in front of people, but it wouldn't stop him from forcing me into his truck where it's more private. It's worth it to me to try. Every day worked is forty more bucks, another week of food.

I crawl inside my sleeping bag, feeling good about my plan. It's not perfect, but it's something. I blow out the candles and let the roar of the falls carry me peacefully into dreamland.

Three

*I*t's been over a week now since the old man mugged me. That still sounds weird to me. No matter how many times I say it in my head, I can't get used to it. It's too dramatic even for my chaotic life. I've laid low from the homefront, and have been spending nights at the cave. I only go to the house to shower after Dad has left for work and before I go to the deli. I did clean the house once so Dad would think I'm still around, but the next time I showed up there, I saw he had trashed my room.

Today is payday, and I've been nervous all day, so I ask to leave early. I don't want to be around at closing in case Dad is hanging around waiting on me. I haven't seen him, but I feel him constantly, probably because I'm so tense waiting for him to pop up. I can't rely on my senses right now. It feels like he's waiting around every corner.

I go out the back door of the deli which opens to the delivery alley. That way I can leave unseen. I walk around the building and scan each row of parked cars. Dad's truck isn't here. I walk to the mall entrance and go the bank to cash my check. Next, I go the public restroom and stuff most of my money in my socks. I keep out enough to get more food and to hit the sales racks for school clothes. I make quick work of my clothes shopping and walk out with new shirts and a heavy coat that's last year's fashion. I head for the Food Mart.

I feel safer out away from the mall and like I dodged a bullet. I cut through town using streets that Dad wouldn't normally use. I start across a street when a car rips around the corner and bullies its way in front of me, barely missing me. It honks, and the driver yells something, then flips me off. It's Rod, from school, driving his mom's green Impala. What a jerk.

"Get on with your bad self, there, Hot Rod!" I yell at him. I hoof it to the cave.

Once I'm in my cave, I realize it's not such a great idea to have my clothes in here long term. The musty-cave smell isn't good for my social life; the one I do have these days. I decide to keep them at the house and just change when I shower there. I'll leave a couple of shirts here in plastic bags for emergencies. I pull the money from my socks and add it to my coffee can. $1050.73, enough to make it through nine months of school, if I'm careful. Anything I earn beyond this point is to make life more pleasant, not for survival. I wear the smile of pride and breathe a sigh of relief. I've made it. I'm actually doing this! I bundle up the clothes to take to the house. I'll drop them off before I meet Chris for hoops.

Later, back at my cave, I'm lying exhausted in my sleeping bag. A smile crosses my face as I think of all my accomplishments, especially that I beat Chris today! What an awesome day! He tried to say he wasn't on top of his game, but he was doing just fine. I'm getting better. I'm so glad he taught me his moves. I'm gonna rock it next year! I did take the sorry loser for a burger. My treat because I won, which feels way better than a loser's buy.

The mall is bustling with people. It's lunch time, and the deli is slammed. We've had a steady line of at least five people all day, and now that it's lunch time, the line is clear out the door. My boss is taking orders, and I'm slamming out sandwiches at a record pace. We keep glancing at each other and grinning because we really are on top of it today. We're just clicking, and everything is full speed ahead. She's calling out orders up to six or seven sandwiches ahead, and I'm maintaining, keeping it all straight. It's fun.

My heart jumps, I feel sick, and my hands begin to tremble. I instinctively know he is watching me. I look up from the prep line straight into his face. He is near the back of the line, standing to the side of the customers just inside the door glaring at me. For a brief second, I'm ashamed of him seeing me in my uniform. I swallow down the embarrassment and his title of 'fairy-boy.' I know that if I'm still here at closing, he'll be here to greet me. We stare at each other for a long moment. I'm paralyzed. He missed my payday, but he'll be here to collect today.

"Ian! Come on! T on rye, the works!"

I grab rye, slap on mayo, toss on turkey and every veggie on the line. I wrap it up, and when I look up again, Dad is gone.

The lunch rush is over, and the mall is slowing down in general. I clean the prep line, cut up veggies, and refill the line. Then I make a fake phone call and tell my boss there's been a family emergency. I tell her this is my last day of work and that I also need to leave early. I apologize for not giving notice and not finishing out the summer. I really do feel bad leaving her at such a busy time for the store. She tells me that it's fine, she'll get her baby sitter's brother to help out. She pays me for the time she owes me, puts it in an envelope inside a bag with a sandwich, chips and a soda. She gives me a hug and makes me promise to visit sometime.

Tears fill my eyes, because I really hoped to earn more cash, but also, because I really will miss her. Nobody else will click with her like I did today, and we both know it. I promise her I'll visit, and head for the back door. Before the door locks behind me, I'm regretting my decision. Maybe I could just avoid Dad and keep my job. As I think this, my feet keep moving forward. I hear the door click shut, and I keep walking. I pick up my pace, then run all the way to my cave.

She paid me in cash, instead of check, this time. Probably, because I only worked a couple of days since my last check. I pull out my coffee can and count out my money. She paid me a full two weeks' wages! Tax free too. Tears fall. I hear the echo of the back door shut on one of the few good people in my crazy world.

My can now holds $1670.73.

* * *

I've stayed hidden in my cave for four days now. I came out a few times to stretch my legs, but only briefly. I won't go into town, or near the house, which means I also haven't been to Chris's to practice. How long can I do this? What happens when school starts? Will the old man show up there? If he does, at least he can't knock me around there. This is such a mess. I don't understand why I can't just have a normal life. Just one more year is all I need to be on my own. Maybe I should just go for my G.E.D. and leave this town behind.

I rub my face; it feels dirty. I pull out my shaving kit and dig around for soap to wash my face. I can smell myself. I need a shower and clean clothes, which means that tomorrow morning I have to go to the house. I'll get my dirty clothes and make a trip to the laundromat too. A thought hits me. The laundromat is near the Boy's and Girl's Club. I can pay for a month's membership, and shower there! I'll never have to set foot in that house again! I can't believe I haven't thought of this before now. I only have four weeks until school starts, then I can shower there, every day after P.E. and even after practice a few times a week. I can make this work! I will make this work!

I wake from the night's chill and the roar of the Falls. It's barely light out, but I'm too cold to go back to sleep. It's already getting colder at night and harder to warm up in the mornings. I drink a soda, my last, and decide to start my day just so I can warm up by moving around. I grab my dirty clothes and stuff them into my garbage bag with handles. I slip down out of my cave and inch across the face of the rock wall.

My muscles tremble from cold and lack of use for the past four days and five nights. I reach the shore and stretch out every muscle. I pick up my bag and jog down quiet streets. As I approach my house, I see Dad's truck is still in the driveway. I sneak into Chris's backyard and wait for the sound of Dad's truck to drive by. I don't have to wait long. I hear him, then watch him roll by. I walk to the sidewalk and watch as he turns off our street on his way to work. I'm back in my old house in under a minute.

The place smells, and I have to hold my breath. It stinks of drunken breath, sweat, rotten trash and urine. This is so disgusting. Was it always like this? No, I think. I used to clean. The thought gives me some comfort. I go to my room. It looks like a tornado hit it. My clothes are ripped from hangers and thrown. Dresser drawers are pulled out and dumped. The mattress is off the box springs.

I smile. "Didn't find what you were looking for, did you?"

My foot crunches something. I look down and see shattered glass over the smiling face that I used to call Mom. I stare at it, remembering the times I've cried myself to sleep with it next to me on my pillow. It used to be a child's comfort to see her face. Now it does nothing for me or to me. I leave it where it lies, where it was thrown.

I gather up the clothes I want to keep and stuff them in my bag. I go to the bathroom and grab a new bar of soap, a nearly full bottle of shampoo, deodorant, and toothpaste. I stuff them in a bag and toss it into the bigger bag with my clothes. I planned on showering here, but I'm so disgusted by this place, that I just want to leave. I go into the kitchen and find clean utensils. There are no clean bowls or plates. I look around at the piles of rotting food-caked dishes and decide there is nothing else here for me. I go out the door, snag my ball from under the porch and head to the laundromat.

I go to the B and G Club while my clothes are in the washer. A cute girl gives me the grand tour of a privileged, paying member. I pay a month's dues, then use the shower. The tile is white and clean. It smells fresh in here. I smell fresh and feel brand-new. I slide my hygiene bag in a locker and pay the rent on that as I leave.

I watch my old familiar and new clothes, toss together in circles of hot air. I can't help but be excited. Me, Ian Oliver Taylor, actually has a pool, sauna, hot tub, and a weight room! This membership is the best idea I've had yet. I fold my clothes neatly, bag them up and take then to the Club. I stack them perfectly in my locker and smile at the rainbow of colors that will look the same next time I come here. It dawns on me that I have never had a safe place for my belongings. Definitely, not at home, and at the cave I have to check every time I go there to see if someone has found my hideaway. Even my locker at school is not really private. The teachers can go in anytime they want. This is the first time in my life that I have a place that is completely private and safe. I decide to buy my own lock to put on it so that if anyone here wants in, they'll have to cut the lock off.

I close the door and press my forehead against the cool metal and grin. I'll get a lock with a key to wear around my neck to always remind me that I have a private, safe place. I go to the hardware store where I buy a lock with a heavy key, and a silver braided chain to put it on.

I know the old man will either be at work or at Grady's until noon, at least. I decide to swing by Chris's to shoot some hoops. He'll probably stomp me; it's been so long since I've practiced. That'll be hard to live down.

I feel excited and good about my life. Dad is basically out of my life, I have my own place and cash to see me through. I realize if my boss hadn't paid me extra, I'd never be able to afford the Club membership. I'm so grateful to her. She has made my life so much nicer, and she has no idea how much she has improved it.

I'm proud of what I have accomplished. I have a pool! A sauna to take the chill off in the mornings! I touch the key around my neck and feel almost normal. No, better than normal. I am free!

I get to my street, no, Chris's street now, and start down the sidewalk. A deep sadness rolls over me instantly. It weighs down my shoulders and pushes through my chest and into my gut. I stop. I don't want to feel this, not now! My life feels too right, now. But, this is Chris's street, and he is my friend; I have to know if it's him. I hesitantly continue toward his house. I get closer and see a strange car in his driveway. Chris is sitting in the yard. I begin to move toward his house when I realize that's not just any car, it's the coroner's wagon! Oh, God.

I stop in my tracks and watch, on full alert. Chris stands as a gurney is brought out from the house. I assume it's old man Tanner. Chris doesn't need this. I listen with my heart wide open. I feel Chris's confusion, fear, sadness and guilt. I recognize all of it; it's familiar to me. It's the same pain as when my Mom left. Only Chris's is more complex, deeper, and has a finality to it. He has no hope of ever seeing his G-pa again.

I watch as the car pulls out and leaves the house. I don't know what to do. I'm not family, or close enough to him to share this time with him. I watch him stand alone, long after the coroner has gone. I feel him shutting down, blocking off his emotions. His heart is emptying out. He's like a hollow shell or a robot, as he moves toward the stairs. I wait and watch. Nobody is coming to be with him.

I walk up the stairs and face the door. I look through the window; he is sitting on the couch. I raise my hand to knock but realize the sound would be a rude intrusion. I pull my hand back and instead, reach for the door knob, turn it and walk in.

Chris is staring at the T.V., watching a black and white movie. He doesn't turn to see who walked in. He has the T.V. muted. The house is dead quiet. I move toward the couch and slowly sit. I don't speak. What could I say to make it better? Nothing. We sit in silence for hours as he stares at the scenes in black and white. I just sit and let my soul tell his, 'You're not alone.'

His silent movie, *Frankenstein*, ends, and I feel the need to do something. Anything to move him out of this robotic state he's in. It's like the power light is on, but the program is deleted. I can't feel anything from him but emptiness. It scares me. Even animals have something I can sense.

I walk upstairs, to create movement in the room's air. Maybe a gentle stir will nudge him back. I get to the top and see what must be G-pa's room. The door is open. I close it. I don't want Chris to see it if he comes up here. I wander until I find Chris's room. I pull the comforter from his bed, hoping some familiar warmth will be some comfort to him. Maybe he's in shock.

I carry it downstairs and see he hasn't moved. He stares at a snow-filled screen. I lay the comforter over his shoulders and guide him against the couch's back. Maybe food will wake up his senses. I go to the kitchen and see five beers in a six-pack. Dad's face flashes in my mind. I throw the image out. I take two of the beers to the couch, and we drink. Chris makes a face on his first sip.

Again, I think of Dad and say, "I hear it goes down easier with practice."

By Chris's second beer, I have only drunk half of mine. But he is talking now. Progress. I switch out his empties with my full ones when he's not paying attention. By the time he has finished all of them, he is talking freely, telling me the secrets that keep him a prisoner. He tells me of finding his twin brother murdered, what he saw in detail, and I see why he went pale that day the blood sprayed from my nose.

I tear up at the knowledge of another person enduring such pain and reliving such horror just to help me with a bloody nose. Nobody has ever sacrificed part of themselves for me before. I never knew until now, that it was absent from my life. This opens up a new dimension of the world to me. Suddenly, it's me who isn't alone here. Chris has no idea what he has done for me. He has made me see that I've been living life alone. I want to cry . . . but I won't.

Momma
You loved me once, I remember thinkin',
But now my memories are rotten, stinkin'.

—Ian

Daddy
Loved you once,
Hated you twice,
To be your son comes with a price.

—I. O. Taylor

Four

I sit in the back pew, overwhelmed by the emotions of all these people. So much loss! It feels like a rogue wave drowning me. Chris's G-pa lays in a coffin, the center of everyone's attention. Attention. It's the one thing I'm sure he never sought out in life.

Chris and his mom are sitting together up front on a hard, wooden bench. They are alone like anchored pilings of a dock during this tsunami. This custom of ours seems odd to me, that out of respect, people aren't allowed to sit next to them, hold their hands or whisper kind words to them while they say their goodbyes.

The service ends, and I leave before anyone sees that I'm here. I don't know what to say to Chris or his mom or to any of these friends of old man Tanner's. I never really knew him, only of him. I came today just to thank him for his love and kindness to my friend, Chris. Also, to fill an empty seat in case there were a lot of them empty. There weren't.

I walk down quiet streets that would normally be active with people running errands, but most everybody in town is at the church. People who aren't are buried in their work, oblivious to all the grief that fills the air. I end up at the park. I have nowhere to go or anything to do. I sit in the grass and absorb the physical and psychic quiet.

Rod's mom's Impala is parked in the far corner, semi-hidden among the trees. Rod is more than likely over there smoking weed, thinking he is incognito. He's such a mess. What a waste of life.

I lie back in the cool grass and watch the clouds overhead. I think of old man Tanner cruising around in that old truck of his and realize that I'll miss seeing him around. His death has changed Deer Falls forever. The simple comfort of familiarity from seeing that old-timer running his errands is gone. The reassurance of consistency has been chipped away, and never again will our souls feel the comfort of his presence.

My heart hurts for Chris. I want to help him somehow, but I don't know how to reach inside and pull out the pain that he carries. I picture my hand dipping into his chest scooping out handfuls of sticky, black tar, then reaching deeper and pulling out a thickened mass of old pain from his brother's death. I wish it were that easy.

Out of nowhere, my chest explodes in alarm! I sit up, looking for any sign of Dad. I only see the Impala snuck away under low hanging tree limbs. The burst hits my chest again—it's fear and panic in full force. I jump up and bolt for the Impala. I hear a scream and tear open the door. Rod has a girl trapped, lying on her, and they are slapping each other.

I grab him by the waistband of his jeans and drag him off her. She is crying and kicking at him as I pull him clear of the car. I smell the reek of weed and the stench of alcohol breath. It's as if I close my eyes and when I open them again, my fists are flying into Rod's face. My eyes open again and I see blood smeared from his nose. The next time my eyes open, Jen, the girl who is with him, is pulling at me, yelling, "Ian! Stop it! You'll kill him!'

I look in Jen's face and see her smeared make-up, her disheveled clothes, and I hit him one more time as hard as I can. He goes out like a light, lying limp on the ground.

Jen is crying and pulling at my shirt. My hands hurt, they're covered in blood, mine and Rod's. I stand up, put my arm around Jen, and she curls into me, trembling and sobbing in my chest, which just makes me want to go rounds on him again.

"Jen, what were you doing with that piece of trash?"

Between sobs, she says, "He said he'd give me a ride uptown, but then he pulled in here to smoke first." She tries to say more but cries instead.

"Come on, let's get you home."

"No! No, Ian! Oh, God. I can't let anyone know what happened here!" She wipes black tears from her face, smearing her make-up even more.

I look at her, confused. I feel her fear, but it's a different fear now. Is she afraid of her family? Hers is the all-American dream family. Hers could be on one of those commercials having game night. I study her face, her eyes plead with me.

"All right, fine. We'll go to the falls and clean up.

I look at my knuckles again; they feel like they're on fire. I take another look at Rod. He's a slumped puddle of disgusting flesh, with a bloodied face and still out cold. I guide Jen with an arm around her shoulder, and we start for the falls, leaving Rod where he lies. I sneak another look at my hand and am sickened by the thought that I'm just like my old man. I didn't even know what I was doing!

Jen and I walk about ten minutes, and I can still hear the tremble in her voice. I pull her in close to me again as we walk. She trembles under my arm. Rod scared her bad. My heart aches for her, knowing that some of her naïve trust in the world is gone. She has lost some of the innocence that makes it possible to imagine her as one of my 'game night families.' The thought makes me angry. Why is there so much pain in the world? Why are people so cruel? Tears fill my eyes. I try to hold them back, but a gasping sob escapes me.

Jen stops abruptly and looks into my face. She grabs both of my arms, "Ian! Are you hurt?" She searches my face.

"No, Jen. It's just . . . what I did back there, what Rod tried to do, all of it. Ya know?"

"Ian, you did a good thing back there. He was drunk and stoned. I didn't realize how bad off he was until I was in his car, or I never would have gotten in. I'm so stupid sometimes. I don't even know why I got in. I can't stand him. I was running late to meet the girls . . ." Tears course down her face again. "I'm just so stupid!"

I grab her shoulders; her face is buried in her hands as she cries. "Hey, Jen, you are not stupid. Far from it."

She looks into my eyes, and I bend close to her face and stare into her eyes. "You're a good person, Jen; just too trusting." My words cut deep into me as I feel I am tearing away more of her blind innocence. "You just trusted the wrong person."

Her phone rings out a playful tune. She pulls it from her purse. It's the friends she was going to meet. She texts them, telling them something came up, and she is out. Her phone sounds out again, and she turns it off without answering.

I take a deep breath, preparing for the worst. "Jen, are you . . .?" I sigh. "I mean, did he . . .?"

She shakes her head no. "He would have, though, if you hadn't stopped him." The pitch of her voice goes high. "Thank you." With those words, she sobs freely. I pull her into a tight hug and hold her.

I whisper into the top of her head, "You are more than welcome, Jen." Tears sting my eyes again.

When she gains control of her sobs, we continue to walk.

"Jen, you know we have to tell someone about this or Rod will keep doing it until he does hurt someone. Maybe he already has."

"Ian . . . please. I'm begging you. You don't understand!"

My anger flairs. "Understand what, Jen?" I grab her arm and spin her to face me. I hold her in both hands, too hard. She winces from the pain, and ducks down into herself to get away from me.

"Jen, he could have hurt you! Bad!"

She nods. "I know, I know! I'll never let myself get in that situation again Ian! I promise! Just please don't say anything," she begs. "Please, Ian." I loosen my grip on her arms.

Her tone turns angry. "This is me! My life, Ian. My choice! And I don't want anyone, anyone to know!"

I shake my head at her. I can't believe she's letting Rod, the bully, the animal torturer, and now near rapist, just slide on this! "Jen, your parents aren't going to be mad at you!"

She looks at me with pure disgust in her eyes. "Is that what you think this is about, Ian? That's soooo not it!"

She starts walking again, and I keep pace.

"What then?"

Her eyes reflect a heaviness that's bigger than her small frame of a body. She covers her face again, and cries so deep and so hard it breaks my heart.

I guide her to the curb, and we sit. I put my arms around her, holding her, rocking her, letting her cry. When her sobs quiet to hiccups, she begins to talk.

"It's my parents, Ian. They're talking divorce. If they found out this happened, they'd blame each other. I'm the only reason Dad is still living at home. If they knew about this, Ian, it would turn into a fight that would destroy our family. It would be me, my stupidity that sends our family over the edge. I can't live with that, Ian, I just couldn't bear it."

"Jen—"

"Ian! I don't want to talk about it right now. I just want to get to the river, wash my face and think this whole mess through. Okay?"

I nod my head, and we continue to the falls. We don't speak, the only sound is our feet slapping pavement and an occasional sniff from Jen. We crunch through gravel as we cut off the street to the river. It's the falls' roar that drowns our pain and anger as we bend to wash our faces and hands.

The cold water burns my raw knuckles at first, but once the skin loosens, I can make a numbed fist. We sit under the footbridge where people can't see us and let the sun warm our river-cold skin.

Jen breaks the silence. "My dad, he is such a gentle, kind man . . . he adores me. My mom, she is just so cool, ya know?" She snorts out an embarrassed laugh. "I know, I'm sixteen and not supposed to think like this about my parents. But, I can't help it; I do. They tried to have a baby for years, even went to those fertility places. They spent a mound of cash just trying to have a child. Then a friend knew someone who had a pregnant teen. They got their miracle; they adopted me."

"I am the center of their world. If my dad knew what happened to me today, it would shatter him. It would kill a part of him inside. We would change; he wouldn't see me as his innocent little girl anymore.

218

His eyes would be different when he looked at me. They really would blame each other outwardly, but blame themselves inwardly. It would be the final straw that breaks my family."

"Give your parents some credit. They're smart; they know there are Rods in the world."

"I'm trying to explain to you—" She sighs. "My family is so fragile right now. Mom let me go alone. Dad hasn't let me get my driver's license yet. They would blame each other. Right now, they just need a little time to work their issues out, without this mess being added to it. I know that in a while, things will be back to normal."

"This isn't something you can just out of the blue report later when it's more convenient. If you don't do this now, you lose credibility. This is a now or never kind of thing."

"Listen, Ian." She lowers her voice. "Rod tried to destroy me today." Her breathing grows rapid with her anger. She grits her teeth. "I will not let him destroy my family. I won't!" She stares at me, and I know she means it.

Life is so complicated sometimes. What seems black and white or right and wrong can shift so easily. I'm angry that Rod will get away with more of his cruelty, yet I feel just as strongly about Jens's right to tell or not and her right to protect those she loves like I protected her.

"Okay, I won't say anything because you've asked me not to, and you have the right to keep what happens to you private if that's what you want. But, for the record, I think you're wrong about losing your family over this. I actually think it would cause you all to stand together and fight. However, it's your life, and I respect that."

She lets out a long sigh. "Thank you, Ian."

"You need to understand something, though, I will not let this happen again. If Rod tries anything with you, or any other girl again, I'm taking him down. He gets a free pass this time, but he won't be so lucky if he does it again. That's a promise."

"Ian?"

I look at her.

"I believe you."

We sit quietly, listening to the falls. Ironically, gentle, peaceful butterflies drink from the river's edge.

"Ian?"

"Yeah?"

"Do you . . ." She clears her throat. "Do you think I caused this? Ya know, am I a tease?"

"No, Jen. You aren't one of those girls. You just trusted a jerk."

She lets out a sigh and nods her head. "He told me I was."

"He lied."

* * *

After Jen is calm and safe at home, I head to the cave. I'm so angry at Rod, my dad and myself that I'm afraid of what I'll do next if somebody crosses me. It's best to go hide out for a while and cool off.

I hear tires slowly crunching the pebbles in the street. I expect it to be Rod. I'm ready for round two. I spin around and see that it's Deputy Dupree. The car stops.

"Ian," He says, as he nods hello.

I don't say anything. He gets out of his car and walks over to me.

"There's, uh, been a complaint made, Ian." He looks at my torn knuckles. "Can you tell me where you were an hour ago?"

I stay silent.

He nods his head because he already knows. "Listen, I don't know why you worked Rod over; I can't honestly say I'm too broken-up over it either. But, his momma brought him down to the station and has filed a complaint against you."

"Deputy—"

He raises his hand to stop me. "Now, Ian, I don't want you to say a word, not yet. Let's take a ride to the station and see if we can't just hash this thing out civil-like." He looks me square in the eyes. "All right?"

I nod my head.

He opens the rear door, and I slide in. As we pull out, tears fill my eyes. This day just keeps getting deeper and deeper.

"There he is! Isn't that him? Let me at him! You're nothing but a juvenile delinquent! Aren't you? Well, buster, now you're gonna pay!" Rod's mom screams at me the entire time Dupree walks me through the main room of the station.

An officer holds her back to keep her from jumping on me. I see Rod quietly sitting in a chair staring at his hands, while his mom flips out. Rod's face is a mess. His eyes are purple, one is swollen shut, and his lips are split open. He has knots and bruises all over his face.

I feel shock and shame at what my hands have done until I remember Jen's face when she got out of his car. I see her trembling and crying, then her stoic anger while protecting her family, and I become infuriated again. My face turns hot as I stare at Rod. Dupree see's this and pushes me forward, moving me quickly to a small room.

I cast a glance over my shoulder at Rod and remember distant, long-forgotten demands of my dad; 'Stick up for yourself,' 'Never leave on the losing end,' 'It's not over 'til the guy is a K.O.' I wonder if Rod's dad tells him the same thing. I wonder if I'm turning into my old man. I wonder if I even care anymore because I know a new side of me was born today.

Deputy Dupree sits me in a chair and closes the door. He sighs a long breath.

"All right, Ian, first I need to read you your rights. You're being charged with assault and battery."

He does that, then asks if I want to call my dad or an attorney. I shake my head.

"So, what happened here, Ian?"

I stare at my mangled knuckles, then at the floor. "He was forcing himself on a girl. I stopped it."

I look at Dupree. His eyes are wide, and his mouth is gaped open, then he pinches his lips shut until they turn white. I realize that he thought this was going to be some stupid name-calling session gone rough.

"What girl?" I hear the anger in his voice.

"I can't tell you that."

He hits the table and yells, "Why the h—not!"

"Because I don't know who she is!"

He looks me in the eye. "Bull spit! Tell me!"

"I can't tell you, Dupree! She asked me not to. I gave her my word."

"Now look here, Ian. That's very sweet and touching, but I don't think you realize how much trouble you're in here. If this is self-defense or defense of another, then the D.A. will drop the charges. But think about this realistically. How can we believe you saved a girl when you won't tell who she is?"

"Well, ya know those scratches on Rod's face? Any marks I left won't be claw marks."

Dupree's mouth twitches the start of a smile, but he stops it. "Enough now, Ian; who's the girl?"

I stay silent.

"Ian, tell me so I can get her statement, and then all of this is over. I'd love nothing more than to send that blonde hurricane out there packing."

I chuckle. "Guess I won't be shopping at the Food Mart for a while, huh?"

Dupree leans back in his chair and rubs his face. "What if you call her, and tell her to call in as an anonymous witness?"

My face drops. I hate that he's trying to play me. I thought he was on my side. I glare at him. "Just how stupid do you think I am? That would be traced, and you'd have her in here in five minutes! Cheap shot, Dupree! We're done here!" I jump up and shove my wrists at him. "Take me to lock-up!"

"Sit down and listen." He waves me back down in my seat and leans forward like we're co-conspirators like we're on the same page, but I'm not buying it. "It wouldn't be you breaking your word. It would be me investigating."

I sit back down in my chair, close my eyes and begin to hum a tune. I'm done.

"Ian! You could get years for this!"

My eyes pop open. I stare levelly at him. He's being honest, I know, because I feel his wave of sympathy roll over me.

"I'm trying to put the right person in jail here. I'm trying to help you, kid. Trying to help the girl!"

"Then you better do your job and break-down that lump of—!" I stop short and continue to hum.

He jumps up, jerks me from my chair and cuffs me, then takes me to lock-up.

We walk past Rod and his mom as we make our way to the hallway that leads to the cells. She makes a remark I don't catch, but Rod reeks of guilt and fear, stronger than the alcohol he drank, or weed he smoked. He stinks up the room with his guilt. Everyone but his mom sees it clearly.

Dupree slams a metal, barred door shut, and I find myself standing in a cell alone.

"You're segregated by yourself because you're a minor, Ian. It's for your protection. Think about what that means while you sit here."

The cell is filthy and smells of old vomit. The concrete floor slants to the center where a drain is. Why is that here? For flooding? I sit on a metal slab that's bolted to the wall. I'm puzzled as to why the bed has holes drilled in it. Then I realize this is the drunk tank, and the holes keep the drunks from drowning in their vomit! My eyes go to the drain in the floor, and I envision them hosing down the room. I jump up and try to count how many times the old man has slept it off in this very room.

I look around. Paint is chipped and worn from every surface in the room. The bars are rubbed clear of paint down to the metal at hand height. There are disgusting pictures scratched into the walls, along with names, dates and crude poems.

I sit on the floor, my back against the wall, and am just dozing off when the jangle of heavy keys brings me back to reality. A female officer smiles, then keys open the door. In an instant, I'm excited that I'm being released. It's about time!

"We need to get your fingerprints and take your picture, Ian.

Really? This is actually happening to me? Dupree is leaving me here? Tears fill my eyes as disappointment overcomes me. I send them back where they came from. I suck it up and feel my heart go stiff.

The officer walks me down a hall and into a room with a machine for prints, a camera, and monitors that show the cells. I see four blobs of orange on the screen before she moves me to the fingerprint scanner.

"We called your dad. I'm sure he'll be here tomorrow to get you out once the judge sets bail."

My heart races. "But, I told Dupree not to contact him!"

She smiles at me like I'm a child scared of being grounded. "It's the law, Ian. We have to notify your parents."

Another deception of Dupree's! The one person I need to trust can't be trusted. My heart grows a little stiffer, a little tougher. My soul says, "Fine," and I become even more determined to survive.

I spend the night in the same cell, but now I have a flat air mattress and a smelly, gray, wool blanket. I'm dressed in orange coveralls, plastic sandals, and am wearing a plastic I.D. bracelet in case I get lost.

The next morning, I'm cuffed and shuffled off to the courthouse. We go through non-descript doors that look like closet doors, which lead us through secret halls that feel like narrow passages between the real walls, and that the public doesn't know exist. I feel like a guarded rat in a maze.

The judge set bail for fifty dollars because I'm a minor and a low flight risk. He doesn't know I've been a flight risk my entire life. I offer to pay the bail, and I hear muffled chuckles behind me. He tells me that my parents must do it so I can be released to them. He isn't aware that I only have one parent and that he's MIA. I'm taken back to jail, and the metal gate slams. Packing my heart down firmer.

It's three days before the female officer smiles, jangles the keys, and says, "You've been sprung, Ian."

Panic hits my chest like a blow. This means that Dad is here. My protectors are feeding me to the wolf. I change into my street clothes and am escorted to the front part of the station. I'm trembling.

"Scared?" The officer asks.

I don't answer, I feel like I'm going to throw-up.

"Don't worry, I've seen this dozens of times over the years. It's always the same. Your dad loves you, he just left you here to teach you a lesson." She smiles at me.

I wonder what lesson that could possibly be. I also wonder how drunk he is. I start my calculations. It's early evening, so . . . They wouldn't release me to him if he was too drunk. Would they?

We round the corner, and I see him. He's mad. I know that anger in his eyes. He's playing nice in front of the cops, but I know what's coming. I glance at the officer. She's smiling until she sees my face. Her smile drops a little, and she studies me. I look away. She tells Dad my court date, and we leave the station.

"You cost me money, you little—!"

I wish his name for me were true, then I wouldn't be his son. We get in the truck, and I can smell alcohol on his breath. He grabs a bottle from under the seat and chugs. I want to run, but I'm too close to the cop shop.

He drives. He drinks. He yells.

"The cops called me at work and told me they had you. I told them to let you rot in there. Then, today, after I worked all day and go to relax at Grady's, that little fairy-boy, Dep-u-ty Du-pree, walks up in front of God and everybody and announces my business! Told me to spring you out! Telling me how to raise my own blood!"

I feel a moment of satisfaction that one, dad was embarrassed, and two, that it was Dupree that did it. Maybe he is on my side.

"Wipe that smirk off your face before I knock it off for you" He screams this with spit flying. He empties the bottle and throws it in the street.

I consider jumping out and running at a stop sign, but we're rolling again before I can get the nerve up.

He grabs the front of my shirt, along with some skin, as we pull into the driveway. He drags me across the seat and out the driver's side while yelling that he'll be getting the bail money and gas money wasted on me. I struggle to get away, but he's too strong and not sloppy drunk. He pulls me up the stairs, shoves me in the house and kicks the door shut. Then he does what he does best.

I wake to groaning and am surprised that it's me doing it. Chris is in my face, calling my name. I startle and look around frantically for Dad.

"Ian, it's okay, he's gone. Can you stand up?"

Chris helps me to my feet, and with an arm over his shoulder, and his arm around my waist to hold me up, we stumble to his house.

He sets me on the couch, then locks the door.

"I saw him drive you home. When I saw him leave a little later, I came over. You were in the newspaper, Ian. Assault?"

I don't respond.

He brings me a wet rag and ice, then sits beside me. My ribs hurt, as he sits. I sense his anger in my gut, but in my chest, I feel his heavy heart. He is crying inside. For me. Ian Oliver Taylor.

"My God, how could he do this to you?"

"Deja vu, huh?" I try to laugh it off. My speech is distorted by a painful and split lip. I wonder if I look as bad or worse than Rod now. "Where's your mom?"

"She had to go handle some stuff about the house. You know, G-pa left it to her. We're staying here. I'm not going back to the city."

I smile, which makes my mouth hurt. "Dang, and I only told you about the old man 'cuz you were leavin'."

"Ian, I think you should report him, have him arrested. I really do."

I shake my head and snort out a laugh. I look at Chris's face, he's serious.

"Look, man, he'd be locked up a few weeks at most, I'd go to a foster home, and the next time he saw me on the street . . ." I sigh. "It's better not to tell anyone. Really. Trust me on that."

From in my cave, I sense the light,
But something lurks that gives me fright.

My heart can see the beckoned beams,
To ride them may bring all my dreams.

My tears are cold, they miss my life.
My soul betwixt pleasure and strife.

While I am safe within this hole,
It's my courage that has been stole.

To ride the bow means I could die,
And yet to live, I have to try

From in my cave, I sensed the light,
My dreams gave strength, my fears took flight

—Ian Sense/In O Sense

Five

It's been five days since the old man bailed me out of jail, and 'taught me a lesson.' I've been holed-up in my cave for a much-needed break from the crazy world. I've only been out to clean up a little. I feel like a bear in hibernation. I need to roam. I need a shower.

I stand in the sink area of the Club and look at my face under the bright lights. My hair is growing out of control, my skin is pale like I've lost my natural tan except where the bruises are. My ribs aren't sore anymore, but the skin on my sides and back is still discolored. My brown eyes are the only thing about me that seem normal, and even they look tired. Tired from too little sleep and too much life. I tell myself the bruises don't look too bad, that people will think it's from the fight with Rod.

I take a swim and let my muscles stretch out and come back to life. The cool water feels good pressing against my body. I do some speed laps that refresh me. I can almost face the world again. I hit the shower and smell human. I grab a new shirt and clean cargo shorts from my locker. I smile; everything is exactly as I left it. I toss the key hanging around my neck under my shirt and head out.

I'm nervous, but it's a normal nervous, not my inner alarm going off as I near Chris's house. I jog up his front steps and knock, watching both directions of the street for Dad's truck to ride up any second. Chris answers the door, grins and snags up his ball.

We only practice for an hour before I'm tired.

"You're turning into a wimp, Ian! I like it!"

I grab the ball from him and head off court in the direction of the burger joint. "I need food. My treat."

Between mouthfuls, Chris fills me in on what he's been up to.

"Mom and I are fixing up the house. Making minor repairs, painting, that kind of stuff. Well, I am. Mom just runs around finding more repairs to do." We laugh. "I need help, man. I really do."

"I'm there. What can I do?"

Chris laughs. "You can babysit Mom so she stays off my back, then I can actually get something done."

"Uh . . . no."

"Well, I had to try." He laughs. "I'm pulling off wallpaper downstairs, painting inside and out, replacing the weather-stripping around the doors and re-caulking all the windows. Oh, and assembling a kit for a backyard swing."

I stare at him. "You? You're doing all of that? By yourself?"

"Yeah, and in two and a half weeks before school starts."

"Wow. Well, do ya 'spose we should start with the swing so your mom is out of the way?"

"Like tonight? Now?" Chris grins.

"Let's do this."

We jog back to Chris's house, practicing our cool fake-out passes. I feel normal again, useful like I have a purpose by repairing some small corner in this crazy world. It feels good to laugh, to be a part of something. But I stay alert to my surroundings, watching for Dad to pop up.

Turns out that old man Tanner has a work shed piled deep with old chests full of every tool made since 1902! Chris and I scrounge around looking for tools made in the last decade that we recognize so we can put the swing together.

"So, Ian, how's it going? At home, I mean." He asks in a quiet, voice.

I stand up from digging in a box and look over at him. His expression is one of trepidation. He doesn't want to pry, but he's truly concerned. I shrug my shoulders, and he nods, accepting that it's none of his business.

"Well . . ." he says, trying to change the subject and erase the awkward moment.

"I haven't been home, Chris. Not since he mugged me."

He stares at me puzzled. "Where have you been then?"

"I . . . I have a place."

"What? Like an apartment?" He's on the verge of being impressed.

I chuckle. "Not exactly, but it's safe."

"Well, if you . . . ya know, you can stay here if you ever need to. Mom will just think it's a slumber party."

I laugh. "Thanks, I think."

"You're eating, right?"

"Usually," I say with a grin.

"Well, I can easily arrange meals while we work on the house. Mom wouldn't suspect a thing, and it wouldn't be a problem at all."

I nod. He's embarrassed to offer, and I'm embarrassed to accept. I take the tools out to the yard.

"Hey, Chris, where are we setting this swing up?"

He points to the neighbor's yard and laughs.

"Boys! I am so impressed! Look at what a wonderful job you've done here!" Chris's mom looks surprised as she walks from her car to the now assembled swing. "Can I sit on it? Is it ready?"

Chris gestures an invite to sit, and she does, carefully. She relaxes and begins to swing gently while sneaking peeks at the bolts for added assurance.

Chris sits next to her, wearing a proud, beaming smile. She hugs him and giggles like a young girl. I can't help but laugh. This is what a real family feels like. I give them their moment and start gathering up tools.

Chris jumps up to help me. "Hey, Mom, we're starving! We don't want burgers or pizza either. We want a real meal!"

"Well, all right. How about fried chicken, mashed potatoes and gravy? There's also cake and . . ." she cocks an eyebrow at Chris, "maybe some ice cream left?"

My stomach gives a loud cheer, and Ms. T. says, "Oh my!" She jumps up to start dinner. "Give me forty-five minutes, guys."

"Oh, by the way, Mom, Ian is spending the night tonight. We plan on working late." Chris looks at me, and I give a nod.

"Honey, that's a lot to do in one day. If you wear him out the first day, he'll never come back!"

"Depends on how good your chicken is, Ms. T."

"Blue ribbon status, Ian. Don't you go anywhere!" She laughs as she enters the house.

"So, I figure if we get the caulking and weather-stripping done tonight, we can have Mom rent a power washer for the outside tomorrow. We should get that done before the weather changes on us. What do you think?"

"I think you don't give a guy a chance to catch his breath."

"I'm afraid if you get your wind, you'll say no."

We hunt up scrapers and putty knives from the shed and go inside the house. Chris pulls out a bag with tubes of caulking and two guns. I cut the tip off a tube and put it in the gun, then look at Chris, he has the other one ready.

"So, tell me, Chris, exactly how long ago did you plan on me helping?" I ask, pointing at the two guns.

He laughs, and Ms. T. answers from the kitchen. "Oh, he knew last week, Ian."

"Really. Last week," I say shaking my head. Chris gives me a cheap smile and shrugs his shoulders.

We work well together and have the living room windows done by the time Ms. T. calls us for dinner.

Over dinner, we discuss our game plan on how best to finish everything before the summer is over. The next two weeks will be non-stop during daylight hours. I'm thinking these two are dreaming if they think we can make it in time.

Ms. T. asks, "Ian, do you have time to do this? It's a lot of work. What will your parents say?"

"I just have my dad, Ms. T. He doesn't care." I glance at Chris and see that he caught the irony of my comment.

"Well, I think we should pay you for your help. Something other than dinner."

"That's not necessary, I'm happy to help."

"Nonsense. I'd be paying anyone else thousands to do this."

"There's no sense in arguing with her, Ian, once she's got her mind set on something, she won't let it go, 'til you're exhausted and give in."

"At least we can help with school clothes. Have you shopped yet?" she asks.

"A little."

"Well, it's settled then, you boys get this all done in time, and I'll take you both shopping. No pressure;" she laughs, "you have two weeks."

"Hmm . . ." Chris and I both say at the same time.

I eat, feeling safe, secure and ecstatic that I'll be able to save all of my stashed money for the school year. This is way better than I thought. Reality hits again, and I realize that Chris and his mom don't know that I could be going to jail in three weeks. I'm more determined than ever to have this job finished before school starts. Then I'll just fade back into the shadows for a while. Maybe a long while.

* * *

During the week that it took us to water blast then paint the outside, we only messed up twice. We painted half a wall with trim color, and then Chris fell off the ladder. He didn't get hurt bad, but Ms. T. freaked out. I thought our project was a done deal, but we got her calmed down, sat her in her swinging chair and convinced her we could do the job without killing ourselves. We finish with paint-streaked hair and all bones still intact.

At dinner, I ask Chris, "So, how did it feel to fly?"

"Smooth, like I was born for it."

Ms. T. chokes on her food.

Chris says, "You know, the outside was a little tougher than I thought it would be, but we did it." He raises his glass in a cheer.

He's right, and it feels awesome to know that we actually did do it. We only have the inside to paint now. Ms. T. finished pulling down the wallpaper, so we're right on schedule.

* * *

I can't believe school starts in ten days. Ms. T. is good as her word and is taking us shopping today before we start the inside painting. We'll take the day off tomorrow, too. She said even the devil takes Sunday off because it's too much work fighting all those prayers in church!

We hit the first few stores in the mall, and I feel awkward. I mean, how much should I spend? Can they really afford this? Also, Ms. T. is used to buying two of everything from when Chris's brother was alive, so she keeps pulling duplicates, but different colors, off the racks for us.

Chris keeps trying to steer her away from doing it by making excuses why he or I can't wear an item. He finally pulls her aside and mumbles, "Mom, um, Ian and I don't want to dress alike."

I know she didn't realize what she was doing, it was automatic for her, something she'd done for seventeen years. I feel her wave of shock as realization sets in, then her grief rolls through her. She does a good job of hiding the extent of her pain. She laughs at herself, she's embarrassed at her flub. I feel Chris's void as he is face to face with the hard, cold fact that he and his mom still have a long way to go to get ahead of this pain. He realizes they share and will continue to share a hundred moments and setbacks, just like this one.

I watch as their eyes meet, in a known and shared pain. They both straighten their backs, stand a little taller, take a deep breath and smile. I think to myself, it's in their family blood—this strength they have. I am proud to call them friends and lucky to be included in their inner circle. They have opened their hearts and home to me this past week. I practically live with them or have been.

Ms. T. doesn't ask questions about Dad or suggest that I go home, and I don't bring any of it up. We just naturally evolve into me being in their home. It's become the norm. I'm careful not to hang out in front of the house, though, in case Dad drives by.

I hear his truck every day, twice a day. That's when my spine freezes, and I wait, scared that next, I'll hear his stomp and stagger on the porch. I don't know what I'll do if that day comes. To run would leave the Tanners in danger. Also, the cops would get involved. To go with him would be . . . well, not good.

We leave the mall loaded down with everything imaginable. Ms. T. was not missing a thing. She even bought cologne and a stud earring for Chris. They tried to talk me into getting my ear pierced. They laughed when I told them I was too chicken. Really, though, I was worried what Dad would do if he saw it. He thinks only fairy boys wear those. I did get a cool chain for my locker key though. Once we get back to Chris's house and haul in our bounty, I slip over to my old house.

Dad isn't here, so I do my part to make it look like I'm still hanging around. Usually, I toss things around so it looks like I still live here. I'll leave empty food wrappers in the living room, a half-full glass, a cup, and even a damp towel in the bathroom. It's fast work, in and out, so I won't get caught here when he comes home.

Today my gut feels ill-at-ease. I'm on high alert, walking like a thief in my own house. The house is so still, so quiet that I jump when the refrigerator clicks on. I shake it off and grab up dirty dishes from around the house to wash. I put Dad's dirty clothes that are heaped on the bathroom floor, in the hamper. I trade out the washcloths and towels for clean ones. I run the shower for a minute to leave it damp, appearing as if I used it. I scoop up scattered newspapers from the living room floor and stuff them in the trash and take it out to the can, then pull the can to the curb for pickup tomorrow morning. I run up the front stairs and grab the mail from the mailbox on my way back in and set it on the coffee table. I make my bed, toss a book on it to make it look like I've been home reading and leave the bathroom and kitchen lights burning as I go out the back door.

My gut tells me Dad is just around the corner; I know he'll be here any minute. I get to the front of the house and am startled by Jen standing on the porch.

"Jen! What are you doing here?" I walk up the steps and take her hand, guiding her off the porch. "Come on, I was just heading out." My heart pounds with fear, knowing Dad will pull up any second.

"Oh, okay."

"Jen, you can't come here, to my house. What do you want?" My tone comes off as anger, but it's not anger, it's fear. "I mean, I'm hardly ever here. If my dad's truck is here, don't knock on the door. He hates company."

Her eyes tell me that she doesn't understand. Our lives are so different.

She never even considered life with an abusive dad or worried what he might do to her friends.

"So, how are you doing? Wait, Rod hasn't . . ."

"No, but I heard you were arrested and that you could go to jail for this!"

"Jen, don't worry about that, okay? It's all going to work out. We have to believe that." I tell her this even though I'm not convinced myself. "Listen, they aren't going to throw me in jail for a fist fight. They just aren't."

"But they already did, Ian!"

"That was only because Rod's mom raised a stink and I ticked off Deputy Dupree because I wouldn't give him your name. Really, it's going to be okay."

"Dad saw all this in the paper. He said you could go to jail for a year! I told him that I knew both of you and that you were a good person." She looks down at the ground and mumbles, "I'm supposed to stay away from you."

My heart sinks at being seen as a hoodlum-type. The guy that parents warn their kids about. I wonder if all adults will view me that way, especially those who can send me to jail.

"Jen, don't worry about your dad seeing us talk, I'll keep my distance. As far as a year in jail goes, well, I've never been in trouble before, and everyone knows what a pain Rod is. They aren't going to lock me away."

"Well, just to be sure, can't you tell them you were protecting some girl you don't know?"

I grin. "I did. Besides, is there any girl in this town that any of us don't know?"

"Well, someone from out of town then. I don't think I can live—"

"Stop already! It's going to be all right! Okay?"

She nods her head but isn't convinced any more that I am.

I put my arm around her shoulder and lead her away from my house. I feel her stiffen under my arm at the same time I see a green Impala come down the street. It's Rod.

"You're okay," I tell her. Rod makes an obscene gesture toward Jen, and I take out after him. He hits the gas, and the only damage I manage is to slap the trunk of his car. I get back to Jen and see her brush a tear away.

"Ian, I have to go. I'm meeting the girls at the mall. They'll wonder where I'm at and ask all kinds of questions."

I hug her and can feel her shame and embarrassment. It makes me all the more determined to protect her, to keep her secret at all costs. She starts to pull away before there is any emotional connection to our hug. I hold on to her, trying to let my soul pull the unease out of her. I feel her fear and dread; she grows almost panicky. She starts to break free again, but I hold her, wrapping my arms tighter around her because she needs it. I mumble in her ear, "Don't worry about me, Jen, it's all good. Let's just work this out between us, like true friends do." Quietly, and trustingly, okay?" I feel her tension relax, and release the hug.

She won't look me in the eyes but nods her head. I lift her chin with my finger. I could kiss this girl if she weren't so broken. Not a romantic kiss, but a comforting, you're normal kiss. My heart is heavy for her. I want her to feel safe, secure and like Jen again.

238

"Jen," I smile at her, "you're gonna make some guy very happy and proud one day."

A tear breaks loose and slides down her cheek. She backs away, nods her head, then turns and walks away.

I jog over to Chris's house and slip into the backyard just as the old man's truck turns onto the street. I slide down the back wall of Chris's house 'til I'm sitting. I rub my face and let out a long breath of the barely escaped.

* * *

It's done. We've finally finished the house. I plop down on Chris's bed, fresh from the shower, with only traces of paint in my damp hair. I hear Chris turn on the shower as I lie here, enjoying the inner reward of a job accomplished and done well. Fresh paint smell fills the house. I stare at the dividing line where the wall meets the ceiling and see where the wall color overlapped onto the ceiling. I didn't do that part. So, I'll be sure to point it out to Chris, even though he'll deny he did it. We're both exhausted and sore. It's been a rough two weeks plus, but we did a good job. It doesn't look like old man Tanner's place anymore. Before you didn't even notice all the carved trim work near the eaves or on the porch. Now it all pops, just like the porch railings and posts. It looks fresh, cheery, like a home. A real home.

Ms. T. is out back grilling up steaks. She said it's our last chance at a summer brouhaha, and a perfect ending to a job well done. Personally, I just love any excuse she has to stuff me full of food.

I'm spending the night again. We've picked out action films with fast cars and hot women. Chris said it's his duty as a son to do the tug-of-war thing on moral issues with his mom. Movies are a great way to combat her dedication to innocence and the naiveté she wants for him. That's their battle; I'm just here to watch the show, be it movie or the Tanners.

Tomorrow it's back to the cave for me. I'd rather stay here, but school starts on Monday, and it would raise Ms. T.'s suspicions if I stayed. Chris and I already discussed it.

I can't believe the summer is already gone. Monday, I'm officially a senior! Top of the local food chain! The b-ball team is gonna rock this year! Tomorrow, Chris and I are having a last summer practice to fine tune our moves before we show Coach what's what. I can't wait to see Coach's face!

My smile drops as I remember I have court the second week of school. I crack my knuckles then look at them. Nobody can tell now that they demolished Rod's face.

The shower goes off, so I get up, comb my hair, put on new clothes and go downstairs while Chris gets dressed.

Six

"**I**f my teacher says anything about me being late, I'm throwing you under the bus, Coach!"

"You were gonna be late anyway, but go ahead, I'll take the hit, one for the team, you know? Wait, which teacher?"

"Daley."

He slaps the air. "She doesn't scare me. So, you're trying out this year, right?"

"You bet. I'm bringing a new guy with me too. Tanner is gonna blow your mind."

I sprint off down the hall as Coach yells, "My mind doesn't blow easy, Taylor!"

"All the better, Coach."

"Be at the gym during lunch. Both of you."

I laugh at his impatience to see Chris, as I give a high wave, then round the corner.

I hit the classroom door just as the tardy bell rings. I scan the already full classroom and see only two empty desks, and only one of them is by a girl. I slide into that one.

"Hi," I say. It's Autumn Riley.

She blushes bright, and it's the sweetest, softest, most innocent thing I've seen in months. My chest surges. She has taken my breath away. I take in her vibrant blue eyes and white-blonde hair and think: *World History just got a whole lot more interesting.* I turn and spark a faux fight with the kid next to me to give Autumn time to recover, and so that I don't embarrass her more. It works. We connect during class, or I think we do until her mom shows up to pull her out of class.

Autumn's face turns bright again. She won't even look at me. She just keeps her head down and writes on her desk. She is slumped down in her seat, wishing she could dissolve. I can feel her extreme embarrassment, shame, and yes, even some anger. I want to reach over into her space and touch her hand. The kids in the class are making it worse. I want to scream at them to shut up, but I know that it wouldn't help, it would just get worse for her.

She leaves the room, and the class settles down. I glance at where she sat and see where she underlined the words: THIS BITES.

Autumn Riley. I say her name in my head, hold it in my mouth. I picture how she had curled into herself, hiding behind her long, blonde hair. I see her sparkling blue eyes lighting up her face when I first sat down. I'm going to know you better, Autumn Riley. I pull out a pencil, slide over to her desk, and draw a rose. I'm hoping that when she comes in tomorrow, it gives her a smile. I want to see her eyes light up again. I want to be the one that makes that happen. Throughout the rest of third period, I see her face in my mind. The prospect of seeing her tomorrow trumps this being the first day of my senior year.

Chris and I meet during lunch in the locker room. We've changed clothes and are heading to the gym. B-ball practice doesn't officially start for a few more weeks, but I know that Coach is already making his unofficial picks for all the teams this year. We go through the double doors and see Coach standing, waiting, with a ball under his arm.

I glance at Chris and grin. "Let's show the old boy how this is done."

"My rep is on the line here, Ian, being the new kid and all, so I do the first fake-out shot. I'm thinkin' the mid-air twist."

"Make it happen." I slap him on the back, and we jog over to Coach. I'm grinning large and buzzing with excitement to show off my find.

Coach points at Chris. "You Tanner?"

Chris nods.

Coach looks him up and down, tosses him the ball, and says while looking at me, "Blow my mind, kid."

Chris does.

It's been three days now since school started, and Autumn hasn't been back to class. At first, I wonder if she dropped World History because I sure put it off as long as possible. Plus, if my old man showed up like her mom did, I'd drop it again, regardless of needing the credits to graduate. I keep hoping to see her in the halls, but I don't. Then I overhear some girls saying she is sick, and won't be back for a long time.

I'm worried about her and disappointed. It's gonna be a long wait, but then, I'm busy enough just trying to keep life on track as it is. It's a fulltime job just dodging Dad, b-ball practice, and catching a bed at night. Then, of course, there's the whole court thing next week, too. If Autumn knew what my life looked like right now, she'd run the other way. Shoot, I'd run from it if that would help!

After practice, Chris heads home, and I jump in the school's shower. I leave the locker room just as I hear Coach locking up his office in back. I slip out quietly.

I get to the river's edge and do my usual scan before ducking behind the falls. That's when I see her. Autumn. She is standing on the footbridge. She is so absorbed by the falls and her thoughts that she doesn't see me. I stand, just watching her, taking in her essence. Her hair shines like an aura around her in the sunlight. Her face tilts down and I know she sees me. She has to. I lift my hand in a wave. I want to talk to her, I want to ask how sick she is, when she'll be coming back to school, but mostly, I just want to stand next to her, to look at her. Just as I move to climb the bank up to the bridge, she turns and leaves. Did she see me? Is she avoiding me on purpose? Does she know about my arrest? Am I a person that her mom has warned her against like Jen's dad did her?

It's early, but I open cans of dinner anyway, more out of boredom than hunger. I sit on my rolled-up sleeping bag, using it as a chair, and eat. My mind won't get off the whole Autumn thing. How sick is she? She's not dying, right? I didn't sense anything like that from her, but then, maybe she didn't know yet. Maybe that's what the 'THIS BITES' thing was about. Maybe that's why she ignored me.

I picture her blushing face hiding in a shroud of blonde hair. Her eyes still brilliant with color. I remember her feel, the sense I got from her. She is quiet, reserved, alone in a crowd, yet resigned to it. She has an innocence about her that others could mistake for naiveté, but they would be wrong. Then, there was her fear once her mom showed up. I focus on that fear now. It wasn't powerful, or an overbearing-panicky fear like mine of my dad, but more like a fear of exposure.

I lean back against the cave's wall and sigh. What's your story, Autumn Riley? Can I be part of it?

I lean out the cave's opening and rinse my fork, then roll out my bed and curl up into it. I feel my body warm the bag, and then the bag warms me back.

* * *

I walk through the courthouse doors and head to the courtroom that I stood in before. I take a deep breath, open the door, and step inside the small, dim, muffled room. It feels like an oversized coffin.

I look around to see if Dad is here. He isn't, but I'm shocked to see Jen! Why is she here? Doesn't she realize people will know she skipped school to be here, and that it points to her being the recued, mystery girl? She gives me a small, scared smile, and I act like I don't know her and take a seat in the front row.

A man stands and walks over to me, hand extended.

"Ian?"

"Yes."

"I'm your public defender."

"I didn't know I had one."

He smiles. "My office sent you a letter." He opens a black leather briefcase and adds, "Your address is . . ."

The man's voice is muffled by my own thoughts and blood rushing through my ears. *An Attorney? Oh God, I am in deep trouble here.*

"Ian?"

"Yes? Yes, that's my address and no, my dad isn't coming."

A frown crosses his face as he looks intently in my eyes. "Like I said, today we are just asking for an extension so we can go over your defense together. Here's my card, please call my office and schedule a time to meet."

"Okay." I turn to leave, and he puts a hand on my arm.

"No, Ian, you have to be here for this."

"Oh, okay."

My name is called out, and I go through a thigh-high gate to where my attorney stands. The judge stares at me, judging me before he hears my case. I feel small, accused and hated. He sets a new court date for next month. The attorney puts a hand on my back to guide me and let me know that I can leave. Another name is called out as I exit through the door. Jen follows me out.

"Jen! What are you doing here? If the wrong person sees you—"

"Ian, I had to. I just couldn't leave you alone to face these people. I just couldn't."

I smile. "Thanks, but listen, if you don't want this thing out in the open, you have to stay away. Okay?"

She nods yes and looks down, chastised.

We walk back to school together, and she tells me that Autumn has mono. She'll be out of school for a month. I take the news, acting like it's just non-personal gossip, but inside, my heart is near ecstatic by the time we reach the school. Possibilities of outlandish luck and timing fill my head. She'll be back when my court thing is a little clearer. Light at the end of my tunnel!

The bell rings, and the halls are instantly flooded with noise and bodies. I get to my locker, and Chris is leaning against it, wearing a huge grin.

"Don't get too excited yet; they postponed."

His grin drops some.

I don't want to lose my great mood, so I say, "Hey, at least I have another chance to teach you my smooth moves!"

"Yeah? What moves would those be?" He laughs.

I punch him in the arm. "Oh! There's one there!"

We head off down the hall and see Rod dragging a kid, half his size, into the restroom. I look at Chris.

"After you," he says.

We go through the door, and Rod has this kid lifted and pressed up against the wall to his eye level. Rod is screaming in the kid's face, and spit is flying disgustingly. The kid is obviously terrified and nearly in tears.

"Rod! Got a problem here?" I ask.

His first reaction is to punch whoever is interrupting his bully-session, then his eyes register Chris and me. His confidence wavers and the kid drops to his feet.

A grin crosses Rod's face. "You out to save the world, Ian? You can't sucker slap me this time."

I laugh, at his attempt to scare me and discount the beating I gave him before.

"There's no saving needed here. He owes me. Don't you Pee-wee?"

The kid looks at Chris and me, then shakes his head vigorously.

I step up close to Rod, nose to nose. In a flash, I see Jen's face and see the disgusting gesture he tossed at her in front of my house. Rod reads it all on my face. He holds up both hands in surrender, and the kid splits out the door.

"Calm down, killer," Rod says, trying to salvage his pride.

I grab the front of his shirt and in a low voice say, "You know, Rod, it's time you grew up and started acting like a human being instead of an animal. Animals get hurt in these parts."

"Is that for real?" He watches Chris and I both.

"But then, you know all about that, don't you, Rod?"

He doesn't say anything and pulls free from my grip. He pushes into and past me and then Chris and leaves.

I start to reach for him because of his insolence, when Chris says, "Ian," and grabs my arm.

I look in Chris's eyes. "I know! I know. Wait 'til court is over."

He points a finger at me as if to say, exactly.

I walk to the sink and splash water on my face to cool my anger down. Chris is watching me with concern in the mirror. I'm sure he's wondering just how much of my dad lives in me. I wonder, too.

"Hey," I say, trying to get us back to normal, "I'm doing laps at the Boy's and Girl's Club after school. Wanna come?"

"Sure. I gotta snag my trunks from the house though.

"Okay."

"Afterwards, we'll see if Mom will scare up some dinner for us. So, short practice today?"

"Yeah."

We make our way to the intersecting hall, then go in opposite directions.

"At practice, I'll demonstrate some of my smooth moves!" I yell out to him.

"What? Like that back there?" he yells back.

I shrug, playing innocent and jog down the hall to class.

After school, we end up skipping practice completely and meet at the Club instead. Turns out he's as good a swimmer as a ball player.

"Is there anything I'll be able to beat you at?"

He laughs, then climbs out and sits on the edge of the pool with me. "I learned to swim over the summer."

"This *summer*?"

He looks at his feet swirling the water. "Yeah, at the river."

"No way! So, you've been swimming what, a month?"

He grins. "I swam across it, actually."

I stare at him, unsure if he's putting me on or not.

He laughs. "Seriously, I did!"

"Nobody's ever done that, Chris. So, tell me, how was the drop over the falls?" I laugh.

"I was far enough up river—"

"Wait a minute, you're really serious. You swam . . . what, the widest part?"

"It took a lot of practice. I didn't just jump in and jet across. I built up my strength and my nerve," he chuckles, "until I made it, that is. I almost didn't."

"I bet! And, why would you want to do that? Just to see if you could? For bragging rights? What? That's just crazy!"

"How am I gonna brag back home about a river down here? Explain how wide it is? I don't think so, Ian. Actually, you're the first to know. G-pa knew, though, the sneaky dog." He smiles. "It's hard to explain why I did it, but the best I can describe it is that I knew if I didn't get across that river, I'd never get over Craig being dead."

"Whoa, that's . . . intense."

"Yeah, it was, but it worked."

I nod my head. "I'm glad."

"Yeah." He gives a chuckle. "Me too."

We sit quiet for a minute. "All right, I told you something private, now I have a question for you."

"What? Like tit for tat?"

"Or, quid pro quo, I guess." He stares at me. "Where are you living, Ian?"

I squirm uncomfortably.

"I know you shower at school," he tosses his head toward the locker room, "Or here, I'm guessing. So what kind of place are you living in that doesn't have a shower, man?"

I look away from his face, I'm in a corner here, and it ticks me off. I look back at Chris, and he hasn't moved his eyes, they're locked on me.

"God, Chris! Does it really matter? I'm doing everything right! I'm going to school and will pull my grades, I'm showing up for my court dates, I'm trying out for sports—I'm the All-American guy here. Okay?"

"Look, I'm trying to help you out. I mentioned to Mom—"

"What! Why would you do that, Chris? Why? You just killed any chance at safety and of actually making it, that I had!" I start to get up. I can't believe he's betrayed me like this. Him of all people! He knows how Dad is! He catches my leg before I can rise and pins it to the floor.

"Hold on just minute!" he yells. "I didn't give any details, man. I wouldn't do that to you."

The echo of our voices bounces around the pool room. We lower our voices. Tears crest my eyes over the loss of trust I had in him.

"I trusted you, Chris," I say this looking him square in the eyes while jabbing my finger in his face. I jerk my leg loose from his grip and start to get up.

"Ian," he says quietly. I pause, leaning back on my elbows. "I stood around and did nothing because you asked me to. Nothing. I watched my best friend get beaten, not once, but twice. I said nothing because you trusted me not to tell. So, why would I tell now?" His eyes drill into mine. "Answer me that."

I stare at him. His eyes are filled with fear. I don't move.

"You're a friend like I've never had before. All of my old friends knew Craig too. We got caught up in this stupid clown act, so after a while, people expected it, we couldn't let it go. We were expected to be the life of the party."

I sit up, and we stay quiet, just watching the roll of the pool's surface.

"Ian, you're the first real friend I've ever had that let me just be me. I'm new at this so I may make some mistakes, but I would never do anything on purpose to jeopardize that."

Chris is honestly afraid of losing our friendship. I sense his fear of losing it, but also of losing the progress he's made getting on with his life without Craig. I realize that I am his first friend and a first step back into his life after his grief. He is terrified of messing this up, and what the consequences will be if he already has. I hold his survival in my hand, just like he holds mine. I nod my head. "Okay, Chris, okay."

"Look, man, I only told her about you because she brought it up. She really likes you. For some reason, she thinks you have a 'good moral compass.'" He gives a gesture of quoting her, then rolls his eyes. "Of course, I set her straight on that." He grins.

I snort a chuckle and say, "Thanks for that, dude."

"Listen, I told her you were staying at a friend's house because you and your dad don't get along. I never mentioned his drinking, or the fights or about you staying at the river."

I snap my head up and look at him. Has he been following me?

"Relax, it's not rocket science. There's the shower thing, some of your clothes are still at my house, and if I were in your shoes, it's where I would go. Anyway, I asked Mom if you could stay with us. You could use the other bedroom. Not G-pa's," he adds quickly. "There's the old sewing room that's empty."

I look at Chris, he is all-out serious.

"Mom asked if you listen to loud migraine music." He grins. "I told her I'd hide your CDs, that it would be no great loss given your taste of music."

I let out a small laugh. I can picture Ms. T., all nervous, jittery and worried over my family life.

"Honestly, she's fine with it."

I let out a deep sigh. Nobody has ever offered me so much before. It boggles my mind; this is all so hard. I know that if I don't accept this, something between Chris and I will be forever sealed off. To do that could take him places in his grief that wouldn't be good. I think of what I sensed that first time I met him, and how he was after G-pa died. He closed himself off, he shut down. I am key to his being okay right now until he turns a corner.

Chris breaks the silence and into my thoughts. "You know, winter snow will be here before long, and your bedroom at the house comes equipped with heat and a roof." He smirks.

"I have a roof . . . of sorts." I grin back. "Listen, if I do this, it would only be until school is out . . . or until I go to jail."

"You stay as long as you want or need, Ian, and you aren't going to jail. You don't know what a ruckus Mom would stir in this little town." He gives a low whistle.

"Does she know about my court stuff?"

"No."

"What if she finds out?"

"If she finds out she'll become a wildcat at the courthouse, police station, even down at the Food Mart with Rod's mom. She won't stop fighting for you until her last breath. The woman is short and sweet until there's an injustice, then everybody steps back! She's got sharp claws and a good aim. She really does like you Ian, probably loves you. She considers you hers already."

I let this sense of protection shroud me. It feels real, not like Dad or Dupree. If I accept this offer, take this gamble and put myself out there again and all falls through . . . well, I've been a solo traveler all my life so I will deal if it all goes south. Something feels different this time, though, and I don't think it will. Chris and Ms. T. are invested in this as much as I am. We all have a lot to lose. I fill the gap for them that Craig left, and they fill the gap my own family never filled.

"Wow. So, what happens when we argue?"

He laughs. "I kick your butt first, and then Mom takes my side. Or she better."

"What if I do something she doesn't approve of? I mean, I just know things can go bad real, quick sometimes, ya know?"

"Well, she'll probably ground you." He gets serious. "Ian, this isn't a trick bag. If it all goes wrong, you can go back to camping in the snow if that's what you want. You're my friend, and I don't take that lightly. Okay?"

I consider all of this and weigh out what happens if Dad or the authorities find out where I am.

"I need your word that you or your mom will never tell my dad where I am or get the authorities involved."

"I'll tell you right up front, Ian, that I can't promise for Mom. If she learns what your dad did to you, it will be all over for him. The authorities would be involved. So, if you tell her any of that, she'll go for the throat. I can promise that on her behalf. I can also promise you that I won't tell her, the authorities or anyone else unless you ask me to. I can promise, too, that I will never tell your dad where you are."

"He's dangerous, Chris. I won't put you and your mom in danger to keep a little snow off my back."

He looks at me intensely. "I know he's dangerous, Ian."

We both let out sighs at the same time.

"Well, then all that's left to do is shower first, so I show up on Ms. T.'s doorstep smelling better than you and creating an edge for myself in her affections."

"Ohh . . . Good luck with that, but please, do try!" He laughs. "She's gonna be so happy that you're doing this, man. I think she misses having two boys around. Nothing you do or don't do is going to shock her or impress her more than I already have!" He laughs.

I get up to go hit the shower, and Chris jumps into the spa and moans like an old man with joint pain.

The water pounds my face and chest, releasing my tensions. Tears, in full release, mix with the water, cascading down my chest. An emptying. A cleansing. Like the falls.

When my tears have stopped their flow, I throw my head back, owning the relief, safety and freedom. It's crystal clear now just how trapped I've been in Dad's violence, Mom's disappearance, and my self-made freedom. I fully understand now why I developed my empathic sense of alarm. I understand why the flying dreams I had as a child were so real. I remember the disappointing moment I realized I couldn't really fly, the way my subconscious had made me believe. It's no wonder Mom left and never came back. Life has so many twists and turns. You never know what is around the corner. I feel my world shift . . . again.

By the time I'm out of the shower, Chris has dressed, and I see his trunks draped over the bench to dry.

"Hey, I guess I'll bring my clothes to your house, huh? We can hang our trunks in the locker to dry."

"Sounds good." He looks in my locker, and his eyes go wide. "Jeez! You have everything you own stuffed in there?"

"No, remember? I still have stuff at your place."

"Our place, Ian."

I grin as I pull clothes out and toss them in my bag. I hang our trunks up, then lock the padlock. "I just paid a month's fees, after that, you're on your own."

"So, do I get my own key then?"

My body tenses, it's still the only safe place I have until I test the waters at Chris's house.

"You can't come here alone unless you're a member. I have to babysit you." I smile. "Besides, I can't have you using my trunks to pick up chicks." Suddenly, it dawns on me, Chris must have membership, because he got in here without me with him earlier. But, he doesn't say anything. Instead, like a true friend, he teases back.

"What? In those there? I don't need nothin', especially those, to keep me sharp with the ladies. Yep, I'm a regular chick magnet. It just comes natural, dude."

"Come on, Mr. Natural, I'm starving."

* * *

For the first time in my life, I'm lying in a new bed, with sheets and a comforter that still smell of starch and the plastic they came in. I smile. I cozy down into it all and breathe deep. So much nicer than the cave. It's much better than my old bed, too, where I'd lay wondering if I'd be ripped out of it in my sleep.

I'm trying to make this room a home in my head, but my life's reality, life as I know it, makes it impossible. So, I lie here, enjoying the temporary moments I have of completely safe sleep in this new bed and enveloped in new fabric smell. I wonder how long I have until Dad sees me walk out the front door, and all of this is ruined. Why couldn't Chris live even one street over? Only three houses separate my old world from this new one. At some point, they will clash. The thought terrifies me. Terror keeps me grounded in reality, and guilt makes me question my decision to come here.

After school, I have to meet with my attorney, which means another missed practice. I've been dreading this meeting. I don't want to go through the whole argument about giving Jen's name again. I'm afraid I'll give it up in a moment of weakness because the closer my court date gets the more scared I am. I just don't have a clear defense without her testimony. I fight the feeling of defeat as I enter his office.

"Ian." My attorney nods and shakes my hand. "Good to see you."

We sit, and he gets right to business. "So, tell me, what is home life like for you?"

My heart skips a beat as I go into full-on panic. It's all I can do to stay in my chair and not run out of his office and out of Deer Falls forever.

"Why?"

"Well, because I have concerns. See, I find it odd that your father doesn't show up for your court date, but manages to find his way to my office while drunk, scaring my secretary to death, and accusing me of hiding you out."

My jaw drops open. This public display is new and out of character for the old man. I find my voice.

"Um, it's okay," I lie.

He folds his hands on his desk and leans toward me.

"Then explain how you got those bruises on your face that I saw a trace of in court. Odd, really, because they aren't there in your booking photo, so they can't be from the fight."

I stare him down. "Well, apparently they just hadn't ripened yet. Are we going to discuss my case or my home life? 'Cuz if this is just therapy, then we're done here."

He looks at me, solidly in the eyes, trying to figure me out. I fight to hold his stare, and don't squirm in my chair.

"All right, Ian. Let's talk defense. What would make you angry enough to beat the snot out of some kid nearly twice your weight, and to do the damage you did?'

I am silent, trying to come up with an answer.

"You see, Ian, I believe you have a turbulent home life, and the stress of living with an abusive, alcoholic father led you to react to your anger in the only way you know. With your fists. I think when the judge understands this, he'll give you anger management classes, and get you somewhere safe." He ends his statement with a slight drum roll on the desk, then leans back in his chair, cheesing at me like it's a done deal.

"No."

"What?" He leans forward, squinting his eyes at me trying to intimidate me.

"No. I . . . I can't do that."

"Why not?"

"Because my Dad doesn't hit me." I feel my face flush with guilt from my lie. I start to escape his stare but hold on. "I mean, he drinks, sure. What grown-up doesn't? He has never hurt me, and I won't accuse him or leave him. Those marks, the bruises, were from another fight." I drop my eyes to the floor, faking guilt. I look back up into his face. He is staring hard into my eyes, unsure whether to believe me or not.

"Ian, listen. I cannot in good conscience, or ethically, let you stay in an abusive home. For one it's inhumane, and two, I could lose my license."

"I'm being honest here. Dad has a drinking problem, and he misses some of my games, but he loves me and would never hurt me."

I bite my tongue until I taste blood. Am I doing the right thing here? Am I throwing away the only chance I may have to legally keep Dad out of my life and myself out of jail? I just want to graduate, save up some cash, then leave Dad and this town and its memories behind me. Forever. I don't want to leave Chris's house, Ms. T., or my new room. I don't want to go to a foster home with strangers and endure court forced visits with the old man. Tears well up in my eyes. They won't push back, and I let out a gasp. Quickly, I use my tears.

"Please don't take me away from my Dad!" I say this like I love my Dad more that life itself. "He's never hurt me. He wouldn't do that!"

"All right, Ian. I had to make sure, you know?"

I wipe my tears. "He's a good dad, really."

"So, tell me what got you so angry that you took on that human tank?"

I snort out a laugh, and he hands me a box of tissue.

"A girl," I answer.

He laughs and slaps a hand on the desk. "Money and women! Problems as old as time itself!"

The meeting goes in a better direction after that. I tell him my story but refuse to give Jen's name. He gets angry and succeeds in scaring me about jail if I lose my case. He tells me that prison is even a possibility and I nearly cave in but manage to sweat it out and hold it together. He ends our meeting by telling me to check in with him next week and he'll let me know what he comes up with for a defense. I walk out, feeling like I've been through a spy's interrogation. I have a shaky future, but I have my integrity . . . I did what I told Jen I would do, I kept her out this.

My soul has heard your silent cry.
I stir but stumble in reply.

I've heard this ode someplace before,
I know it deep within my core.

Silence sits upon your tongue.
For me, your sorrow's clearly rung.

Key the lock of misery's door,
Together we'll win this ugly war.

                      —Ian

Seven

---

*I*t's been a few days since I've had time to myself. I'm craving it. I'm thankful to Chis and Ms. T. for a place to stay. It's just that I'm used to spending a lot of time alone. I just need some room to breathe, I guess. I tell Chris I have things to do after school and that I'll be home later. Home. The word slips out, and the realization sneaks up on me. I really am feeling at home here.

I hoof it to the Falls and take in the powerful crashing sound. I haven't stood and just listened to them for a while. They feel like an old friend, or like sliding into a favorite, comfy sweatshirt. I do a quick scan, then disappear behind them into my world.

It feels different in here. Everything is still in its place where I left it, and I can't quite put my finger on it, but something has changed. I pull out my sleeping bag and can smell the damp-earthy odor in it. I use it as a chair and pull out some jerky, and my money can. I count out just over $1600. I slide a fifty in my pocket and stash the rest in my can. I sit back against the cave wall and watch the blur of water speed past my doorway.

If I do go to jail, will I ever come back to this cave? How old will I be when I get out? Eighteen? Nineteen? Everybody else will move on with their lives while mine is on hold. Chris, Jen, Autumn, even Rod will all be so busy living, I wonder if they'll even think of me. I let out a long breath.

There's this fight going on inside of me. When I promised Jen I wouldn't tell, I didn't actually believe that I could end up in jail! And for a year, according to Jen's dad. Is it still my responsibility to save her if my own ship is sinking? When does Jen have to own up to her part in all of this, when it would keep me from going under? Is my promise forever? No matter what happens? Where is the line drawn that allows a person to break his word and still live with a clean conscience himself? Is it my responsibility to help save her parents' marriage? Is it even Jen's? Has there been enough time for them to work it all out? Is it disloyal of me to even ask such a question? Loyalty, honor, integrity, my word—these are honestly all that I own in my life except for a few clothes. If I don't have these, then who is Ian Taylor? People say, 'be true to yourself.' What does that even mean? Am I true to myself by being a loyal friend, or, by protecting my own interests? If I choose self-protection in order to be true to myself, then I lose everyone else in my life by my disloyalty. What happens if giving Jen's name doesn't work? Then, when I do get out of jail, do I just step out of the prison gates, knock the dust from my shoes and leave everyone behind? What happens to me if I chip off a little piece of me, as a sacrifice, to save my life as I know it now? What will that cost me five, ten or fifty years from now? Where will these people be then? Still in my life? Are Jen, Chris or Autumn people I want in my life that long? Chris, I can see as a life-long friend, but Jen, not really. Autumn? Well, that remains to be seen, but it would be nice.

My thoughts wander to Autumn, and what she is doing right now. I picture her face, her hair, her smile, and her blush. Her blush . . . I remember when I sat next to her, how her face bloomed sweet as a rose. I have to get to know her, jail or not. I need to know about this girl, everything about her, and see if she wants to know me. I decide that I will walk by her house. Maybe she'll be outside. If she isn't? Then I'll just go up to her door and knock.

I put the sleeping bag back into its garbage bag and look at my money can. I pull out all of the bills and push them deep into my pocket. I get it now, what's different here. This isn't home anymore. Just like when Dad's place wasn't home anymore, and I just knew. I look at the cans of food lined up against the wall, then slip out of the cave.

I walk to Autumn's house, half afraid that she'll think I'm nuts for showing up. After all, she barely knows me. Worse yet, maybe she doesn't want to see me. I try out different ice-breaker topics in my head. Everything I come up with involves her being sick. I'm sure that's the one thing she doesn't want to talk about. I mean, who opens a conversation discussing mono? She's so shy and quiet that the conversation would close her off for sure. I shift gears and think; I could tell her how beautiful she is, and that because she doesn't realize it, she makes me crazy over her and I can't stop thinking about her. "Stalker." I could always say, 'Hey, so did you see me in the paper?' I let out a long breath.

How do I get to know this girl better? She's real; a bit of a loner of sorts, like me. I don't want her to be alone in a crowd anymore. I remember what that's like. I want to help her bloom. She has strengths hidden under her shyness. I felt her power resonate under her embarrassment that first day of school. I want to see her laugh, really laugh. I want to see her eyes shine bright. I want the world to be a good place for her.

I turn onto her street, and my eyes pick out her house. My heart beats like crazy, Dang it! What am I going to say? Hi, remember me? I sat by you in World History while the class turned you into a putz? It's then that I realize her mom's car is in the driveway, so I walk on by. *Weasel! Punk! Wuss! God, I'm pathetic!*

* * *

It's getting late. The house is quiet, but I can't sleep. I've been tossing around in my bed forever. I look at my watch: 10:40 p.m. I slip out of bed, get dressed and creep downstairs. I need to walk. My soul is chaotic, and I need to break free from all of this, whatever 'all of this' is. It borders on panic, like claustrophobia. It's past curfew, and I consider the consequences of Ms. T. catching me leave, but the impulse to walk is too intense. I slip out the door silently.

The air is cold, and the night is lit by a full moon. A crisp clarity fills my heart and mind. The panic recedes slightly. This is what I needed.

I'm drawn to the falls, I feel if I can just stand near them, then their roar will pound away some of this tightness in my chest.

I walk onto the footbridge, but someone is already here, standing near the railing. I hang back, letting them have their moment. I sense their hurt, confusion and anger. It is balled up into a tightness that slams against their chest, searching for escape. I watch and wear the extreme power of this person's emotions. I am in awe over the strength and intensity of them. As I allow myself to relax and absorb the sensation, I realize this is the claustrophobic feeling that urged me to leave the house. My senses picked up on this person. My chaotic restlessness was not mine at all! I am a witness.

I am on high alert now, waiting to see why I am here. The silhouetted figure stands on the bottom rung of the guard rail. A breeze stirs, moving the figure's long hair. Obviously female, her image is ingrained in my mind forever, also, in my memory. Black against gray, backlit by the silver moon. The moment is magical, the image fairy tale-like. Her face is turned up to the moon as she spreads her arms as if receiving the sky, the falls' mist and moon's radiance, which are all tangible to her alone. I need to see her face, I have to.

I walk slowly, mesmerized by the sad beauty of this situation and the immense power of her emotion. I sense the indescribable, controlled chaos of her being. This extreme intensity is a new phenomenon to me. I have never encountered this number or intensity of emotions meshed together at once like this before.

She steps gracefully up to the next rung, almost floating as if balanced purely by air. Before I realize it, I am standing, breathless and in awe beside her. She isn't aware of my presence. I feel the controlled chaos within her take form, like a laser beam, as it nears escape from her chest. Trance-like, she gently leans forward. A cloud now passes from over the moon, and I see her face clearly.

"Hi, Autumn."

She startles and nearly goes over the rail. I grab her hand and guide her down. Her touch is soft, yet as powerful as a static shock. The moon's light on her face shows me her confusion. A tear's trail shines on her cheek. My thumb gently wipes it away. I dare not even breathe, or something will break. I want to hold her and absorb that chaos into myself, to give her relief. I know that if it disappears, she will awaken to parts of herself she doesn't know exist.

She moves back away from me, without a word, startled, confused, and walks across the bridge. I watch her leave and understand that she wasn't even aware that she was about to end her life. I watch as the night swallows her in silver-edged darkness. My soul weeps.

* * *

I wake groggy, my mind still wrapped in last night's images. I sigh.

My watch reads 7:30 a.m. I leap up and throw on clothes. I wash my face, brush my teeth and wet my hair so it lays down. My stomach knows there is bacon cooking in the house and tells me all about it. When I get downstairs, Chris is sopping up the last of his egg with toast.

"I figured you were a no-show, so I ate your breakfast." Chris grins. "Mom just kept cooking more, so it's lucky your mug finally popped in, or I'd be in serious pain. Probably have to take the day off." He gets up from the table, puts his plate and glass in the sink and kisses his mom on the cheek.

"Ms. T., can I just toss some bacon on bread and eat on the run?"

"Don't listen to him, there's time for you to eat, Ian."

"I have some things to do before school."

Chris and his mom trade glances. "Sure, here." She piles layers of bacon high on bread and hands me a glass of o.j., which I chug down.

"See ya at school, Chris," I say with my mouth full as I run out the door.

I jog down the sidewalk while stuffing the sandwich down my throat. Dad's truck is gone, but still, I go up the stairs cautiously. Old feelings of fear rise and I remember acutely why I swore never to come back here. However, I need to call my attorney, and I want the caller I.D. to show my home number so it appears I still live here.

I pull mail from the box and walk in. A wave of stench rocks me back. The place smells like urine and stale alcohol breath. My eyes jerk to Dad's room. The bed is a mess, but empty. I leave the front door open to air it out for a minute, but my paranoia of him showing up makes me close the door. I move to the kitchen and am shocked by the mess. Dishes are heaped and teetering on every surface, while the smell of burnt fish permeates the air. I toss the mail that is still gathered in my hand on top of the mess. And it causes an avalanche that shatters on the floor. I stare, stunned, that any human could live like this, and that it's my old man doing it.

I leave the kitchen as it is and go over to the phone. I pull out my attorney's card and dial. He is in early and answers his own phone. He tells me he needs to see me today so we can go over some things. Suddenly, there is a loud crash and I yelp. I spin around, but nobody is there. The pile in the kitchen worked itself loose, and gravity won.

"What was that!?" comes blaring over the phone. Adrenaline has blasted me, so now my hands are trembling. I think fast. He doesn't need to know the mess this place is in.

"Um, my dad just dropped something."

"Is that a fact." It wasn't a question, and I knew something was up. "Ian, I was just going to tell you that I got a call from Dupree last night, he arrested your dad for DUI."

I quickly say, "Cat!" I said my cat knocked some dishes off the thing, the . . . Get! Get down, Harvey! Where were we?"

"You didn't notice he wasn't home last night, Ian? Or this morning?"

"I crashed early last night, and he leaves for work before seven, when I get up. What is this? Another interrogation?"

"No, no. All right, listen —"

His voice drones on, but all I can do is feel relief that the old man won't be busting in on me right now. I can see the drunk tank cell in my head. I wonder if he's reading the poem I scratched into the wall. The one about living with a drunk. The thought hits me, what will this mean for my living arrangement? Will this attorney or Dupree contact family services and try to put me in a foster home?

"Are you there?"

"Yeah, sorry. I'm a little shocked about Dad. What time do you want me there?

"I leave early today, so around 2-2:30."

"Okay, I'll cut my last class and get there by 2:45."

"Hmmm, cut the last two classes and be here by 1:30."

"That class ends at 1:30."

"Just come after lunch! All right? I'll call the school and tell them."

"Whatever you say. You're the guy holding the get-out-of-jail-free card."

I hang up and look around the stinking mess the old man lives in. I'm disgusted and so done with all of it. I go to my room, it's still trashed. Maybe even worse than when I walked out weeks ago, it's hard to tell.

"Jerk."

I stare at Michael Jordan suspended in mid-air, on my wall. I decide I don't need any reminders of this place in my new room. There's nothing here for me anymore. I close the bedroom door and know in my soul that I'll never enter this house again.

I walk through the house toward the front door, taking a final look at familiar walls, floors, tables and Dad's recliner. A cockroach scurries past my foot. I step on it. I stop in front of Dad's room. It's a pigsty. Greasy clothes cover the floor, the blanket and sheets are blackened with dirt and pushed half off the bed. On his nightstand lie some bills—two singles and a five. I put them in my pocket. A bottle of clear booze, half empty, sits uncapped beside the spot where the money was. I pick it up, look at the label, sniff the bottle, and a familiar scent wrenches my stomach. I throw the bottle, slinging booze over the room before it shatters against the wall. Tears blur the room.

I walk out the front door. I breathe deep to take in clean air. I stand tall and unafraid for the first time in my life. I go down the stairs and look back at the ugly, painful, hateful house. I close my eyes, turn toward the sun and feel its comfort on my face. I walk, sun in my face, fresh air in my lungs, and, as a new person, I head out for school. I start to jog, with a smile on my face. I go by my new home.

"That is one fine paint job there. Yes, it is!"

The tardy bell rings just as I hit the door. I decide to play it off by going straight to the office to create an alibi with the secretary.

"I have to leave today, after third period, to meet with my attorney."

The gray-haired sentry gives me a look like I'm a criminal and says, "He just called."

"Okay, just thought I'd let somebody know."

"We know," she says, implying that nothing gets by her.

I pat the countertop, "Well, good to know."

I step into class and hear the teacher. "Taylor, you're late. The bell rings at the same time every day."

"I was in the office. Ask the secretary. She knows. All of it. Everything." I nod my head like an honest child and wave my hand at the phone on the wall. "Really, call her. She knows."

Snickers break out around the room, and the teacher gives me a look that says, 'that's enough.'

Third period comes and goes; the bell rings, and I mentally dump my school day. I stuff my books in my locker and hold out the ones I'll need for homework, pushing them into my backpack, then go hunt down Chris. I find him at his locker talking with Jen, Julie and Terri.

"Hey, guys, how's it going?"

"Hey, Ian," the girls say in sync. Jen smiles, then avoids my eye. I sense her embarrassment over me knowing her secrets and her guilt for jeopardizing my freedom.

"Jen, you look nice today." It's my way of telling her again that she dresses fine and what happened isn't her fault, but it kind of backfires. Everybody gets quiet. Her friends nudge each other, and Chris stares at me with a half-grin on his face.

"Chris, can I talk to you a minute?" I pull him by his sleeve.

'What was that all about?" He chuckles.

"Nothing. She just looked kind of sad or something. It came out all wrong."

"Uh-huh."

"It's not like that. Listen, I have to leave, I'm meeting with my attorney, so I won't be here for practice."

"Okay. Everything cool?"

"Yeah. They, uh, arrested my dad."

"Yes!" He yells, punching the air. "Wait, not for . . ." his eyes search my face for marks.

"No, no. I didn't bump into him or anything. Look, I'm not sure, but I think my attorney wants to use the old man's drinking in my defense somehow. I'm concerned that if he does everything will come out; you know, about me staying at your place because he hits me."

"Do it, man! Take him down. He doesn't hit you, Ian, he beats you, bad. I've said from the start you should tell someone and get a restraining order against him. I know Mom would apply to be your foster mom. It could all work out, Ian!"

I shake my head. Chris doesn't get it. "A restraining order won't keep him away. What happens if he gets out and shows up when you and I aren't there?"

Chris's face pales.

"Oh! You get it now!" Tears burn my eyes. I'm afraid he'll throw me out of their home for putting his mom in danger.

He nods and looks down the hall. He's processing all that he and Ms. T. have taken on.

"What if we make a trip to your old place and discourage him on ever showing up?" The anger in Chris's voice is seething. I search his eyes to see if I am a target of this anger and start reconsidering my cave.

"Ian, he can't do this to you ever again, and so help me, if he comes to my house—"

"Chris," I snap my fingers in front of his face. "Reality here, man; come on." I sigh. "For now, what do I do about this attorney?"

His eyes focus on me again, and he's more rational. "Lay it out straight about the fight with Rod, tell who this mystery girl is and keep denying that your old man is a piece of—"

"Okay, okay, I get it. I can't give the girl's name, though; she needs more time. I just needed to make sure there wasn't another way to handle it. Ya know?"

He grabs my arm, "Hey," I see something click in his eyes. "It's Jen, isn't it?" I stare at him.

"See ya at home."

I head out to the attorney's office, cutting through the mall parking lot. I'm way early, so I swing by the deli to have lunch and to keep my promise to visit my former boss.

"Ian! What a great surprise to see you!" She comes from behind the counter and hugs me, making a long line of customers wait. "I've missed you. Hey, you aren't skipping school, are you?"

I laugh. "No, I have an appointment. Hey, can I help for a few minutes?" I ask while scanning the impatient line of people.

"Please! Yes!" She laughs.

"What happened to your babysitter's brother helping?"

"Ah, you know, good help is hard to find."

I see the service line is nearly empty so I wipe it all down and make fast work of chopping vegetables to fill the line with. I restock wrappers, styro boxes and cups. Then, like old times, we get into our groove and slam out sandwiches. In only fifteen minutes we have the line of customers cleared out. She won't let me clean the area; instead, she makes us lunch, and we sit down to visit.

"Ian, you really need to come back to work."

"I just don't have the time in my schedule now. I have practice every day, and things are just crazy."

"What about on the weekends? I'll even give you a raise," she grins, "and all the free food you can stuff down, at least until you break the bank," she laughs.

"I love that you're willing to let me come back, especially after the way I quit, with no notice and all. By the way, I appreciate the extra wages you paid me when I left."

"I paid you extra? Then you should owe me, um . . . four weeks of labor!" She grins.

"Maybe I'll stop by once in a while and play the hero again."

I stand up to leave, and she hugs me tight. As I walk out the door, she yells, "Don't be a stranger. I've missed you."

I wave a hand and head out into the mall.

I was right. One of my attorney's concerns was where I'll stay while Dad is locked up. The other concern was Dad's abuse. He tried to wear me down so that I'd admit it. I tell him I'll spend a few nights at a friend's house, and denied again any abuse from Dad. I know there's nothing he can do about it without evidence.

"The court date has been bumped up too, Ian. We go to trial next week."

My gut clenches. The thought of being back in jail by next week makes me dizzy with fear. My thoughts race. Will I be there with the old man? No, he'll be out by then. I feel nauseous.

"Ian, I'm going to use a protective defense. I'll say this kid was picking on someone and you intercepted it. However, the amount of damage you did was overkill, and that will hurt us. To counter that, I'm using your Dad's arrest record to lay evidence of a stressful home life, which explains some of the excessive measures you took. I was hoping this kid would come clean, and the mother would drop the charges, but that isn't happening. I'll request probation and anger management classes. We'll hope for the best."

"And if our hopes aren't met?" I ask.

'You're looking at eighteen months in jail. You'd go to the Juvenile Detention Center until you're eighteen, then finish you're sentence in prison."

Tears hit my eyes immediately. *Oh, Jen, what now? We've run out of time here.*

"Ian, that's the worst-case scenario. I expect you'll be released from Juvenile when you turn eighteen if you don't get into trouble while you're at the center."

I nod and wipe my eyes.

"I need more to defend you! I'm not blowing smoke here, Ian. This isn't a game. Tell me who the girl is!"

I stand up to leave. "I promised her."

He uses profanity as I walk out of his office.

I go to the Club and swim out my anger and fear to a controllable level. I get out and drop into the hot tub exhausted. I close my eyes and melt into the massaging heat, escaping the world. Chris's voice startles my eyes open. He is in the water sitting across from me.

"Thought you'd be here," he says.

I close my eyes again to shut out his voice. It doesn't work.

"So, how'd it go?"

I look at him and can tell he's scared for me, for his mom, and for himself.

"I didn't break under pressure, if that's what you mean," I snap.

"Whoa; I'm not the enemy here."

I sigh. "I know. Sorry."

Tears fill my eyes again, and I shake my head. "He needs the girl's name, needs her to testify. He's gonna try for probation, but I could go to prison. I'm scared, Chris. I really am. I'd be in the Juvenile Detention Center for nine months, until I'm eighteen, then transferred to prison for nine more months."

Chris is quiet.

"I want to run so bad, man. Just leave here and go where nobody can find me—not my dad, not the law. Go somewhere like New York or L.A.; just hide in the masses of people. I'm so tired of looking over my shoulder for Dad all the time, and worrying about jail for saving a girl from being raped! It's crazy, all of it! I don't get why life is so hard!" I punch at the water, and it sprays the concrete ten feet away. Chris stays quiet and lets me cry.

When he does speak, it's in a quiet tone. "Ian, I, um, have some cash that G-pa left me. We'll hire you a good attorney, not that public defender."

I smile at his kindness. "Thanks, Chris, but the fact remains—the girl needs to testify no matter who defends me. Ironic, isn't it? I go to prison for abusing an abuser, who remains free."

I leave the warm tub, and the reality of the cold world slaps my skin. Chris walks beside me.

Eight

*Y*esterday, I pulled Jen aside in the hall. I told her my trial was this week, and that I'm facing a year and a half in JDC and prison. I asked if she's had enough time for her parents to work things out and if I could give her name for my defense.

She told me that she talked with her Dad, and he wasn't sure yet about a divorce, so she didn't tell him about Rod or me. She cried and said that she'd call Deputy Dupree herself. She just couldn't look her dad in the face and tell him. I'm not convinced that she'll really do this on her own, but she needs to in order to gain control over her self-worth and to feel human again. So, I won't give her name. She has to do this herself.

Official practice started this week. It looks like the guys didn't practice all summer, or do any sports at all! Their muscles are tight, and they're easily winded. We have a team of couch potatoes whose bodies need to wake up. Chris and I will be carrying them the first few games it looks like, but I suspected as much going in. I'd really like to place in finals this year, but team is the operative word here, and it's not looking good. Coach isn't happy either, and when he's not happy, he works us to death. Guys have been dropping like flies all week. Even Chris and I, who only missed a few days of off-season practices, are like beaten dogs by the time drills are over.

At least I've been too tired to stress over my trial. Which happens to be tomorrow morning, 9 a.m. sharp.

* * *

Judge Michaels breaks the silence of the crowded room.

"Mr. Taylor, I have yet to see your parents in my court room. Where are they?"

"The mother—"

The judge cuts off my attorney. "I'm speaking to Mr. Taylor, Counselor."

I clear my throat. "Mom isn't here."

"I can see that."

"I mean, she left when I was little."

He nods. "And, your father?"

"Arrested, sir."

"On what charges?"

"Um . . ." I look at my attorney, and he whispers in my ear. "Drunk and Orderly—" My attorney whispers again. "Disorderly conduct with intent of criminal mischief."

He nods again. "So, who is your guardian?"

A voice from the audience answers. "I am, Your Honor."

My head spins, and I'm shocked to see Ms. T. standing a few rows behind me. I didn't know she was here, or that she even knew about my court, and I'm suddenly ashamed that she knows.

"My name is Patricia Tanner. Ian has been staying in my home for the past six weeks or so."

"Weeks?" The judge asks.

"Yes, sir. I did some snooping around—sorry, Ian—and found that in my opinion, Mr. Taylor was not doing justice to Ian. I suspected that Ian was basically living on the streets to avoid his father. God knows how long it's been going on."

My attorney whispers in my ear, "Why, Ian! I underestimated your acting skills!"

"I initially met Ian as a friend of my son's. Ian helped with repairs on our home—which you did a wonderful job of, Ian—and he has been staying at my home since. He has his own room, he attends school, and is on the basketball team."

I feel my attorney's stare, and my face heats up.

Another voice sounds out, it's Coach. "That's true, your Honor, he is one of my top players. He's dedicated to his team and practiced in the gym even before the season started. If he has been homeless, that would explain why last year he showered at the school. Quite often too."

"Last year as well?" The judge asks staring at me. I don't answer.

My attorney whispers again, "You're a natural!"

"Shut up!" I whisper back. His mouth twitches back a smile.

I hear another familiar voice, and turn to see my former boss. "I own the deli in the mall, and Ian worked for me over the summer until he had what he called a family emergency. Ian, why didn't you say something? He is a loyal, honest, trustworthy and hardworking employee. I would love to have him in my shop again."

"Enough, people!" The judge yells. "This is not a town meeting! This is my courtroom!"

The crowded room goes instantly silent, not even a cough is heard.

"It appears, Ian, that you will need to go into the Children's Protective Services Program, where the state will evaluate your case and find a home if indeed it renders itself needed at the closing of your criminal case."

"He can stay with me!" Ms. T. yells.

"I'll gladly take him in," Coach adds.

"I have extra room at my place, and he can have gainful employment at my deli as well."

"He's already established at my home, though!" Ms. T. argues.

"Order!"

The room goes silent again.

"We are hearing a case of assault! This is not a custody hearing!" The judge pauses, staring, scanning the audience, daring anyone to speak.

"Now, the court notes that the defendant is highly regarded in the community and that there are a number of homes available to him, should that be necessary." He looks at me, then continues. " Mr. Taylor, as far as these charges go, they are very serious."

"Your Honor, I would like to point out the fact that Ian has not had proper guidance—"

The judge holds up a hand to stop my attorney.

A small voice speaks from the back of the room. "He did it to protect me."

There is a shuffling as people turn to see who is talking. Jen stands alone in the aisle, arms crossed and hugging herself. I whisper under my breath, "Thank you, Jen."

"Rod was . . ." She looks to the floor, then back up at the judge. "Ian helped me. I asked him not to tell anyone." She starts to cry. "But now he might go to jail if I don't tell what happened!"

"Liar!" Rod's mom screams.

Everyone's head snaps back up front.

"These are just a couple of delinquents, trying to frame my son!"

"Order! Bailiff, bring that young lady, the plaintiff, without his mother, and the defendant to my chambers! The rest of you go home. You've turned my courtroom into a circus, and these proceedings are now closed to the public."

"I have the right to be with my son!" Rod's mom yells.

Judge Michaels snaps back, "In my court, I say who has rights and who doesn't. One more word from your mouth gets you the right to ten days in jail for contempt!" He snatches up the file from his throne-like desk and storms down the steps of the platform.

"All rise!" the bailiff announces.

"Bailiff! Get these people in my chambers. Now!" The door behind the judge's desk slams.

I stare, gape-mouthed at all of the confusion around me. People are mulling and mumbling. I see the bailiff pointing Jen to the door that Judge Michaels just went through. She looks scared to death. I catch her eye and mouth, 'It's okay, Jen.' I see Chris now, standing beside her. He nods and gives a small smile. Jen walks through the thigh-high gate into the business part of the room.

My attorney is as excited as a little kid. He's telling me what to say when I get in there. "This is going to be good! Man, I wish I was a fly on the wall right now. Just tell the judge everything, Ian. All of it. Pull out some of those tears you do so well," he snickers.

I shrug his hand from my arm as the bailiff pulls me away. I scan the crowd and see familiar faces everywhere. From people I barely know at school to the principal himself. Everybody has skipped school to be here! Half the town is here, even the gal who works at the Club!

Deputy Dupree slaps cuffs on Rod in front of his mom and hustles Rod across the court while ignoring Rod's mom's protests. The bailiff walks me through the door behind Rod and Dupree. I stare at Rod's hands, which are cuffed behind his back, as we squeeze our way down a narrow, dark-paneled hall.

Dupree stops Rod and gives him a look of disgust as he opens the door to a large, leather and wood furnished room.

The judge has unzipped his robe and is pouring a cup of coffee.

"Sit," he says without turning around.

We all sit, and he nods at Dupree, who then unlocks Rod's cuffs before leaving the room.

The emotions in the room are thick and make the air hard to breathe. I can feel the electricity in the air. My own fear is mingled with what I sense from everyone else, except the judge, who is so angry that his neck and face are flushed red. It's like I can feel the heat come off of him in waves. Jen is so scared she is trembling. She's afraid of the judge and of disappointing her parents, but she's terrified of Rod. Rod boils with a rage that seethes continuously inside of him. It is a constant state of existence for him. To be this close to him, in this room, is more than disturbing. It's like waiting for the crash of a Jack-in-the-box. You know it will happen, and all thought is suspended, waiting for the inevitable. He is volatile, and I wonder if the judge and I can take him if we have to since he's sober and so angry.

There's a light tap on the door, and a short, blonde woman pokes her head in. "Judge, do you need a witness to any statements?"

"No, Becky, thank you. If I ever get this mess sorted out, I'll get them written . . ." he looks each of us in the eye, "and signed."

I see Dupree and the bailiff standing guard at the door in the hall. It makes me feel better, especially when I see that Rod has seen them too. Becky closes the door, and the three of us spend the next hour in that airless room, telling our story to a big man who is in charge, and not at all happy with any of us.

We all finish, and the judge tells Rod that he doesn't believe that Jen gave him permission to kiss her, nor does he believe that kissing was Rod's only intention. Judge Michaels steps to the door and mumbles something to Dupree. Dupree and the bailiff enter and stand Rod up. Dupree cuffs him, reads him his rights, and they escort Rod out. I hear Rod crying as the door closes. I wonder if he will be left in jail to learn a lesson or if his mom will bail him out A.S.A.P. I'd place bets on the latter.

Next, Judge Michaels tells Jen that what she did was irresponsible and dangerous. He tells her also, that not coming forward sooner caused much grief to me and wasted the court's time. He says that in the future, to consider how her actions, or non-actions, will affect others. He ends by telling her she is only allowed to accept rides from people her parents approve of. He then excuses her from the room and sits eyeing me for a long, uncomfortable time in silence. I wipe sweat from my upper lip.

"Well, Mr. Taylor, now it's just you and me."

I don't respond.

"What is going on at home?"

In a flash, my new home comes to mind, before I realize he means Dad's house. The one I don't consider home anymore. I take a deep breath. I am emotionally exhausted, scared, yet relieved, but also confused. I break down in tears. He lets me cry, which is even more embarrassing.

When I get ahold of myself, I tell a story that sounds more like fiction than fact. However, the feelings I have while laying it all out are anything but fiction. I explain how Mom had left just before my tenth birthday and how Dad's drinking made him mean. I told him about Dad's old boxing days and how he knocked me unconscious several times over the years. I explain that for as long as I could remember, I've tried to avoid him and that when I got older, I just started staying away. I tell how I'd go to the house and move things around or clean to make it look like I still lived there. I explain the mugging when he found out I was working and how he showed up at the deli one day, on what he thought was my payday, so that's why I quit my job. I explain that the last time he did a K.O. on me was the day he bailed me out of jail, and it was then that I finally put him out of my life for good.

Judge Michaels asks, "Why haven't you told anyone this until now?"

At first, my years' old excuse comes to mind: that I didn't want to miss Mom if she came for me. Then I dig deeper and realize that's not true anymore, that the reason had changed.

I look at the judge. "Sir, it used to be in case my mom came back to get me, but now it's because I live with my best friend and his mom. If I told, the courts would have to tell Dad where I live, which is only three houses down from his house. I'm scared of what he might do to them if he knows I am there. I'm afraid he will hurt them. He can really mess people up."

I sit back in my chair, and let out a deep breath, and feel the heartache of years gone by, leave me. I feel the weight of the entire world has just been lifted from my shoulders and chest. It was a weight that had built for so long that I hadn't known its full burden. Until it was gone.

"Judge Michaels?"

He tilts his head at me.

"I think also, that I didn't tell anyone because . . . well, he's my dad."

Judge Michaels nods, stands up and refills his cup. His back is turned to me when he says, "Ian, I am ashamed of our community because none of us saw this. None of us put the pieces together, so you were forced to make survival choices that no child should have to make." He turns to me. "For that, I am truly sorry. We have failed you. It is my job as a judge to ensure the innocent are not punished, just as surely as it is my job to punish the guilty. If there were a way to punish our community for being passive to the detriment of another, I'd order it. To make matters worse, you were nearly sent to prison for doing the very thing we adults should have been doing for you: protecting the vulnerable."

I start to thank him, but he cuts me off.

"Now, about your living arrangement. I am going to push through the paperwork to have you placed in a safe home. I promise you, Ian, your father will not hurt you or your foster family on my watch."

Panic hits my gut, knowing that now that Dad is exposed, I will pay for it. Various scenarios flash through my head in an instant.

"How can you guarantee that? You can't watch my house every minute of every day! He'll find me, and when he does—"

"Ian!"

Tears have poured from my eyes. I wipe them away.

"I am a man of my word and a man of power in Deer Falls. People do what I tell them, no questions asked. If I order 24/7 surveillance on you, trust me, it will be done. Diligently. You are now and will be, safe, Ian, and so is your new family."

I'm not convinced, but it's good to know that others will be helping me stay alert to Dad's presence.

"Now, there were people out there that stepped up and want you to live with them. You have choices to make. You can choose one of them, or you can go to a foster home the state chooses. What do you want to do?"

I sit, a little dazed. An hour ago, I thought I was going to prison. An hour ago, I didn't know how many people cared about me or how much they cared. An hour ago, I learned I am not the solo flyer I always thought I was. I consider what life would be like with each person who spoke up in court.

I look at Judge Michaels. "You swear to me, on the Bible, and with every breath in you, that they will be safe?"

"I swear to you, Ian, on a stack of Bibles, and with my dying breath, you and your new family will be safe."

"Because I really care a lot about each of those people who stood up for me out there today," I say while standing and pointing in the courtroom's direction.

Judge Michaels nods. I sit back down.

"Coach is proud of me. He pushes me to be the best I can be; he nearly kills me some days," I snort out a laugh. "He makes me physically strong. He doesn't just want me to do well, he convinces me that I *will* do well. My boss from the deli makes me do what's right, ya know?"

"What do you mean, Ian?"

"Well, she's nice, so I want to help her make as much money as possible so she can keep the deli open. She's a stickler on giving people huge sandwiches for a fair price. She won't cut corners either. If the serving line isn't at temp, or if cut veggies aren't used in two hours, she tosses them! She trusts me to do my job right and her way. She trusts me with the cash register, and she's even left me with keys to lock-up a few times when she couldn't. She's shown me how hard it can be to do the right thing sometimes, but you do it anyway, even if nobody's looking. She's taught me how good it feels to do the right thing; it makes me feel clean inside."

"She really throws two-hour old vegetables out?"

I nod my head. "It used to drive me crazy. Now I just make sure I don't cut too much at once, or actually, I used to."

"Does she deliver?"

"No, now it's just her in the shop, no employees."

"Both she and Coach see promise in me; they've both helped me be a better person. To choose one over the other is insane. I wouldn't know how to do it. Besides, I don't have to. You see, Ms. T., well, she treats me like her own son. She opened her home to me even though she didn't know my circumstances. She just trusted me from the start. She trusted me to fix and paint her house. A kid! She would pack up and leave Deer Falls if she needed to in order to keep me safe. Ms. T., well, sir, she loves me, and I love her and Chris. They are my family now."

Judge Michaels sits back in his chair, listening intently to what I say. His elbows rest on the arms of his chair, and his fingers are tee-peed in front of him. The silence is thick as he stares at me. I want to squirm but fight it.

Finally, he lowers his hands and says, "Ian, I will set that up for you. Legally."

He punches a button on his phone and Becky answers on the speaker. "Yes, Judge?"

"Becky, do a background check on Patricia Tanner, and then call Ed Baker at Children's Services and tell him I need to see him today at . . ." he checks his watch, "12:30."

"Yes, Judge."

"Becky, do you know the deli in the mall?"

"Yes, sir, they serve nice sandwiches."

"Call in an order for me, Ed and yourself. We'll all be eating here today."

"Yes, sir."

"Oh, and Becky?"

"Yes?"

"Come to my chambers' door, please."

Almost immediately there is a light tapping, and Judge Michaels steps out into the hall but leaves the door ajar. I can hear him talking with Becky.

"Reschedule my hearings for today, I have an errand to run at the jail. Do you have any cash on you? Like fifty bucks?"

"There's money in petty cash, Judge."

"Good. Pull that out for me."

I sense something in Judge Michaels. It's not fear or rage like I usually pick up from people, I don't know what it is. It's almost like an uncertainty or a restlessness. Is he doubting his ability to keep me safe from Dad?

Judge Michaels re-enters the chamber and sits down. "Ian, I've given this situation some thought, and I have decided to leave you in the custody of Ms. Tanner. Starting today, it will be on record that she has sole custody of you. She is your legal guardian. Once her background check has been completed, there will be forms to sign, then it will be a binding agreement between you and her, and your father will have no legal say on your life. If you change your mind for any reason, or if complications arise, I want you to call Becky and tell her you need to see me. Understood?"

"Yes, sir." I manage to choke out, "Thank you."

"You are welcome. Ian, you are free to go." He waves his hand toward the door in invitation.

I look at him. His words, 'free to go,',' sink into my chest, my gut, and then my soul. I am free. I am safe. I stand up, a smile cresting my lips. "Sir, I have wanted to go for years. And never more so than when the court wanted me to stay." Judge Michaels chuckles. "Now that I am free to go, I believe I will stick around for a while longer." He laughs a deep laugh as I close the door behind me.

I walk out the front doors of the courthouse and see about twenty people hanging out on the steps. People begin clapping. Laughter and a few cheers go up. I feel embarrassed by the attention but happy. Chris, Ms. T. and Jen pounce on me, giving me hugs. I feel ridiculous as tears roll down my face. They usher me down the stairs toward the car.

Chris says, "Jen approached me at school this morning in tears. She told me everything. We called the police, but Dupree wasn't there, he was at the courthouse. So, we rallied the troops and came here ourselves."

Jen says, "Ian, I am so sorry I put you in that situation, how can you ever forgive me? Your friendship means so much to me, and I am so sorry." Jen's dad walks up beside her and puts his arm around her shoulders. "Deputy Dupree called Dad from the courthouse while we were in Judge Michaels's chambers."

I look at her dad; he has a kind face, kind eyes that have obviously been crying. He reaches for my hand and shakes it, firmly. "Thank you, Ian Taylor."

"You are welcome, sir. And Jen, I value your friendship as much as you value mine. You were forgiven from day one."

She hugs me and whispers in my ear, "Dad said that he and Mom are going to work harder at their marriage." She lets me go and smiles. They walk off together, and Chris punches me in the arm.

"Get in the car already, man!"

I look around at the people watching us, I wave to my boss, and Coach. "Wow, Chris, you really did rally the troops."

I told you Mom would turn this town upside down if she had to. I guess I've got a little of her blood in me."

As we pull out, I turn and see Becky and the judge in a second-story window. I hold up my palm in a wave, then lose sight of them.

Chris and I take the rest of the day off from school. We're all too excited to do business as usual. Ms. T. takes us out for sodas, and I tell them everything that happened in chambers. I explain how Judge Michaels is speeding up the foster home process and that he promised to make sure we were all safe from Dad.

Later, with a packed lunch, we go to the river just to get away from the ringing phone and all the well-wishers popping in. We need to adjust to us. It is a little chilly, but the sky is clear. The river is raging, it all feels so clean, clear and awesome. I am full of life.

Chris shows us where he swam across the river. It is staggering to think it would even be possible, given the river's width and strength of current. Then again, this is Chris we're talking about. Ms. T. flipped out because it looked so dangerous. I called him a liar, told Ms. T. that he was fooling her.

"Stop teasing her. Chris! You're scaring her." His eyes take me in, and I feel a brother's bond between us because Chris and I both know I will protect his mom as if she were my own.

After lunch, we walk down river and to the base of the falls. We leave Ms. T. on shore as I take Chris to my man cave.' His eyes are serious as he looks around the cramped, dirt hole. What used to be a comfort, an accomplishment, even a place of pride for me, is now a stark picture of reality and an embarrassment. Instantly, I regret showing Chris my cave.

I rush gathering my personal items, and finally decide to leave the sleeping bag and the pop-top cans of food. I pick up my note pad of poems and my clothes and tuck them in my trash bag, then sling the handle over my shoulder. I grab the money can and stuff a ten spot in it. Chris gives me a puzzled look. "For the next kid's emergency."

He nods his head and points his finger at me, gesturing it's a smart move. We hoist ourselves down and inch along the rock wall. We get to shore, and I drop the trash bag.

Ms. T. looks puzzled, then realizes where we are. She takes a deep breath, and whispers a breathy, "Ohh." Her eyes water, she nods her head up and down in reluctant acceptance as if to say, 'This was bad, but also good, and now it's done.' She hugs me tight and says, "Come on, let's go home, boys."

I have a family. I have a place. I have a home. I belong.

Dream Catcher

There, right there, a glimmer I see.
Can't make it out, what could it be?

I feel its presence, its majesty.
Leave me! You're merely fantasy!

You sing of destiny, purpose, and hope.
You're not for me, not in my life's scope.

Hold on, wait a moment, was that a gleam?
Ahh, I know you, you're my long-lost dream.

Come closer, please; I can almost touch you.
I'd forgotten your appeal, I'm made brand-new.

So here you return, on more solid ground,
Asking me to travel the road you've found.

Yes, I will travel, to the heavens above
In search of my life, in search of my love.

—Ian Oliver Taylor

Nine

At 6 a.m. my alarm screams me from sleep, and I slap it quiet. A thrill hits my heart as I remember the rumor is that Autumn is coming back to school today. I plan on being there when she leaves her house.

I jump in the shower and scrub extra well. I wash my hair twice and use Ms. T.'s good conditioner. I use a double portion of antiperspirant, then smear some on my palms too, just in case.

I comb my hair and put on cologne. I stare at my face in the mirror. I look scared. My eyes are all buggy. I squint slightly, and it helps. I make a mental note to squint when I see Autumn. A pounding on the door makes me jump out of my skin.

"Okay! Okay! Jeez."

I open the door to a puffy, pillow-marked face with blood-shot eyes. "Wow, yeah, fix that," I say as I swirl my fingers in front of Chris's face.

He pushes me aside and closes the door. I grab my backpack from my room, glance at the time: 6:45 a.m., and head downstairs. I stop halfway and go back up to the bathroom, where the shower is already running. I poke my head through the door into a cloud of steam.

"Chris."

"Get out!" he snaps.

I grin. "I'm cutting out early; see ya at school."

"Fine. Out!"

I jet downstairs, pop bread in the toaster and pour a bowl of cereal.

Ms. T. steps up beside me. "Ian? Don't you want some eggs?"

I look at her, her eyes still bleary from sleep. I smile and shake my head as I hit the brew button on the coffee maker. I chow down and head out the door before the coffee is brewed.

I glide down the sidewalk trying to come up with something smart or funny to break the ice with Autumn. It's a lost cause. Everything is either pretentious or cheesy. I better not blow this!

I get to her street and scope out her house. The front window curtains are partially open, but I don't see any movement. I look at my watch: 7:10 a.m. She wouldn't have left already. Would she? I stand on the sidewalk in front of her house turning in circles like a doofus, wondering if I should stay or run to school and try to catch her.

I put my pack on the sidewalk and sit. I wait. I look at my watch again: 7:12 a.m. I sigh. *No, she didn't leave this early. Should I run and see if she did? How far could she have gotten? What if she comes out while I'm chasing a ghost? Nope, I'll wait. I'll leave at 7:50. I'll have to run to school then, but—she's here, she has to be. I sit and wait.* I pick at my fingernails and try not to stare at her curtains, watching for movement, like a pup. I practice my eye squint, squish some ants, look at my watch again. 7:20 a.m. . . . 7:22 now. I hear a noise, and see her door move. I stand up, sling my pack over one shoulder, squint my eyes and watch the most beautiful girl ever, hop down the stairs.

She hasn't seen me yet. She gets to the walkway before she looks up. Her eyes are startled at first by someone standing in front of her house. She smiles, blushes, drops her eyes, but then looks up at me square in the face. So gorgeous! She's wearing a huge white smile, and her eyes are sparkling as she comes close.

"Hi, Autumn!" It's all that will come out of my mouth, and it's breathy, like total desperation when it does. My hand grabs for hers before I know what it's doing, but I pull it back before she notices, I hope.

She takes my hand, and I instantly feel her joy and excitement because I'm here. Relief! I squint my eyes a little and smile. She's still wearing her smile.

"So, can I walk with you?" I manage.

She laughs and shows me our clasped hands.

"I'm glad you're back at school."

"Me too. It's gonna be a great year."

I grin. "Yep, sure is. Hey, by the way, you didn't drop World History, did you?"

She laughs again. "You didn't give my chair away did you?"

"Not a chance."

After school, Autumn hangs around to watch us practice. This is huge because her friends had plans to go shopping, but she chose this instead. I walk her home, and she talks about how different school is for her this year. It's exciting, fun, and the first time she's really enjoyed it. She feels like a part of everything, instead of just an onlooker.

I ask her If I can call her. She says yes, but that she wants my number for insurance, in case I chicken out. I laugh at her ability to see straight through me and watch as she enters my number into her phone. She watches closely as I write hers on paper.

The phone rings and I dash to get it, hoping it's Autumn.

"May I speak with Ian Taylor please?"

I recognize Judge Michaels's voice. "Yes, your Honor, this is Ian."

I hear him chuckle. "Outside of the courtroom, Judge Michaels will suffice."

"Oh, sorry."

"I'll get right to the point here, Ian." My heart beats hard wondering if he has changed his mind about jail or living here. "I'm calling to inform you that your father was arrested today, a few hours after his release. He was driving intoxicated, and this is his fourth arrest on this charge."

"Okay."

"Because he has four of these charges and he's still waiting for court on the last charge I suspect he'll serve a mandatory one-year sentence. I just want you to know that you can relax. You are safe."

I picture the old man getting released and going straight to Grady's where he got drunk. I wonder where he got the money since his pay day isn't until another two days. My mind flashes to the day I sat in Judge Michaels's chambers, and the sense of doubt I felt from him.

"Wait a minute here. Did you do have something to do with this? Oh my god! You did. What did you do?" My stomach feels sick.

"I kept a promise that I made, Ian."

Guilt fills my heart knowing that because of me, my dad will go to jail for a year. I see the cell in my mind. "But, I avoided him for a long time. I could have stayed hidden!"

"It's the law that the parent knows where the child has been placed unless there is a verified threat to the child's life. We didn't have that. All we had was your word. There were never any police reports, hospital records, or eyewitness accounts that we could find. Think about it—you hid not only from him but from the town as well, so nobody would know. We only had your word to go on."

"So, what did you do? I mean to get him arrested?"

"I'm not going to discuss this with you. I just wanted you to know that you and your new family are safe. You are a smart kid, use this situation wisely and make this an opportunity to get on with your life unhindered."

"I remember now. This is about your errand to the jail that day I was in your chambers, isn't it? You took money to the jail. You put money in his belongings, didn't you? You knew when he got released, if he had money, he'd go get drunk and drive. This was a set up! How could you do that?" Tears choke my voice. "Tell me, how? Does this make you feel clean inside? Because I feel like sludge."

"Listen, Ian. Before you go throwing blame and judgement around, listen to me. I have lived many years doing this job, this job of judging situations and people. There isn't always a clean way out. Not every choice is right and wrong or black and white. Sometimes, the choices I have will leave one or the other party hurt. In times like those, like in this case, I had to choose between a kid who was doing everything right, as far as he understood it, and protect him from an adult that was intent on hurting him and possibly others. Your father has a history of violence, not just with you, but at Grady's, and he has several DUIs, most of which were never reported by the police. He skated for a long time. He would have driven drunk again, the minute he got any money in his hand, and he would have come to you for that money. He would have had access to where you are. Which, do I need to remind you is only three doors down?" He released a heavy sigh. "I made a promise to protect you and the Tanners. I am a man of my word, that's what keeps my conscience clean. This was the only way to insure my promise was kept. In this situation, I believe I made the best choice possible."

I know he is right. I know that dad would have come after me, if not to the Tanner's, then he would have waited for me around the corner and jumped me. I feel sick, about how all of this ended up, and the part I played.

"Judge Michaels?"

"Yes?"

"I get it. I don't like it, but I understand it."

"I don't like it either, Ian. But I like it better than the alternative. His new case is being heard by a different judge, so I don't know the date, but you can call the courthouse clerk to find out if you want to attend."

"No, sir, I don't believe I want that."

"Well, that's your prerogative. Goodnight, Ian, and good luck to you."

"Sir?"

"Is there more, Ian?"

I turn my back to Chris and Ms. T., then mumble so they can't hear me. "Where would I have gone for, you know, those anger classes? I mean is it a school or something?"

"Don't worry about that, you don't have to go. The court found that your actions were justifiable."

"Well, is there a place in the phone book or something?"

"Do you feel you have problems controlling your anger?"

I shrug, even though I know he can't see me. I glance around, and Ms. T. calls Chris into the kitchen, I'm sure to give me privacy. "I just know that after I dragged Rod from the car, that alone may have stopped him, but it was like I'd close my eyes and when they opened again, I'd be hitting him. After Jen stopped me, I felt just like my old man. I hated that."

"All right, Ian, listen. I think it was a one-time event for you. I suspect the years of stress and anger from living with your father made you react that strongly. However, if classes will help you to start a new life for yourself, I will make a call and see that you get enrolled."

"I'd feel better. Um . . . how much does it cost? I have some money saved from my job at the deli."

"The Children's Protective Services will foot the bill. You don't need to worry about that. Let's just get you to a place where you trust and like yourself better. Okay?'

"Okay. Thank you."

"Goodnight, Ian."

"Goodnight, your Hon—Judge Michaels."

I hang up the phone and look up at two pairs of eyes staring, waiting. My first instinct is to keep the call private. "So, are we ever going to step into the new millennium and get me a cell phone? Or at least one without an anchor?" I joke.

They don't laugh. Their eyes, waiting nervously and worrisome, tell me they care. I feel their anxiety, and I know they deserve to be part of my life as openly as I am theirs.

I throw a thumb toward the phone. "That um . . ." I clear my throat, "was Judge Michaels." I look to the floor and back at their piercing eyes. "He said they arrested my dad. I guess this is his fourth DUI, so it carries a one-year mandatory sentence.'

"Yes!" Chris yelps.

Ms. T. puts a hand on his arm while keeping her eyes locked on me. "Ian? Honey? How do you feel about that?"

Maybe it's her voice or the way she asks, or maybe the way she looks in my eyes, all worried and searching for the real me. Maybe it's all of it pulled together, but tears fill my eyes, then leak out. I try to talk, but my throat has closed shut with a lump. She reaches me and pulls me into her soft, plump, mom arms and holds me while I cry. She doesn't slacken her hold even briefly until I get control of myself.

I glance at Chris, embarrassed, but he is busying himself picking at something stuck on the table.

"I, um, it's my fault he's in that terrible place. I let the judge know how scared I was of Dad. Now he'll be locked up for a year."

"Ian, he chose to drink and drive, repeatedly. It really was only a matter of time."

"I just think that if I would have thought about it, I could have warned him, so he could change."

"Honey, if previous arrests didn't change him, then your warning wouldn't have either."

I nod my head. "I just don't understand how it all had to come to this. I mean, I just wanted him to be my dad, to go to my games, to be proud of me. To stop hitting me. I just wanted him to love me. He's my dad! I love him! I don't know why he can't love me back." I look into Ms. T.'s eyes. "He's all I've ever known."

"Of course, you love him! No matter what our family does, we still love them. They are part of us, and we are part of them."

Chris stares intently at his mom, listening closely.

"You've been around him your entire life, good or bad. Now that he's not around, you're going to grieve over him, no matter what he's done. Ian," she takes my face into her palms and looks into my eyes, "it is perfectly normal to feel the loss, but you can't blame yourself for the loss or for his actions. He has a sickness, and that's how you must see his alcoholism. It's a destruction that takes down everyone and everything near it. You can't rescue him. This is the chance you have to rescue yourself. And a chance for him to rescue himself."

I nod. She lets go of my face, "That's my plan, Ms. T." I drape my arms over her shoulders, and she hugs me, patting my back.

Chris sits at the table, deep in thought. I feel a wave of guilt wash over him, and I know he still has something huge buried deep inside of himself. It's going to be a rough road when it comes to the surface. I plan to be here for him when it does. I step back and say, "I'm really tired right now; think I'll go upstairs for a while."

"Okay, you go on up if you want, but I want you to think about the positive changes opening up for you, as you are closing this chapter on your life. All right?"

I go upstairs, knowing she is right, but I don't have a clue as to how to go about it. I enter my room and gently close the door. The smell of new bedding, curtains and paint still give my chest a small charge of unbelievable hope. Even after all these weeks. I switch my lamp on, and its soft light brings out the deep color of green and burgundy that decorate the room. It feels warm, heavy, stable and calm. My room. I turn on the stereo that Chris is jealous about and remember his dancing fit over me getting it. I laugh again. I unroll new posters and begin tacking them to the walls. As I put each one up in its perfect spot, I let the room soak into me. My home, my bed, my desk, computer, stereo, clothes . . . all mine, for as long as I want it. I'll never be ripped out of a deep sleep and plunged into violence here. I'll never come here and find everything tossed, broken or stolen. I'll also never see my mom standing in my doorway.

I sit on the foot of my bed and look around. I watch the screensaver on my computer roll through the litany of an exploding universe, with tumbling meteors and newborn stars. I watch it run the entire show and begin its cycle again. Astrophysics would be cool.

I sit in the chair in front of my desk and touch the mouse. The universe disappears. I do a search of astrophysics and astronomy. All kinds of information come up, and I read for a long time. This is way cool. I search for universities that offer a science curriculum. Turns out, my state's university is one of them. It's only a couple hundred miles from here. It offers astrophysics! I can have a new town, away from Dad, yet close enough to visit Chris and Ms. T. I feel freedom, the freedom I've always dreamed of is right here and accessible.

I sit back in my chair, my mouth open, in shock. I have my freedom, my direction, and I can feel destiny taking hold of me. Suddenly, everything has fallen into place, I feel . . . right. I just know that for this reason, I had to have the childhood I had, to teach me what life will be if I don't work hard for my dreams. I ask myself, why the beatings then? And my mind answers its own question. Because I had to learn how to overcome terrifying obstacles and become independent so I could learn to think for myself and find my true life. My true life that is being true to myself! I get it now. Judge Michaels was right. The world isn't made of perfect choices; the decisions are often gray. I chose to leave Dad behind, long before the first time I ducked into that cave. I've just accomplished what my soul had in sight for me all along.

I don't know how I'll pay for college but I know I'm going. I close the search and get ready for bed.

I lay for hours. Ms. T. tapped on my door once, but I faked sleep. I lie here in the dark, thinking of my life, the world, and what it will be like at college. I imagine the excitement, the people from all over the state, the town and the dorm or apartment I'll have. It's all new, all fresh, and so far removed from working at the deli and living in the cave, while saving money to escape. This isn't a frantic escape or running away from problems. This is opportunity, destiny and purpose.

Ms. T. is right. It had to go down like this for Dad, in order for me to be rescued. His choices, his violence, are finally paying for my chance in life. I wish he'd given me my chance in another way, though. I promise myself, for Dad's sake, that I won't squander this chance I've been given. I have finally come into myself. In a year, I'll be ready to set out on my own life's journey.

* * *

We've been practicing hardcore all week for this game. Luckily, for us, our first game of the season was with a team we were pretty even with last year, and we smoked them! Tonight, we go up against Green Valley High, last year's champs. I'm so pumped up for this that the adrenaline is flat-out screaming through my veins!

We hit the court, while Autumn and Jen pump up the crowd with their practiced cheers. Then it's game on.

Chris breaks out, making the first two points of the game. I steal the ball and bump our score again. The game is smooth as glass, as Chris and I run it hard across the court in a familiar exchange that's become second nature to us. Toward the end, our team is tired and sweaty, but Green Valley is discouraged and barely loping down the court. The scoreboard reads 64-42 with only three minutes left on the clock! We're slamming these champs!

"Chris!" I nod at the board.

He looks and grins. He gives me a double fist bump, our signal to shine.

I steal the ball again, pass to Chris, and he fakes a pass that Green Valley leaps for, as he does his mid-air twist, pocketing two points. The crowd explodes to their feet in cheers. Next, Chris steals the ball, passes to me, and we toy with Green Valley, taunting them to get the ball as we pass between us along the court's length, running out the clock. I miss a shot that rims, but the shortest kid on our team rebounds it just as the buzzer sounds.

Chris and I high-five, and the team is jumping and hugging each other, We did it! We creamed last year's champs! I see that Chris's lip is bleeding pretty good. I point in a way that asks, 'What's that?'

"I think I ticked off Finley."

We look at him as the other team is leaving the court. The big, blonde, Finley turns and glares at us. We laugh.

"Maybe next time you should stick to rubbing a smaller guy the wrong way."

"What, this?" Chris asks as he dabs his lip with a towel, "This is my trophy."

Coach calls Chris and me over to him. I glance in Autumn's direction, she's obviously proud of me. She's glowing. I give her a huge smile and a wink. We get to Coach, and I see Judge Michaels walk up with another guy I don't recognize.

"Ian," the judge says. "This is my brother-in-law." The man extends his hand, and I shake it, then Chris does.

"My name is Roger Jeffries. You boys tore it up out there."

"Thanks," we both chime.

"I'm a scout for State." He hands us both his business card. I quickly see the name of the university he's from. It's the one that offers my astrophysics program! I stare, gape-mouthed like a complete idiot.

"Don't lose those, and call me just before graduation. I'll get you up there for tryouts on next year's team. Unless you clowns are holding out for the Globe Trotters."

We all laugh.

"Could be full scholarships in it for you."

I burst out with, "Astrophysics! I want to study astrophysics!"

Chris laughs and covers my idiot move by saying, "We'll be there!" He laughs and slaps my back in camaraderie.

"We could use a couple of guys like you. Keep practicing."

We shake hands again, and I reach for Judge Michaels's hand. I shake it firmly, look him in the eye and say, "Thank you, for everything."

"It's all you, Ian, always has been." The men turn and leave, and Chris and I run into the locker room whooping and hollering all the way.

We're both on a natural high, and Ms. T. can't get a word in, all the way to the burger joint, where the team will meet up. She did manage to cry though when we shoved the scout's cards in her face, yelling, "Full Scholarship!"

The next night she declares a celebration 'man's meal,',' and cooks steak, large cut fries, pull-apart rolls and apple pie. Chris teases her that G-pa would be appalled that the only thing homemade are the steaks.

She slaps him with her hand towel and tells him, "If you boys stopped doing things to celebrate all the time, maybe I'd have time to cook from scratch."

As I sit at the table loaded with a king's feast, and enjoy the laughter and teasing, everything feels so . . . right. I look around the table and take it all in.

"Ian, honey, what's wrong?" Ms. T. asks. She jumps up and comes to my side of the table, and puts her hands on my shoulders, and bends over looking at me, her face only inches from mine.

I chuckle. "Nothing."

"Well, something's not right!"

I shake my head. I look at Chris and then Ms. T., "Everything is right. It's just never been so right before."

She hugs me tight. There's no escaping her when she's on a mission. "I know, Ian, everything is perfectly, right, isn't it? It is for me, too. I'm so glad you're here."

"Hear, hear!" Chris says raising his soda in a toast.

"Hear, hear!" we chime in.

Chris changes the subject. "So, Ian, are you sweet on Jen?"

I choke on my soda, spraying it through my nose. Laughter breaks out.

"Well, are you?" Ms. T. asks. "Who is Jen?"

She thinks for a minute, "Oh! Ian? Are you? Should we have her over for dinner? How exciting!"

"Wait a minute! Hold on." I stop everyone. "No, I'm not sweet on Jen. She's just a friend."

Ms. T. slumps back in her chair. "Oh."

Chris grins big. "Great, 'cuz I am."

We all start talking at once, and before the meal is over, Jen has been called and invited to the movies next weekend. Chris refused to have her over for dinner, which I totally get.

"I want to go, too!" I say.

The expression on Chris's face sends Ms. T. and me into laughter until we have tears in our eyes. Chris jumps up and puts me in a head lock, while Ms. T. slaps us both with her towel.

* * *

It's taken a little while, but Autumn and I are more comfortable with each other now. She doesn't blush quite so often, and I don't have to remind myself to squint anymore.

Our group is standing near Jen's locker, and I have my arm around Autumn when Chris points at us. It finally dawns on him why I've been hanging so close to Jen's friends.

"I'm telling Mom! I can't believe you let me go through her interrogation the other night about Jen! You're a dog, Ian! A dog!"

I laugh. "You tried to hang me out to dry first, dude! You just threw it right out there on the dinner table. Made me blow soda out of my nose!" I turn to Autumn, "Hey, how would you like to come over for dinner?"

"Don't do it, Autumn! This dog is just using you to get in good with Mom!"

"Ian, I'd love to help you win points at home," Autumn smiles sweetly.

"Ah, man. I'm done for. Just done," Chris whines. "Jen, want to come over for dinner? Tonight?"

We all say, "Tonight?"

"If I can get you there before Ian brings Autumn, I can save some face here."

I squint at Chris, whisper in Autumn's ear, and she hands me her phone. "Ms. T.? Can I bring a girl home for dinner tonight?"

Chris isn't standing for any of this. "Seriously, Ian? Is that how it is?"

"'Fraid so, buddy, I've got a reputation to uphold, being the new kid and all."

Chris points at me, jumping up and down. "Oh! Oh! And the dog throws the master's own line back at him!" Chris yells toward the phone, "Mom, I'm bringing Jen tonight! You remember Jen?"

We're all laughing so hard we barely hear the bell ring. Autumn starts to move toward her classroom, but I hold on to her hand and pull her back to me. I give her a quick kiss on the lips. "We make an awesome team!"

She laughs as she walks off.

* * *

The house is calm tonight. I go upstairs to my room. I open the door and realize that I've been here long enough now that the fresh paint smell is gone. The room smells like the dryer sheets Ms. T. used on my bedding. I slide my fingers over the comforter as I walk to my desk. A college application lies across my keyboard. I sit down and pick it up. This is something I never really saw myself doing until a few months ago: applying for college.

I look at the newly framed photograph of my mom that I salvaged from the front yard the day a clean-up crew emptied out Dad's house. I wonder what Mom would say if she knew . . . any of it. She probably, honestly wouldn't care. I think of how far I've come without her, managing the life she left me to.

I know that most people would think I must hate Dad for the way he treated me, but I have to look at the whole picture because I lived it. What I see is that he forced me, by default, to explore basketball, to learn a sensitivity to other's emotions, and to survive on my own. Because of Dad, I learned what it cost someone to love me, me—Ian Oliver Taylor, and that I am worth the sacrifices that love costs.

Because of him, I have a hunger for life and love that I wouldn't have gotten from a childhood filled with family game nights. Like Mom, he no longer does anything for me, or to me.

I toss the photograph in the trash beside my desk, and I fill out the application to my life, on my own terms.

Epilogue

My visitor pushes pages of legal work in front of me. I scribble *Vera A. Drexell* on the x'd lines. I'm surprised by how spidery my scrawl has become over the years. I stand, look him solidly in the eye and shake his hand to seal the deal, just like Roy taught me. I have just signed over the deeds to Roy's and my land to the community of Deer Falls.

As I enter my room and lay on my bed, my memory flashes through people I've known.

There was the Mexican family that settled on the backside of one of our hills. The government didn't know they were here, and nobody told either because they were good folk and didn't cause a ruckus. One of their daughters married the Taylor kid. That boy was always mean as a snake, drank a lot too. One day that Mexican family just up and left without so much as a fare-thee-well, leaving that Taylor kid to stew in his own juices while raising a small boy alone. I always suspected they got wind that Taylor was going to turn them in to the Feds. I don't know why they left that young boy, though. I suppose because they were a peaceful clan by nature and scared.

I'd get calls from the small boy the first couple of years, asking for his momma. I don't know how he got my number, or why he thought I'd know where she was. She used to help out up at the old place to earn a little money, so maybe he saw my number written by his Momma's hand. Later, after I moved to town, he became my paper boy. I'd tell him stories about his kinfolk. I never let on that it was his family I spoke of, though. Maybe one day he'll figure it out when it doesn't hurt so bad. He's a young man now. He's a handsome kid who turned out good. Took after his momma's side on all corners.

There was a young girl, Rita, who walked into town one day. She had no car and had walked from a place that only she and God know. She carried a crying baby in her arms. She was exhausted, dirty, scared and hungry. I pulled her into the house, took care of her until the sorrow left her, then marched her down to the Food Mart and told the kid that owned it, that she would be working for him now. He knew better than to argue with me. That little baby of hers turned to be a young version of her beautiful momma.

Then, of course, there's Reggie, my own boy's friend. When his wife passed on, he closed himself off from everyone; well, except for me. I guess I was his stand-in momma. He just shut off any emotion he had, until his grandson showed up. Now that boy was in a bad way, but it saved Reggie. More good comin' from bad. They hid something on the hill up on our old place.

So, that's proof. All through life, there's good shining from under the bad. My own days are numbered now, I feel it. So, I gave this land to the generations of people who have lived, loved, hurt and died here. It's as much theirs as it ever was Roy's and mine. It's as it should be.

My body feels light. Someone keeps hollerin' my name. "Vera! Vera!" They're so far away, so their yells are faint. I ignore them. If they want me, they'll find me.

Humph. Well, I'll be . . . I don't have all those aches that over the years I've grown so used to. I only notice them now because of their absence. Even that hip that earned me a limp and a shuffle moves like brand new!

I feel happy, but I'm not sure why. Oh my! Will ya take a look at that! There's my Roy over yonder! Look how handsome he is. And there are my boys, and my baby girl Lila!

Why, there's Reggie! Lily, his wife, is standing next to him, and a young man also. I wave, and a light leaves my hand and envelopes them all in a glow, that illuminates other groups standing nearby. Some of these people I haven't seen since I was a child!

"Vera." My name is called softer, closer. I look at Roy, he holds his hand out to me, and like a young girl of thirteen, I leap into his arms.

About the Author

"I am the fortunate mother of an awesome daughter and am a grandmother. I have a soft spot for teens and 20-somethings who have battled and are still battling the effects of bad childhoods. I heard many heartbreaking stories as I tutored math to such a group for five years. I have lived in several states across the U.S., and have a difficult time deciding on my favorite. Currently, I'm checking out Virginia."

—Samantha Lady

Coming Soon!

The second volume in the *Deer Falls Series*!

Don't miss what Jen has been up to, and find out more about Rod, and how he fights life!

A tiny hint just for you, *Deer Falls* fan!

Jen becomes a successful musician, while Rod grows into a shadier character. Autumn, Chris and Ian are in college, and there just might be romance in the air. Chris and Ian have the final battle of their consciences as they clear up their own secret pasts.